GOOD BONES

What Reviewers Say About Aurora Rey's Work

Roux for Two

"Rey (*Roux for Two*) stresses the importance of building something to last in this torrid home renovation romance. Rey makes the chemistry between Maddie and Sy obvious and immediate, leading naturally to plenty of creative and exciting sex scenes, but tempers the hot-and-heavy goings-on with emotional intelligence that makes the relationship feel as sturdy as a load-bearing wall. Readers will never doubt that a happy ending is on its way, but they'll love watching it come together."—*Publishers Weekly*

Greener Pastures

"I was hooked on this from the very first moment and enjoyed it so much I couldn't put it down. It had everything I want from a romance and everything I have come to know and love in Aurora Rey stories. Definitely recommend this amazing story and for romance readers, it's another must read!"—*LESBIreviewed*

You Again

"*You Again* is a wonderful, feel good, low angst read with beautiful and intelligent characters that will melt your heart, and an enchanting second-chance love story."—*Rainbow Reflections*

Twice Shy

"[A] tender, foodie romance about a pair of middle aged lesbians who find partners in each other and rediscover themselves along the way. …Rey's cute, occasionally steamy, romance reminds readers of the giddy intensity falling in love brings at any age, even as the characters negotiate the particular complexities of dating in midlife—meeting the children, dealing with exes, and revealing emotional scars. This queer love story is as sweet and light as one of Bake My Day's famous cream puffs."—*Publishers Weekly*

The Last Place You Look

"This book is the perfect book to kick your feet up, relax with a glass of wine and enjoy. I'm a big Aurora Rey fan because her deliciously engaging books feature strong women who fall for sweet butch women. It's a winning recipe."—*Les Rêveur*

"The romance is satisfying and full-bodied, with each character learning how to achieve her own goals and still be part of a couple. A heartwarming story of two lovers learning to move past their fears and commit to a shared future."—*Kirkus Reviews*

Ice on Wheels—*Novella in* Hot Ice

"I liked how Brooke was so attracted to Riley despite the massive grudge she had. No matter how nice or charming Riley was, Brooke was dead set on hating her. A cute enemies to lovers story."—*Bookvark*

The Inn at Netherfield Green

"Aurora Rey has created another striking and romantic setting with the village of Netherfield Green. With her vivid descriptions of the inn, the pub, and the surrounding village, I ended up wanting to live there myself. She also did a fantastic job creating two very different characters in Lauren and Cam."—*Rainbow Reflections*

Lead Counsel—*Novella in* The Boss of Her

"*Lead Counsel* by Aurora Rey is a short and sweet second chance romance. Not only was this story paced well and a delight to sink into, but there's A++ good swearing in it and has lines like this that made me all swoony because of how beautifully they're crafted."—*Lesbian Review*

Recipe for Love

"*Recipe for Love* by Aurora Rey is a gorgeous romance that's sure to delight any of the foodies out there. Be sure to keep snacks on hand when you're reading it, though, because this book will make you want to nibble on something!"—*Lesbian Review*

Autumn's Light—*Lambda Literary Award Finalist*

"Aurora Rey is by far one of my favourite authors. She writes books that just get me. ...Her winning formula is Butch women who fall for strong femmes. I just love it. Another triumph from the pen of Aurora Rey. 5 stars."—*Les Rêveur*

"Aurora Rey has shown a mastery of evoking setting and this is especially evident in her Cape End romances set in Provincetown. I have loved this entire series..."—*Kitty Kat's Book Review Blog*

Spring's Wake

"[A] feel-good romance that would make a perfect beach read. The Provincetown B&B setting is richly painted, feeling both indulgent and cozy."—*RT Book Reviews*

"*Spring's Wake* by Aurora Rey is charming. This is the third story in Aurora Rey's Cape End romance series and every book gets better. Her stories are never the same twice and yet each one has a uniquely *her* flavour. The character work is strong and I find it exciting to see what she comes up with next."—*Lesbian Review*

Summer's Cove

"As expected in a small-town romance, *Summer's Cove* evokes a sunny, light-hearted atmosphere that matches its beach setting. ...Emerson's shy pursuit of Darcy is sure to endear readers to her, though some may be put off during the moments Darcy winds tightly to the point of rigidity. Darcy desires romance yet is unwilling to disrupt her son's life to have it, and you feel for Emerson when she endeavors to show how there's room in her heart for a family."—*RT Book Reviews*

Crescent City Confidential—*Lambda Literary Award Finalist*

"This book blew my socks off... [*Crescent City Confidential*] ticks all the boxes I've started to expect from Aurora Rey. It is written very well and the characters are extremely well developed; I felt like I was getting to know new friends and my excitement grew with every finished chapter."—*Les Rêveur*

"*Crescent City Confidential* pulled me into the wonderful sights, sounds and smells of New Orleans. I was totally captivated by the city and the story of mystery writer Sam and her growing love for the place and for a certain lady. …It was slow burning but romantic and sexy too. A mystery thrown into the mix really piqued my interest."
—*Kitty Kat's Book Review Blog*

"*Crescent City Confidential* is a sweet romance with a hint of thriller thrown in for good measure."—*Lesbian Review*

Built to Last

"Rey's frothy contemporary romance brings two women together to restore an ancient farmhouse in Ithaca, N.Y. …[T]he women totally click in bed, as well as when they're poring over paint chips, and readers will enjoy finding out whether love conquers all."—*Publishers Weekly*

Winter's Harbor

"This is the story of Lia and Alex and the beautifully romantic and sexy tale of a winter in Provincetown, a seaside holiday haven. A collection of interesting characters, well-fleshed out, as well as a gorgeous setting make for a great read."—*Inked Rainbow Reads*

"One of my all time favourite Lesbian romance novels and probably the most reread book on my Kindle. …Absolutely love this debut novel by Aurora Rey and couldn't put the book down from the moment the main protagonists meet. *Winter's Harbor* was written beautifully and it was full of heart. Unequivocally 5 stars."—*Les Rêveur*

Visit us at www.boldstrokesbooks.com

By the Author

GOOD BONES

by
Aurora Rey

2024

ISBN 13: 978-1-63679-589-8

THIS TRADE PAPERBACK ORIGINAL IS PUBLISHED BY
BOLD STROKES BOOKS, INC.
P.O. BOX 249
VALLEY FALLS, NY 12185

FIRST EDITION: APRIL 2024

CREDITS

EDITORS: ASHLEY TILLMAN AND CINDY CRESAP
PRODUCTION DESIGN: SUSAN RAMUNDO
COVER DESIGN BY INK SPIRAL DESIGN

Acknowledgments

It felt like a fun premise, writing a romance about a romance writer who doesn't believe in happily ever afters. It was fun to write, too, coaxing Kathleen out of the shell she'd built around her heart. But it also made me wrestle with my own hang-ups around love and commitment and expectations. Not always a pleasant endeavor, but a worthwhile one. This story bolstered my belief in the kind of love that lasts (even, or maybe especially, if it's not the traditional monogamous, married kind). I hope it does that for you, too.

It feels a bit redundant to always thank my amazing editors, Ash and Cindy, and the folks at Bold Strokes Books who create the books and get them out into the world. But their work is essential and valuable and often hidden, and I remain deeply grateful for the passion and energy that goes into getting so many important stories published.

The same, I suppose, could be said of thanking readers. But none of this would matter without you, so thank you. Thank you for reading and reaching out and being a part of my life. It's a thousand times better with you in it.

Dedication

For all the jaded romantics out there. Keep believing.

CHAPTER ONE

"Hello, beautiful." Kathleen tipped her head one way, then the other, willing her brain to overlook the peeling paint and sagging front porch. "I told you I'd be back."

The house, of course, did not respond. But Kathleen was accustomed to one-way conversations. Or, perhaps more accurately, filling in both sides herself. If she could do it with her characters, she could do it with her house.

"We're going to have so much fun together. And we're going to make you so pretty."

She lifted her shoulders and let them fall, allowing the zing of infinite potential to course through her. All the more thrilling since she didn't often indulge it outside the confines of her writing. But she'd finally turned that writing into a career that afforded her a decent living and a gorgeous old farmhouse, so it seemed fitting to let all that possibility out to play.

That said, it was barely thirty degrees out and her imagination didn't keep her warm. Time to take her flights of fancy inside. She picked her way up the icy and uneven sidewalk to the front porch. She fished out the keys the Realtor had handed over that morning at the bank and gingerly made her way up the slippery steps.

The roof over the porch needed replacing, but it was still intact, meaning the wood planks underneath were dry. She added a snow shovel and rock salt to the running list in her mind, then stomped to dislodge the snow from her boots. And promptly fell through.

Well, not all the way through. One leg. To just above the knee. She let out a yelp, as much surprise as pain, and dropped both the keys and her purse. "Shit."

After a moment of getting her bearings, she wiggled her toes and moved her foot from side to side. A light sprain, maybe, but nothing worse. A minor miracle, all things considered.

Except for the fact that she was stuck. As in, really stuck. The splintered wood caught her jeans, and her free leg did not have enough leverage or strength to force the matter. She'd promised herself she'd start Pilates now that she had the time to, but she'd yet to actually do any. "Fucking Pilates."

There was also the matter of being in the middle of nowhere. Well, not technically nowhere. The tiny town of Bedlington was only about ten minutes away, but her house sat on a quiet road with zero neighbors in direct view. One of the main reasons she bought the house, even if it was shaping up to be a major liability today.

"Are you okay?" an unfamiliar voice asked.

Relief at being rescued—potentially at least—warred with embarrassment over her current situation. Oh, and the fear of being snuck up on by a complete stranger while completely helpless. She did her best to turn, settling for an awkward torso twist, and found herself looking at an androgynous redhead who could have passed for one of her students. "I think so. Though I seem to be stuck."

"That's better than hurt," the stranger said. "Can I help?"

She didn't see as she had much choice. "Yes, please. Be careful, though. The steps are slippery." And the last thing she needed was a slip and fall lawsuit before she'd even moved in.

"Got it." They made their way up and assessed the situation. "Do you want me to try to pull you out first? Or I can go snag some tools and we can do it more delicately."

It was hard to imagine tools bringing delicacy to the table, though she appreciated that this random passer-by had some at the ready. "I think if I can brace my foot, it'll release me."

Her knight in carpenter pants and plaid smiled. "Let's give it a go."

Kathleen put both her hands and her fate in the hands the stranger extended. The next thing she knew, they were both standing on the part of the porch that hadn't collapsed yet and she'd all but fallen into their arms. She reached for the railing to get her balance, but it literally gave way in her hand. Strong arms came around her, at once holding her steady and pulling her close. Without meaning to, she let go of the rotted wood and grasped the decidedly sturdier shoulders in front of her.

"All right?" they asked.

Other than the utterly disarming green eyes and woodsy scent invading her senses and making her woozy? "Good. Yes. Sorry. And thank you."

They released her but seemed almost sorry about it, a fact that made Kathleen more self-conscious rather than less. And then they smiled, leaving Kathleen scrambling to ignore the swoony feeling dancing around in her belly.

"Glad I could help. And glad you're okay. That could have gone way worse."

She nodded. "I'm not sure what I would have done if you hadn't come along."

"Kathleen, right? Kathleen Kenney?"

The discomfort of falling into an attractive stranger's arms gave way to an entirely different sort of unease. "How did you know that?"

"Sorry. Jeez. Didn't mean to be creepy. I'm Logan Barrow. Barrow Brothers Construction?"

The dots connected. "Oh. Yes. We're supposed to meet tomorrow, aren't we?" Had she mixed up the day on top of everything else?

"We are. I was just, you know, doing a drive-by." Logan looked sheepish now, like she'd been caught at something.

For better or worse, having Logan slightly off-kilter helped Kathleen relax. "Scoping out the job ahead of time?"

"Something like that." Logan grinned.

"I like knowing what I'm getting myself into, too." Not that she'd done a bang-up job of that here. Or in life, for that matter. But in principle, sure.

"Well, I know you bought it as-is, so I wanted to make sure it felt safe enough for a walk-through."

A snort of laughter escaped before she could stop it. "Now she tells me."

Logan glanced down. "Are you sure you're okay? I think you're bleeding."

Kathleen dropped her gaze. Her jeans had a tear that would render them useless for anything besides cutoffs—not that she wore cutoffs—and a smear of red covered both the fabric and her skin. "Oh, God."

Logan's hands came to her arms once again. "Don't pass out on me, now."

She laughed. "I won't. Not dizzy, just surprised, I promise. I didn't even feel it."

"Adrenaline will do that to you."

The gash didn't look serious enough for stitches, but she should probably go take care of it rather than traipsing through whatever other dry rot booby traps might be lurking inside. "Yeah, now that I know it's there, it hurts like a son of a."

"My house is close by," Logan said. "The Barrow Brothers office is, too. Both have first aid kits."

The thought of Logan on the ground tending to her was a step too far. She shook her head. "No, no. I'll be fine."

"You're not staying here, are you?" Logan seemed genuinely concerned by the prospect.

"I've got an Airbnb over in Bennington." The closest she could find that didn't involve sharing bathroom and kitchen space.

"Okay, good. I feel bad about you driving in this state, though."

Being fussed over left her even more uneasy than being flirted with, so she straightened her shoulders and ignored the burning sensation in her leg. "I'm fine."

Logan seemed reluctant to agree but didn't argue. "I'd feel better if you didn't walk through alone. Do you want to meet earlier so you have some time to do that before our official meeting?"

The thoughtfulness struck her before she realized she was about to drop a boatload of cash and it was in Logan's best interest to make her feel good about that. "It's all right. I did before I put in the purchase offer. I just wanted the experience of doing it again now that it's mine."

"Well, I promise you'll have plenty of chances to do that, now and every step of the way." Logan offered a playful shrug. "Assuming you want that, of course."

She never understood the big reveal on home shows. Like, sure it was cool to see it all done, but how were people not involved in literally every decision? She sure as hell planned to be. Even if she had no intentions of getting her hands dirty along the way. "I certainly will."

"So, not to be pushy, but will you wait for me to go in tomorrow? It would make me feel better."

She wanted to ask if that was contractor code or butch code talking. Assuming, of course, Logan identified that way. These young queers had so many more options for defining themselves than her generation did. But that was a personal question, and she'd already gotten more up close and personal with Logan than she wanted to. "I will."

Logan looked genuinely relieved. "Thank you. Ten o'clock?"

"Ten o'clock." That would give her a solid three hours for writing beforehand. Which was good since she fully anticipated spending the rest of the day trolling websites and home stores for materials and fixtures and all the other things she'd get to pick out to make her house perfect.

"Can I walk you to your car?" Logan asked.

A little heavy-handed in the chivalry department, but she had technically started it with needing to be rescued, so it seemed wrong to bristle. Besides, she was hiring Logan—her company, at least—to do her bidding for the next few months. There'd be no mistaking who had the upper hand then.

❖

Logan wasn't running late, but she was the last to arrive for the weekly meeting of the Barrow Brothers brain trust. Of course, with her parents at one of her dad's physical therapy appointments, the staff meeting consisted of her siblings and her. Jack sat at the table with coffee and a crossword puzzle, and Maddie flipped through one of the binders stacked in front of her.

"Hello, troops." Logan settled in her preferred chair and opened her laptop.

Maddie looked up. "Oh, good. You're here."

"And on time, I might add. I can't help it if you're early."

"All the worms for me." Maddie grinned.

Logan made a face. "You can keep them."

"Ha ha." Maddie rolled her eyes. "Anyway. Since some of us have jobs to get to, let's get started."

Jack closed his crossword. "I'm pretty sure we all have jobs and all know what we're doing on them."

"Not true." Maddie lifted a finger. "Logan has a meeting with a new client tomorrow and has no idea what she's doing."

"I know what to do with new client meetings," Logan said. "Even if I don't know what the client wants yet."

"Yeah, but you don't know what the scope of work is going to be or what the client is like." Maddie's tone wasn't condescending, but it reeked strongly of bossy big sister. Even though they'd all been working for the family business for over a decade, she'd been there the longest and took lead on most of their projects. That combined with a lifetime of being the oldest and pretty damn imperious about it and, well, there was Maddie.

"I met her just now, actually." Logan lifted her chin, indulging in the satisfaction of a moment of knowing something Maddie didn't.

Maddie frowned. "Wait, she's scheduled for tomorrow. How did you meet her today?"

"I did a drive-by and she was on the porch." In the porch, if they were being literal about it, but Maddie and Jack didn't need to know that.

"So, you stopped and talked to her?" Jack looked slightly horrified at the prospect of talking with a client when it wasn't absolutely necessary.

Maddie wrinkled her nose. "It does seem a little creeper."

Okay, so maybe they did need to know. "Her foot had gone through a rotted board on the porch and I saw it happen, so I stopped to help her out."

"She was stuck?" Maddie sounded more amused than concerned.

"Technically, yes."

Jack let out a snort. "This is going to be fun."

Though she'd only spent about ten minutes total with Kathleen so far, her protective instincts kicked in. "She seems really nice. I think it's going to be a great project."

"Did you do a walk-through?" Maddie asked.

"No, she'd scraped up her leg a bit and wanted to get back to where she's staying to clean it up." No need to mention the weird flirty vibe that was maybe just her but definitely felt mutual.

"Poor woman." Maddie shook her head.

"I hope she doesn't feel like her reno is jinxed," Jack said.

"I'll make sure she doesn't." Logan would have said that about any client, but she felt it extra about Kathleen.

"Okay, so rotted porch." Maddie, who'd opened her own computer, typed furiously. Well, as furiously as one could type with two fingers. "You'll make a note of any other structural issues when you go through."

Logan ignored the comment since it insulted her intelligence. "You know there are apps now, that can teach you to type."

"If I typed all day, I might bother learning. But since I don't— thank God—it's not worth the effort." Maddie continued pecking at the keyboard.

She'd learned from their mother, reluctantly, before heading off to college. It earned her plenty of teasing from her siblings and her friends, but she got the last laugh when it came time to crank out all those papers. And all those client emails now.

"Speaking of." Not a graceful segue but whatever.

"Speaking of what?" Maddie asked the question, but both she and Jack eyed her with curiosity.

"I want to take lead on this project."

Jack folded his arms. "What does that have to do with typing?"

"Well, if it was my project, I'd be the one taking notes." A reasonable deduction if not the most compelling argument.

"Why this one?" Maddie asked.

They'd been discussing it for months. She typically handled the design side of things, both because she had the best design eye and because she'd gone to school for it. But she'd been itching to do more, to see a project through from start to finish. And she was technically the age Maddie had been when she supervised her first job. "Because it's time."

"You don't have the hots for the client, do you?" Jack's face made it clear he was joking.

"Of course not." She crossed her fingers under the table, a fibbing habit she'd never kicked from childhood.

"It's settled, then." Maddie gave a decisive nod. "Mom and Dad will be so pleased."

She smiled because they would be. And making her parents proud mattered. Probably more so because they were proud of their kids no matter what. "I've been fiddling with the project management software, but I'll plan to run everything by you before presenting it to Kathleen. Ms. Kenney. The client."

Jack laughed and Maddie looked incredulous, like she might be regretting her decision. "You've got to figure out what she wants first," Maddie said.

She ignored the flush that warmed her cheeks. "I'll ask her, of course. And default to formality until she tells me otherwise."

"I was talking about her house."

Oh. That. Logan smiled, not even having to fake confidence on that front. "Piece of cake."

CHAPTER TWO

After a stop at her apartment to bandage her leg and change clothes, Kathleen decided she'd earned a little retail therapy. She meandered the aisles of the home store, resisting the urge to put things in her cart at random and reminding herself it was a matter of delayed gratification more than denied. What she needed was inspiration. And then a plan. And then she could buy all the obscenely soft throw blankets and chunky brass asterisks her heart desired.

Though, maybe, the asterisk could come home with her today. She'd never seen one before and what if she couldn't find another when the time came? It spoke to her writer nerd soul. Into the cart it went. Along with the mug that declared "I'm a grown ass lady and I do what I want."

Because she was. And perhaps more importantly, she finally had the bank account to back it up. Well, within reason. Financial freedom was relative after two decades of hustling between adjunct gigs and shoestring freelance work.

She continued to wander, snapping photos and taking notes. She didn't plan to decorate her house lavishly, but she had every intention of decorating it on purpose. With vision, not with random things she'd been able to pick up on the cheap.

Satisfied with the outing, and her display of self-control, she headed to the registers. She let a bag of dark chocolate covered cherries snag her attention and added them to the pile of purchases. She deserved a treat after her brush with death that morning.

Even if it wasn't anywhere near a brush with death. The fact of the matter was that brushing up against Logan left her more frazzled than her fall through the porch had. Even now, hours later, she could feel the warmth radiating from Logan's body, her firm grip as she held Kathleen steady. A fact that was utterly and absolutely not okay.

"Ma'am?"

Kathleen's attention crashed back into the moment and the bright-eyed cashier with big glasses who reminded her of her favorite student. "Sorry?"

"Your total is seventy-three twelve."

"Oh. Yes. Sorry." She tapped the card she'd already pulled out to the screen.

"You're fine. Would you like a bag?"

"Yes, please." Because all her reusable ones were stuffed in one of the straggler boxes of things she scrambled to pack after the movers had come and gone. She needed to find those.

She strolled out, shopping bag in each hand. She'd no sooner loaded them into the trunk than her phone rang. She groaned, thinking it might be her mother, only to be pleasantly surprised by Trudy's face smiling on her screen.

"Aren't you supposed to be at work?" Kathleen asked in lieu of a hello.

"Who says I'm not?" Trudy, her best friend but also the interim dean at one of Kathleen's former adjunct gigs, laughed. "I swear, the higher up the food chain you go, the less work there is to do."

The assertion didn't surprise her, though she had no doubt Trudy hustled plenty, trying to do right by both her students and her faculty. "Yeah, but you have to hang out with the provost."

Trudy let out a snort. "Truth."

"Seriously, though. Is everything okay?" They were old enough to talk on the phone still, but not so old that random calls in the middle of the day were a thing.

"That's my line, new homeowner. How was it walking through now that it's yours?"

She climbed into the front seat but didn't start the engine. "I wouldn't know."

"What is that supposed to mean?" Trudy asked, instantly suspicious.

"I didn't actually make it into the house. I was too busy falling through the front porch." She reached down and patted her leg lightly. Even through the bandage and clean jeans, she could tell a doozy of a bruise was forming.

"Oh, my God. Are you okay?"

She relayed the highlights, from getting stuck to Logan showing up and saving the day.

"That's one hell of a meet-cute." Trudy might be a Black feminist scholar, but she loved a romance as much as Kathleen did.

"Stop." Though even as she protested, she filed away the idea.

"I'm serious. Rescued by the contractor you'll be working in close quarters with for the next several months? Having that contractor be butch and rugged and chivalrous?"

"Who said anything about butch and rugged?" She very specifically hadn't, even if the description suited Logan to a T.

"You didn't have to," Trudy said.

A sniff of dismissal would have been more effective, but what came out was a snort of laughter. "She's like half my age."

"Age gap."

Kathleen rolled her eyes. "And I have no intentions of getting involved, with her or anyone else."

"Ice queen." Again, no hesitation.

"You can't just keep throwing tropes at me," Kathleen said, even as she laughed at the assessment.

"Sure I can. I don't really see you as an ice queen, though. Maybe grumpy and sunshine."

She shouldn't take the bait but, damn it, how could she not? "Are you calling me grumpy?"

"Stubborn. Set in your ways. Jaded when it comes to love." Trudy paused. "Hmm. Maybe you are an ice queen."

"I'm hanging up now." Kathleen started the engine.

"Wait. When are you going back to the house?"

"Tomorrow morning for my meeting with the contractor." Meet-cute—or meet cringe—aside, she was counting the hours. She didn't have enough of a design eye to know exactly what she wanted, but she couldn't wait to figure it out. And Barrow Brothers promised to deliver both the vision and the finished product.

"With Logan, you mean," Trudy said.

Kathleen groaned. "Either tell me about you or I really am hanging up."

"There was a brouhaha at Faculty Senate last night, but we should both be drinking a glass of wine for that story. You busy tonight?"

"I have a hot date with my outline." Because she couldn't start writing the next book until she had a solid sense of where it was going and how it was going to get there.

"Take a break for virtual happy hour with me?" Trudy asked.

"Always." Because work should always be balanced with play. And because she might write happily ever afters for a living now, but friends were her true love, and Trudy topped that list.

❖

Logan pulled up to Kathleen's house, just as she had the day before. Only this time, Kathleen wasn't lodged in the floor of her front porch like some errant weed sprouting from a crack in the sidewalk. She stood on the crumbling path to said porch, arms folded, and seemed to be staring it down.

Logan parked and got out. Kathleen turned and offered a wave before turning her gaze back to the porch. Logan joined her. "It wasn't personal, you know. Rot chooses its victims at random."

Kathleen laughed. "How did you know that's what I was thinking?"

"Lucky guess. Good morning, by the way."

Kathleen faced her fully. "Good morning."

"Thank you for waiting for me. I feel better going in together." Because she'd feel that way about any client, not just this one.

"Well, it seemed more practical than paternalistic. You can't very well get on with your job if I've fallen through the floor or am lying trapped under a collapsed wall."

Kathleen said it lightly, but the mere thought had Logan's stomach turning. Again, because she cared about the safety and well-being of all her clients. "Let's hope we don't have to worry about either of those things."

"We shouldn't. I bought the house as is, but I did have it inspected. The porch got flagged, but the rest of the structure is solid." Kathleen gave a brisk nod, all business. "It might be a fanciful purchase, but it's not a foolish one."

She wanted to ask what made it fanciful. Along with what brought Kathleen to Bedlington in the first place and if she was moving here alone. But first things first. "Let's go in, then, and see what we're working with."

Kathleen led the way, stepping gingerly up the porch steps and reaching over where she'd fallen through to slide her key into the lock. Then she did this adorable little leap, over the hole and into the house. Logan followed, more because her legs were too short not to than wanting to be cute about it.

Kathleen turned with a grin. "Welcome."

"Thank you." Logan took in the foyer's details and filed them away. The carpet on the stairs had crossed the line from tired to sad, but the newel post and banister had escaped painting. High ceilings and an ornate chandelier she hoped Kathleen decided to keep. A narrow hall presumably led to the kitchen, and a pair of French doors opened to the living room.

"Most of the rooms just need cosmetic work." Kathleen eyed Logan. "If you consider stripping and refinishing the floors cosmetic, that is."

Logan nodded. "I do."

"I had half a mind to knock down the wall between the kitchen and living room, but I'm worried it will feel too modern." Kathleen gestured behind her. "I'd love to know what you think."

Kathleen led the way to the kitchen, a medium-sized room whose layout was not helping it in any way. "I can see why you'd want to open it up, though."

"There's also this." Kathleen opened a door on the opposite wall, revealing a butler's pantry with built-in drawers and glass-fronted cabinets.

"Nice."

"Right?" Kathleen beamed. "Maybe it would be more practical to take out this wall and turn it into a breakfast nook? Even though I really love it as it is."

Logan prided herself on being able to walk the line between steamrolling clients and letting them make terrible design choices, though she'd had moments of straying too far in one direction or the other. "It's perfect. You'd lose a lot of character without gaining much usable space."

"Yeah." Kathleen sighed. "But as cliché as it is, I want an island."

Of course she did. "Islands are super practical, which exempts them from being cliché."

"That's a nice way of putting it," Kathleen said like she actually believed it, too.

"It's true." Logan turned one way, then the other, taking measurements in her mind. "Planning to entertain a lot?"

"Oh, God, no."

Logan couldn't help but laugh at how immediate and emphatic the denial came. "Sorry, sorry. Didn't mean to assume."

Kathleen lifted a shoulder. "Can you tell I'm an introvert?"

"I hadn't figured it out before, but I get it." A person couldn't spend more than half an hour with her brother Jack and not get it.

"I do love to cook, though. And I've never had an island. I promised myself I'd have that if nothing else."

Like she did with lots of clients, Logan wondered where Kathleen had lived before. If she'd ever owned a home or always rented. Whether she'd lived alone or with someone else. And, perhaps above all, why she'd chosen to put down roots in a tiny Vermont town out of the way to pretty much everywhere. "Then you shall have it. And a whole lot else, if I have anything to do with it."

"I suppose that's why I hired you." Kathleen's smile looked victorious, maybe even a little smug.

Logan couldn't decide whether that smile had anything to do with her, but it was hard not to take it as a compliment. "You won't be disappointed."

Kathleen folded her arms and lifted her chin, clearly sensing the shift in Logan's energy. "So, what are you going to do about my kitchen?"

God, she loved this part of the process. With or without a gorgeous client spurring her on. "Well, I'm thinking we create a cased opening that matches the one from the foyer into the living room. Maybe French doors for cohesion, maybe not if you want the wall space. It will give the feeling of openness without feeling out of place. Then, unless you're attached to having a formal dining room, we combine that with the kitchen and create an island that goes across like this with some seating and a smaller dining table in the corner there."

It was probably too much information too fast. She had a habit of doing that when she got excited. But one look at Kathleen made it clear she'd kept up. And liked what she heard. "Yes."

"Keep the sink under the window, add some open shelves." She spread her arms to indicate both sides. "Then uppers along that wall and a surround for the fridge."

Kathleen nodded. "Do we get to talk materials yet, or is that getting ahead of myself?"

She flipped open the leather-bound journal she'd brought to take notes. "It's never too early to talk materials."

"I'd love an enamel sink with drainboards, but I'll settle for apron-front if that's not gettable."

Logan jotted it down. When Kathleen didn't continue, she looked up. "And?"

"And I haven't decided on anything else yet. I just feel really strongly about the sink."

That was a first. "Ah."

"I want a farmhouse aesthetic. I mean, obviously. I bought a farmhouse."

"Those two things don't always go together." Much to her chagrin.

"Well, they do in my book," Kathleen said with emphasis to imply judgment of anyone who disagreed.

"Then that's exactly what you'll have. White cupboards are probably the most traditional, but you could do a color and get away with it. I can work up a few options, but if you're leaning in a particular direction, I'll use that as my starting point."

Kathleen turned a slow circle. "In my head they're colored, but light. Like a green or blue. With quartz counters and a white backsplash."

That was easy. "Excellent choices."

"I don't know enough to come up with it all myself, but I know what I like when I see it."

So that settled that. "Okay, I'm going to take measurements so we can get the blueprint right, and then I'll pull together pictures and samples to go through."

"That sounds amazing." Genuine delight shone in Kathleen's eyes.

"Shall we walk through upstairs and get an idea of the rest of the work you want done?"

Kathleen nodded again. "Of course. Though, if you give me my dream kitchen, the rest will be gravy."

Kathleen likely hadn't meant it as a challenge, but Logan couldn't help but take it as such. "Nothing against gravy, but my goal will be to give you your dream everything."

"Everything?" Kathleen raised a brow.

"Well, everything I can that's within your budget." Because that might be an arrogant answer, but it was an honest one. And one that didn't cross any other lines that might get her into trouble.

"I see." Kathleen smirked.

Were they flirting? It sure as hell felt like it. Maybe she shouldn't be so worried about those other lines. Logan tipped her head, wanting to open a door but knowing better than to walk right through. "And maybe a few things that aren't."

CHAPTER THREE

L ogan clicked and dragged, adjusted and scaled. Once she had the measurements entered, it took hardly any time at all to get a basic rendering of Kathleen's house on the screen. They'd be doing some basic work on the exterior. Well, not basic, but a mixture of structural and cosmetic that would be more about restoring the original look of the house than inventing anything new. Nothing wrong with that, but not what got her juices flowing.

She toggled to the floor plan, cracked her knuckles, and smiled. This was where the magic happened.

For not having precise ideas of what she wanted her house to look like, Kathleen had fairly strong opinions of how she wanted it to feel—bright but cozy and, more than anything, serene. Logan had teased out the fact that she'd be working from home. And that this area of Vermont was where her grandparents had lived, which was why she chose it over western Massachusetts, where she'd been living before.

Logan hadn't managed to suss much else. Nothing about what kind of work. Nothing about Kathleen's hobbies or interests. And no clue at all about whether she had a partner of any kind, though she had used exclusively I statements about the house, so that implied plenty. It didn't strike her until after the fact that Kathleen managed to keep so much to herself without seeming aloof or unfriendly. Warm, but reserved. It made Logan want to get to know her better. Coax her out of her shell.

"I swear I can hear your wheels turning all the way over here. What'cha working on?" Maddie's voice came from across the room and cut through the cloud of her reverie.

"The design for Kathleen Kenney's place." Which was true, even if she hadn't technically gotten past pondering Kathleen herself.

"Nice. What are you thinking?" Maddie got up from her desk and came to hover over Logan's shoulder.

She toggled over the file of inspiration photos she'd begun to compile. "She wants farmhouse without kitschy or country."

"Sure, sure."

"And an office slash library because she works from home." Lots and lots of books was how Kathleen described it, with almost as much enthusiasm as she'd had for antique enamel kitchen sinks.

"I'd wondered what she did for a living." Maddie laughed. "Lord knows there aren't that many options around here."

It was true. Bedlington didn't boast any major industries of its own and was too far away to be a reasonable bedroom community for any of the surrounding cities. The school probably employed more people than anyone else, along with the little independent grocery store. Even growing businesses like Grumpy Old Goat Dairy were small potatoes, where the recent doubling of the staff meant hiring two people. "Her grandparents lived near here. Good memories, I think."

"That's not a lot to hang a hat on," Maddie said.

"Well, I think she lived in the Berkshires before, so it's not completely out of left field."

"And markedly cheaper." Maddie shrugged. "So, what's the scope of work?"

It could be curiosity, or it could be a test. Either way, Logan didn't mind. "Major kitchen and bath overhaul. Floor refinishing. Paint and lighting everywhere. Not taking out any full walls, but adding cased openings two places downstairs. Wait, I lied. We're taking out the tiny bedroom upstairs to add an en suite and larger closet to the main bedroom."

"Mm-hmm. Mm-hmm."

"She's got a healthy budget, so as long as we don't go extravagant on the finishes, she should be able to get everything she wants." It might be her first time taking lead, but she had plenty of practice when it came to getting the most bang for a client's buck.

Maddie folded her arms. "Exterior?"

Oh, right. That. "Rebuilding the porch, full paint job, new shutters. Roof is in good shape."

"What about landscaping?"

Logan blew out a breath. "We haven't gotten that far yet."

"Well, don't get too far without it. It'll swallow up more cash than you think, even if it's basic."

"I know, I know." She'd sort of forgotten, but she knew.

"And don't forget to work in a contingency. At least ten percent. You're not usually there when it has to get used, but it's so much better than hitting the homeowner with unexpected costs that add to the bottom line."

She'd sort of forgotten that, too. "I got it."

"Sorry. I don't mean to go all Dad on you." Maddie grinned. "Though, to be fair, he went all Dad on me."

"Yeah." He really hadn't with her. Something about being the baby of the family. The thing was, she wouldn't have minded. She'd much rather be taken seriously, be considered an equal, than be spoiled and not held to the same standards, the same expectations, as the rest of the family.

"I'm going to ask you to run everything by me, but only because Dad doing that with me saved my ass more times than I care to admit in the beginning."

"That's fair. Honestly, I want to do it myself, but I want to do it right even more." Which would be the case generally, but it felt especially true when it came to Kathleen. Maybe because Kathleen would be her first, and she had a lot riding on it. But maybe, also, it had the tiniest bit to do with the fact that Kathleen was gorgeous, and she had the feeling it might be Kathleen's first, too. Logan wanted to make her happy. Happy with the project, obviously, but happy with her as well.

❖

Now that they'd established the walls wouldn't crumble around her—or the floor give way beneath her—Kathleen got to the house early to wander the rooms before her second meeting with Logan. She took pictures and notes, a few measurements. Just enough to start shopping for furniture and other fun things. By the time Logan's tires crunched in the driveway, she'd worked herself into an almost giddy state.

Since giddy wasn't the vibe she wanted to convey, especially with the project budget on the table, Kathleen took a few steadying breaths and pictured her mother's disapproving face. It never failed to sober her right up. It dampened her mood only a little today, which felt like a good omen. She opened the door wide and smiled. "Logan. It's great to see you again."

"Likewise." Logan lifted a roll of paper. "And I'm very excited to show you these."

"Not as excited as I am to see them." As in, she'd been awake since before dawn knowing today was the day she'd get to.

Logan stepped inside and they headed to the kitchen, where Logan slipped off the rubber band and unfurled the plans on the somewhat cramped existing counter. "That island can't come a minute too soon, can it?"

She chuckled. "It can't."

"So, downstairs first." Logan swept a hand across the paper to smooth it.

Kathleen did her best to ignore the shape of Logan's fingers and the confidence of the move. Just like she ignored the way Logan's flannel shirt and carpenter pants made for a perfect butch contractor aesthetic, something Trudy would have a field day with. Instead, she studied the lines of the floor plan—familiar but slightly changed. The placement of cabinets and counters, the tiny curves and boxes that represented doors and windows, plumbing fixtures and appliances. Her brain raced, trying to take in the whole of it while capturing every detail at the same time. "It's beautiful."

"I love that you say that, even though it's just lines and numbers at this point."

She shrugged. "I make things up for a living. I have a good imagination."

Logan nodded, curiosity seeming to mix with enthusiasm. "Right. So, here's the new opening. Here's the island. Cabinets and appliances."

"Mm-hmm."

"Any questions?"

"Other than how quickly can you make it happen?" She lifted a hand. "Kidding."

"No, no," Logan said. "It's a perfectly valid question. And we'll get to that as soon as we finish going over these."

"Yes, of course." She'd meant to joke. But of course she and Logan didn't know each other, and Logan would take her seriously. Which was for the best, really. Keep things straightforward and professional.

"Any questions about this level?"

Kathleen cleared her throat. "No, it all looks good."

If Logan sensed any change in her demeanor or tone, she didn't let on. "Okay, so second floor has the bathroom and closet work."

"Yes." Because another mm-hmm might come across as rude and she certainly didn't want that.

"I pretty much split the square footage evenly between the two, but if you want a few more feet for one or the other, we can do that."

She steepled her fingers and pressed her palms together. "So, I've been thinking."

Logan lifted her chin. "Is that code for changing your mind?"

"This is the time, right? Before work begins?" It sure as hell better be. For what she planned to drop on this remodel, she was going to get what she wanted.

"It's the perfect time." Logan gave her an encouraging smile, which promptly made her feel like a jerk. "What have you been thinking?"

"I wasn't going to go for the walk-in shower and separate tub, but I think it makes sense. Especially with all this space." And especially since she wasn't getting any younger, though she didn't feel the need to say that part out loud.

"Definitely a great choice. Easier to keep clean and fantastic for resale value if you ever went that route."

Logan either didn't think about it as a safety feature for older people or she knew better than to say so. Kathleen appreciated either. "Great."

"We'll be moving plumbing anyway, so it shouldn't add significantly to the budget." Logan pointed to the space drawn in for the tub. "I'd leave the shower here and put the tub under the window."

She nodded. "Yes, please and thank you."

"You're easy." Logan winked.

She attempted a subtle clearing of her throat, the kind that would acknowledge the possibilities of a comment like that while pointedly refusing to engage in them. Unfortunately, it turned into a coughing fit. Logan looked at her with a mixture of apology and alarm, which only made things worse. "It's fine. I'm fine," she said in a hoarse whisper that did little to bolster the assertion.

"Sorry. I was being cheeky. I didn't mean to overstep."

And she was being a prude. Ugh. "It really is fine. Thank you for making the adjustments."

"In all seriousness, this is your project. There will be a point when changes will cost you time and money, but you should never hesitate to ask. I'll let you know what it entails, and then you can make an informed decision. Okay?"

"Okay." There. That was better. Professional. Grown up.

"Now, I didn't bring any samples today, but I did bring some pictures." Logan fished a tablet from the messenger bag she'd set next to the plans.

"I have some saved, too, if they'd be helpful. I've been gathering ideas for decor, but they speak to design, too."

"I'll take anything and everything you want to share. In the meantime"—Logan tapped the screen—"let me know what you think of these."

As Logan scrolled through, Kathleen felt herself begin to nod. "All of it. I love all of it."

"Oh, good."

"How did you know?" It was like her collection, only better.

"Well, you gave me a lot to go on."

She hadn't thought so. "Can I just say I want exactly what you come up with?"

"For now." Logan grinned. "This gives me enough to gather samples for the next round of decisions."

Kathleen tapped the tips of her fingers to her lips a few times then held them there, as though doing so might hold in the swell of emotion that threatened to burst out of her. Not that she needed a physical gesture to accomplish that. She had years of keeping her feelings neatly packaged and out of public view. Sure, she had more experience with frustration and disappointment, but she was ready to embrace joy and delight, even if she had every intention of keeping that to herself as well. It was safer that way. Neater. "You're very good at this."

Logan smiled, confidence radiating from her. "Well, it is my job."

"Still. Learning the technical aspects of design and knowing how to apply them in ways that speak to your individual clients are two different things. You have skill but also talent."

That got her a knowing smile. "You sound like a teacher."

Kathleen tipped her head. "You found me out."

"Is that what you do? Did? What grade?" Logan searched her face as though she'd been trying to figure that out.

"College, actually. Some community college, some university." Which she did love, at least the few magical semesters when she taught full-time at a single institution.

Logan continued to study her. "Did you move around by choice or were you stuck in the adjunct industrial complex?"

She raised a brow at the phrase—one she'd certainly heard but considered a bit over the line, even with the borderline inhumane employment practices some universities relied on.

Logan chuckled. "Sorry. The contingent faculty were organizing a union where I went to college while I was there and I got involved."

"Ah." She'd stayed out of the political fray herself, more because she hated confrontation than not believing in the cause. Knowing Logan had been involved gave her a strange mix of satisfaction and unease. "I tended to think of it more as a hamster wheel, but yes. I worked mostly as an adjunct."

"But obviously you're not doing that anymore if you're moving here. Unless you're teaching online."

She took a deep breath, still unused to the words she was about to say. "I'm a writer now."

"Oh, wow. That's really cool." Logan seemed genuinely delighted by the prospect.

Just like before, it left her feeling satisfied but ever so slightly off kilter. "I confess I'm still getting used to it."

"What do you write?"

She braced herself. Why was this part harder to say? "Romance. Queer romance, actually. Women, not men."

"For real?"

That's why it was harder. Way too often, people were either incredulous or judgmental. Even if they managed to be polite about it. "Yes."

"I'm not a huge reader, but I've picked up a few that my friend Clover told me I had to. I'm so going to look you up."

Would it be rude not to tell Logan she wouldn't find any books under the name Kathleen Kenney? Maybe. But what were the odds Logan would actually do it? Slim. "So, to answer your question, yes. Recovering teacher. Who now gets to hole up like the introvert she really is and write all day."

"Which is why the office is so important."

Kathleen reminded herself to be glad Logan rolled with the conversation shift. While she was at it, she also reminded herself to ignore how attractive Logan was when she smiled. "Second only to the kitchen."

"Obviously."

Logan continued to grin, and Kathleen continued to pretend to ignore it. "So, what else do you need from me?"

"Just a signature and a big fat check."

Good-looking and charming. Definitely a dangerous combination. "And it's okay that we haven't finalized all the materials?"

"Everything is a range at this point. And your estimate is at median price. The cost can go up or down along the way based on your decisions."

Made sense. "And what about unforeseen calamities?"

"I'm hopeful we won't have any of those, but there is a ten percent contingency fund worked in for unexpected issues that pop up. Because some invariably do."

The lingo made her feel like she was on one of the home improvement shows she watched to break the monotony of marathon grading sessions. "Right. Yes. Good."

"We have you penciled in to start demo next Tuesday if that works for you."

She swallowed the flutter of excitement, promising herself a happy dance when no one was around to witness it. "It's perfect."

CHAPTER FOUR

K athleen hadn't planned on spending much time at the house during the demolition phase, but when Logan texted her a confirmation and a *See you there!* she thought maybe she'd missed the memo of needing to give a final sign-off or approval of some kind. She didn't mind, really, since one of the coffee shops she'd scouted for writing happened to be in Bedlington, not a half mile from her house, and she had every intention of spending her day at the keyboard.

She pulled up to the house, but the driveway was already full of pickup trucks, so she parked on the street and made her way up to the front porch. A large piece of plywood had been set over the hole, making her smile.

"Temporary fix." Logan's voice came from behind her. "I promise the final version will be much nicer."

Kathleen turned. "I have no doubt."

"Come on in. The crew is just getting started." Logan opened the door but waited for her to go in first.

She stepped over the threshold and found herself in the company of a half dozen men, most of whom were twice Logan's size and probably twice her age. "Good morning."

They returned the greeting, but their attention immediately shifted back to Logan. Logan pulled out her tablet and started giving directions, clearly at ease with being in charge. The men didn't seem to mind and quickly scattered to do her bidding. When they'd all gone, Logan turned to Kathleen with a smile. "And we're off."

Exciting to be sure, but not something she needed to witness. "Did you need me to sign something?"

Logan regarded her with curiosity. "No. You signed the contract and paid the first installment. You're all set."

Now it was her turn to look confused. "So, why am I here?"

"Oh." Logan grinned. "Demo. I figured you'd want to get your hands in it, at least a little."

"Get my hands in what?" Even without knowing exactly what Logan had in mind, she was pretty sure she didn't.

"Put holes in walls. Break things," Logan said, like it was the most obvious thing on the planet.

"I don't think so."

"You don't want to swing the sledgehammer? Not even once?"

Kathleen made a face. "I really don't. Is that a thing?"

Logan gave her a bland look.

"Okay, fine. I watch enough HGTV to know it's a thing. But it feels kitschy. Like, they're doing it for TV."

Logan shrugged. "Maybe. But it's also a fantastic way to work out some rage. Do you not have any of that?"

Well, that was a loaded question if ever she heard one. "I tend to keep to more mild-mannered coping mechanisms."

"Yeah, but this is your chance not to." Logan wiggled her eyebrows comically.

A tiny part of her was tempted. To swing the hammer and see things crumble and splinter. To unleash years of disappointment and pent-up frustration, of feeling like she'd never be good enough. But the much bigger part balked. Scared of what might happen if it all came tumbling out. Or scared she'd be a klutz about it and look like an idiot. Either way, the sane and sensible side won out, as it always did. "I'm good, but thanks."

"Totally your call." Despite the deference of her words, Logan's face registered disappointment.

What did she care if Logan was disappointed? She didn't. Especially when it came to something like this. "I guess I'll get out of your way, then, so you can get to work."

Logan's demeanor changed. "You know you're always welcome on site, though, right? It's your house. You have a right to be here."

Probably the professionally appropriate things to say, but Kathleen got the sense Logan meant it personally. Neither sat particularly well. "I'm sure I'd slow things down. Don't hesitate to call or text me if you need anything. Otherwise, I'll steer clear."

Logan nodded. "Okay. We do need to set up a meeting to settle on the design elements."

Again, she couldn't shake the feeling Logan wanted to spend time with her. Silly. And likely a figment of her overactive imagination. She had spent more than a passing moment thinking about spending time with Logan. "I'm literally free any time."

"Let's plan end of the week. Friday afternoon? I'll be able to gather all the samples by then. And the house will feel more like a blank canvas than it does now."

Kathleen went for a brisk nod. "Sounds good."

"We can do it at the office if you'd feel more comfortable, but it's nice to see materials in the space."

"Here is fine." It wasn't like she didn't want to be in her house. She just didn't want to be in the way. Or, you know, get dirty.

"Excellent. I'll look forward to it."

Logan walked her out despite Kathleen's assurances she could find her way. She got to her car and started the engine, only to realize Logan still stood on the porch, as though waiting to see her off. Suddenly self-conscious, she shifted into gear. Only she missed and landed in neutral, revving the engine but going nowhere. Heat rose in her cheeks, and she was grateful Logan couldn't see. She shifted again and pulled away. Apparently, she didn't even need to fumble big tools to feel like an idiot.

By the time she got to the Sugar Shack, a whole two minutes later, embarrassment had settled into the sort of unease she could use. She'd decided on a meet-cringe rather than a meet-cute for her next book and needed the low-grade mortification that comes with a flub in front of exactly the wrong—or in the case of her characters, oh so right—person.

Kathleen parked and headed in with her laptop, ready for some caffeine and maybe a hit of sugar to get her brain in gear. She was instantly charmed by the café's interior: wood-paneled walls that had likely been in place since the seventies, mismatched tables and chairs, and a curved-top glass case full of baked and fried delights.

The expected aromas of coffee and donuts enveloped her, the notes of maple reminding her of her childhood. She closed her eyes for a second, just to soak it in.

Hopefully, they didn't mind folks who lingered, because she had every intention of passing many hours here.

"Morning. What can I get you?" The woman behind the counter had to be in her seventies, with white hair pulled back in a bun and a pair of reading glasses hanging from a chain around her neck.

"Coffee please, the bigger the better." She did a quick perusal of the case. "And I think one of the maple bacon Danishes."

"Excellent choice," said a woman behind her.

Kathleen turned and found herself face-to-face with a longhaired version of Logan. Or at least a close approximation. She was older, and her jeans and flannel fit a bit more snugly than Logan's. "Are you a Barrow?"

"I am." The woman's eyes narrowed briefly. "Wait. Are you Kathleen Kenney?"

She couldn't decide what felt stranger—recognizing someone in town or being recognized. Though, honestly, it was part of the allure of moving to Bedlington. She might want to hide away from people in general, but being in a town small enough to feel a sense of community registered high on her list. "I am."

The woman stuck out her hand. "Maddie Barrow. Logan's sister."

Kathleen took the hand. "Pleasure to meet you."

"Work starts at your place today, right?" Maddie asked.

"Yes. I think Logan wanted me to participate."

Maddie laughed. "She wants everyone to be as excited for demo as she is."

"I'm excited." She tipped her head. "I just prefer to experience that excitement at a safe distance."

"Homeowner prerogative."

It was nice to have that decision validated, whether or not Maddie truly meant it. "I'm going to tuck in here and get some work done."

"Don't let me keep you." Maddie lifted her chin in the direction of the register, where Kathleen's coffee and Danish sat waiting.

"Oh. Jeez. Sorry," she said to Maddie before turning to the woman waiting patiently for her to pay. "Sorry."

The woman waved her off. "Don't you worry. We always have time for a little chitchatting around here."

Kathleen pulled out her credit card. "And can you add whatever she's having?"

"You don't need to do that," Maddie said. "If anything, I should be buying your coffee."

"How about you get next time? I have a feeling we'll be running into each other if you're a regular."

Maddie grinned. "Deal."

She gestured for Maddie to order, then paid for both before taking hers to a table by the window. Maddie handed over her travel mug to be filled. "I gotta find the box where I put those," Kathleen said.

"I'll tell Logan to bring you a Barrow Brothers one."

"Oh, you don't need to do that." Because as easy as it was to be friendly and casual with Maddie, she couldn't quite pull it off with Logan. Trying would only draw attention to the fact that she wasn't.

Maddie waved her off. "Just some swag for a new client. And free advertising for us."

"Yes. Okay." That made it seem mutual somehow.

"I have to run, but I'm sure I'll end up at your house somewhere along the way. And, like you said, I'm sure I'll bump into you."

"I'll look forward to that." It struck her how much she meant it.

Maddie took her now full mug and lifted it in Kathleen's direction. "Have a good one."

She pulled out her laptop and thought about the home and the friends and the life she wanted to make here. And it struck her, not just that she meant it, but that she was making it happen. "I think I will. You, too."

❖

Logan pulled her buzzing phone from her pocket. She didn't even have to unlock the screen to see the entirety of Maddie's pithy text. *Met Kathleen. You have the hots for her, don't you?*

Curiosity won out over witty retort, at least in terms of priority. *Where and nuh-uh.*

Sugar Shack and you're a liar. Then, *Passing by so stopping in.*

Logan groaned. Not because she resented the check-in. That part actually made her feel better. She'd been involved in so few demos before this one, she wasn't sure where to look for potential issues. No, it was Maddie's assertion that she already harbored a crush on Kathleen. One, because Maddie could be so obnoxious when it came to stuff like that. Two, because it would be harder to play off since it was true.

She stuffed her phone back in her pocket, clipped her measuring tape to her belt, and left the laser level where she'd set it up to mark the new edge of the doorway. She didn't even make it to the front door before Maddie pulled up out front. And Maddie didn't even make it up the front walk before she started in.

"Couldn't convince her to pick up a sledgehammer, eh?"

Logan shrugged. "I offered. She wasn't interested."

"In your hammer?" Maddie smirked.

"Did you seriously come here just to harass me?"

"Of course not." Maddie bounded up the porch steps. "I came to check out progress and see if you needed anything. Harassing you is bonus."

She rolled her eyes but laughed. Truer words were never spoken. "I'd love to show you what we have going."

"Lead the way."

Logan headed upstairs first, pointing out the bedroom to be demolished and describing the new bathroom layout. "She decided to go for the walk-in shower and a soaker tub under the window."

Maddie nodded knowingly. "Nice. Especially for someone her age."

"Wait." Logan frowned. "What do you mean her age?"

"Middle age. Not old, but not getting any younger. Walk-in showers are safer, especially for people who live alone." Maddie narrowed her eyes. "Pretty sure I'm quoting you on that, accessible design guru."

She had made that exact argument on more than one occasion. And she was pretty sure Kathleen planned to live in the house by herself. It was the middle age part that tripped her up. Kathleen was older than they were for sure, but not by that much.

"What?" Maddie asked.

"I just wouldn't put Kathleen in that category."

"Uh, she's definitely in her forties. Early, maybe mid. That's middle age, kid."

Logan shook her head, filing the assessment away to pick apart later. "Whatever."

Maddie let out a low whistle, her way of letting it go but not without having the final say.

"Let me show you the kitchen." Most of the crew was there, pulling up laminate countertops and ripping out the old cabinetry. She showed Maddie the butler's pantry Kathleen had decided to preserve, then took her through to the living room where the wall would come out. "She hasn't decided on doors or not yet. I'm going to see if I can find a set that match the ones leading in from the foyer, though, because I think the symmetry would be good."

Maddie nodded her approval. "You've done good, kid."

"Good enough for you not to call me kid?" She had to ask even though there wasn't a chance in hell the nickname would die.

"Maybe when you have kids of your own." Maddie winked.

"Great. I'll get right on that."

"Speaking of," Maddie said, all casual. "How bad do you have it for her?"

"I don't. I mean, I think she's beautiful. And smart and all that. But that's it." Well, that and just reserved enough for Logan to want to get past her walls.

"I'm going to hold you to that."

She didn't like to admit she had a type, but she did, and Kathleen was it. And Maddie knew it. "I'm holding myself just fine, so that won't be necessary."

Maddie smirked. "Then I'll hold you to that."

"Fine. Is there anything else, boss, or can I get back to work?" Because she really did want to see what taking that wall back would do for the space.

"That'll be all. Do you want a hand?"

She imagined she would at some point. No point taking it when she had things under control, though. "I think we're good."

"Okay, text me after lunch with an update. I may steal Ange for the Lynch project if you can spare her."

Logan offered a casual salute, and Maddie left. She finished marking her lines, donned her safety glasses and gloves, and got to work.

Despite the chill in the house, it didn't take long to work up a sweat. For all that she'd nudged Kathleen to give it a go, swinging a sledgehammer was no joke. She made good progress but had no doubt her shoulders would ache the next day.

After taking a break to mark and cut exactly where she wanted the new edge of the wall to be, she started the dirty work of pulling back the plaster and lath. Unlike drywall, it crumbled at every touch, and it didn't take long before she was covered in dust. She stopped again, this time for water and a minute to check on progress in the kitchen.

Satisfied, Logan pulled her dust mask back into place and resumed work. Since this part didn't demand precision, her mind remained free to wander. Though, to be fair, it didn't get very far. It swerved right back to Kathleen and the look of skepticism on her face when Logan tried to talk her into participating in the demo. The way her smile softened when Logan tried to offer assurance. And the look of mischief when Logan needled her about having rage.

God. For all her teasing, if Maddie knew she genuinely had the hots for a client, Logan would never hear the end of it. Which was ironic considering Maddie was practically living with the client she'd developed the hots for—and started dating and fell hardcore in love with—while working on her house. Of course, Maddie and Sy had done a lot of the work on the house together. She wouldn't have the luxury of all that forced proximity with Kathleen.

Besides, that was Maddie. Maddie didn't have anything to prove. Logan did. So, she'd make do with admiring from afar. With a little harmless flirting thrown in here and there. Because what harm could that do?

CHAPTER FIVE

After yet another productive afternoon of writing at the Sugar Shack, Kathleen headed to the house. She couldn't wait to see potential colors and textures in the space, even if poring over tile samples and paint chips with hammers banging and saws buzzing left something to be desired. But when she pulled into her driveway a little after four, the air was quiet and only Logan's truck remained.

Logical, really. Preferable, even. Letting the crew knock off early rather than trying to carry on a conversation with people milling and tools going. But knowing that didn't stop the flutter of anticipation in Kathleen's chest at the prospect of being alone with Logan. Of being the center of Logan's attention and getting all bashful and weird because she couldn't stop staring at Logan's hands and wondering what they would feel like on her skin.

If she only had to contend with her own attraction, she could deal. For all her time writing racy scenes and characters who couldn't keep their hands off each other, she had a solid track record of proper if not downright prim behavior. No, that wasn't her problem. It was the fact that Logan seemed more than happy to flirt with her, sending her imagination six ways from Sunday. Kathleen had no illusions Logan harbored any particular attraction to an awkward, slightly frumpy, middle-aged woman, so the whole thing left her feeling foolish and self-conscious.

But as her new favorite mug so succinctly put it, she was a grown-ass lady. And she had paint colors to pick, so she'd get over herself and get on with it.

With a decisive nod for no one's benefit but her own, she got out of the car and strode to the front door like a woman on a mission. Because she was. Well, a woman on a mission who stopped short of the front door and tiptoed over the plywood covering the hole in her front porch just to make extra sure she didn't plummet through it again, but still.

"Knock, knock." She knew it sounded silly but was unsure how else to announce her presence.

"Hi." Logan emerged from the kitchen with a warm smile that went all the way to her eyes.

Kathleen blushed, remembered she was a grown ass woman, and cleared her throat. "Hi."

"So, I've got some good news, and I've got some bad news." Logan went to the makeshift worktable, made from a pair of sawhorses and a piece of plywood, expression suddenly serious.

Kathleen folded her arms. "Is there actually good news, or are you just saying that to soften the bad?"

Logan frowned. "I would never trick you with good news that didn't really exist."

The earnestness made her smile. "All right, then."

"I got a call from my salvage guy today."

She tried to decipher whether that counted as good news or bad news. "And?"

"And he's got a pair of doors that are a perfect match for the ones in your house, but he's only willing to hold them until the end of the week."

Kathleen nodded. "Okay, so what's the bad news?"

Logan frowned. "The part about him only holding them til the end of the week. I told you that you wouldn't need to decide whether you wanted doors for at least a month."

She laughed. "That's the best bad news I think I've ever gotten. Please tell me all your bad news will be that caliber."

The frown became a pout that was way cuter on Logan than it had any business being. "I can't promise that."

"I'm kidding."

Logan perked right up. "Does that mean you want the doors?"

"I wanted them all along. I just worried mismatched ones would look weird."

"Oh." Logan let the word hang, then grinned. "Why didn't you say so?"

Why hadn't she? Because she hadn't wanted to disappoint Logan one way or the other—a fact she only realized that moment and one that decidedly didn't sit well. "I was waiting to have an opinion until I knew my options."

"Yeah, okay."

Since Logan took her answer at face value, she didn't elaborate further. "Do I need to go get them?"

Logan waved her off. "Now that I know you want them, I'll take care of it."

Damn if she didn't love being able to hire people who'd simply take care of things. "Well, that was easy. What else do you have?"

"Options. Options upon options upon options."

Some people might find that overwhelming. Hell, when it came to other aspects of her life, she might, too. But when it came to her house and getting to pick from a plethora of lovely things laid out neatly in front of her? Bring it on. "Lay 'em on me."

Logan chuckled, but Kathleen was too excited to be embarrassed. "Let's start with the kitchen."

Logan had procured the sink of her dreams, so that was sorted. She went with the lightest quartz for the counters, but chose a variation with a subtle glittery vein in it, because who didn't love a little sparkle now and then? Cabinets proved more of a challenge, since she was splurging on custom and that meant literally every color was available to her. She settled on a pale sage that Logan assured her would look fantastic with the antique brass hardware and faucet she picked. A simple shaker style because she loved clean lines, and the fact that they'd be easier to clean.

Backsplashes proved even harder than cabinet color, at least on first glance. Traditional or modern? Statement or subtle? "What would you choose?" she eventually asked.

Logan seemed to hesitate. "For myself or for you?"

Curiosity became as compelling as making a decision. "Both."

"Well, I'm a sucker for herringbone, but that feels maybe a touch masculine for you." She dug through the pile of samples that had taken over the makeshift table. "For you, I'd pick the fish scale. Elegant but the tiniest bit whimsical. And if you did a grout that had a hint of glitter, it would pick up the shimmer in your counters."

She could see it instantly and loved it almost as quick. Like a mermaid, but subtle. "Yes. That. Exactly."

Logan smiled with confidence that toed the line just shy of smug. "It'll be great."

Bathrooms came next. Logan assured her using the same tile in the shower would provide a moment of continuity rather than cross the line into kitschy. And she took Logan's suggestion of a classic penny tile for the floors in both of the upstairs bathrooms and the half bath downstairs.

"Super fitting with the age and style of the house," Logan said.

"And not redundant? Or boring?"

"I don't think so." Logan lifted a shoulder. "You could stick with that style and mix up the colors if you wanted. It'll cost more not to get one in bulk, but not much."

"I like that. Maybe black and white downstairs?"

Logan made a note. "Done."

Since the sun was beginning to set, they made their way from room to room with paint swatches, making a few choices and narrowing down the possibilities in others. "I just don't know," she said, feeling weirdly torn between shades of blue and green for the bedroom.

"Well, I can leave my swatch book here and you can make a point of coming by at different times of the day. Or…"

"Yes?"

"Or I can get samples so you can see them on the wall before you decide."

The option appealed, but she hesitated. "That's high maintenance, isn't it? That's what you're thinking and not saying."

"It's only high maintenance if you request more than four. Or narrow it down to four, then decide you don't like any of them." Logan lifted a finger. "Though neither is as high maintenance as picking a color, then waiting until the whole room is painted to change your mind."

"I see." The tone might be teasing, but she sensed a kernel of been there, done that truth in it.

"But even when it comes to that, you're allowed one."

"Seriously?" She couldn't imagine being that much of a diva.

"Every now and then, the color that seems perfect is utterly wrong once it's up."

She made a tsking sound.

Logan chuckled. "It happened to me when I did my place, and I immediately painted over it, so it only feels fair to give clients the same latitude."

"Ah. Well, then." She smirked, oddly charmed by the admission.

They spent another half-hour poring over the paint chips, debating the relative merits of neutral tones. Logan's enthusiasm seemed to match hers, and it was easy to get carried away—hands brushing and shoulders bumping.

"You're very good at this," Logan said when they'd finished. "Your enthusiasm is infectious."

Kathleen smiled. "That's mutual."

"I have to confess I had a hard time looking at the paint instead of you."

The hairs along the nape of her neck stood up, and a tingling sensation danced along her spine. She didn't want Logan's words to thrill her, but they did.

"You're incredibly beautiful." Logan's lips parted, like she'd maybe startled herself, but she didn't look away. "I hope you don't mind me saying that."

She did. Of course she did. Even as her pulse raced and she fought to keep her gaze from lingering on Logan's mouth. "It's fine. I mean, thank you."

"I didn't mean to make you uncomfortable." Logan smiled with the same confidence and charm from earlier. Only now it had nothing to do with the house and everything to do with her. "It's just that I've been wanting to say that since the day I met you and, well, I'm not always the best at keeping my opinions to myself."

Everything about this crossed some line or another. Not that she'd been on the receiving end of unwanted advances often, but she'd worked with college students long enough to recognize the impulsivity of youth and the trouble it had the potential to stir up. "I'll take the compliment, then, and not worry about the rest."

Logan seemed to search her face, though she couldn't fathom what Logan was looking for. "Would you like to grab a drink together? Maybe talk about something other than business?"

In an instant, Kathleen found herself longing for the grinding screech of a saw. Or a drill. Anything, really, to drown out the buzzing in her ears. And the voice somewhere deep inside that screamed yes. She shook her head.

"No?" Logan asked, a mixture of surprise and dejection on her face.

"No." It came out sharp, almost like an accusation.

Logan didn't say anything.

A thousand possibilities ran through Kathleen's mind. Logan feeling sorry for her. Logan angling for a personal relationship that would somehow benefit her on the business side of things. Far-fetched, probably, not to mention unfair. But somehow easier to cling to than having to navigate Logan being genuinely attracted to her and not having the sense to put a lid on it. "I don't think that's a good idea."

"Oh." Logan, to her credit, looked genuinely disappointed.

"For many reasons, not the least of which is the fact that you work for me." Much like the "no," the assertion came out harsher than she intended. Which, in turn, made her feel small.

Logan nodded.

She cleared her throat. "We're working together, I mean. It's simply not appropriate."

"I understand."

A comment about being old enough to be Logan's mother bubbled up, but she swallowed it. One, because it was an exaggeration. Two, because it made her feel icky on top of all the awkward. "I think professional boundaries are best."

"Yeah." Logan nodded again. "Yes. I'm sorry if I overstepped."

It was Kathleen's turn to nod. If only it was as simple as that.

❖

It had been subtle, but Logan had zero doubt Kathleen had been flirting with her. Well, flirting back. To be fair, Logan had started it. Though she'd been subtle, too. Wanting to make sure the feelings were mutual. And wanting to avoid anything that might earn her a dress down from Maddie. And yet, somehow, she'd stuck her foot in it.

The worst part was, she hadn't even meant to. But Kathleen had been so delighted with her design ideas and looked so freaking gorgeous in the late afternoon light. The compliment had come tumbling out, and when Kathleen had gotten slightly awkward, what did she do? Did she back off and play it cool? No, of course not. She'd doubled down and asked Kathleen on a date. Things had gone from awkward to worse, and by the time they wrapped the meeting, she had more than a small worry that Kathleen would fire her from the job.

She hadn't, thank God. But she had gotten almost painfully formal in their text and email exchanges. And when Logan offered to show her the revised design mockups with the colors and finishes Kathleen had chosen, Kathleen had asked if they could do the meeting at the office. She wasn't exactly sure what to make of the request, except to know it couldn't be good. All she could hope was this meeting would go smoothly enough and Maddie wouldn't pick up on whatever weird frosty vibe had descended upon their interactions.

Her plan backfired about ninety seconds after walking into the office—long before Kathleen was due to arrive. Maddie took one look at her foot bouncing under her desk and knew something was up. A mere minute of needling and she was spilling her guts.

She'd never been good at bluffing.

"Should I apologize again?" Logan asked, hating that she needed advice from her big sister as much as she hated being in this predicament in the first place.

Maddie shook her head. "That will just draw attention to it."

Right. "So, I pretend nothing happened?"

"No, you act like the consummate professional."

The door to the office jingled.

Maddie lifted her chin. "As opposed to the consummate flirt."

Logan barely suppressed a groan as Kathleen walked in, looking gorgeous as ever, with the big purse Logan had learned doubled as her laptop bag slung over her shoulder. She wore tall boots over black leggings and one of those oversize sweaters that could pass for a dress. Her hair was done up in a twist, her cheeks flushed from the cold. If Logan didn't already have the hots for her, she would have developed them then and there. Which, of course, was the exact opposite direction her thoughts needed to be going.

"Hi, Kathleen." Maddie stood from her desk and crossed the room. "I didn't know you were coming in."

Logan wondered if the lie was for Kathleen's benefit, or hers.

Kathleen accepted Maddie's hug without hesitation. "Just doing a review of the final design now that I've made a million decisions."

Maddie laughed. "Come on, now. I'm sure Logan forced you to make a hundred thousand decisions, tops."

"Maybe two." Kathleen spared a brief glance at Logan before giving Maddie a warm smile. "Or one fifty."

"Ha ha." Logan got up and joined them. As much as she wanted to give Kathleen a friendly hug, she knew better than to press her luck. "Thank you for coming in. I'm excited to show you the final design. I think it's fantastic, and I hope you'll be pleased."

Kathleen gave a nod that could only be described as curt. "I'm looking forward to it."

Maddie's eyes narrowed ever so slightly. In other words, she noticed. Which meant Logan would have been screwed either way. At least she got the benefit of a pep talk before wading in.

"Well, as much as I love a good haggle over cabinet hardware, I've got to get to a site." Maddie put a hand on Kathleen's arm, as if to highlight the ease and comfort they shared. "I'll see you soon I hope."

Kathleen's smile at Maddie was just as easy. "If by soon you mean the next morning you stop into the Sugar Shack, then yes. I'll see you."

Logan's gaze bounced between them, a mixture of confusion and consternation. How had Maddie made her way into Kathleen's good graces so quickly while she'd managed to flub them so epically? Oh, right. Because Maddie didn't have the hots for Kathleen.

Maddie left, and Logan continued to stew in her own regret. At least she did until Kathleen said her name. "Huh? Oh, sorry."

Kathleen, who'd gone to stand behind one of the chairs at the little table they used for both staff and client meetings, regarded her with irritation. "Is this a bad time? We can reschedule."

Since the look seemed more accurate than the casualness of Kathleen's tone, Logan steeled herself to spend the next hour awkward and uncomfortable. "No, no. I'm great. This is great."

Kathleen quirked a brow. "Okay, then."

Perhaps if she acted like enough of an idiot, Kathleen would take pity, and they could move on quicker. The problem with that plan was, when push came to shove, she still wanted Kathleen to like her. Or at least respect her. "Please, have a seat."

Kathleen did, and Logan took the seat next to her. She opened her laptop and pulled up the plans. "The new renderings should give you a sense of how the colors and fixtures will work together, but they won't really help you tease out the subtle color variations you're considering in some of the rooms."

Kathleen nodded. "Of course. I've ordered enough things online to know the color on screen rarely tells the whole story."

Logan chuckled despite her nerves. "Exactly. But I'm really loving the play of cabinet and counter colors you've got going on in the kitchen."

Kathleen oohed and aahed over the images, seeming to relax in the glow of her own enthusiasm. Logan relaxed, too—in response to Kathleen but also because grooving on a design that clicked got her endorphins going better than any runner's high. "I love that you love it."

"I really do." Kathleen didn't say it begrudgingly exactly, but she did seem surprised.

"I'll bring over the paint samples and get them up. We won't get to the painting for a while yet, so that will give you time to really consider them."

"I appreciate that." Kathleen hesitated. "I appreciate all of this. You've listened to and incorporated everything I wanted and yet made it better than I ever could have on my own."

If Logan had a top ten list of compliments—well, professional compliments at least—that one would be at the top. "That's exactly what I'm going for, so thank you."

"Now what?"

Logan gave her a rough outline of what projects would be tackled when. Kathleen soaked it all up and, for a brief second, Logan forgot all about sticking her foot in her mouth only a couple of days before. Then she remembered and decided to go out on a limb rather than adhere to Maddie's advice. "I really am sorry about the other day. I didn't mean to overstep or make you feel uncomfortable."

Kathleen stiffened, and Logan immediately regretted her choices. "It's fine."

It so wasn't fine. But without an exit strategy, Logan couldn't see another route but to plow on. "I swear I'm not in the habit of asking clients out. We just seemed to be on the same page, and I let myself get carried away."

Kathleen didn't recoil, but she may as well have. Her shoulders straightened and she very pointedly refused to make eye contact. "I think it would be best if we set it aside and focused on the work."

Ugh. Exactly what Maddie said. "Okay. Yeah. Sure. I just..." When elegant words didn't come, she decided to cut her losses. "Yes. You're right."

"Great." Kathleen stood, probably more abruptly that she would have otherwise. "So, you'll be in touch with anything else you need?"

"Absolutely."

Kathleen picked up her bag and headed for the door.

When it looked like she might leave without another word, Logan called out a rather feeble, "Take care."

Kathleen turned back for a mere fraction of a second. "You, too."

CHAPTER SIX

K athleen managed to avoid Logan gracefully for three whole days. She didn't manage to keep Logan from her thoughts—or a couple of her sexually explicit daydreams—but no one needed to know that but her. She was a romance writer, after all. An active imagination came with the territory.

In those days, the first hints of spring—snowdrops, a few exuberant daffodils—gave way to tiny buds of green on the tips of trees and patches of grass that leaned more alive than dead. It put her in a good mood in spite of herself. In spite of the fact that she couldn't seem to set boundaries without coming off bitchy.

But her luck had run out. She pulled up to the house to find Logan's truck among the three parked in her driveway. Its presence taunted Kathleen and left her in a tangle of indecision. What was worse—having to interact with Logan or driving away like a coward?

In the end, she parked her car and pulled out her laptop, balancing it half on the steering wheel and half on her slouched stomach. Sure, it would be easier to sit in the passenger seat and use her actual lap, but that would have legitimized her decision to write in her car rather than go in the house and see Logan. This way, she could simply pretend that inspiration had struck, and she needed to get the words out before they flitted off in search of a writer who would pay attention and get them down immediately. Quirky artist more than skulking coward.

There was one problem. There were no words, inspired or otherwise.

She studied the screen, fingers poised over the keys. She read what she'd written that morning. Decent, but a scene that left her needing to sort out where to go next rather than creating a tidy little path into the next chapter.

Why had she come in the first place?

Because Logan had said the paint samples were up, and Kathleen was an eager beaver. But also because Logan specifically hinted she wouldn't be there much this week. With the electricians and plumbers working on the guts of the house, there was nothing for Logan to oversee. And Kathleen had taken that as a perfect opportunity to poke her head in and check on progress. A little treat to keep her going even as the close quarters of her rental felt closer and closer by the day.

The rap of knuckles against the window just about sent her flying out of her skin. She jumped. She screamed. And after a quick glance told her it was Logan lurking on the other side of the glass, she blushed.

Since she'd dawdled long enough for the car electrics to go to sleep, she had to fumble with the key before she could fumble to put the window down. Because that was how her life worked. At least when it came to being in close proximity to Logan.

"Everything okay?" Logan asked.

Vigorous nod. "Yep. Totally."

"Were you coming in?"

There was no way to say no without looking like an idiot, so she nodded again. "Yes. I just…needed to get something down."

Logan gestured to the screen. "I hope I didn't interrupt the genius at her work."

If only overthinking her life choices counted as work. "No, no. Just a few notes I didn't want to forget."

"I swear I don't know what I'd do without the voice memo thing on my phone." Logan stepped back so Kathleen could get out. "Do you use that? Like when you have an idea when you're driving?"

"Sometimes." As in twice, both after Trudy teased her about being a dinosaur for pulling over to jot things down.

"Well, I'm glad you're here. I'd love to show you a few things before we close up the walls. And, obviously, the paint samples."

Kathleen resisted a groan. Or perhaps multiple groans. One at the prospect of having to smile and nod over pipes and wires she couldn't care less about. Another at the prospect of having to do it with Logan. "I hope there aren't any issues."

Logan gestured for Kathleen to lead the way. "Not a one. At least so far. I can't promise it'll all be smooth sailing, but it is today."

Inside, sheets of drywall and boxes of tile for the bathroom sat stacked next to sawhorses and a very large and scary saw. Banging and the high-pitched whine of another saw carried from upstairs. "Looks like progress."

Logan offered an easy smile. "You don't have to say that. It looks like a mess. But we're done tearing apart and we'll get to start putting things back together soon."

"You can't edit a blank page."

Logan's smile became a look of curiosity.

The last thing she needed to be doing right now was opening the door to friendly banter. "It means most first drafts are shitty, but they're a necessary part of the process. Get the guts on the page, then you can make it look pretty."

"A perfect analogy for a renovation." Logan grinned. "Come on. Let me show you the kitchen guts."

They wandered the rooms. Despite her presumed disinterest in what happened behind the walls, she couldn't help but marvel at the intricate maze of pipes and wires. And knowing they'd been looked at and, in some cases, upgraded gave her the peace of mind she wouldn't be ripping into any of her nice new walls anytime soon.

Logan seemed perfectly at ease, leaving Kathleen to wonder whether it had more to do with being in her element or an uncanny gift for dusting herself off and acting like things had never gone sideways. If the latter, Kathleen envied her. She might have the confidence to do that in the classroom, but in purely social situations? She'd be stuck rehashing every second for weeks if not months.

When they got to studying the paint samples, Logan had them start in the kitchen. Since most of the noise came from upstairs, she was surprised to find a male version of Logan, complete with a flaming ginger beard, attaching wires to the fancy GFCI outlets Logan insisted were required to pass code in modern kitchens. If the look on his face was anything to go on, he was even more surprised—and rather less pleased—to see her. He lifted his chin rather than putting down the outlet or the screwdriver.

Kathleen smiled, amused and empathetic at the same time. "You must be Jack."

He grinned, then. "I take it my reputation precedes me."

"Well, that and the family resemblance."

Jack laughed at that, but Logan looked genuinely confused.

Kathleen waved a finger back and forth between them. "Family resemblance?"

Logan's eyes narrowed for a second, and she shook her head. "Yes. Resemblance. Definitely a shared gene pool here."

No longer sure whether she should be amused or irritated, Kathleen straightened her shoulders. "Don't let us disturb you. We're looking at paint."

Jack nodded and seemed happy to be let off the hook. "Better you than me."

She chuckled before shifting her attention back to Logan. "So, show me my choices."

Logan pointed to the roughly one-foot-square blocks on the opposite wall. She ran through each one, as though the name might factor into Kathleen's decision. Kathleen nodded, trying to imagine each on a larger scale. Logan observed that morning light was different from afternoon, and Kathleen might do well to stop by again to experience it. "Artificial light will change the look, too. Obviously we can't fully mimic your chosen ambient light at this point, but I can leave a few work lights on if you want to come after dark."

She could. She might even enjoy the exercise and the excuse to get out of her apartment. But the winners were obvious in her mind, and there was the matter of bumping into Logan when she least expected it. It wasn't that she couldn't handle it; she simply preferred not to. "I don't think that will be necessary."

"There's really no rush. We won't be painting for weeks yet, and you can stop by anytime."

She'd sort of imagined doing that. Writing in the café in the morning, popping by the house on her way home for lunch. Or driving by late in the afternoon when the work was done for the day. And now it all felt—what? Not icky. Just awkward. Like going to that end of semester party at her department chair's house and having half the tenured faculty have no idea who she was. She'd honed her skills in handling situations like that, but she'd also promised herself she'd stop putting herself in them in the first place. "Like I said, that won't be necessary."

She rattled off her selections—summer sage and crystal bay and mushroom bisque—and took more satisfaction than was probably fair watching Logan scramble to write it all down. Logan asked her about finishes and she rattled off those preferences, too.

"Are we done here?" she asked.

"Um. Yes. I think so."

"Great. I'll get out of your hair." She hadn't meant to be curt, but that's how it sounded. A fact solidified by the look on Jack's face.

Logan nodded, either unfazed or eager to look it. "I'll walk you out."

She bit back the refusal, if for no other reason than it would make her look petulant rather than self-sufficient. And at this point, what was ten more seconds?

❖

Logan resisted the urge to linger and watch Kathleen drive away. She let out a sigh, wondering if they'd taken one step forward or two back. She retreated to the kitchen, knowing Jack wouldn't want to weigh in but wanting him to anyway. "So, Kathleen is nice, right?"

Jack paused putting away his tools long enough to give her a pitying stare. "Damn, dude. What did you do to get on her bad side?"

Logan sniffed, regretting that she'd asked and deciding to play dumb. "What are you talking about?"

Jack gave her the look he usually reserved for when she came home with yet another piece of furniture she'd salvaged from the side of the road. Funny how quickly a look could go from pitying to don't patronize me.

"Was it that obvious?" she asked. It had to be for Jack to notice.

"I'll ask again. What did you do?"

"I didn't do anything." Other than put her foot in it and set Kathleen permanently on edge in her presence.

He folded his arms.

"I asked her out."

"You didn't."

"Oh, no. I absolutely did. I didn't mean to. It's just, we were having a moment and it sort of slipped out before I could stop it." Which made it even worse than if she'd been suave about it.

"That's not a thing." Jack pointed a wire stripper her way. "You don't accidentally ask a woman out."

She let out a sniff. "Curmudgeonly sods like you might not, but sometimes the more social among us get some good banter going and get a little ahead of ourselves."

"Nope. That's like saying you accidentally ate a whole sleeve of Girl Scout Cookies."

She thrust both arms out to the side. "Also a thing."

"They might not be premeditated actions, but you're not doing them without awareness. Unless you're, I don't know, moving through the world high all the time." He sniffed his disdain at the prospect.

She didn't make a habit of getting high, but eating entire boxes of Thin Mints while under the influence wasn't a bad time. Not to the point of this conversation, though, nor something stuffy Jack needed to know. "I'm sorry, did you go to law school when I wasn't looking?"

Jack zipped his tool bag shut. "Does Maddie know?"

"Does Maddie know?" She curled her lip with the parroted reply and gave it extra obnoxious inflection for good measure.

"I take that as a yes."

Logan let her head fall back and waited a beat. Though that was likely a sufficient answer, she righted herself and added, "She was in the office the morning Kathleen came in for her final design review. She noticed how squirrelly I was being and called me out. I confessed with the hope she'd take pity."

"Did she?" Jack asked.

"Not really."

Jack let out a whistle. "How bad did she lay into you?"

"Not too bad, but Kathleen arrived before she had the chance, and then Maddie had to go to a job site."

"You know that's a lecture delayed and not avoided, right?"

"I know." She sighed. It would probably be worse given the easy rapport Maddie and Kathleen seemed to have.

Jack tutted. He never got into situations like this. Like, ever. At least his default response was a sort of world-weary pity rather than scorn.

"The worst part is Maddie told me to let it go, and I swear I tried to take her advice, but then I wound up apologizing and it was like I'd crossed a line all over again." Her mind held the image of Kathleen stiffening at her words, and it left a knot of regret sitting like a stone in her stomach.

"What were you thinking?" Jack asked.

"The first time or the second?" Not that it mattered. She really couldn't seem to get out of her own way.

"Either. Both." Jack scratched his beard. "The first. Asking her out in the first place was the bonehead move."

Logan groaned. "I wasn't thinking. Haven't you ever been so attracted to a woman that your rational brain stops working fully?"

He shrugged. "When I was twenty, maybe. But even then, I blame starting T. I had legit raging hormones."

She laughed at the memory. Jack was Jack several years before he transitioned physically, but that first year on T had been a learning curve for all of them. "So, you're equating me to a teenage boy."

He tipped his head. "If you're gonna go and act like one."

"It wasn't like that. I'm telling you, she was flirting with me. It was mutual." Logan frowned. "Until it wasn't."

"Such is the way of women." Jack sucked his teeth. "That's why you only ask out women you never have to see again if they turn you down."

It was both the most logical and most depressing advice she'd gotten in a while. "Yeah."

"Chin up, kid. You only have to see this one for a couple more months, then you can avoid each other the way nature intended."

Ostensibly true and, by rights, something she should find reassuring. Only she didn't. Though she couldn't quite put her finger on why. Maybe it was because there'd always be this blemish of unprofessionalism on her first job as lead. She clung to that explanation because the alternative—that she'd somehow managed to get herself genuinely hung up on Kathleen in the short time they'd known each other—left an unpleasant pinch at the base of her skull.

"Come on. Let's finish up here and I'll buy you a beer."

They didn't hang out very often just the two of them, mostly because Jack was both an introvert and a homebody. The fact that he was offering meant more than just a distraction for the evening. "You buy the beer and I'll get the nachos."

"And wings?"

She grinned. "And wings."

CHAPTER SEVEN

If she had any sense, she'd avoid Bedlington altogether. Kathleen posed the argument to herself even as she steered her car in that direction. Not entirely, but until the dust settled—literally and figuratively. Once she was in her house, she'd rarely run into Logan. And once they no longer had to awkwardly navigate working together, she could manage said run-ins with a brief nod and a half smile and be on her way.

To be fair, she'd never bumped into Logan at the Sugar Shack. Whether that had to do with timing or Logan getting her legal addictive stimulants elsewhere, she didn't know. Either way, it was starting to feel like her place, and she liked it. And damn if the words didn't flow when she was there. She wasn't genuinely superstitious, but she'd had enough dry spells in her decades of on-again, off-again writing that she had no intentions of tempting fate on that front.

Which was all well and good until she pulled into her usual spot in the ten-space municipal lot and all but ran into a Barrow Brothers truck. Fuck.

Wait.

Chances were much higher it belonged to Maddie. They'd run into each other twice already since that first time, and it was becoming a bit of a running joke. And unlike the weird vibe she had with Logan, every interaction with Maddie had been easy. Too bad Maddie couldn't be in charge of her renovation. Then she wouldn't have to deal with the complicated mess of being attracted to Logan, trying to deny said attraction, and sticking her foot in her mouth in the process.

Not something to dwell on. No, this morning was for hot coffee, a maple donut, and a steamy first kiss. And not just any steamy first kiss, the best kind of steamy first kiss. One that happened when neither character expected it. One she crafted. One she controlled.

With all that to look forward to, and with the day's snow flurries showing no signs of yielding to April showers, she hurried inside. And found herself at the tail end of a line that stretched practically out the door. "What the…"

"Excuse us." A woman, probably mid-thirties, herded a pair of little boys in matching wool hats.

She stepped aside to let them pass and shuffled up in the line. The whole place was packed with people she'd never seen before. Mostly parents with kids in tow. Field trip, maybe? No, too many chaperones for that. And a mix of ages.

Despite the line, she got her order in and filled in a matter of minutes. Finding a place to sit was another matter. She scanned the small eating area, but there wasn't a table to be had. She might have to drink her coffee in the car and finally get around to checking out the local library.

"Kathleen, over here." Maddie's arm waved above her head.

She picked her way over—which felt like a strange yet accurate way to describe walking the twenty feet that separated them. "Did I miss that it's National Take Your Kids Out for a Donut Day?"

Maddie laughed. "First day of spring break. It's a bit of a tradition to kick it off with a treat."

"Better than day drinking in Daytona, at least for the under ten crowd."

"Okay, that's a mental image I didn't need." The woman sitting across from Maddie stuck out a hand. "I'm Clover."

"Kathleen." She shook Clover's hand and tried to place her. "Oh, you're the goat lady."

Both Maddie and Clover laughed. Clover gave a decisive nod. "I am. And you're Bedlington's newest resident."

"Well, soon to be. As soon as my house is finished." Which couldn't come soon enough, even though technically the work had only just started.

"You should stop by the farm. I'll give you a personal tasting." Clover lifted a hand. "Assuming you like cheese, of course."

It was her turn to laugh. "I'm not sure I trust people who don't like cheese."

"Hear, hear." Maddie pointed to the empty chair at their table. "Will you join us?"

"I wouldn't want to intrude."

"We insist," Clover said.

Since they seemed genuine, and since she hadn't gotten her coffee to go, she took the chair. "Thanks."

"How's the renovation going?" Clover asked.

An innocent enough question, and since it came from Clover and not Maddie, she assumed it didn't come with subtext lurking beneath the surface. "So far, so good, I think. The demo part seems done, and all the big decisions are made."

"Logan's lead on that one, right?"

She couldn't tell whether the question was directed at her or at Maddie. Maddie seemed torn, too, and her smile forced.

"She is." Maddie looked squarely at Kathleen. "How's that going?"

"It's great," she said, perhaps a little too quickly. "Logan has such a great design eye. She's suggested things I never would have come up with on my own, but that are exactly what I want."

Maddie's eyes narrowed slightly, and Clover's gaze darted between them. Kathleen bit the inside of her cheek and reminded herself that ten plus years in the classroom with college students had honed her ability to sit in—and wait out—uncomfortable silences.

Clover suddenly sat up straight. "Oh, my God. Does Logan have a crush on you?"

Okay, so they'd sailed right past uncomfortable and landed squarely in Kathleen wishing she could melt into the floor. "No, no. Nothing like that."

Clover looked to Maddie, who cringed.

"Okay, it's a little bit like that. She asked me out. I declined. No big deal." It was a huge deal to her, but they didn't need to know that.

"Poor Logan." Clover shook her head. "I mean, poor you, too. It's so awkward to have to turn someone down. It's just that Logan wants so badly to be taken seriously, and she is legit never going to live this down."

Maddie pressed her lips together like she was trying not to laugh. Kathleen, on the other hand, wasn't sure how to react. She'd crafted this version of Logan in her mind—confident, dismissive of social conventions, someone who didn't worry at all about being taken seriously. Clover's take threw that up in the air and left her with more questions than answers.

"I hope you won't hold it against her," Clover said. "She's a really great person but gets a little ahead of herself sometimes. Eager, you know? And I know I just met you, but you're seriously her type."

Kathleen blushed. "I—"

"Don't have to say anything. It's none of our business." Maddie looked pointedly at Clover. "And we're definitely overstepping."

Clover bit her lip, looking only slightly cowed. "Sorry."

If a small part of her bristled at the presumed familiarity, the rest of her reveled in it. It reminded her of meeting Trudy, of just getting to know one another and yet feeling like they'd been friends for ages. "It's okay."

Maddie looked incredulous. "Is it? It isn't our business personally, but if it's affecting how you feel about the work being done, it's one hundred percent my business to fix it."

"Let's say I took it as a compliment and leave it at that." Because she liked the easy banter but wouldn't mind changing the subject. And whatever her feelings for Logan, she didn't want to cause any actual trouble.

"Fair enough." Clover gave a decisive nod. "Maddie mentioned you're a writer. What do you write?"

Sort of like she had with Logan, Kathleen fumbled a bit but reminded herself to take pride in the kind of stories she told. And boy did she find a receptive audience. Both Maddie and Clover read romances. Maddie was pretty stuck on sapphic since discovering their existence, while Clover read anything and everything under the sun.

"The dirtier the better." Clover lifted a finger. "But nothing too dark."

After some gentle needling, Kathleen gave up her pen name. It wasn't like she wanted to keep it a secret. More like sharing it felt like roundabout self-promotion and she still got antsy about that. Clover squealed and promptly slipped into fangirl mode, having read and loved the book that opened the door to Kathleen being able to write full-time. Kathleen blushed, a mixture of delight and discomfort. "Thank you, truly. The attention makes me uncomfortable, but I'm a sucker for praise deep down."

Clover shook her head. "Girl, aren't we all."

"Why is that a thing?" Maddie asked. "Being uncomfortable, I mean."

Kathleen shrugged. "Because patriarchy."

Everyone tutted their disapproval. Clover sighed and said she needed to get back to the farm. Maddie agreed that the day was wasting away. Clover lifted her chin at Kathleen. "What about you? You going to sit here and write sexy things?"

She looked around. In the time they'd chatted, much of the crowd had cleared out. "Only first kisses today, but I'll get them in the sack soon enough."

"I'm already looking forward to it." Clover stood.

"Me, too." Maddie grinned. "I haven't read your first yet, but I'll be rectifying that situation immediately."

"Wait. Does Logan know?" Clover asked.

"Know what?" Though Kathleen was pretty sure she knew what.

"That you write." Clover made little circles with her hand. "What you write."

"Yes, but we never got around to the fact that I don't write under my real name."

Clover nodded slowly. "Do you not want her to know?"

It felt like a silly line to draw in the sand now, though she didn't plan on any grand announcement about it. "I don't feel strongly one way or another."

Clover continued to nod, but Maddie's expression held mischief. "So, you're not opposed," Maddie said.

"Not opposed." It's not like she and Logan were having enough personal conversations at this point for it to be a thing.

Maddie grinned. "Good to know."

❖

"What do you mean you hung out?" Logan paced the length of the office and back, stopping in front of Maddie's desk. "When?"

"This morning. At the Sugar Shack. Clover and I were having coffee, and she came in. It was a chance run-in."

"Clover was there?" Logan pinched the bridge of her nose and did another lap of the room. "How long were you all there?"

"Together?" Maddie asked, all innocence.

"Yes, together."

Maddie shrugged. "Half an hour, maybe? Clover and I headed off to work and Kathleen stayed behind to write."

Half an hour might not seem like much, but it was officially more time than she'd spent with Kathleen in the last week, including the design review. "What did you talk about?"

"Grumpy Old Goat, her books, you. It was all very friendly."

Friendly. Not a word she could currently use to describe her own interactions with Kathleen. Of course, that was shaping up to be the least of her worries. "What do you mean you talked about me?"

"Just in passing. Clover guessed that you'd developed a crush and was very emphatic that while Kathleen is totally your type, you're not the sort to go around hitting on women at random."

She stopped dead and spun to face Maddie. "What?"

Maddie waved her off. "It was cool, though. You know how Clover is."

She did. Clover could get away with saying just about anything to anyone and making it seem okay. It didn't mean she wanted to be the subject of said uninhibited running commentary. And most definitely not about her and Kathleen. In front of Kathleen. "I don't suppose it occurred to you to steer the conversation elsewhere?"

Maddie's shoulders straightened. "I'll have you know I did exactly that. We started talking about Kathleen's books. Turns out Clover is a huge fan but didn't know Diana Davenport was really Kathleen Kenney. So that had us going for a while."

She hadn't had a chance to go hunting for one of Kathleen's books yet, so she had no idea Kathleen didn't write under her own name. "Wait. Have you read her book?"

Without hesitation, Maddie fished a paperback from her bag and held it up. "Clover has and lent it to me. I'm going to put my feet up in front of a fire with a nice glass of pinot this weekend and devour it."

Logan snatched the book from Maddie's hand. A graphic of two women, one in a dress and the other in a suit, standing back-to-back adorned the cover. *The Kissing Clause.*

"I'm sure Clover will let you borrow it, too, but I have first dibs. I'm going to see if I can get Sy to read the spicy parts with me." Maddie waggled her eyebrows.

So many things about this threatened to make Logan's head explode, she wasn't entirely sure where to start. "Please stop talking."

Maddie cackled. "You're the one who started it with so many questions."

"And I have serious regrets." Though, as much as she didn't like all the specifics, she'd rather know than not.

"Come on, just because you went and made things awkward with Kathleen doesn't mean the rest of us might not want to be friends with her."

In the grand scheme of things, having Maddie and Clover befriend Kathleen should help smooth things over. Even if her attraction remained unrequited, she wanted that. Kathleen deserved to make friends in town, and Logan wanted to be part of that. Or, at the very least, not have things be tense and uncomfortable every time they happened to be in the same room at the same time. "You're right."

"I'm sorry. I don't think I heard you. Could you repeat that?" Maddie's expression made it perfectly clear she'd heard.

"I think it's nice that you've become friends."

Maddie pursed her lips at the roundabout concession. "Does it really bother you?"

Maddie might enjoy goading her, but she'd never do anything intentionally hurtful. Which meant she deserved a generous answer if not an entirely honest one. "No."

"Not convincing."

Logan blew out a breath. "I just regret biffing things in the first place."

"Yeah." Maddie got reflective for a minute, as though remembering her own missteps through the years. "Live and learn, kid. Live and learn."

"For the record, that's the worst advice ever."

Maddie smirked. "It's not advice. It's a platitude. They're different."

Touché. "Got any useful advice?"

"Be the consummate professional. Things will blow over."

She sure as hell hoped so. "Thanks."

"I'd say get yourself a copy of that." Maddie pointed to the book Logan still held. "But I'm not sure you can handle it."

Logan studied the cover once more. She wondered if the clause in question required kissing or prohibited it. And then, entirely without meaning to, she wondered what it would be like to kiss Kathleen. Not now, not with Kathleen so reserved and aloof. But in some alternate universe where Kathleen was willing. Eager even. Soft lips that yielded, invited Logan in. Or maybe they'd be insistent, demanding. Would she taste sweet, or would there be a hint of spice?

"Logan." Maddie's stern voice yanked her back.

"What?"

Maddie shook her head, as though knowing exactly where Logan's thoughts had gone. "Never mind."

She handed the book back, but not before committing the details to memory. She might very well regret discovering the various sexy scenarios Kathleen's mind cooked up, but it was a price she'd pay any day of the week. Even if Maddie's advice to keep things professional was sound, her imagination would have a field day no matter what. Might as well give it something to go on, since it was the only part of her that would be seeing any action for the foreseeable future. "I'm going back to work."

"But you just got here." Maddie seemed genuinely confused.

"But now I'm restless. I'm going to go do some manual labor and bring my laptop home for later."

"You always make fun of me for saying that." Maddie folded her arms.

"Yeah, but now I get it." Truth be told, she wasn't a fan. Hopefully, the sort of physical exertion Maddie swore by would do the trick. Or at least take the edge off.

"Aw, kid. I'm sorry."

Logan waved her off. "Live and learn, right?"

Maddie chuckled. "Live and learn."

CHAPTER EIGHT

K athleen switched the phone to her other ear and willed her
leg to stop twitching. "I'm in the little apartment I rented
short-term. I told you about it."

Her mother made a sound of disapproval. "That was weeks ago.
You haven't moved in yet?"

She closed her laptop, as though doing so would protect her
work from the bad mojo of the conversation, and got up to pace. "I'm
having major work done. It takes a while."

"I still don't understand why you didn't buy something that was
move in ready." Another tut. "Or less in the middle of nowhere." Her
mother had a habit of pretending not to understand things she didn't
like. Kathleen's choice of profession, for example, or her choice about
pretty much anything else. The only thing Patricia Kenney had ever
approved of was Susan, the professor of Medieval literature who'd
happily let Kathleen play doting domestic partner the entire time
she'd been on the tenure clock, only to dump her for a PhD student
the moment she got it.

"I wanted something with character, that I could put my own
stamp on."

Patricia sighed. "Well, send us some pictures. Your father is
anxious to come for a visit when it's all done."

Doug Kenney could be as much of a hard-ass as his wife, but
he had a sentimental streak. Especially when it came to his daughter.
And anything having to do with Vermont. "I will."

"And the contractor? You're not worried about being swindled?"

She chuckled at the choice of phrase. "No, I'm not worried."

"Good. It's hard to get good help these days."

She had half a mind to call her mother out for being a snob, but Patricia wouldn't have taken it as an insult. "Barrow Brothers has an impeccable reputation. And they're currently fourth generation."

"Family business. That's good. I'm sure whichever of the current brothers you got knows his stuff."

"I've got a sister, actually. And she does."

"Well, isn't that interesting," Mom declared, as though she'd never heard such a thing.

She refrained from mentioning that Logan had to be twenty years her junior. Or the fact that Logan had hit on her. No, she and her mother didn't have that sort of open, share everything relationship. Which was fine. Even if she suffered the occasional pang of disappointment that they didn't share much of anything. "Quite."

"Did I tell you that your brother is being recognized by the local medical association?"

Only three times so far. "You did. That's great."

"We're so proud. It's important to be a good doctor, but to be so dedicated to the community, too."

Kathleen could feel her mother beaming through the phone. Hopefully, the telepathy didn't go both ways, and she was managing to keep her eye roll to herself. Not that she begrudged Brian his accolades, but she was pretty sure the majority of his community service came in the form of charity golf tournaments. "I'm sure Britney and the kids are excited, too."

"Oh, yes. It's going to be presented at a luncheon at the country club and we've bought a whole table. It's a shame you can't make it out so the whole family could be together."

There was little she could imagine wanting to do less than fly to Virginia to sit around the table at some country club catered luncheon with the sole purpose of further stroking her brother's ego. "I'm on a pretty tight deadline here. And I need to be close in case something comes up with the house, of course."

"Of course." Mom hummed her approval. "It's important to keep an eye on things. Just know you'll be missed."

The thing was, she didn't doubt it. Nor did she doubt that her parents loved her and, in their own way, were proud of her. It was simply the double whammy of being both the black sheep and the ugly duckling in a family of smart, beautiful, and talented gazelles. They couldn't help what they were any more than she could help being quirky and queer and all the other adjectives her mother used to describe her, her work, and her life choices. "I was actually heading over to the house now to check on progress. I'll take pictures for you and Dad while I'm there."

"Oh, that would be lovely. You know your father loves seeing the guts of things."

Kathleen laughed at the assessment. Her father did love a project, though his interest sat squarely in the world of vintage cars, and his work on them happened in a garage more pristine than most of the apartments she'd lived in over the last twenty years. "I'll get lots, and I'll send a few of the colors and finishes I've picked so far."

"Yes, do that. I'm excited to see how the design is coming together."

They might not have the same style sensibilities, but decor was at least a language her mother spoke. And they weren't so far apart on that front that her mom would nitpick each and every decision. She chuckled to herself. Only the more eclectic ones. "Okay. I'll text you later. Give Dad a hug for me."

Perhaps a tiny bit abrupt, but Mom didn't call her out. She probably had a luncheon or a round of golf of her own to get to. "I will. Love you, darling."

"Love you too, Mom."

She ended the call and set down her phone. Eyes closed, deep breath. Requisite replay to make sure she hadn't said anything that would come back to haunt her later. All good.

She opened them but immediately squeezed them back shut. Going to the house would likely mean running into Logan. Not that she couldn't handle that, but did she really want to? It was getting more difficult to keep up the cool and indifferent act with Logan's unflappable bending over backward to be attentive yet professional, enthusiastic but reserved.

Maybe she should stop trying. Logan showed no signs of hitting on her again. And as Trudy kept insisting, was it really so bad if she did? Kathleen's answer was yes, of course it was. But that had more to do with her own baggage than Logan. And that baggage had a lot more to do with Logan's age and Kathleen's prohibition on relationships than the fact that they were working together—neither of which Logan could have known.

She opened her eyes and gave a decisive nod, even though no one was there to see it. She'd go over and be friendly and take some pictures. Maybe more chance encounters and casual conversation would buff out the lingering rough spots. Because even if she and Logan didn't become friends, it was a small town, and they were sure to run into one another. On top of that, she didn't want things to be weird with Maddie and Clover, whom she considered friends.

Yes, two birds with one stone. It would be perfect. As long as she kept herself from staring too long at Logan's hands and imagining the way they felt on that first day they met—holding her steady and fueling fantasies that left her feeling anything but.

❖

"Knock, knock."

Kathleen's voice carried into the kitchen. Surprise, delight, and concern flicked through Logan in rapid succession. "In here."

Kathleen appeared a moment later. "Am I interrupting?"

Logan smiled because, as ridiculous as it sounded, she couldn't seem to help herself when Kathleen walked into a room. "It's your house, remember? You can come and go as you please."

Kathleen blushed. "But I don't want to be in anyone's way."

"I promise you're not. Unless you literally insist on dancing a jig on a floor that's being tiled." Which made for an adorable mental image.

Kathleen cracked a smile. "Noted."

"Since you're here, let me introduce you to Leah. She's working with me as an intern for the next few months."

Leah stepped forward and extended a hand. "It's so nice to meet you."

Kathleen's gaze flicked ever so briefly to Leah's increasingly obvious baby bump, but the smile she offered was warm. "Likewise. Are you learning design or construction?"

Leah tipped her head back and forth. "I'm going to school for design, but I'm taking a year off because of the baby. Logan offered me an internship, so I'm getting to see both sides of the equation."

"Good for you," Kathleen said without so much as a trace of condescension.

"And Leah is teaching me all the cool new things the kids are learning these days," Logan added.

Kathleen gave her an incredulous look. "You're not that far removed."

"Far enough. A decade is a lifetime, at least in terms of what the software can do." She inwardly kicked herself. Any ground she might have gained in distancing herself from her undergrad days evaporated in equating a decade to a lifetime.

Kathleen probably wasn't keeping literal score, but she offered a wry smile. "No argument there."

"So, what brings you by?" Logan coughed. "I mean, is there anything you need from me? Us?"

Leah's side eye managed to channel both unimpressed teenager and Maddie's disapproving older sibling vibe.

"I wanted to take some pictures. My parents are interested in how the renovation is going." Kathleen seemed a little awkward, too, and Leah definitely picked up on it.

"Oh, I love that," Logan said, not even trying to hide her enthusiasm. The sharing with parents, but also Kathleen being proud of her home and the progress they were making.

"They're not really project types, but they do appreciate the process. Almost as much as the finished product."

Well, that explained some of Kathleen's disinterest in getting her hands dirty. Not having experience had a way of stifling interest as much as confidence. Logan decided to work that angle and see if it got her any traction. "Sometimes the process makes the finished product even more impressive," she said.

Kathleen shook her head. "That's what my editor says when I'm slogging through revisions."

"Are you a writer?" Leah asked with enthusiasm.

Kathleen stood a little taller. "I am."

"That's so cool. What do you write?"

Leah and Kathleen went back and forth for a bit, clearly hitting it off. Logan tried and failed not to be sad over losing that easy repartee with Kathleen. Though she'd still swear there had been flirty energy between them, and obviously there was none of that with Leah. Maybe they'd get back there at some point. Or maybe pigs would fly.

After Leah finished fan-girling and Kathleen finished brushing off compliments, they toured the house. Logan took the lead updating Kathleen on the progress but let Leah explain how they'd determined where lights and outlets should go. Kathleen soaked it up, asking questions and doling out praise, though Logan couldn't tell whether it had more to do with excitement about her house or deeply engrained teacher tendencies.

"It's really coming along," Kathleen said after they'd finished the loop and Kathleen had snapped several dozen photos.

"We're on track," Logan said. "Cabinets will be in later this week and, after they're in place, the guys will take final measurements for the countertops."

Kathleen clapped her hands together, a show of lighthearted delight that had anything but a lighthearted effect on Logan. "I can't wait."

"You should definitely come over the day they arrive," Leah said before Logan could.

"I think I will." Kathleen said it like it was a revelation, this casually dropping by to check on things. "In the meantime, I'll get out of your hair."

"Why don't I take a picture of the two of you?" Leah pointed to Kathleen's phone. "You, know, in the work zone."

Logan expected Kathleen to deflect, but she nodded instead. "Yes. That would be lovely."

"How about over there?" Leah pointed to the corner of the kitchen that had been completely gutted. "That'll be a dramatic spot for a before and after."

They shuffled into place and Logan resisted putting an arm around Kathleen's shoulder. Kathleen didn't try, but she did stand close enough for their arms to touch. Even through Logan's flannel and the lightweight sweater Kathleen wore, Logan would swear her skin warmed at the contact. Not the kind that spread slowly, like the first sip of coffee on a cold morning. No, this was more of a zing that zipped through her and made her think of the cheesy lines in the romance novels Maddie lent her, the ones about sparks and jolts of electricity. Maybe they weren't so cheesy after all.

"Logan." Leah's curt call yanked her back to the moment, and to the fact that she'd been caught staring off into space.

"Sorry."

Leah shook her head but laughed. "You were thinking about cabinetry, weren't you?"

"Uh-huh." A dorky admission but a hell of a lot better than the truth.

Kathleen bumped her shoulder to Logan's. "It's okay. I was, too."

Logan cleared her throat and wondered what chance Kathleen's thoughts had been the same as hers. Slim to none. "Sorry," she said again.

"Okay, you two. Smile." Leah lifted the phone, and Logan did as she was told.

Kathleen must have, too, because a second later Leah handed the phone back.

"Thanks," Kathleen said.

"It's a super cute pic."

Kathleen blushed more than when Leah had gushed over her work, making Logan wonder if maybe it wasn't as unlikely as she thought. It sucked that she didn't know. Couldn't possibly know. Much less ask.

Either way, Kathleen didn't linger. When she'd gone, Leah gave her a look that reminded her so much of Maddie, she laughed. "What?"

"Why didn't you tell me you had a thing for the client? It would have been way easier not to laugh if I'd been prepared."

"I don't," Logan said way too quickly.

Leah simply stared.

"Cripes. Have you been talking to Maddie?"

"No, I spent more than ten seconds in the same room as the two of you."

"Ha ha." She'd been going for dismissive, but it came out way too stilted to fly.

"I'm serious. And it's clearly mutual. You should totally ask her out."

"Lesson for you. Don't date clients." She didn't add that it was a lesson she'd learned the hard way.

Leah frowned. "What about when you're done with the project?"

"Me or in general?"

Leah's hands went to her hips. "Both."

"It's probably fine in general, if not ideal." Assuming the client said yes.

"Why not you?"

She could come up with some professional BS, but it wasn't her style. Besides, she really liked Leah. Had known her since she was born. Trusted her. And unlike Maddie, Leah wasn't likely to give her a painfully hard time at every turn. "Because I stuck my foot in my mouth and did ask her out."

"And?"

"And she shot me down, and things have been weird ever since." Ugh.

"Ouch." Leah shook her head. "That sucks. I'm sorry."

She was, too. "Yeah."

"But she's totally into you."

Logan shrugged. "I think you might be reading that one wrong."

"Nope." Leah pointed right at Logan. "She may have turned you down, but it's not because she's not into you."

Did that make her feel better or worse? Did it matter? Logan sighed. Yeah, it did. Not because she imagined Kathleen might change her mind, but because it made her feel like less of an asshole. It soothed both her ego and her good guy sensibilities. Even if it left the rest of her hanging.

CHAPTER NINE

If it's not too much of an inconvenience, I'd prefer to meet in person," Logan said, her voice sounding far away, like a bad connection on an old landline.

Kathleen frowned, more over the ominous tone than the request for a face-to-face. "Of course."

"And it involves something we ordered for your house, so I'd like to be able to show you what we're working with. Would you mind coming here?"

Again, she had no issue with the request itself. It's whatever lurked underneath that gave her pause. "How bad is it?"

"Not a disaster but more than a snag."

She appreciated the straightforward delivery on top of the honesty. "I'll be right there."

On the drive over, she conjured a few dozen doomsday scenarios. Burst pipes, collapsed walls. But then she reminded herself Logan said "not a disaster." Whatever else she felt about Logan, she trusted that Logan wouldn't downplay the situation. If anything, Logan would be the under promise, over deliver sort. She respected that, liked it, in spite of the firmer boundaries she'd set between them.

Maybe it was an issue with the new windows. Those were due to come in this week. Or the porch. The ground had begun to thaw and Logan said they'd be able to put in the new foundations soon.

When she got to the house, the usual vehicles sat in the driveway. Or at least what she'd come to think of as the usuals. Logan's truck, of course. Leah's bright red hybrid. And one Barrow Brother's truck that ferried anywhere from two to five crew members scheduled for the day's projects. She took the absence of the plumber's van as a good sign. Perhaps because it was farthest from her wheelhouse, but plumbing loomed large in her fears of what could go wrong.

She went to the side door and resisted the urge to knock. Inside, Logan and Leah stood in a sea of boxes, a few of which had been opened to reveal kitchen cabinets. Her mood lifted despite the reason for being summoned. "Hi."

Leah's "hi, Kathleen" came out with significantly more enthusiasm than Logan's.

Kathleen tried not to stare at the perfect corners and pristine finish of the cabinet in front of her, but it was a tall order. "Whatever the bad news is, I'll take it much better with these beauties around me."

Leah smiled, but Logan's expression remained serious. "You'll need to look closer," Logan said.

She shifted her gaze back to the cabinet closer to her, tipped her head one way, then the other. "These aren't the color I chose."

Logan nodded in sober agreement. "They are not."

Her lips pursed and she studied them with a more critical eye. "It's the same shade but darker than what I picked. Bolder."

"It is." Logan blew out a breath slowly. "And it was my error. I selected the wrong color code when I ordered them."

Kathleen nodded slowly, instinctive disappointment warring with the reality of loving the color in front of her.

"Barrow Brothers will one hundred percent make it right."

"What do you need from me, then?" Surely, Logan didn't want simply to display the evidence of her blunder.

"There are two options for moving forward, and I want you to be the one who decides which is preferable."

Ah. "Okay. What are the options?"

Logan cleared her throat and looked even more uncomfortable than when admitting her mistake. "The most obvious is to order the correct color. We would cover all the costs associated with that, obviously. It would, however, set us back two weeks."

And there was the rub. "Not a complete calamity."

Logan managed a half-smile. "Like I said, not a disaster but more than a snag."

"What's the other option?"

"Bring in a painting crew. They'll do a custom color match, and their work is impeccable."

"But?" She assumed there was one based on Logan's dour expression.

"But if you hold the samples up to each other, you might be able to tell the difference." Logan sighed. "And that's still a one-week delay."

In the grand scheme of things, neither was that big a deal. Sure, it would mean another week or two in her rental, which had a cost. Sure, it meant a delay in the happily ever after she'd concocted for herself, consisting of endless days of writing and cooking, of curling up in cushy chairs with books and wandering from room to room with the sheer delight of it being all hers. But compared to the countless other disappointments over her forty-three years, hardly a drop in the bucket. "What happens if we used them as they are?"

Leah perked up, but Logan just looked confused. "They aren't what you wanted," she said.

Kathleen shrugged. "They aren't. But I might like them better."

Logan was not swayed. "You don't have to say that. You don't have to compromise."

The word niggled her the way a mosquito bite would—unpleasant and triggering. But would it be a compromise if she really did prefer the accidental color? "Could you unbox a few of them so I could see them in the space?"

"Of course, but only if you genuinely want to."

She gave a more decisive nod. "I do."

Logan and Leah got to work. Kathleen resisted the urge to tear into some of the boxes herself, mostly because she didn't want to look like a toddler on Christmas morning. Leah broke down the cardboard and Logan dragged a section of three cabinets into a line. "More?" Logan asked.

"No, that's good." She angled her head one way, then the other.

"Look, I really don't want you to even consider settling for something that isn't what you want," Logan said.

She appreciated that, even if Logan's adamant tone bordered on edgy. "I wouldn't be."

Logan frowned, though it made Kathleen think of a kid pouting over an impossible choice.

"I like them. I want them." And never would have been bold enough to pick them.

"You're sure?" Logan asked.

She turned to Leah. "Am I not being clear?"

Leah shot Logan an apologetic look. "You sound clear to me."

"Excellent. Then it's settled. No delay, no fixes needed." She lifted her shoulders and let them fall. "I'm happy."

Logan sighed.

"Now what's wrong?" Kathleen asked.

"Nothing." Another sigh.

"But?"

Logan's face remained solemn. "It was still a mistake. I don't like making mistakes."

Boy, could she relate to that. As someone who worked with teenagers for sure, but also in her own life. She'd certainly made her share. "What if we called it a happy accident, then?"

"Like this little nugget here." Leah pointed at her stomach. "Not my best move, but I can't bring myself to regret it."

Kathleen smiled, a wave of affection for both of them. Not maternal, but more the older, wiser, been around the block a few times kind. Which, in turn, made her sigh.

Logan pounced. "But you're still allowed to regret this decision. Or change your mind. Do you want to sleep on it?"

She bit her lip and considered her options, then decided to take a chance. "Would you fall all over yourself trying to make this right for any client, or are you still overcompensating for the fact that you asked me out?"

Leah guffawed and Logan blanched, making her freckles appear almost stark.

"It doesn't matter one way or the other, but I'm curious." She paused. "And knowing the answer will make dealing with each other easier moving forward." Another pause. "At least I think it will."

"I…"

Her unabashed frankness had rendered more than a few students and even a couple of deans and department chairs speechless, so it shouldn't surprise her to have that effect on Logan. Disappoint, perhaps, but not surprise. "It's okay. You don't have to answer."

Logan lifted her chin, as though accepting an unspoken challenge. "In the spirit of full disclosure, both. But your satisfaction with the work—Barrow Brothers' as a whole but mine in particular—is most important. I do want you to like me, but I need you to like your house. Love. You should love your house. And it's my responsibility to make sure that happens. Above all else."

She'd already started to soften where Logan was concerned. Clover and Maddie had given her enough insight to put things in context, and it wasn't as though she'd disliked Logan to begin with. More the opposite of dislike, which stirred up all the shit that made her slam on the brakes and slap up her defenses. But there was more to it now. This passion, this drive to do her job well and to give Kathleen exactly what she wanted? Well, she'd have to be heartless not to be swayed. "I love these cabinets, and I want them in my home."

Rather than seeking yet another verbal confirmation, Logan studied her for a long moment. Kathleen mirrored Logan's chin lift from a moment before. Eventually, Logan nodded. "Then that's what you'll have."

❖

With the cabinet decision sorted, Logan and Leah unboxed the rest of the order, as much to have it ready for installation as to give Kathleen the pleasure of seeing them all in a nice row. Okay, and maybe to double, triple, and quadruple check that Kathleen genuinely wanted them. Kathleen pitched in and, by the time they finished, delight radiated from her. Not quite enough to leave Logan pleased with the kerfuffle, but the gnawing pain had left the pit of her stomach, so that counted for something.

"While you're here, do you want to get your hands dirty?" Leah asked Kathleen with all the genuine enthusiasm and naiveté Logan had brought to the table a few weeks prior.

Logan bit the inside of her cheek, hoping Kathleen would be gentle if not agreeable.

Kathleen looked up from the cabinets she'd gone back to studying. "Like what?"

Logan choked on nothing more than her own saliva. It turned into one of those loud, hacking coughs that left her red in the face and both Leah and Kathleen looking at her with concern. "Sorry," she said with a wheeze.

Kathleen narrowed her eyes, like she knew exactly what triggered the fit. Leah, blissfully ignorant, asked, "Are you okay?"

Logan nodded. "All good."

Kathleen took mercy and turned her attention to Leah. "Besides fretting about my cabinets, what are you working on?"

"The tiling in the bathrooms is done, and Logan wants to put up the trim before the sinks and toilets get installed so we don't have to work around them." Leah rubbed her hands together. "We get to use the nail gun."

Finally trusting herself enough to speak, Logan added, "It's not all that dirty, honestly. You're welcome to stay and give it a try." She shrugged. "Or just watch."

She expected Kathleen to make a face, then politely decline. Only she didn't. She gave yet another slow, pensive nod. "All right."

It bugged Logan ever so slightly that Kathleen said yes to Leah after saying no to her. Though, watching some trim go up and maybe tacking on a few pieces herself didn't really land in the same ballpark as knocking out a wall. And now that pieces of the house were coming together, Kathleen's enthusiasm to see and be part of the process would naturally increase. That's what she told herself, at least, as the three of them filed upstairs.

"What else is going on today?" Kathleen asked.

Logan pointed to the newly expanded main bedroom. "Drywall is going up in the closet and where the new wall will be."

Kathleen peeked in. "Wow. It's even bigger than I expected."

"It helps that we claimed an extra window. Having natural light from two sides makes a huge difference." A difference she'd mentioned but downplayed, not wanting Kathleen's expectations to outpace reality.

Kathleen stepped inside to take it in. Mark and Della stopped working long enough to offer hellos, and Kathleen slathered them with compliments. It highlighted just how much Kathleen didn't do that with her and gave Logan yet another pang of regret for ruining whatever chance they'd had at easy rapport. Kathleen apologized for interrupting and returned to the hall. A moment later, the three of them stood together in the bathroom.

"This is huge, too. I've never had a bathroom that could hold three people before." Kathleen turned a slow circle, pleasure evident on her face. Then she quirked a brow. "At least not without one in the tub and one on the toilet."

Leah laughed. Logan did, too, but with wonder more than amusement. Who was this woman and what had she done with the stiff and formal Kathleen she'd resigned herself to?

"You could practically host a dinner party in here. Or maybe just entertain a private guest." Leah winked at that last part and Logan cringed, fully expecting the insinuation to set Kathleen off.

"I'll be sure to add 'tub for two' to my dating profile," Kathleen said casually, sending Leah into a fit of giggles.

Logan shook her head, more confused than anything else.

Kathleen glanced her way and seemed to catch herself. She cleared her throat. "Anyway. Tell me about trim."

Logan picked up a piece of the simple one-by-four Kathleen had selected for her baseboards and a comparable length of quarter-round. "We primed and painted these yesterday, so they'll only need touching up where the nails go in."

Leah lifted a finger. "Having painted the trim of my bedroom on my hands and knees, I can vouch for this being the better method."

"Has it been cut to size already, too?" Kathleen asked.

"Yep." Logan flipped the wood. "And marked with the corresponding wall."

Kathleen looked duly impressed. "I would not have thought to do that."

"I didn't on my first job, and Maddie promptly gave me a lecture and lesson on tricks of the trade." Which she probably would have admitted either way, but something told her Kathleen would respond to humility more than cleverness at this point.

Kathleen nodded with what appeared to be appreciation, confirming she'd made the right call. "So, tell me about this nail gun."

Leah picked up the cordless model that Maddie made fun of but Logan preferred for small spaces. "I don't plan to be on the tool end of the equation most of the time, but I think it's important to know how to use them."

"It's always good to have a diverse skillset," Logan said.

"And a construction crew has more respect for a designer who isn't afraid to jump in when needed."

She'd said as much when she agreed to take Leah on as an intern. She loved that Leah not only remembered the advice but took it to heart.

"Interesting." Kathleen seemed to be taking it to heart as well.

Logan offered an encouraging smile. "That's true for designers but not clients. Clients get to do what they want and should be respected no matter what."

It sounded way cheesier than she meant it to, and Kathleen's smirk confirmed it landed that way. "Unless the client is overly demanding, mercurial, and impossible to please, right?"

Was Kathleen teasing her? She'd genuinely thought that ship had sailed. It might not be the flirty vibe she'd hoped for—or the dating that might ensue—but she'd take it any day of the week after where they'd been. "We respect those clients, too. At least to their faces."

Both Leah and Kathleen laughed, and Logan felt lighter than she had in days. Even before the cabinet debacle. Kathleen watched intently as Leah attached pieces in the corner where the toilet would go, then nodded solemnly when Logan indicated it was her turn, as though accepting a dangerous mission from a commanding officer.

Logan knelt next to the wall where the tub would be, and Kathleen positioned herself opposite, so they faced each other. "I'll hold the board in place," Logan said. "Just press the contact trip until it's flush, then pull the trigger."

"Is it weird that the firearm terminology freaks me out a little?"

"Nope," Leah said from the doorway. "I don't like it either."

Logan tried for an encouraging smile. "I promise this is about a billion times less dangerous."

"Right." Kathleen set down the nailer and wiped her hands on her jeans. "So, top and bottom, doesn't matter where?"

"Yes. I'd say about half an inch in for the best hold, but it's pretty hard to mess up."

Kathleen chuckled. "Don't say that. You'll jinx me."

Logan willed herself not to put a hand on Kathleen's shoulder. "I mean it, though. You got this."

"Yes. Okay." Kathleen picked it up again and positioned it with both hands. "Here goes."

The nailer did exactly what it was supposed to do. Kathleen squeezed her eyes closed. She also squeaked. An honest to God, ridiculously adorable squeak.

"Are you okay?" Logan asked.

Kathleen opened her eyes and blinked a few times. "That was so cool."

"Yeah?" She needed to break this habit of second-guessing Kathleen at every turn, but damn if Kathleen didn't keep surprising her.

"Do you feel so handy?" Leah asked.

Kathleen looked up. "I'm not sure I'd go that far."

Logan hesitated for a second, then took a chance. "If you do at least six nails, you get the title officially."

"Is that so?" Kathleen hefted the nail gun and stared it down. "All right, then."

Logan scooted along the wall and Kathleen worked her way down the board. It took ten to get it in place, and Kathleen did them all. "Nicely done, Ms. Kenney."

Kathleen smirked, though her eyes held a softness Logan hadn't seen before. Or at least not since those first couple of meetings. "Thank you."

CHAPTER TEN

H ow's progress on the Kenney house?" Maddie asked. "It feels so weird to have a job site I'm never at."

"You can come by if you want," Logan said more confidently than she might have a few days before.

"I don't need to check up on you. I know you're doing great." Maddie nodded, encouraging to the brink of condescending without crossing the line.

"Okay, Mom."

Maddie huffed. "I was trying to be nice. You don't need to get snarky."

"I'm not. You sounded just like Mom, and it was cute."

Maddie frowned, trapped. She couldn't take issue without implying something less than complimentary about their mother. And since Mom was there—along with Dad and Jack—she knew better than to go there.

"Is it going great?" Jack asked. Not snarky, but definitely suspicious.

"Yes." Logan straightened her spine. "Electric is done, thanks to you, other than some new light fixtures that haven't come in yet. Bathroom fixtures are set to go in today, along with kitchen cabinets. Crew is coming out to do a final measure for counters at the end of the week."

Maddie nodded her approval, along with Mom and Dad. Jack remained incredulous. "House sounds like it is great. How about the client?"

Everyone knew about her cabinet gaffe—not to mention that other gaffe, with the exception of Dad—so no point getting defensive or playing dumb. And for all that her family might tease her, she didn't doubt they had her back. Since only Maddie knew the outcome, though, she explained. "And she stuck around for a bit after. Leah and I were putting up trim in the bathroom, and Leah convinced her to have a go with the nailer."

Jack made a face, not even pretending to hide his disdain for getting chummy with clients. Well, chummy with anyone, really. Maddie looked impressed, if slightly uneasy. "And how did that go?"

"She enjoyed it. She's been really hands-off, so it was great to have her jump in and participate, even a little."

Maddie shook her head. "I meant with you, not the nail gun."

"Oh." Logan was tempted to gush but knew better than to overplay her hand. "Good. It was good."

Not enough to satisfy Maddie. Mom, either. Even Dad looked mildly suspicious.

"I think we're in a good place. She genuinely loves the cabinet color. I think it made her realize she could go a little bolder than she initially planned."

"Uh-huh," Maddie said. "And?"

"And I think the rest is water under the bridge. She seemed happy and relaxed."

"Well, that's how we like our clients," Mom said in her chipper, look on the bright side way.

Dad frowned. "What's water under the bridge?"

Jack jumped in before Maddie could. "The fact that Logan finds the client super pretty and made her feel momentarily uncomfortable."

A magnanimous explanation, and more generous than Maddie would have given. She shot Jack an appreciative nod. He rolled his eyes but smiled.

"Ah." Dad nodded like that was plenty enough detail for him.

"She and Leah hit it off, and I think that's helped smooth things over." No need to admit the pang of envy it left her with.

"I'm so glad." Mom, who was best friends with Leah's mom, had orchestrated the internship when Leah got pregnant.

Happy to have the focus shift away from herself, Logan pounced. "Not that Leah isn't great all the time, but I think Kathleen worked with college students long enough that she's super comfortable with people that age."

"Makes sense." Mom smiled.

"And I'm sure Leah didn't ask her out, so that's a win, too." Maddie smirked.

Had she been sitting close enough, she'd have kicked her sister right in the shin, and Maddie would have one hundred percent deserved it. Since she wasn't, she went for a wholesale conversation change. "Any word from Uncle Rich?"

That got a collective groan from the group.

"What? What did I miss?"

"He's bringing his fiancée up to meet the family," Dad said as though he'd been summoned to testify before a grand jury.

"And take inventory," Maddie said, lip curled in disdain rather than defeat.

"Wait, for real?" Uncle Rich was the other half of her dad's generation of Barrow Brothers. He'd gone to Florida for a trade show and not come home. In the few months since his departure, he'd gotten himself engaged and decided to cash out his share of the business and retire. Which was all well and good aside from the fact that, even with pooled resources, they didn't have the liquid assets to make that happen. It was all very stressful and gross, and she spent most of her time blocking it from her mind.

Dad sighed. "He wants us to meet Cherry."

"Cherry?" she asked.

"As in Charlene," Mom said.

"Oh."

Dad continued, "He wants to show off the Barrow Brothers operation."

"Even though he doesn't want anything to do with it." Jack shook his head.

Maddie lifted a finger. "He wants enough to do with it to get what it's worth to him in dollars."

"Yikes. I'm sorry I asked." She wasn't, really. She needed to know what was going on. It just sucked that it had to play out like some cartoon villain scheming to get rich and leave everyone else high and dry.

"I'm hoping we might be able to talk some sense into him," Dad said.

"And see if he's secretly been brainwashed by some gold-digging floozy." Jack pointed at Maddie. "Her words, not mine."

In spite of the suckiness of it all, Logan couldn't help but laugh. "Do we think that's a legitimate possibility?"

"Nah." Dad waved a hand. "He's pretty good at coming up with harebrained ideas all on his own."

Maddie wagged a finger. "Yeah, but if she's convinced him to do this so she can rob him blind, we might be able to pull back the curtain and save his sorry ass."

She hadn't considered that possibility and didn't want to. Again, it all felt a little too cliché to seem real. "When are they coming?"

"Next month. They're planning to fly up so they can drive Rich's car down." Dad shook his head.

"Filled with everything valuable the floozy can get her hands on," Maddie said. "Assuming, of course, she is a gold-digging floozy."

"Maddie." Mom's scolding tone got everyone's attention. "She might be a perfectly lovely woman. We should reserve judgment until we've had the chance to meet her."

Everyone nodded, duly cowed.

They resumed business talk, running through the list of current and upcoming projects. Logan scribbled notes to herself about the design work she had on her plate in addition to Kathleen's renovation. The meeting wrapped and everyone scattered to their respective desks and job sites. Logan lingered, using the office Wi-Fi to get the details of a couple of upcoming antique shows she wanted to check out. Maddie did, too, typing away with all the fervor of someone who hated that part of her job.

"Do you really think she's going to be awful?" Logan asked, quiet enough for only Maddie to hear.

Maddie looked up, scowl firmly in place. "Let's just say I've got my 'I told you so' dusted off and ready to go."

❖

Kathleen pulled up to her house and found Logan standing on the front porch, smile on her face and hand raised in greeting. It gave her a flash of coming home—home to her house but also home to Logan. The clarity of the sensation belied the absurdity of it and left her unsteady. She shook it off and forced her focus to the reason she stopped by the house in the first place: her new front porch.

"What do you think?" Logan called before Kathleen had even shut the car door behind her.

She hurried up the walk so she could stand on it herself. "It's perfect."

Logan jumped up and down a few times. "And solid as they come. You could host a dance party on this porch."

"I think I'll pass, but it's nice to have the option." She preferred her dance parties to be parties of one, thank you very much.

"We still need to add the railing, but it's otherwise ready for rocking chairs and lemonade."

Kathleen cringed. "I might be too old for a dance party, but I'm not sure I'm ready for rocking chairs. Isn't there something in the middle?"

Logan lifted a finger. "One, you're never too old for a dance party." She added a second. "Two, rocking chairs are both ageless and timeless. I'll have you know I have a pair on my front porch."

She didn't know why, but she imagined Logan in an apartment. Well, no, that wasn't true. She did know why. It never occurred to her that someone as young as Logan, and as single, would own a house. Much less one with rocking chairs. "I stand corrected."

"Though, maybe you're a porch swing sort of woman. That's legit, too. If you are, I can go ahead and put in some eye bolts to make it easier to hang when the time comes."

"I honestly hadn't gotten that far."

Logan grinned. "I won't hold it against you since it's not porch weather yet, but I hope you plan on wiling away some time out here when the weather's good."

She did like to take her laptop outside. Though, she'd want a table and chairs for that. Would that look strange? Maybe that should be out back on the patio. She didn't plan to do much wiling, but a swing might look nice. Good for outlining and brainstorming. With a cup of coffee. Or, even better, a glass of wine.

"Is that a no?" Logan asked.

Kathleen cleared her throat, slightly embarrassed to be caught daydreaming. "I'll think about it."

Logan nodded. "No rush. We'll do the exterior painting next week. It's supposed to be dry and in the sixties."

A minor miracle for late April. "I'm looking forward to seeing that finished. And thank you for letting me know the porch was done. Definitely worth a trip over."

"I confess that's not the only reason I asked you to stop by." Logan's smile managed to be a little shy and a little sly at the same time.

"You didn't get the wrong color of something again, did you?"

She'd meant to be funny, to show Logan she wasn't stiff and uptight all the time. Only it backfired and Logan looked utterly horrified. "No. Not at all. I hope you don't think I make mistakes like that often. I really don't."

Kathleen cringed. "Sorry. I was trying to be funny." And failing epically.

"Oh. Ha ha." Logan's affected laugh was followed by a real one. "Actually, it is funny. If I wasn't so busy being overly sensitive about it, I would have gotten it."

Perpetually crossed wires and missed signals. That summed up Logan and her in a nutshell. It was too bad, really, even if it was for the best. "Still. I didn't mean to make you feel bad."

"Let's chalk it up to good-natured teasing, shall we? I can take my share of that."

"Because of your siblings?" She swallowed the sigh that bubbled up, not wanting to give the wrong impression.

Logan chuckled. "My whole family, but especially my siblings. Are you an only child?"

She did sigh then. "I have a brother. He's a doctor."

"Not close?" Logan seemed curious more than judgmental.

"He's the golden child. I'm…"

"Not?" Logan offered.

"By a long shot. More interested in books than ballet lessons." Which she didn't regret now, exactly, though it would be nice to have a hobby that supported things like strength and flexibility and grace.

"I don't see anything wrong with that."

"No, but it doesn't show well. My parents are particularly interested in show." And she never failed to disappoint.

"I'm sorry." It was the obvious nice thing to say, but Logan seemed to mean it.

"It's fine. I know they love me. I'm just the black sheep of the family." She angled her head. "On top of being the rainbow one."

"For what it's worth, I never took to ballet either." Logan shrugged. "Though my artistic streak threw both my parents for a loop."

"Did you choose design as a compromise, then?" Only after asking did she realize what a personal question it was, but Logan didn't seem to mind.

"Yes, but of my own making. I always wanted to go into the family business. Design was a way to do that and play to my strengths."

So logical. So tidy. It made Kathleen wonder if she would have made different decisions had she embraced that sort of mindset. "Well, you seem to be very good at all aspects of it now."

"Maddie would beg to differ, at least when it comes to wielding power tools. But the girl can barely draw a stick figure, so it all comes out in the wash."

"I wish I could say the same about my brother, but he's good at everything." Literally. She didn't resent him for it, but damn it made him insufferable sometimes.

"Something tells me you're infinitely more charming."

"A matter of opinion, I suppose." And not something she felt compelled to dissect. "Anyway, that's not why you called me over. Is it good news or bad news?"

Logan's face registered the abrupt shift, but she didn't comment on it. "It's more of a present."

"A present?"

"Not something we put in the original design, but I saw it and thought of you. If you like it, we can incorporate it." Logan shrugged, as though trying to downplay the whole thing, while also holding back excitement.

"I hope you didn't feel obligated."

"I didn't. And you might not even like it." Logan shifted from one foot to the other, the way an impatient child might. "Do you want to see it?"

She shouldn't be charmed, especially without even knowing what the gift was. Or if it was reasonable and appropriate. But Logan's enthusiasm proved infectious, and Kathleen couldn't remember the last time someone surprised her. Well, not in a good way at least. "I do. Lead the way."

Logan opened the front door and, as was her habit, gestured for Kathleen to go first. Kathleen did, then hovered awkwardly in the doorway since she didn't know where to go. "It's in the office," Logan said.

Hearing it called the office felt like a gift. Because even though it didn't need a lot of work, she planned to splurge on nice bookcases and an antique rug to go with the desk she'd already bought and had crammed into the living room of her rental. "All right."

She stepped into the space with absolutely no idea what to expect. What she saw was an old wooden ladder propped against the far wall. Only it wasn't any old ladder. It had scuffed up casters on the bottom and matching tarnished bronze rigging on the top. "It's a library ladder," Logan said.

Kathleen nodded slowly and walked toward it. "I know."

"You'll have to spend a bit more on custom shelving that can accommodate the track." Logan came up beside her. "I can have a track made by a metalworker I know, but you'd have to pay for that, too."

She continued to nod, words stubbornly refusing to form.

"Come to think of it, maybe it feels more like a burden than a gift. You shouldn't feel obligated to keep it if you don't want to make that extra investment. Or if you don't like it."

She put a hand on Logan's arm. "I love it."

"You don't have to say that. I know I've overstepped once before. I really didn't want to do that again. It's just, I don't know. I saw it, and I thought about you all tucked up in here with your computer and your books, and it just felt right. I couldn't help myself. Does that ever happen to you?"

"Logan." It came out more stern teacher than sentimental writer.

"Yes?" Logan asked.

"I love it."

"It seemed like such a book lover's thing to have, you know? Like, not to be a dork, but I grew up watching *Beauty and the Beast* and even I was a sucker for the library. Oh, and that scene in the beginning. In the bookshop?"

The tears came and she fruitlessly tried to hold them back, though it was laughing at Logan's rambling admission that tipped her over the edge. Because she had too, obviously. She grabbed Logan's hand, unable to resist the moment of connection. "Yes. It's the best part."

Logan looked at their joined hands for a beat before locking eyes with Kathleen. "You like that movie, too?"

Something crackled in the space between them, like the spark of static electricity but everywhere. Kathleen shoved it aside, along with the almost irresistible urge to grab hold of Logan and pull her close. To kiss her. To touch and taste and take everything Logan had to offer and see if the chemistry between them had even half the heat of her fantasies.

No. No kissing. Definitely none of the stuff that came after kissing. It didn't matter if her imagination or her libido wanted to, had been wanting to all along. It was her brain that ran the show and her brain that kept her safe. She needed to get a grip.

"I watched it so many times I wore out the VHS tape, and my mom had to buy me a new one," she said.

Logan smiled. "I love that."

Kathleen dabbed at her eyes, then rolled them, then laughed—this time at herself. "Not that you even know what a VHS is."

"Hey, I'm not that young."

Kathleen resisted asking exactly how young and went for an incredulous look instead.

"And I have older siblings."

She believed the latter over the former, but really, it didn't matter. It wasn't like they were dating. "Well, I love that you love it in whatever format you had it." She took a deep breath and worked to keep her emotions in some semblance of order. "And I love that you thought of me."

"You're okay tweaking the plans?"

"I confess I considered asking for one, but it seemed over the top in such a small room."

Logan shook her head. "Nothing that gives you joy is over the top."

That wasn't universally true, obviously. But what if she let it be true a little more often? Not only with her house, but in life? Something to ponder another day, with the help of her therapist. Today, she'd simply delight in making the leap from home office to genuine library. And maybe, she'd delight in the fact that Logan made it possible.

CHAPTER ELEVEN

L ogan pulled into her driveway and let her head fall back. What a roller coaster. She'd gone from giddy at the prospect of giving Kathleen the library ladder to terrified Kathleen wouldn't like it to thinking—once again—that Kathleen might be on the verge of kissing her. It was a lot for a body in the span of a single afternoon.

"That bad, huh?"

She jumped at the sound of Jack's voice, muffled through the closed window of her truck. "Jesus, you scared me." He shrugged and she got out. "Good day, actually. Just intense."

Jack chuckled. "Dude, same. Let's pop a couple of beers and put our feet up."

"Your place or mine?" she asked.

Jack narrowed his eyes. "Depends. You got any good beer?"

"Just some Cold Snap I haven't drunk yet. I've been on wine lately."

He tipped his head toward his side of the duplex they shared. "Come over to mine. And bring your own bottle if you're feeling fancy."

They parted ways on the porch, and she let herself into her place. Kiwi got up from her bed and trotted over to say hello. "Hi, girl. How was your day?"

Kiwi stretched and yawned in response. To be fair, it was one of her primary modes of expression. Being fourteen took a lot out of a dog, though—even a scruffy little mutt like Kiwi—so Logan neither worried nor blamed her. "Wanna go see Uncle Jack?"

That got a butt wiggle and a happy dance, complete with the tippy-tap of her nails on the floor. Kiwi loved Jack almost as much as she loved Logan. Logan untied and kicked off her boots and slid her feet into the fleecy slippers she lived in at home, which extended to Jack's place. She grabbed an open bottle of Syrah, and she and Kiwi padded the ten or so feet from her front door to Jack's.

She let herself in and didn't wait for Jack to come downstairs to help herself to a glass from the cupboard. Jack appeared in sweats and his own pair of fleecy slippers—Christmas presents from their parents—and grabbed a bottle of something way too dark and malty for her tastes from the fridge. Since it wasn't warm enough for the back deck without getting a fire going in the chimenea, they parked on the worn leather sofa in Jack's living room.

She clinked her glass to his bottle. "Cheers."

"Cheers." He took a long swig. "So, what made your day so intense?"

She relayed the highlights and Kathleen's ultimate happiness with the ladder.

"You got it bad, dude."

"What do you mean?" She kind of already knew. Okay, no kind of about it.

Jack's look said he knew she knew and didn't appreciate her playing dumb.

"I still feel like I'm digging myself out of a hole, you know? I want her to know I'm not a creeper, and that I can be friendly and professional without crossing lines." That sounded slightly better than trying to win Kathleen over.

"And buying a client an expensive antique for their home that they didn't ask for is that?"

"How is it you can make anything sound bad?"

Jack shrugged. "It's a gift."

She let out a humph that summed up her opinion on the matter. "The ladder wasn't that expensive. And I offered it as an option. The install will be on her dime."

"Oh, I see. So, really, you're just trying to upsell her."

Logan groaned. "You're the worst. You know that, right?"

Jack grinned. "I know."

"Enough about me. What are you getting up to that I can harass you about?"

Jack leaned back and propped his feet on the coffee table. "Not a thing in the world. I work, I putter, I read good books. I did try a new eggplant parm recipe last night. I think it's a keeper. You want some leftovers?"

"Yes. Yes, I do." Because she'd been so busy putting in extra hours at Kathleen's, she'd been living on frozen pizza and sandwiches.

"Got fifteen minutes for me to make a salad and garlic bread to go with it?"

"Always."

"Like I had to ask." Jack hefted himself off the couch and Logan followed.

"You know, you could use your culinary skills to impress your own lady friend instead of your bachelor sister."

Jack's lip curled. "No, thank you."

"Seriously, are you going to be a celibate hermit your whole life?"

"Of course not. I have the occasional hookup. It's just all that relationship stuff. So much drama."

Logan shook her head. "That is such a guy thing to say."

"Look, do I want to settle down and have kids someday? Of course I do. But I'm not in any hurry. When I stumble on the low-key, laid-back girl of my dreams, I'll make the effort. Until then? Too much work."

They'd had variations of this conversation countless times. Jack always played the crusty bachelor, Logan the hopeless romantic. "But what if you don't stumble upon her? Or what if you do and she isn't the low-key, laid-back girl you were expecting?"

"Then she's not the girl of my dreams, is she?" Jack handed her a cucumber and an orange bell pepper. "Chop those."

Hard to argue with that logic, even if she wanted to. "You're such a curmudgeon."

"Yep." He'd stopped being offended by the descriptor in high school.

"Fine. What are you puttering on?" She pulled out a cutting board and went to work.

"I picked up a vintage turntable at a garage sale and I'm rewiring it." He smeared roasted garlic and butter onto the baguette he'd split longways. "I'd love you to refinish it for me when I'm done. Split the proceeds?"

They'd done that before—merging skills sets on random junk finds and making a tidy little profit. "I'm game."

"Maybe you could buy it for your lady friend."

Logan groaned. "You have to stop calling her that."

"Why?" Jack slid the bread into the oven and pulled a lidded baking dish from the fridge. "That's what you called my nonexistent one."

"Exactly. It implies things." Things she was pretty sure she and Kathleen would never get up to.

"Now who's the curmudgeon?"

"Naw, man. I have the feelings. They're just unrequited."

Jack paused, raised the spatula he was using to dish up the leftovers. "And that, my friend, is why I'm the curmudgeon."

He had a point. She'd tortured herself over her attraction to Kathleen, knowing it wasn't reciprocated, and having to find out that fact in the most cringey way possible. But damn if the look on Kathleen's face this afternoon didn't make it all worthwhile. There might not be any hope for them as a couple, but it was enough to keep Logan's faith alive. "I'm going to remind you of that when a pretty girl comes along and turns your world upside down."

"You go right ahead." He scooped out a second helping before jabbing the spatula in her direction. "But I wouldn't hold your breath."

❖

Kathleen wrapped both hands around her coffee mug and propped her elbows on the table. The screen in front of her sat blank, save the blinking cursor. Most mornings, she loved the potential of a fresh page, a new chapter. Especially when the morning's chapter included her characters getting hot and heavy for the first time. The explosion of all that pent up potential, the release of sexual tension that had been building day after day, page after page.

Too bad she was too busy being haunted by her own pent up sexual tension to enjoy it.

She'd literally been writing around the sex scene for days. Skipping ahead, reworking earlier chapters. It was becoming problematic—for her writing schedule but also for her own sanity. And worst of all, it showed no signs of letting up.

She'd tried exercise. Nothing. A cold bracing shower? Nope. A relaxing hot one? Even worse. She'd even tried masturbating. The orgasm took the edge off briefly but did little to chase away the images of Logan that lodged in her mind. The fantasies. The longing.

It was almost enough to make her wish for a stack of poorly written Comp 101 papers to take her mind off things. Almost.

The problem was, for as unsuitable and inappropriate as her attraction to Logan was, she had not a shred of doubt that it remained mutual. Sure, Logan had become the unflappable professional, respecting each and every boundary Kathleen laid out. Hell, Logan seemed to be respecting boundaries Kathleen hadn't even come up with. But for all her default doubts that someone had the hots for her, Logan's energy hadn't changed. If anything, it came in louder and more clearly than ever.

The worst part? She was pretty sure Logan didn't have a clue she continued to send those signals. And since she was practically tripping over herself to keep things on the up-and-up, Kathleen didn't have the heart to tell her. All of which was to say, she found herself drowning in sexual frustration with the added burden of knowing she could, with a single word, end her misery.

Trudy, of course, proved zero help. She'd taken to asking Kathleen daily if she'd decided to sleep with Logan yet. Yet being the operative word. And as much as she enjoyed her burgeoning friendship with Maddie and Clover, talking to them about Logan felt completely off limits. One, because it didn't seem fair to Logan. Two, because she had a sneaking suspicion they'd be no better than Trudy.

It sucked being an adult all the time.

She set down her coffee and sighed. She was, though. An adult. All. The. Time. Sure, an adult who pursued a painfully impractical academic career, then quit said career to write queer kissing books, but still. When it came to things like principles and integrity, she didn't waver. Not a trait she had any intention of changing anytime soon.

And yet, the more time she spent with Logan, the more she believed it was a trait they shared. Yes, Logan had crossed a line. But, if Kathleen was being honest, she'd probably been sending all sorts of confusing pheromones. Because as much as she'd never seriously considered hooking up with Logan, her imagination had jumped on that bandwagon from the get-go. Was it fair to blame Logan for picking up on those signals and acting on them?

Ugh. Okay. Enough. She could waste an entire day chasing this particular circle. Might be a nice way to pass the time, but it didn't get books written. She had a deadline and a couple of characters overdue for tearing each other's clothes off. Besides, getting them hot and heavy might manage to distract her from the fact that she wasn't.

Kathleen laced her fingers together and pressed them away from her, arching her back and getting a nice shoulder stretch in the process. She cracked the knuckles of one hand, then the other. Time for sexy time.

"Are you sure this is what you want?" Bette's eyes fixed on Ava's, intense and dark.

Ava flicked her gaze to Bette's lips. The confident smirk made it clear she already knew the answer. But Bette wanted her to say it, ask for it. "Yes."

Bette's hand, already on Ava's thigh, swept higher. Ava spread her legs, inviting Bette in. But Bette had other ideas. She lazily caressed the curve of Ava's hip, the swell of her ass.

"Please."

"Please what?" Bette asked.

"Please be inside me."

Bette shifted, her fingers skimming over the patch of hair at the apex of Ava's thighs before sliding into her wetness. Bette hissed, and Ava took profound satisfaction in the sound. In knowing Bette wanted her with the same ferocity, even if she played it cool.

Once, twice around Ava's clit. "You're wet for me, baby," Bette said.

Ava nodded.

A few more slow circles had Ava on the verge of begging, but Bette didn't torture her for long. She eased one, then a second finger into Ava. Ava moaned. "You like that, don't you?"

She nodded again, unable to form words.

"Can you take more?"

"Please," she said, though the hoarse whisper bore little resemblance to her normal voice.

Bette shifted onto her knees before adding a third finger to her long, slow thrusts. Ava arched to meet her, basking in the way Bette's fingers curled inside her. Stroking. Beckoning almost. "Do you want another?"

They'd discussed it—four fingers, a whole fist—in the endless text threads that kept her up into the wee hours so many nights. Curiosity and comparing notes had given way to full-on sexting. Elaborate fantasies that had her riding her vibrator and wishing for more. So much more.

And now she had it. Maybe for tonight and maybe for forever. She'd stopped worrying about which it would be before they'd finished dinner. All she knew was that she wanted everything Bette would give her. "Yes, please."

Bette worked Ava slowly, using Ava's wetness but adding some lube, too. She circled Ava's clit, coaxing two orgasms out of her in quick succession. Ava rode them, losing track of herself and the sounds she made, clinging only to the feel of Bette's hand and the promise of being filled in a way she never had before.

"Try to relax for me. Let me in."

She let out a shaky laugh. "I'll try."

The press of Bette's hand intensified. Ava's body strained, wanting but resistant. She let out a breath and braced herself to ask for a break. Only she didn't have to. Bette's hand slipped into her like it was made to. The fit, the fullness—it was otherworldly.

"Fuck. Yes. Loga

"Fuck." Kathleen hit the delete key with vigor, typing the correct name in its place. She scrubbed her hands over her face and let out a sigh before reading over the words on the screen. Too much for a first time. Way too much. But she could retool it for a later chapter. Maybe? Probably?

Her own arousal was a different matter. Kathleen shifted in her chair, more keyed up than she had any business being at eleven in the morning and exactly zero idea what to do about it.

So much for distraction.

CHAPTER TWELVE

K athleen didn't see Logan for more than a week. They texted, though. Updates about the house, some decisions about the shelving in the library. Library. It still gave her a little thrill to think she was going to have one all her own. Not so different from a home office and yet, worlds apart. The stuff of fantasies.

Kind of like Logan.

Oh, God. She did not just think that. But, yeah, she totally had.

Logan had been invading her thoughts more and more. With the awkwardness—edginess?—mostly behind them, it had been all too easy to let her guard down. Get friendly. Unfortunately, the friendliness led to thoughts and even a few dreams that embraced a much more euphemistic use of the word.

And now she was a bundle of nerves, no longer afraid that Logan would hit on her, but stuck in the sinking realization that Logan absolutely wouldn't. It was beyond frustrating. Not to mention next-level pathetic.

And then Logan texted asking if she had some time to drop by. Something Kathleen needed to see, to weigh in on. After assuring her it was nothing bad, Logan refused to elaborate further, leaving Kathleen to wonder if she had another surprise up her sleeve that would leave Kathleen breathless. Or worse, breathing heavy.

She groaned at sinking to such a terrible line as she pulled up to the house. This was what she'd been reduced to. Perhaps she should warn her editor.

Only Logan's truck sat in the driveway, so she didn't expect a cacophony of buzzing and banging, but when she walked in, the quiet felt almost eerie. "Hello?"

"In the kitchen," Logan called.

She headed that way. "Are you here by yourself?"

Logan stood at the nearly finished island, laptop open. "You caught a rare moment of calm. Construction is mostly wrapped. Tile guy and painters are in tomorrow and the rest of the week."

"I hope that didn't sound like a complaint. I didn't mean it that way."

Logan smiled. "It didn't. I just wanted to give you an update. Leah would have been here, but she had a doctor's appointment."

"Everything okay?" Kathleen hadn't spent much time with Leah, but she'd developed a fondness for her. Not motherly, exactly, but cool aunt. Cool in ways Brian's kids would never find her cool.

"Just routine. I swear the appointments come almost weekly when you're pregnant." Logan shrugged affably.

Kathleen suppressed a shudder. She'd had a brief phase of wanting children in her twenties, influenced perhaps by falling head over heels for Susan and spinning every happily ever after scenario known to man. The desire dried up when the relationship did, and at this point in her life she was grateful not to be negotiating custody with someone she could barely stand the sight of.

"Is it the doctor part or the pregnancy part?" Logan asked.

"Yes," Kathleen said with a laugh.

"Maybe don't mention that around Leah?"

She conjured her best insulted look, and Logan's sheepish expression told her it landed as intended. "So, what's this update?"

"I wanted to show you the library."

Her heart fluttered at the prospect even as her brain told her to keep her expectations low. "Did the shelving arrive?"

"It more than arrived. The crew got it in yesterday, and I spent the afternoon installing the ladder hardware."

"Seriously? You said it would be another week at least."

Logan smiled, almost bashful. "But you were so excited about it, I wanted you to have it done sooner."

A flutter of an entirely different nature started in her chest. It flitted down her spine and made the tips of her fingers tingle. It ventured south, too, situating itself most inconveniently. "You didn't have to do that."

"I wanted to."

The simple statement left her shaky on top of tingly. What the hell was wrong with her?

"Normally, I'd wait until the end to do a reveal. You know, get all your books in, the furniture. Really stage the room."

Kathleen grasped at the promise of levity. "I'm familiar."

"But all the floors are being done at once and, you know, your furniture isn't here yet." Logan lifted a shoulder and let it fall. "It's actually not that much of a reveal at all."

The flash of vulnerability, however brief, made Kathleen's insides go melty. It was all she could do not to kiss Logan right then and there. She settled for a hand on Logan's arm. "It's a reveal to me."

Logan looked up, eyes fixing on Kathleen's. Kathleen's pulse ticked up a few notches, her throat tightened. Logan's gaze flicked to Kathleen's mouth for less than a second, then she blushed at being caught. Kathleen's lips parted, words of reassurance and desire fighting in her mind and tangling on the tip of her tongue.

Logan wanted to kiss her. Kathleen knew it as clearly as she knew her own name. As clearly as her own longing thrummed through her. But as clearly as she knew that, she knew Logan wouldn't. Kathleen had drawn a line in the sand and Logan wouldn't cross it. At least not without invitation.

Would she do the inviting?

A thousand words of warning swarmed her mind like bees whose hive had just been kicked. Practical ones, ones about being a hypocrite. A few came from the part of her heart she'd kept locked away for as long as she could remember. The part that craved connection but found it always left her lacking. Or worse, convinced the lacking resided in herself. But for all that fear, all that silent screaming for self-protection, the loudest roar came from her own longing. From the part of her she funneled into her writing but kept safely tucked away when it came to her own life. And for reasons she'd maybe never be able to explain, that was the voice she listened to.

Kathleen covered Logan's lips with her own. Logan seemed to yield and yet meet her at the same time. How novel.

When was the last time she'd initiated a kiss?

The question faded, along with all the others and their surroundings and everything else. All that remained was this perfect melding that satisfied her even as it demanded more. Logan's hand came to her cheek, threaded into her hair. Kathleen sighed at the sheer perfection of it. Logan seized the opportunity to slip her tongue in, to tease and taste and promise. Promise there was, in fact, so very much more. If only Kathleen would let herself take. Let herself go.

When Logan's other hand slid to the small of her back, pulled their bodies close, it no longer felt like a matter of if.

❖

Logan searched Kathleen's face, trying to figure out what had just happened. Well, not what, exactly. The what was a kiss, and a doozy of one at that. No mistaking that. It was the how and why and can we do it again tripping her up.

"Are you okay?" Logan asked, not entirely sure she wanted the answer.

"Yes." Kathleen gave a decisive nod. "Yes."

"But?"

Kathleen squared her shoulders. "I didn't intend for that to happen."

"For what it's worth, I didn't either."

Kathleen looked incredulous.

"You may choose not to believe me, but when a woman tells me she isn't interested, I back the hell off." It fell pretty high on her list of things required to not be an asshole.

Kathleen bit the inside of her lip, like maybe it was herself she couldn't believe. "I believe you."

Logan blew out a breath, the wave of relief stronger than she cared to admit. "Thank you."

Kathleen took a deep breath of her own and let it out slowly, as though the acknowledgment came as a relief to her as well. "Yeah."

"But I'd be lying if I said I regretted it." And she wasn't in the habit of lying.

Kathleen frowned. "I don't either."

"But?" She eyed Kathleen hopefully. "Or maybe and?"

Kathleen smiled. "And I'm not sure what to do now."

She could think of several things—starting with kissing again and ending up in bed back at her place—but that's likely not what Kathleen had in mind. "I think agreeing we both enjoyed it is a good first step. You did enjoy it right?"

Kathleen let out a soft chuckle. "Understatement."

Delight and desire zinged through her in equal measure. "So, we're in agreement there. Excellent. I'm open to it happening again. Are you?"

Kathleen chewed her lip, the move reminding Logan of a kid being called on in class not knowing the answer. "Maybe?"

"Okay. I'll take that." Anything more than flat-out refusal counted as a victory. "What do you need to help you decide? Anything from me?"

Kathleen seemed surprised by the question. "Um."

"I totally respect if you need time alone, or something along those lines. To think or whatever. But I'd love it if we could spend time together outside of working on your house. Maybe that would help?"

"Like a date?" Kathleen seemed genuinely alarmed by the prospect.

"Like dinner and conversation with no strings or expectations."

Kathleen smirked. "Sounds a lot like a date."

"Yeah, but the no pressure part saves it, right?" Logan went for a cheesy smile to drive home that her semi-hard sell wasn't meant as pressure, either.

Kathleen tipped her head back and forth. "Yes, but simply saying no pressure doesn't undo the inherent expectations that arise when two people who've kissed embark on what is, by all social standards, a date."

"You sound like such a college professor right now." She knew better than to say it was hot.

"I fall back on intellect and reason when emotionally uncomfortable." Kathleen sighed, but a smile still played at the corner of her mouth. "At least that's what my therapist says."

Logan laughed then, because how could she not? "I don't have a therapist, at least not at the moment, but mine would say I use humor, which ironically undermines my self-interest since I'm forever hustling to be taken seriously."

"Wow."

"I know, right? I'm working on it. Maybe I should go back to therapy." Not an easy feat in a town the size of Bedlington, but that was no excuse.

"I actually meant I was impressed by that level of self-awareness. I'm not sure I had that at your age. In fact, I'm sure I didn't."

Logan stood a little taller. "That's a point in my favor, isn't it?"

"It is." Kathleen seemed reluctant to admit it, but she didn't recant.

"Look, I think it's beyond obvious that I find you attractive. Physically, but in a lot of other ways, too. I'd like to spend more time with you. If it goes somewhere, great. If not, that's okay. Sharing a good meal and good company is never a bad way to spend an evening." All true, even if it came with a dose of disappointment. Of course, that would prove less disappointing than if Kathleen didn't accept the invitation to begin with. That would mean Kathleen had turned her down twice, and she was pretty certain there was no going back from that.

"All right. Yes."

"Yes, you're agreeing with that statement or yes, you'll have dinner with me?" Man, did she hope it was the latter.

"Yes. To both." Kathleen gave another decisive nod. "No pressure, and to the extent possible, no expectations."

Logan stuck out her hand before thinking better of it. "Deal."

Kathleen accepted the handshake, looking more amused than put off. "Deal."

"So, tonight?" Jumping the gun, maybe, but she didn't want Kathleen changing her mind. Which sounded better than wanting to strike while the iron was hot, though that was the adage that came to mind. "If you don't have other plans, obviously."

Kathleen hesitated.

"Or tomorrow. I'm eager, not pushy. An important distinction in my book." She went for another cheesy smile and hoped Kathleen felt the same.

"I appreciate you making it." Kathleen chewed her lip again. "How's tomorrow?"

Would saying she'd take any day of the week make her sound desperate? "Tomorrow is great. We could go out. Or…"

"Or?"

"Or you could come to my house and let me cook for you."

Kathleen raised a brow and Logan cringed.

"Too much?"

Kathleen considered for a long moment before saying, "No. That sounds really nice. Are you okay cooking?"

She liked that Kathleen phrased it as a preference instead of questioning whether she knew how. "I am. Nothing fancy, but I enjoy it. And not to be weird, but I feel like conversation can be easier when you're not in public."

Whether Kathleen agreed or simply decided to go along, Logan couldn't be sure, but she nodded. Then she angled her head. "Do I get to see my library now?"

Logan laughed. "Can I say it was a damn good kiss to make me forget about that completely?"

Kathleen smirked. "Yes, because I did, too. But now I've remembered, and I want to see it."

"That makes me feel good on both counts." Really, really good.

"Should I close my eyes?" Kathleen asked, playful expression still firmly in place.

She didn't know if the reveal warranted it, but if Kathleen was volunteering an exercise in trust—even a tiny one—she wasn't about to turn it down. "I'd love that."

Kathleen's eyes closed and her hands extended, inviting Logan to take them. Logan did, a giddy thrill dancing up her spine. She released one just long enough to open the door, then guided Kathleen into the space and turned her to face the wall of floor-to-ceiling bookcases. "Can I open?" Kathleen asked.

"Open." Logan stepped to the side and held her breath.

Kathleen gasped. "Oh. They're perfect."

Logan beamed, joy coursing through her as much as pride. "I'm glad you like them."

"I more than like them. I love them." She walked over to the shelving and trailed her fingers along the wood, stained to match the ladder. "It's exactly what I imagined and somehow better at the same time."

"That's the ultimate compliment for a designer, you know." One she'd heard before but felt extra keenly this time. Like Kathleen's words validated her—validated whatever might be growing between them—as much as her work.

Kathleen turned to face her. "I feel like I'm the one who should be making you dinner."

Logan grinned. "I'll let you as soon as your kitchen is done."

Kathleen nodded and returned her attention to the bookcase. She slid the ladder back and forth. "Can I climb it?"

"Yes, but I wouldn't recommend a full Belle sweep. That's a smooth cartoon move, but I'm not sure how well it would translate to real life."

Kathleen laughed. The sound—rich and full and carefree—sent Logan's heart tumbling to places it had no business going. It was how she worked, though. She felt things fully, even when it got her into trouble. And maybe they'd never get where her imagination had already gone, but Kathleen had technically just agreed to not one but two dates. Surely, that had to count for something.

CHAPTER THIRTEEN

Logan opened the door with a dish towel thrown over her shoulder and a warm smile. "Hi."

Kathleen returned the smile. "Is it my imagination, or are you surprised to see me?"

"Not surprised." Logan gave a playful shrug. "Okay, maybe a little surprised."

She shook her head. "I'm not some millennial who'd ghost you without the courtesy of at least a text."

Logan raised both hands. "I never meant to imply you were."

"But you did think I might cancel." She couldn't hold that against Logan, since she'd considered it more than once since agreeing to dinner the previous afternoon.

"I knew you were reluctant to say yes in the first place. How's that?"

"Fair."

"I'm glad you're here, though." Logan stepped back. "Please come in."

She might have enjoyed a moment of proving Logan wrong, but it was short-lived. A scruffy little nugget of a dog ambled over to say hello, prompting introductions and Kathleen falling immediately and intensely in love. On top of that, Logan's place—which she'd expected to resemble a college apartment on steroids—was clean, cozy, and impeccably decorated. "Your home is lovely."

"Thank you. Sourcing items for clients affords me lots of opportunity to scout bargains for myself." She gestured to a small bench next to the door. "Feel free to leave your bag there."

She set down her purse and took off the raincoat she'd thrown on against the cool spring drizzle that had started and not let up. "It smells wonderful in here."

"Okay, now you're the one who sounds surprised." Logan's grin was teasing, confident. It suited her, like that was her natural state. Like she'd worked to turn the volume down and finally didn't have to anymore.

"I am." She cleared her throat. "Was. But I'm learning to expect the unexpected with you."

"Or maybe you should expect something different."

It could have been a jab, but it didn't feel like it. No, if anything, it was a gentle nudge not to judge a book by its cover. Exceptionally attractive cover notwithstanding. "Perhaps I should."

"For what it's worth, a lot of people assume things about me."

Kathleen cringed inwardly. She liked to think she was better than that. "Why is that, you think?"

"I'm always the youngest. In my family, in my social circles. And masc, which I know sends teenage boy, don't take me seriously vibes." Logan shook her head. "People think all sorts of things about me because I have short hair and wear boxers."

An image of Logan in nothing but a pair of boxers—plaid, maybe, or with little tools all over them—invaded Kathleen's mind unbidden. She chased it away, shooing it out of her head like she might go after a mouse with a broom. "I'm sorry."

"Oh, it's fine. I mean, it's dumb but comes with the territory. I'm sure you haven't had that sort of experience."

Kathleen laughed. "No, I'm relegated to the societal scorn reserved for middle-aged women without husbands or children."

"I think that's worse." Logan gave her an appreciative look. "Though, for what it's worth, you don't look middle-aged to me."

Logan clearly meant it as a compliment. And yet it bugged her a little that looking younger was meant to be some sort of accomplishment or point of pride.

"Or maybe the more accurate thing to say is that I find you beautiful, and the fact that you're ever so slightly older than me only adds to that."

A nice save, even if an exaggeration. "Ever so slightly, huh?"

"I'm twenty-nine," Logan said with the sort of disdain only a person under thirty could muster. "Are you a day over forty?"

"About twelve hundred days, actually."

Rather than put off, Logan's appreciation only seemed to intensify. "You wear it well."

At least it was on the table now. Nothing like a heavy dose of reality to keep things in perspective. "Perhaps, but a fifteen-year age difference ticks the bad idea column in my book."

Logan gave a dismissive wave of her hand. "We're just having dinner together. No pressure, no agenda. Remember?"

She nodded, gave herself a swift mental reset, and remembered that, in addition to a no-pressure dinner with someone shaping up to be a rather delightful human being, she had things to celebrate. "Right. No pressure, no agenda. Plus I signed a new book contract today."

"You did? That's huge." Logan's whole face lit up, and Kathleen had to fight the urge to kiss her. For reasons.

"Well, not huge. My publisher made it clear they wanted it. I just had to send them a compelling synopsis and first chapter to seal the deal." A far cry from the mountain of queries and rejections that preceded her first contract. Or the second, which she'd angsted over for weeks because the proposal required her to include a draft delivery date.

"You might be this jaded, famous author now, but let me be clear. It's a really big deal."

Given the hips wiggling, arms flailing happy dance she'd done after the call with her agent, it seemed disingenuous to argue. "Okay, fine. It is."

Logan grinned. "I knew it. I'm sorry I don't have any bubbly in the house, but I hope you'll let me pour you a glass of wine."

She'd celebrated her first book deal with Trudy. Her second and third, alone in her apartment near Amherst with a bottle of cheap Prosecco. If she'd told herself on the drive to Logan's she no longer needed to feel special about these things, the half-baked argument evaporated in the warm glow of Logan's attention. "I'd love that."

Since they hadn't made it out of the foyer, Logan led the way to the kitchen. Much like the living room, with its eclectic but thoughtful furnishings, the kitchen radiated personality and style. The cabinets were oak but most of the uppers had glass doors, giving the space a craftsman, rather than dated, feel. Sage green tiles for the backsplash and quartz counters that looked just like the ones she'd picked for her own house, minus the shimmer. A row of terra-cotta pots overflowing with herbs crowded the windowsill over the sink, and an array of antique copper pots and pans hung from a rack overhead. "If I had doubts about your design chops, you could have invited me here."

"Did you?"

"No." Plenty of doubts about other things, but never that.

"Hopefully, my cooking will impress just as much."

She smirked, enjoying herself. "I should warn you it's a tall order."

"Given the schooling and training I have in design, I'm okay with that." Logan poured from a bottle she had breathing on the counter and gestured for Kathleen to sit.

Kathleen slid onto one of the stools. "So, what are you making?"

"It's this chicken dish I had at a restaurant once and spent months trying to re-create. It's got sun-dried tomatoes, chèvre, and a lemon basil sauce."

Not a combination she'd have considered, but it sounded delicious. "Wow."

"I usually try to impress women by saying I know the owner of Grumpy Old Goat, but since you're already friends with her, I made garlic potatoes to go with it."

"Clover is pretty great, so it's still impressive you're friends with her."

"Ha." Logan peeked into a glass bowl she'd set up double-boiler style and covered with foil. "Are you hungry?"

"I missed lunch, so I'm not shy about saying yes."

Logan's eyes narrowed. "You're not one of those forget to eat people, are you?"

"No. I was too busy playing in my new library and signing that book contract." A banner day, really, by any stretch of her imagination, even if it paled in comparison to the kiss the day before.

"Never good to miss lunch, but at least you had a compelling reason." Logan winked as she handed Kathleen a glass and raised her own. "Here's to big deals."

She clinked her glass to Logan's. "And to friends who help us celebrate."

For an impromptu celebration, it felt plenty festive. The wine was dry but not heavy, perfect for the time of year. Logan's cooking skills might not have surpassed her design acumen, but they weren't far off. And true to her word, Logan didn't try to get flirty or make up excuses to brush her hand or cozy up closer. Though, truth be told, Kathleen wouldn't have minded if she had.

After eating, they lingered at the table. Kiwi, who had a bed in every room, snored softly from the gray donut pillow next to the sideboard. Logan refilled their glasses while Kathleen looked on with amusement, and Kathleen remembered that, while there was not a single thing wrong with eating alone, good company had lots to recommend it. Her body relaxed, her brain followed, and she stopped thinking about what time it was or whether things were going okay or when she could make her excuses and leave.

"Shall I open another?" Logan lifted the now empty wine bottle.

"Oh. No. I'm good." Not that sharing a bottle between them counted as a lot, but two glasses was her limit most nights.

"I regret to say I didn't have time to whip up dessert. I've got ice cream, though. Lemon ricotta and chocolate covered cherry."

"I'm good, thanks, though I approve your options." As in, would have happily devoured either.

"There's a local place over in Brattleboro," Logan said. "Teeny tiny, but they pack pints of some of their flavors and it's all to die for."

She smiled, imagining a summer night on her back patio with a pint and a pair of spoons. Because of course she'd let her guard down and Logan invited herself right in. "I'll remember that."

"Well, I'm in no rush to call it a night, but I don't want you to feel like I'm keeping you," Logan said.

"That's a very elegant line."

Logan's eyes went wide. "I swear it's not a line."

"I'm joking." It was fun to be on that side of the table for a change. She blinked a few times, willing her vision to focus and the fuzziness in her brain to clear. "I'm also not sure I should drive."

"Are you okay?" Logan asked, all concern.

"I think having the first glass on an empty stomach was a bad idea." Or at least a foolish one.

"Would you like me to take you home?"

It would mean an hour's drive, there and back. And then she'd be stranded the next day and need to be picked up. "I don't suppose there are ride shares around these parts?"

"Some, but less so evenings during the week. And it would cost a small fortune to get to Bennington, I'm sure."

Perhaps, but a small price to pay if it kept feeling foolish at bay. "I don't mind."

Logan frowned. "But I do. Especially after I'm the one who topped off your glass."

Kathleen reached across the table and put a hand on Logan's arm. "I got myself tipsy. There's no need for you to take responsibility. Or to feel bad."

"You're totally welcome to stay." Logan ran a hand through her hair. A tell of her own discomfort, but it drove Kathleen to distraction. "I should have led with that."

"I couldn't."

"I mean, you could. Literally. Would you like me to take away your keys?"

The absurdity of the question made her laugh. Not once in her entire life had someone needed to take her keys from her. She wasn't about to start now. "No."

"Then you need to let me drive you. I wouldn't forgive myself if anything happened to you."

What kind of woman would let a person drive an hour out of their way on a work night? The kind hung up on maintaining the illusion of boundaries but who was really just unnecessarily uptight. When had she become that kind of woman? Since Logan. Since Logan waltzed in and got her insides all stirred up thinking about flirting and kissing and falling for people she had no business falling for. But to what end? Self-preservation? She was a pro at that and had no intentions of letting her guard down any more than it already was. And certainly not so much that she'd get herself into trouble. "No, I meant you don't need to take my keys. I'll stay. Just to crash, though."

Logan nodded but her eyes held a hint of mischief. "Just to crash. I promise I'll be on my best behavior."

Kathleen nodded, in agreement but also to remind herself that's what she wanted. Even if the prospect of best behavior left a twinge of disappointment rubbing uncomfortably at the soft edges the wine had so nicely given her.

❖

Logan led Kathleen upstairs and went to her linen closet in search of a spare toothbrush. She turned, wielding the package like a prize. "I knew I'd bought a bunch when they were on sale."

Kathleen stood in the short hall that separated the two bedrooms, one of which Logan used as an office and workout space. Her brow furrowed, and she frowned. "You only have one bed."

Logan cringed. "Yeah."

Kathleen chewed her lip.

"I confess I don't often have company." At least not the kind that didn't want to share.

Kathleen nodded. "Of course."

"I can sleep on the sofa," Logan said. It would be torture, but perhaps less so than sharing a bed with Kathleen and not getting to touch her.

"That's not right."

"Are you saying you want to sleep on the sofa?" She wouldn't hesitate to play the chivalry card if she had to.

"I don't."

"It's settled, then." A vaguely disappointing resolution, though she wasn't about to complain about Kathleen relaxing enough to get tipsy.

Kathleen laughed. "Just one bed."

"Yes. I really am sorry for that." Logan crossed the room to tuck Kiwi—who hadn't waited for them to sort it out to climb into her extra poofy bedtime bed—under her preferred blanket.

"No, no. Don't apologize." Kathleen ran a hand through her hair, and Logan did her best not to notice her very kissable neck. "I was laughing because we're a trope."

"Trope?" She knew the word, but not enough to piece together meaning. Especially with so much of her attention elsewhere. Like Kathleen's neck.

"It's like the basic premise of a story. A category. In romance, just one bed is a trope. The two characters are dead set against sleeping together but wind up in a situation where they have to spend the night together and there's only one bed."

"Right." Logan laughed. "I knew that. I mean, I'd never given thought to this particular trope, but I'm familiar with the concept."

"The thing is, my best friend has been teasing me about how you and I are a whole mess of classic romance tropes."

"I'm trying to decide if that's a good thing or a bad thing." Or a thing that in any way increased their chances of falling into bed together.

Kathleen folded her arms. "Honestly, I'm not sure."

And there it was. "Just like you're not sure whether dating me, or having sex with me, is a good idea."

Kathleen laughed then. "Exactly."

She tried to tell herself joking about it counted as progress. Compared to the stiff and formal vibe they'd been rocking, it had to be. "So, what other tropes are we?"

"You don't want to know." Kathleen shook her head and smiled, but color rose in her cheeks.

"Oh, but I do. Come on, if I'm going to sleep on the couch in my own house, the least you could do is let me in on the joke."

Kathleen laced her fingers together like she was bracing for high-stakes negotiation. "Age gap."

Logan nodded slowly, pretty sure laughing was not the appropriate response. "Sure, sure."

"Ice queen." Kathleen cringed lightly.

"Wait, what's that?"

"One of the characters is aloof, emotionally unavailable, and usually bitchy." Kathleen accompanied the description with an eye roll.

"You're not bitchy," Logan said.

"Just aloof and emotionally unavailable."

Since a smirk played at the corners of Kathleen's mouth, Logan didn't panic. Well, didn't completely panic. "Reserved."

"That's generous. But since I can joke about it, I'm not too far gone." Kathleen laughed. "If I were truly an ice queen, we wouldn't be having this conversation."

"Right." She got it. Sort of. "And what's the other character then?"

"The one who melts her."

She could think of more than a few ways she'd like to make Kathleen melt. Most of them involved being naked. Though, that wasn't the whole of it. She'd love to get Kathleen to relax around her since she seemed to have no trouble relaxing around everyone else. "And how would she, the character I mean, do that?"

For whatever it was worth, Kathleen seemed on board with playing along. "Different ways. It's a premise more than a script."

"How would you?"

Kathleen hesitated, as though debating whether to reveal anything intimate or simply play the conversation out. "Patience. A willingness to look past the frosty exterior and slowly chip away at it." The explanation walked the line, answering the question but giving nothing away. "But like I said, a real ice queen wouldn't even be having this conversation, so it's strictly hypothetical."

At face value, the argument closed the conversation and any implications that might go along with it. But Logan sensed it was Kathleen's way of stepping away from that type, of distancing herself from it. "Thanks for the lesson. I'll have to be on the lookout next time I pick up a book."

Kathleen smiled, seeming to acknowledge the out Logan offered. "There are all sorts. Friends to lovers. Enemies to lovers. Secret baby."

They might have been on the verge of a moment, but curiosity won out. "Secret baby?"

"More a thing in straight romance. Guy hooks up with a girl and leaves town. She's pregnant but doesn't tell him, or can't. That's the backstory. Chance brings them back together and there's lots of angst before they live happily ever after."

"You're serious." Not an impossible story line, but was it that common?

"Oh, yeah. Not a fan, personally, and not only because it's harder to pull off in a queer story."

In for a penny, in for a pound. "Wait. How is that even possible?"

"I've read a couple of surrogate setups. Egg donors. Even a bisexual one-night stand whose protagonist proceeded to fall in love with her hookup's best friend. Surprisingly well done, given how convoluted it all was."

Logan shook her head. "Wow."

Kathleen shrugged.

"Do you have a favorite trope?" It suddenly seemed important.

"I like small town, fish out of water, and enemies to lovers." Kathleen smiled. "And no, we never counted as enemies."

So much for that plan. Not that she had a plan. No, she was flying by the seat of her pants and hoping for the best. "I never would have said we were."

"Good." Kathleen's expression grew serious. "I never meant for us to be anything close to that."

More than the cozy dinner, more than the playful banter about romance plots, the simple declaration gave Logan hope. "Me neither."

"Which brings us back to the matter at hand. Just one bed."

Logan sighed. So close, and yet so far. "I don't mind sleeping on the sofa. You're the guest, after all."

"Which means I shouldn't kick you out of your own bed."

"It really isn't all that comfortable, though. I wouldn't feel right inflicting it on you." She'd traded in the college futon for something more grownup but hadn't sprung for the pullout.

"We should share the bed."

She waited for the punchline. Or the caveat. "But?"

"But I'm still not sure we should sleep together."

Sleeping together clearly being code for having sex. "I'm capable of keeping my hands to myself."

Kathleen gave her a once-over. "What about the rest of you?"

"And the rest of me, too. But you can't look at me like that if I'm going to stand a chance."

"Like what?" Kathleen asked, all innocence.

"Like you don't really want me to keep my hands off you."

Kathleen blushed. "Sorry."

"Don't be sorry. Just have mercy. Contrary to my clumsy moves a few weeks ago, I'm all about respect and consent."

Kathleen took a deep breath. "For what it's worth, I want to."

"Want to?" She thought she knew but wanted Kathleen to say it.

"I want to go to bed with you." Kathleen's eyes closed briefly. "Have sex with you. I really do. And that's what worries me."

A dozen assurances of nothing to worry about flitted through Logan's mind. She swallowed them, because she actually meant that bit about respect and consent. And going for the hard sell would likely send Kathleen scurrying in the opposite direction. "I don't want you to feel worried. Or pressured."

Kathleen nodded. "I know. I wouldn't be here if I did."

That counted for almost as much as knowing Kathleen wanted her. "Do you want to borrow some pajamas?"

Kathleen looked her up and down again but caught herself. She cleared her throat. "If you have some old sweats or something, that would be great."

"I do. I also have some leggings Maddie convinced me were more comfortable than the thermals I had for cold days on job sites." She lifted a shoulder. "If you'd prefer."

"My occasional nighttime hot flashes certainly would. Thank you."

With the easy back and forth, she could almost pretend they were merely friends, negotiating an unplanned sleepover after a few too many glasses of wine. Almost. But when she handed Kathleen a pair of leggings and an old UVM T-shirt, and Kathleen shyly excused herself to the bathroom, the truth of the situation hit her like a ton of bricks. Sleeping next to Kathleen would be torture. Exquisite torture, perhaps, but torture all the same.

CHAPTER FOURTEEN

W ait. You stayed over, but you didn't sleep together?"
The question came from Clover, but Maddie looked
equally interested in the answer. They sat in a row, cross-legged on
their mats, waiting for the other attendees of Sunday morning goat
yoga to trickle in. A few of Clover's baby goats wandered, bleating
and hopping and collecting nose rubs from anyone willing to dole
them out.

"I mean, we slept." She hadn't meant to sound cagey, but she
totally did. The thing was, even now, the memory of Logan's body
pressed against hers sent her poor deprived libido into overdrive.
Because after an eternity of lying there not talking about how weird it
was to share a bed, they'd fallen asleep side-by-side, and she'd woken
up with Logan curled around her big spoon style. And she hadn't been
able to stop thinking about it since.

"In the same bed," Maddie asked.

"It's weird to talk about, isn't it?" Clover asked before Kathleen
could answer.

"Um." Obviously. Not only because they knew Logan but
because the very premise of sleeping with someone and not sleeping
sleeping with them was borderline ludicrous.

"Is it weird weird or weird because it's Maddie?" Clover gave
an exaggerated head jerk. "Because I can ask her to leave, and you
can tell me."

Kathleen laughed and Maddie made a show of being offended.
"I think it's weird weird," Kathleen said.

Clover tutted. "You write sex scenes for a living."

"Yeah. Imaginary ones." Ones where she got to keep a nice tidy distance between herself and the messiness—literal and figurative—of being with another person.

"Oh, come on. You can't tell me you slept over and didn't even think about doing more." Again, the comment came from Clover, but Maddie regarded her with rapt attention.

"I had a couple of glasses of wine, and I'd skipped lunch. They went right to my head, and I wasn't fit to drive. Logan offered to let me crash." All true, if not the entirety of the truth. Or anything close to it.

Clover laced her fingers together and gave a few affected blinks. Maddie mirrored the move.

Kathleen sighed. "She wouldn't let me sleep on the couch, and I felt bad relegating her to it."

Clover nodded knowingly. "Just one bed."

Kathleen snorted.

Maddie's gaze darted between them. "Hold on. What's that?"

Clover shook her head, a look of pity on her face. "Amateur."

Kathleen cleared her throat. "It's when the two love interests aren't planning to sleep together but find themselves in a situation where there's only one bed."

Maddie's eyes went wide. "Oh, my God. That's totally a thing."

Clover nodded. Kathleen made a point of averting her gaze.

Maddie's hands went to her hips. "Wait. Does that mean you and Logan hooked up or you didn't?"

Clover lifted a finger. "They didn't hook up but they both wanted to. It was probably this weird combination of awkward and hot." She looked to Kathleen. "Was it?"

Kathleen pressed her lips together, as much an affirmation as a spoken yes.

"So, extended foreplay." Clover gave another knowing nod. "How long til you put Logan out of her misery?"

Maddie raised a hand. "Not to make it weirder, but I do have a vested interest in this answer."

Curiosity beat out mortification. "Wait. Why?"

"Because Logan is trying so hard to be cool and it's getting painful to watch."

Kathleen frowned, the prospect of playing the tease sitting even more uncomfortably than having this conversation in the first place. "Does she think I'm leading her on?"

"Oh, God, no." Maddie's denial came fast and vociferous enough that Kathleen didn't doubt her sincerity.

She could pretend to be indifferent or deny just how close she was to diving headfirst into a reckless affair, but it felt disingenuous. And it wasn't like Maddie and Clover would even believe her. Yes, they were biased to a certain degree, but maybe they could offer more nuanced advice than Trudy's increasing insistence to just fuck already.

"What is it?" Clover asked gently. "You look legit stressed and not just vaguely uncomfortable."

"There's nothing vague about my discomfort." Kathleen laughed, then sighed. "I'm so much older than she is."

"Is that what's bothering you about all this?" Clover asked, clearly surprised.

Kathleen tipped her head back and forth. "That and the fact that I don't do hookups. Or relationships. Or anything in between, really."

"I don't understand," Maddie said.

"Are you ace?" Clover asked.

She appreciated the question, along with Clover's non-judgmental way of asking. But as tempted as she was to take the out, it seemed wrong to hide behind an identity not authentically hers. "Only if you count middle-aged and jaded as a subset of ace."

"Shut up," Clover said.

"Wait, wait, wait." Maddie raised her hand yet again. "You're a romance writer who doesn't do relationships?"

Kathleen shrugged.

Clover's eyes narrowed. "Do you not believe in happily ever after?"

Coming out as a cynic felt on par with coming out as queer. Not that she doubted Maddie and Clover were a safe space, but damn if the stakes didn't feel just as high. "I..."

"You don't." Clover might as well have pointed a finger and declared, "*J'accuse!*"

"I like the idea of it. And I believe in happy for now."

Clover shook her head. "But Nik and Nora. You gave them forever. Or at least implied it."

"I know. It works out so well on the page. Real life?" Kathleen shuddered.

As all this unfolded, the spots around them filled and the yoga instructor walked in. Clover went over to say hello and check on the five kids she'd selected to bring their unique brand of carefree enthusiasm to the class. Kathleen shot Maddie an aw-shucks shrug and prepared for sixty minutes of poses that would leave her feeling still middle-aged, but limber.

The instructor was gentle, with more focus on breath and alignment than a marathon of sun salutations that would invariably make her want to die. When the class ended, Clover slipped into hostess mode with a side of goat wrangler. Kathleen thought she might seize the opportunity to sneak out, but Maddie reminded her they were all going to her house for brunch.

When they got to Maddie's, the aromas of coffee, bacon, and cinnamon wafted through the house. Maddie's partner Sy puttered around the kitchen, reminding Maddie and everyone else that she'd always cook if it got her out of doing yoga. Kathleen accepted a cup of coffee, complimented the pan of sticky buns that looked like heaven on a plate, and crossed her fingers there'd be a thousand other things to talk about while they ate.

No such luck.

"I just need to understand," Clover said after bringing Sy up to speed.

Kathleen took a fortifying breath. "I love love in theory. And I think it's possible to build the sort of relationship that will stand the test of time. It's just not for me."

Maddie shook her head, not buying it. "But why not?"

"Did you have your heart broken?" Clover asked.

"You don't have to answer that," Sy said. "These two have the best intentions and hearts of gold, but boundaries aren't their strong suit."

Someone kicked Sy under the table, though Kathleen couldn't tell if it was Clover or Maddie.

"I haven't had one of those soul-crushing breakups, if that's what you mean." That involved falling hard in the first place. She was more versed in the false starts and the it's not you, it's me sort of relationships. Well, and Susan, who fell somewhere in the middle. Kathleen still wondered if she'd fallen more for the idea of the life they could have more than Susan herself, a fact that heavily influenced her hindsight.

"That's all you're gonna say, isn't it?" Clover shook her head, obviously disappointed but at least slightly cowed by Sy's admonishments.

"There's not much more to tell. I'm simply not built for it."

"What do you mean by 'it' exactly?" Maddie's tone took on a protective edge.

"Marriage, kids, growing old together. I don't see it in the cards for me. I'm not unwilling to date or have physical relationships with people. I just go in with my eyes open and my expectations low."

Sy let out a low whistle. "Damn." Then her head jerked up, as though realizing she'd spoken out loud without meaning to. "Sorry."

Kathleen waved her off. "No need. It's fine. I know it feels extreme for the romantics at heart." She tipped her head. "And for someone in my line of work."

Clover let out a forlorn sigh. "I still think you should hook up with Logan."

"Because she's not a romantic either?" Kathleen asked before she could stop herself.

Clover winced. Maddie did, too. Great.

Eventually, Maddie spoke up. "I don't think I'm overstepping to say she doesn't have any agenda. And she's certainly in no hurry to settle down."

She'd spent so much time thinking about all the reasons dating someone much younger would be a terrible idea, she hadn't really considered the potential perks. Namely, that Logan wouldn't be looking to get serious. Maybe that was worth taking into account. Not a justification, exactly. Merely an entry in the plus column of the pro/con tally she had going. "I'll keep that in mind."

❖

Logan could think of about a thousand things she'd rather do than have a family dinner with her gallivanting uncle and his new fiancée. A feeling exacerbated by the fact she had little confidence they'd make it through the meal without her sister using the words "gold-digging" and "floozy" within earshot of said fiancée.

There was also the matter of not being able to get Kathleen out of her mind. Kathleen's shyness as she climbed into the bed—facing Logan but teetering almost precariously close to the edge. The way she'd relaxed under the covers, probably helped along by the wine as much as fatigue. Waking up with Kathleen curled against her little spoon style, getting all shy again but kissing Logan's cheek before hustling off to goat yoga with Maddie and Clover. The whole thing left her happy, hopeful, and more sexually frustrated than she'd been since high school.

So now she resided in limbo land, with a vague sense she'd get to see Kathleen again soon, but no firm plans to. Even less firm was her sense of exactly where on the will they/won't they spectrum she and Kathleen sat. All that paired with Maddie promising to go off the deep end if Uncle Rich so much as hinted at selling his half of Barrow Brothers outside the family.

It was going to be a very long evening. At least the food would be good.

She showered and dressed, a little sad to wash away the traces of Kathleen she was convinced lingered on the T-shirt she hadn't bothered changing out of when Kathleen left. She stepped onto the porch just as Jack did. He looked even more dubious about the whole thing than she was. Great.

"How bad do you think it's going to be?" he asked as they got into his truck.

"I'm not optimistic, I can say that much."

Jack shook his head. "You're supposed to balance my cynicism."

"Sorry, pal. You're on your own with this one."

He pulled out of the driveway and didn't even try to hide his scowl. "Want to bet on how young she's going to be?"

"Ew. No." Not that she had issues with an age difference, obviously. It was just the prospect of her uncle acting all suave and some woman they'd never met lapping it up like an eager puppy.

"Twenty bucks says not a day over forty-five."

"Dude. Don't even." Logan scratched the back of her neck. She didn't know Kathleen's exact age, but she imagined it was somewhere in the vicinity. The prospect of her uncle wooing someone who might resemble Kathleen gave her the heebie-jeebies. Mostly because Uncle Rich was so smarmy, but still.

"Okay, twenty bucks Maddie says something inappropriate before dessert."

She rolled her eyes. "Why would I take that bet? I might as well just hand you twenty dollars before we get there."

Jack let out a snort. "Yeah, good point."

"Too bad Sy is scrambling to fill that massive order and had to bail. She's always level-headed, and Maddie absorbs that." She didn't worry Maddie would say anything truly heinous. It was just that, of all of them, she took her role and her stake in the business the most seriously. And even though their stakes were technically all the same, she had that protective thing going from being an older sister the last thirty or so years. "Maybe this Cherry woman will be nice," Logan said.

"But then what would she see in Uncle Rich?"

It was her turn to snort. Rich and Cherry would likely be two peas in a pod. What remained to be seen was how flashy and brassy a pod that turned out to be. "There is that."

She and Jack pulled up to their parents' on time but were the last to arrive. Introductions were just getting under way, so she braced herself and joined in.

"It's such a pleasure to meet y'all." Cherry's shoulders undulated with the cadence of her South Carolina drawl—clearly authentic and oddly charming. "Rich has done nothing but gush about the three of you and his two kids from the moment I met him."

Logan took her turn shaking Cherry's hand. Warm and soft, it exuded the same energy as her words—relaxed but bubbly, in no hurry but wanting to be everywhere at once. "He's done plenty of gushing about you, too."

Not a lie, even if most of what she'd heard had been secondhand.

Not one to waste time or tempt fate, Mom corralled everyone into the living room so she could finish dinner. To her credit, Cherry offered to help and only backed down when Logan and Jack insisted they were well-trained in the ways of the kitchen and happy to do their mother's bidding.

There wasn't much left to do, so she and Jack took turns eavesdropping on the conversation while chopping vegetables for salad and turning the loaf of fresh Italian into garlic bread. She didn't catch all the conversation, obviously, but she didn't detect a single raised voice or snarky aside. When Maddie laughed—long and loud—Jack shot her a raised brow. Mom shrugged.

After getting settled at the table, Mom dished out lasagna while Maddie cleared her throat and assumed her predetermined role of digging for details.

"Well, my first husband, Charlie, he passed away two years ago. Florida was his dream. And even though it wasn't mine, I couldn't quite bring myself to leave, if that makes any sense."

Mom offered a sympathetic smile. "We're all so sorry for your loss. And, yes, it makes total sense."

"The funny thing is, I spent most of my childhood reading *Little Women* and daydreaming about New England." Cherry laughed. "And here I go and fall for a fellow from Vermont."

Logan stole a glance at Maddie, who seemed charmed, if somewhat reluctant about it. Even Jack appeared swayed, smiling at the reference to a book he refused to read as a kid based solely on the title.

Dinner gave way to coffee and cannoli from Sugar Shack. Cherry told the story of how she met Rich at the convention center. She was running around to check on vendors as part of her job as an event manager, tripped, and literally fell into Rich's arms. For his part, Rich made goofy smiles and was all deference—a notable departure from his usual blather and bluster.

By the time they parted ways a little after nine, everyone's mind was effectively blown. She said as much to Jack, who confirmed the sentiment on their ride home. Maddie chimed in over text, all agreement. Not only was Cherry impossible to dislike, she somehow made Rich more pleasant to be around, too. It didn't solve their problem of Rich's burning desire to be bought out, but it made the situation way less icky and angsty than it could have been.

Once home, Logan fed Kiwi and let her out before changing into pajama pants and the UVM shirt she'd lent Kathleen the night before. Appreciative, right? Not creepy. She made a cup of tea and took her tablet to the couch, pulling up Kathleen's book—the one she'd downloaded but hadn't had time to read yet. Kiwi curled against her thigh and grumbled until Logan covered her with the couch blanket. Logan picked up her tablet again but just as quickly set it down, grabbing her phone instead.

Was it weird to text Kathleen? Or weird not to check in at all after last night? She had a flickering thought of What Would Maddie Do but quickly abandoned it.

Hi. Send. Ringer on. Phone down. Wait. Wait. Wait.

Hi.

Okay. That was a start. *Is it okay to text you personally?*

Logan hit send reflexively, then cringed. Personally? Could she be any less smooth? Though, even as she asked, she cringed again at the prospect of tempting fate.

We have shared a bed, so I'm thinking we're safely in the text zone. Kathleen added a winky emoji to the end.

Well, when you put it that way. Logan smirked. Kathleen could have said friend zone and didn't.

I was actually going to text you...

Oh, that was interesting. *Yeah?*

Looking for the best antique spots in a two-hour radius.

Logan rocked her neck side-to-side, sort of for show but letting out a happy moan when it cracked. *My specialty.*

CHAPTER FIFTEEN

L ogan sat on her porch, glad that shifting her weight forward and back in a rocking chair didn't count as fidgeting, and reminded herself this wasn't a date. Though it wasn't technically not a date, either. Kathleen had simply texted her to ask about good spots for antiquing. And then accepted Logan's invitation to go together.

They hadn't really talked about whether they were going to date. Or sleep together. Kathleen had been bashful after spending the night, though Logan couldn't tell if that had more to do with waking up in a full cuddle or the fact that she'd had enough wine to warrant staying over in the first place. Despite a borderline desperation to talk it out and know exactly where she stood, being pushy was what got her into trouble in the first place. She needed to chill the fuck out and let Kathleen take the lead. Or at least let things play out naturally.

When it came down to it, Kathleen might simply be trying to make nice now that they'd tiptoed into friendly territory. And maybe make use of Logan's pickup truck and ability to lift heavy things. Not that Logan was complaining. She'd take time with Kathleen any which way. If it involved kissing again—or more—she was obviously game. If it didn't, well that was okay, too. At least that's what she kept telling herself. Not successfully, mind you, but she kept at it anyway.

Kathleen pulled in and parked in the empty spot to the side of Logan's truck. She got out, wearing a flowy skirt, a light blue sweater, and a bright smile. Logan returned the smile and reminded herself to breathe. *Any which way.* Logan jogged down the steps to meet her.

"I feel bad for commandeering your day off," Kathleen said in lieu of a hello.

"When it comes to antique shops and flea markets, you don't really have to twist my arm." Though she'd be just as inclined to tail along with Kathleen on an errand to the post office.

Kathleen's eyes danced with mischief. "Since I'm in personal possession of proof of this, I won't argue."

"It's a fine line between hobby and obsession," she said, not overly bothered to fall on either side.

"Perhaps it's better to embrace the gray area."

It felt like maybe they were discussing more than shopping habits, but Logan didn't know how to find out without being obvious. "I'm going to tell Jack that next time he ribs me for bringing home a piece of furniture from the side of the road."

"I'm happy to be quoted." Kathleen swept her hand down her torso. "I'm dressed, okay, right? We're not going to be picking through big piles of things, are we?"

"No salvage yards, today, I promise. Though I know a couple of good ones if you ever want to check one out."

Kathleen wrinkled her nose, but it seemed like a playful declaration more than a rigid one. "I'm happy to leave that level of picking to my contractor."

They walked to Logan's truck, and she instinctively followed Kathleen to the passenger door. "It sticks," she lied.

Kathleen didn't argue, but her brow quirked with obvious skepticism. Logan cleared her throat and waited for Kathleen to climb in so she could shut it with extra force and bolster her assertion. When she'd gotten herself situated and had them on the road to their first destination, Kathleen shifted to face Logan. "So, where are we going?"

"This old, converted barn about an hour south of here. It's a mishmash of antique consignment and flea market. A bunch of different sellers all under one roof." Her go-to for random finds and inspiration pieces.

"Oh, that sounds like fun."

"You can't go in looking for something specific, but I've never left empty-handed." She pulled onto the road, not bothering with GPS.

A smile played at the corners of Kathleen's mouth. "Does that say more about the quality of the finds or your self-control?"

A week ago, that would have stung. A dig at her impulsiveness, her immaturity. Now? Now it felt like teasing on something resembling equal footing. She liked the feeling. "I'm going to plead the Fifth."

"Not a judgment either way, for what it's worth."

Logan quirked a brow. "No?"

The smile bloomed into a full-blown smirk. "I may embrace self-control in some areas of my life. Antiques aren't one of them. Especially now that I can shop without obliterating my weekly take-home pay."

She didn't know how much Kathleen made from her writing but loved that it afforded her latitude. Her own salary wasn't anything to write home about, but it covered her expenses and left some for savings and the little luxuries that made life fun. "Are you a serious collector?"

"Oh, God, no." Kathleen laughed. "I like quirky things and things I can take home and polish up. I don't do real restorations, but I'm not afraid of a little elbow grease."

"What about a little sandpaper?" And why did such innocuous conversation hint at more than furniture rehab?

Kathleen gave a wistful shrug. "I'm afraid that exceeds my skill set."

"It doesn't have to."

"No?"

"I could teach you," Logan said, perhaps a little too suggestively.

Kathleen folded her arms. "Is that so?"

"If you were interested, I mean. No pressure." She fixed her eyes on the road and repeated the mantra to herself. *No pressure.*

"I might be. With the right teacher."

"You find something you want, and we'll make it happen." So much for pressure. Kathleen was flirting with her—completely sober and in broad daylight. If that didn't scream potential, she didn't know what did.

❖

"Are you sure you don't mind holding this stuff at your place?" Kathleen asked, unable to shake the feeling she was imposing.

"I absolutely don't mind. I've got the space, but more importantly, I have the setup for refinishing. It'll be way easier than you trying to make your own."

Considering she also needed Logan's help to do said refinishing, it felt foolish to argue. "I hope you'll let me do something nice to thank you for the help, today and whenever we get around to all that sanding and staining you've promised to teach me."

"It's my pleasure," Logan said with feeling. "Truly."

For not the first time that day, she got the sense Logan meant more than the conversation at hand. It left her wanting to be brave, wanting to tell Logan that they should just fall into bed already. Naked this time. And with less emphasis on sleeping. But still she hesitated.

"What?" Logan asked.

"Nothing."

"If you look that intense over nothing, I'm worried what will happen when it's something."

It was a gentle tease, with a built-in escape hatch. She could claim anything—from overstimulation to an empty stomach. "Fine. I was thinking about how long ago lunch was."

Logan laughed. "I have some grilled chicken we could put on a salad. Or maybe I could talk you into ordering a pizza with me."

They hadn't discussed dinner, but it offered the perfect excuse not to part ways just yet. And if Logan was offering, it was reasonable to deduce she felt the same. "Both have their merits. Do you have a preference?"

"My head says salad, but my heart says pizza."

She laughed. "That's such a middle-age thing to say."

Logan pulled into her driveway and cut the engine. "How many times do I have to tell you? I'm an old soul."

Kathleen might not be ready to cede the point, but she no longer felt compelled to argue it. "What if we ordered a pizza and had a little salad on the side?"

"Genius. Sold. Let's go in and order it, then we decide whether to unload now or after we eat."

She followed Logan inside and to the kitchen to let Kiwi out and study the menu Logan kept secured to the fridge with a magnet.

"Can I offer you a glass of wine?" Logan eyed her hopefully.

She lifted a finger. "One. Otherwise, I might end up crawling into your bed again."

Logan, who'd reached into the drawer for a corkscrew, froze. She turned slowly, gaze intense. "It's not nice to joke about such things."

She swallowed the apology that leapt to the tip of her tongue. If she didn't take a chance now, would she ever? Was that a risk she was willing to take? "What if I wasn't joking?"

Logan just stood there, bottle in one hand and corkscrew in the other. "Are you serious?"

"That's usually the definition of not joking." She bit her lip, wondering when she'd last been a tease. Um, never. That's when.

Logan set the wine down. "Look, I don't usually need to be told something multiple times, but given, you know, I'm going to have to ask you to clarify."

She could. Or she could tell Logan what she wanted. What she wanted Logan to do. "I think you should kiss me."

Logan searched her face, as though looking for clues or, perhaps, a catch.

"I know it's really uncool of me to put the brakes on so hard. Then kiss you. Then put the brakes on again. You have every right to say no thanks at this point, so—"

"You want me to kiss you." Logan made it sound like a statement more than a question, which Kathleen took as a good sign.

"I'd like you to do a lot more than kiss me, but kissing seems like a good place to start," Kathleen said, heart in her throat.

"I…"

"Don't find yourself speechless very often?" She chuckled.

"Well, no." Logan frowned. "But I don't know what to say."

"You can say the moment has passed. You can say you're no longer interested. Or, you can say nothing and—"

"Kiss you."

Kathleen nodded. "Yes."

Logan angled her head and studied Kathleen. Kathleen did her best not to talk. Or fidget. Or grab Logan's face between both hands and initiate the kissing herself. Eventually, Logan smiled. She brushed Kathleen's bangs to the side with her finger, then trailed that finger along her hairline, down to her jaw. "I can't tell you how many times I've wanted to do this."

Kathleen swallowed. "You should tell me. Later."

Logan's mouth pressed to hers—not aggressive but not delicate, either. Kathleen's lips parted, a gasp of surprise chased with longing. Logan slipped inside, her tongue gentle but inquisitive. Persistent.

A moan escaped and Kathleen almost pulled back in embarrassment. Logan, however, seemed to take it as encouragement. Her free hand cupped the back of Kathleen's neck, grasp firm. Confident. Sexy.

Kathleen stopped worrying about whether Logan still wanted her. Or whether her breath was okay or whether she'd regret all this come morning. In fact, her entire mind emptied and all that remained was the heat of Logan's mouth on hers and the press of their bodies and the infinite potential of deciding to let go for once in her life and simply enjoy the ride.

Logan eased away, her eyes searching. "Was that okay?"

The question felt like a check-in more than any lack of confidence, which was nice. Since words had vacated along with the worries, she nodded.

"Would it be okay if I did it again?"

Another nod.

The second kiss held no hesitation. Only desire. For all the kisses Kathleen had written through the years, she had no idea a kiss could convey quite so much desire. As though Logan's entire life force distilled into wanting, and she channeled every drop into that one point of connection.

When Logan pulled back again, Kathleen was breathless. Full-body breathless. Pulse tripping, skin tingling, clit throbbing breathless. "Wow."

"Good wow?" Logan asked.

"Yep."

Logan studied her but this time with amusement. "You're sure?"

"You've rendered the writer speechless. Are you pleased with yourself?"

Logan took her time answering. "Very. But only if the writer is pleased as well."

"Let's call that an understatement," she said.

"I like that. So, you'd be open to more?"

More. Such a simple word. Often a throwaway. And yet it summed up the situation perfectly. "More."

"What about dinner?" Logan asked.

"Turns out I'm not all that hungry."

Logan took her hand and led her in the direction of the couch. "I promise we'll eat after."

"Whatever," she said, trying to sound more chill than she felt.

"Well, if I do it right, we should both work up an appetite." It came out like a line. Butch bravado that may or may not live up to the hype. Only it didn't land that way. Logan said it like an observation of the obvious, like she had no doubt in her mind that they'd both have a good time and come up for air and fuel at some point.

"In that case, maybe we should skip the sofa and go right to your room."

Logan hesitated, revealing the tiniest chink in the armor of her confidence. "I want you to feel like you can change your mind if things get too heavy."

She wanted to tell Logan the only heaviness she was interested in was the weight of Logan's body on top of her, but even in the heat of this moment, she couldn't quite pull it off. So she settled for the next best thing. "I won't change my mind."

Logan's mouth opened then closed, like she thought better of disagreeing. Or questioning. "Okay."

Logan squeezed Kathleen's hand and started up the stairs. Kathleen's mind raced, and it occurred to her that she hadn't bothered to shave her legs that morning. And she hadn't shaved above the knee in longer than she cared to admit. "Shit."

Logan stopped. "What's wrong?"

"Just realizing I would have done my morning routine differently had I known this was going to happen."

Worry vanished. In its place, a rather satisfied smirk. "You mean you didn't wake up planning to seduce me to within an inch of my sanity?"

Kathleen laughed. "Yeah, no."

"You're really good on the fly, then." Logan gave her hand another squeeze. "Really, though. If you want to do this but don't feel ready, it's cool. I can wait."

They'd danced around each other for so long, she worried any further delay would jinx the whole thing. "No, it's not that."

"It's?" Logan's brow lifted.

"A moment of feeling self-conscious."

Logan's expression turned serious. "You have nothing to feel self-conscious about."

Arguing would make her hate herself, worse than feeling self-conscious. "It'll pass. As soon as you touch me, I'll be too distracted to think about anything else."

Logan smiled, then. "I guess that's what I'll have to do."

Upstairs was mercifully dim, with no lights on and the late afternoon sun long gone. Kathleen relaxed, at least a little.

"Anything I should know?" Logan asked.

"Know?" Her mind raced.

"Likes, dislikes. Relevant health and hygiene matters. Recent sexual partners."

She let out a snort before she could stop herself. "Sorry." She cleared her throat. "No recent partners. Clean bill of health. You?"

Logan regarded her curiously. "No one for a few months. I had a physical a few weeks ago."

She wondered if Logan wondered about her definition of recently. The fact of the matter was it had been close to two years. Did that count as recently at her age? A stretch, but no point splitting hairs. "I guess that means we're good."

Logan's expression remained intense. "I am if you are. I mean, I've wanted this all along. You haven't. I want you to be sure."

Kathleen laughed. "I've wanted it, too. I've just been pretending otherwise."

"And now?" Logan raised a brow.

"I'm done pretending. I confess I'm out of practice, but if you still want me, then I'm all yours. All in." She cringed. "Not all. In. You know what I mean."

"Are we having the consent talk right now?" Logan asked. "Because if we are, I'm digging it."

Kathleen covered her face with her hands and laughed. "Yes. Though I'd like to state for the record that my characters do this more gracefully than I'm managing right now."

Logan took both Kathleen's hands in hers. "I don't need it to be graceful. I just need you to mean it."

She lifted her chin, letting Logan's confidence rub off on her. "See? That's a good line. I'd use that."

Logan mirrored the gesture. "If you like my lines, wait until you see my moves."

It was just cheesy enough to chase away the rest of her nerves. She tutted. "But that one was terrible. You're back to square one."

"Do not pass go, do not collect two hundred?"

She shook her head, feigning disappointment. "Exactly."

"Hmm. I'll have to try another tack." Logan tipped her head one way, then the other. "Hey, Kathleen?"

"Yes?"

"Would it be okay if I more than kissed you now?"

They weren't keeping score, but damn. Point to Logan. Kathleen took a deep breath. She had no doubt Logan would stop if she asked, but as far as she was concerned, there was no going back now. "I'd like that very much."

CHAPTER SIXTEEN

L ogan paused her revving libido long enough to process Kathleen's words, along with the shaky breath that accompanied them. Like, really process them. All that hesitation, all that reticence. It wasn't about whether or not Kathleen was into her. As hard as she found it to believe, what Kathleen lacked was confidence. Even as her desire ticked up a few more notches, her desire to take away those shadows surged. "I really, really want you."

Kathleen nodded.

"I'd like to spend the next several hours showing you, as a start. If at any moment you change your mind, you just have to tell me. Yes?"

Another nod.

"Good. Now, come with me." Since they'd paused at the top of the stairs, she led Kathleen into her bedroom. "Lights or no lights?"

Kathleen's hand tightened on hers. "No lights."

She might prefer to bask in every inch of Kathleen's body, but now that she understood, putting Kathleen at ease took precedence. Besides, the soft glow that spilled in from the streetlight would offer enough to see what she needed to see. She pointed to Kathleen's sweater. "May I?"

Kathleen gave a little smile with her nod, then lifted her arms.

Under other circumstances, she might tease the novelist for being a woman of so few words. At the moment, she was too busy appreciating the way Kathleen's pale skin glowed in the low light. "So beautiful."

She kissed Kathleen's neck, her collarbones. When she dipped lower, right to the line of lace at the top of Kathleen's bra, Kathleen gasped. Logan reminded herself not to be too precious, too reverent. Not for her own benefit but Kathleen's. If Kathleen was half as stuck in her head as she seemed, she needed urgency more than adoration.

Logan ran her fingers up Kathleen's side, sliding around to unclasp her bra. When she did it with a single flick, Kathleen laughed. "Smooth."

Logan looked up. "I try."

"You're wearing too many clothes," Kathleen said.

"Maybe you could help me with that."

Kathleen nodded, seeming to appreciate having a task. She rid Logan of her Henley and undershirt, then went to work on her jeans. She pushed them down, leaving Logan's boxer briefs at least temporarily in place. "Much better."

Since Kathleen's skirt had a stretch waist, Logan mirrored the move. "Much."

Kathleen tipped her head toward the bed. "Can we?"

"Of course." She pulled back the duvet and gestured for Kathleen to get in first. Kathleen obliged but moved to tug the covers over herself. "Oh, no. Allow me."

Instead of covering Kathleen with the duvet, she blanketed Kathleen's body with her own. Kathleen all but purred, and it took considerable restraint not to grind against her.

"Is this okay?" Logan asked.

Kathleen nodded. "You don't have to keep asking. And you don't need to take your time."

So many ways to read that. But the one she took was Kathleen's need for sensation, the kind that made it impossible to think too long or too hard about much of anything. For better or worse, she knew how to do that. Besides, if she played her cards right, she'd get the chance to take her time later.

She kissed Kathleen again, hard enough to leave no doubt of her intentions, or her desire. Kathleen arched into her, consent and encouragement and invitation all rolled into one. Logan took one of Kathleen's taut nipples into her mouth, letting out a little moan at the way it hardened under her tongue. Kathleen's hands moved restlessly over her back, scratching lightly at the base of her neck and driving her absolutely bananas.

She lapped and sucked, alternating between Kathleen's breasts until Kathleen literally whimpered. Logan lost herself in the rhythm of it, of Kathleen's soft flesh and the way her skin smelled like a meadow of wildflowers on a hot July afternoon. Logan worked her way down, kissing across Kathleen's belly and the patch of hair at the opening of her thighs. Kathleen's legs parted and Logan settled between them. Kathleen's scent was subtle but intoxicating at the same time. Logan could lose herself in that scent, in the restless shifting of Kathleen's hips.

Kathleen's head popped up. "I'm sorry I didn't—I mean, I didn't know we were going to—"

"Shh." She wasn't sure of the exact source of Kathleen's self-consciousness. She only knew there was no need for it. "You're perfect."

"I—"

Logan pressed her tongue gently to Kathleen's clit, and whatever argument or observation Kathleen may have been attempting melted into a moan of pleasure. Logan let out a moan of her own. Weeks of pent-up wanting, of Kathleen's frosty formality, of not knowing if this moment would ever happen. Her clit twitched with a sort of pre-release.

Kathleen moaned again, this time with glorious abandon. God, she loved that sound. She wanted more of it—louder, longer, and with more abandon. She wanted it over and over until Kathleen erupted for her, called out her name.

Mission in mind, Logan tuned into Kathleen's body. The way the muscles in her thighs tightened on the long strokes, the way her belly clenched when Logan increased the pressure. Kathleen writhed and arched, her body undulating with the kind of urgency that had nothing to do with trying to look sexy and everything to do with mindless pleasure. Of course, the abandon was sexier that any erotic intention.

Normally, she'd try to draw the pleasure out, get the orgasm to build slowly. But she didn't know Kathleen's body yet, didn't want to chance getting her too wound up to find release. So as Kathleen chased her orgasm, Logan chased her, happy to follow wherever Kathleen led.

It didn't take long. Kathleen's fingers grasped Logan's hair and her whole body tensed. It was fast and fierce and Logan did her best to ride it out alongside her.

"Fuck," Kathleen said, her voice breathy and spent.

"Yep." Logan stayed where she was, wondering if she might be able to coax Kathleen up again.

Kathleen crooked a finger. "Come here."

Logan abandoned her half-baked plan, perfectly happy to do whatever Kathleen wanted. She crawled up Kathleen's body and kissed her. "You're ridiculously sexy."

"You're generous."

"Biased, maybe, but not generous. Well, at least not about that."

Kathleen smirked. "You're a sweet talker."

She grinned. "Sometimes."

"Are you going to let me reciprocate?" Kathleen asked.

The thought of Kathleen going down on her sent Logan's already throbbing clit into a frenzy. "Yes, but only if you want to."

Kathleen rolled onto her side. "I'm offended you used the word if."

She perhaps shouldn't have smirked, but she did. "Hey, I try never to presume."

"Fair." Kathleen got to her knees. "But I'm still offended."

"You could teach me a lesson. Show me exactly how much you want to." It was a risk to play the challenge card, but the look on Kathleen's face told her it was the right move.

"I'll see what I can do."

Kathleen situated herself between Logan's legs. She licked her lips and it was all Logan could do not to come right then and there. But then Kathleen's mouth was on her and thoughts of coming warred with wanting to stay exactly like that forever.

Kathleen's tongue was magic. Soft but insistent, eager yet unrushed. Logan's resolve didn't stand a chance. Combined with all the weeks of waiting, of wanting, of not being sure it was ever going to happen, Logan succumbed, tumbling into orgasm like free fall. She soared for what felt like eternity and landed, not with a crash, but as though she'd fallen into one of those massive rescue mattresses— softened impact but one that left her breathless all the same.

"Fuck."

"I already said that." Kathleen lifted her head, her hair deliciously tousled.

"It's all I've got, though." She swiped the back of her hand across her brow. "I'll be sure to cite my sources."

Kathleen giggled. "MLA, if you don't mind."

"Whatever you say, Professor." She'd had her fair share of hot for teacher moments, but nothing like this.

"Whatever, huh?" Kathleen scooted up the mattress until they were facing each other.

"Pretty much."

"So, if I said I needed to have your fingers inside me?"

"I'd say fuck yes." Just the thought had her jagged pulse revving again.

"I guess I'll have to cite you back, then."

She slipped her hand between Kathleen's legs and found her hot and slick. "I'd be honored."

She fucked Kathleen, slowly at first and then with an almost frantic intensity, spurred on by a glorious litany of expletives and encouragement. Kathleen returned the favor, asking enough deliciously explicit questions about what Logan wanted to make her wonder where dirty talk had been all her life. The second orgasm was even better than the first, leaving Logan wrung out and revved up all at the same time.

Logan propped herself on her elbow, mostly so she could enjoy the view of Kathleen, still breathing heavy and with a light sheen of sweat where the sheet she'd draped across them hadn't covered. "I could eat you up right now."

Kathleen shook her head slowly, eyes still closed. "Please don't tell me you need another round. You might actually kill me."

She laughed. "No, I'm perfectly sated. You're irresistible is all."

Kathleen let out a sniff.

"I mean it. Of course, I'm also sex-starved." She lifted a finger. "Starved from sex, not starved of sex."

Kathleen chuckled.

"If I can't talk you into another orgasm, can I talk you into dinner?"

Kathleen opened one eye, then the other. "Yes, but I don't want you to go to any trouble."

"We're ordering pizza, remember?"

As if on cue, Kathleen's stomach rumbled. She threw and arm over her torso. "Apparently."

"Preference on kind?"

"Any and all veggies you tolerate and sausage if you require meat."

"That's the most adorable way of conveying your topping choices." She leaned in and kissed Kathleen—quick, but it left her wondering if she could maybe talk Kathleen into another round after they ate. "Seriously."

Kathleen blushed. "I didn't mean to be."

"Clearly, you can't help it."

The blush faded, and Kathleen frowned.

"What? You don't like being called adorable?"

"It's such a young word."

Logan was tempted to insist Kathleen wasn't old, but something told her that would make things worse rather than better. "It's ageless."

"Stop."

"Kind of like how hot you are," Logan said. Kathleen's mouth opened, but Logan bounded from bed before Kathleen could argue, pulling on a pair of boxers and grabbing a T-shirt from the basket of clean laundry she'd yet to put away. "Your pajamas from last time are in there. Help yourself."

❖

"Why is this the best pizza I've ever eaten?" Kathleen asked after taking her first bite of sausage, peppers, and mushroom.

"Because pizza after sex is always the best pizza you've ever eaten."

She chewed slowly, weighing the merits of the argument. "I think you're right."

"It's a double whammy of feel-good chemicals. Plus comfy clothes and couch."

She had that exact combo plenty of nights without the sex and had no complaints. Doing it with Logan after sex? She might be ruined. "I confess I feel about twenty-two right now."

"In a good way? Or bad?"

"Neither. Just strange." Though, if she was being honest, she hadn't had that much sex in her twenties either.

"For what it's worth, I'm happy to take you somewhere nice. Classy, sophisticated. The whole nine yards."

"I don't require that." Wasn't even sure she wanted it. But she appreciated that Logan would offer.

"It doesn't mean you might not like it sometimes. Deserve it sometimes."

Kathleen shook her head. Funny word, deserve. It had so much potential to be liberating, but mostly it stirred up forty-year-old feelings of being not quite pretty enough, not quite smart enough. Definitely not social enough or charming enough or driven enough. Not that her brother started establishing his superiority the day he was born, but he might as well have.

"Why are you saying no?"

"I'm not. I just…" She stared at her pizza and sighed. No way was she killing her sex buzz with childhood trauma talk.

"What?"

"Forget fancy dinners. I don't really do this. Any of it." She kept her tone light, wanting to be honest without weighing down the conversation.

"The pizza, the sex, or the pizza after sex?"

Kathleen chuckled. "The last two."

"Oh, good. If you never ate pizza, I'm not sure we could keep seeing each other," Logan said casually.

"I'm overthinking this, aren't I?" She took a long sip of wine. She overthought everything.

"I don't know. Are you?"

"Yeah. I am. But I'm going to stop now and enjoy the best pizza ever and this lovely pinot noir." She locked eyes with Logan. "And this exceptional company."

"Don't forget the sex buzz."

Kathleen gave into a full laugh, relief spreading through her like the satisfaction of post-coital carb loading. "And the sex buzz."

She went in for a second piece and, by some skill or magic, Logan kept her out of her head. Conversation about books, questions about Kathleen's writing process. Balancing creativity with the need to produce.

"I wouldn't have thought writing and design had much in common, but they do." Kathleen pondered that and let herself slide the rest of the way into a warm sex-carb-wine afterglow.

"Would you write what you write if you didn't have to pay the bills?" Logan asked.

"Honestly, I'm so thrilled that writing is paying the bills, I haven't even stopped to think about it."

Logan smiled. "There's something wonderful about making money doing what you love, isn't there?"

She'd never hated teaching, only the fact that it felt all but impossible to get a single, stable version of it. Writing might not promise stability, but it was shaping up to give her more than she'd had in a long time. And, with the exception of her editor and agent, it left her to her own devices. "Yeah."

"Will you stay?" Logan asked when their wine glasses were empty and only a couple slices remained.

She eyed the bottle, not quite empty but close. "I should, right?"

"Can I ask you something?"

She stiffened, not sure she was going to like the question. "What's that?"

"Would I be able to talk you into staying even if we hadn't had wine?"

She didn't know what she'd been expecting, but the flash of vulnerability wasn't it. Subtle, but vulnerable. She reached over and covered Logan's hand with her own. "You wouldn't have to talk me into it."

Logan's smile spread slowly, like she might not want to admit needing the answer but liked it all the same. "I'm glad."

She wouldn't have said she needed that from Logan, but she liked it all the same, too. "I'm going to have to leave a toothbrush here at this rate."

Logan gave a little shrug. "I'd be cool with that."

She hadn't meant to imply they were dating in earnest, but it hit her that's how it sounded. She swallowed the knee-jerk protest because it seemed unnecessarily rigid. And because Logan had been so sweet in her reply. Oh, and because sex buzz.

She didn't have a lot of experience with those, but turned out they were pretty damn awesome. Maybe Logan—and Trudy and Maddie and Clover—were right. She didn't need to have all the answers. Maybe, just maybe, she could sit back and enjoy the ride.

"Hey, Logan?" she asked.

"Yeah?" Logan regarded her with amusement but also a little like she'd happily fuck Kathleen again.

"Take me back to bed?"

"Of course." Logan's eyes narrowed. "To sleep or for more shenanigans?"

The word choice made her smile. Maybe Logan was an old soul after all. "Shenanigans. Most definitely."

Logan hopped up from the sofa and held out her hand. "Right this way."

CHAPTER SEVENTEEN

Logan woke when Kathleen stirred at dawn. The soft light and feel of Kathleen's naked body against hers made her never want to leave the cocoon of bed.

"I'm sorry. I didn't mean to wake you," Kathleen said.

Logan took advantage of the situation, caressing and kissing Kathleen's warm skin under the covers. "Don't apologize. Just tell me you don't have to go quite yet."

"I should," Kathleen said without a whole lot of conviction.

"Hear me out." Logan kissed her rather than making a verbal argument, then slid her hand between them. Kathleen's thighs parted, though it seemed like Kathleen was operating more on instinct than intention. She was warm and wet and impossibly soft, and Logan couldn't imagine a place she'd rather be.

Kathleen sighed, and any argument she might have been inclined to make disappeared. "God, you're good at that."

Logan pressed a kiss to her shoulder. "I'm just listening to your body. It's telling me everything I need to know."

Kathleen smirked but didn't argue. In fact, she went along, riding Logan's hand until her whole body tensed. She bit Logan's shoulder—not hard enough to leave a mark but close. Which of course drove Logan crazy and made her wish for nowhere to be.

"I want nothing more than to stay in bed and do this all day, but I'm due on a job site at seven thirty."

Kathleen pulled away and half sat up. "Oh, no. What time is it?"

She put a hand on Kathleen's back. "Not even seven. Relax. I just know if you get me started, I'll be done for."

Kathleen flopped back onto the mattress. "I don't come in the morning."

Logan ran a finger between her breasts. "Is that your way of telling me you faked it? Because I can take it, but I'd rather you be honest. We can have plenty of fun that doesn't end in climax."

Kathleen smacked Logan's arm. "No, it's my way of saying you've got me doing things I never do."

"Oh." Well, that was a pleasant surprise.

Kathleen's expression turned serious. "I appreciate you saying that, though. I've faked plenty to spare people's egos and I always feel gross about it." She covered her face with her hand. "I can't believe we're having this conversation at six-something in the morning."

"But it's a good conversation to have." One that managed to stroke Logan's ego in several ways. "Shall we make a no faking pact?"

Kathleen nodded slowly, as though the proposal was equal parts absurd and appealing. Which it kind of was. "Yes. Okay."

Logan stuck out a hand, and Kathleen shook it. "Excellent. Now, can I offer you some coffee?"

"Only if you're making it for yourself," Kathleen said.

"Only if I'm making it for myself." Logan shook her head. "So many things wrong with that statement, so little time."

Kathleen let out a little huff. "I was being polite."

"I'm guessing you don't want to dissect that at six-something in the morning, so I'm going to put the pot on and jump in the shower. If you want one, too, you're welcome to join or have one of your own."

"No, no. I need to head home for fresh clothes anyway."

Logan climbed from the bed and pulled on her robe. "For what it's worth, you look super cute in mine."

She didn't wait for a reply, hustling through her morning routine so she'd have time to enjoy at least one cup of coffee with Kathleen. Which they had at the little table in her kitchen, with Kiwi lazily munching her breakfast and the cool, dewy air slipping through the open window promising that spring really was springing.

"Do you know where I could hire someone to build me some raised garden beds?" Kathleen asked, both hands wrapped around Logan's favorite mug.

"I'd do it."

"I'm sure that's not normally within the Barrow Brothers scope of work."

Logan set her own mug down. "It can be. But I didn't offer Barrow Brothers. I offered myself."

Kathleen shook her head. "You don't have to."

"What if I want to?"

Kathleen chewed her lip. "As in, I'd pay you directly."

"As in, I'd like to do something nice for you." She lifted a hand. "And not because I want you to have sex with me again."

"Oh."

"I mean, I want you to have sex with me again. More than sex, really. But I'd like to do it for you either way, if you'll let me."

"You want to date me?" Kathleen seemed genuinely surprised by this fact.

"Have I not made that abundantly obvious?" She wasn't sure how else she could.

"You've made it clear you're attracted to me."

Logan dropped her shoulders, trying for playful exasperation. "And spending time with you."

"It's just so, I don't know—"

"Please don't say mature."

Kathleen laughed. "I was thinking sweet. Old-fashioned. Like courting."

"What exactly do you think millennials do when it comes to dating?" Did she want to know the answer to that?

"You know," Kathleen said with exasperation.

"I don't."

Kathleen flipped her hand back and forth. "I know saying Netflix and chill is passé, but the principle still holds, no?"

Logan let out a snort. "It does when you're twenty maybe."

"You're still in your twenties," Kathleen said, as though accusing Logan of a crime.

"Barely. And as we've discussed, old soul." Which was legit, not simply something she'd thrown out there to make Kathleen feel better.

"So, you want to date and to build me garden boxes?" Kathleen looked genuinely befuddled by the prospect.

"Yes." A possibility hit her. "Do you think I invited you over just to hook up?"

Kathleen shrugged.

She smacked her hand to her forehead. "Idiot." She dropped it to look Kathleen in the eye. "Me, not you. Definitely not the vibe I was going for. If you recall, I went out of my way to cook you something nice that first time. And we didn't even have sex then."

Kathleen laughed. As in, really laughed. Hard. "Oh, man. What a mess."

She'd started to laugh, too, but stopped short. "What's a mess?"

"This. Us." Kathleen frowned. "Me."

"I don't think you're a mess." Probably the furthest thing from it.

"I am, but it's okay." Kathleen gave a decisive nod. "Everything's okay."

It sounded like a platitude more than a statement of fact, and Logan scrambled for the right words. "I'm sorry if I wasn't clear. I'd like to date you. And I'd like to build you beds for your garden. Would you be on board with both those things?"

Kathleen hesitated.

"Or, if that feels like a lot, how about being willing to consider the dating part?"

Kathleen smirked. "But not the garden boxes?"

She shrugged, playing it cooler than she felt. "Well, if you're going to plant them this year, it needs to happen soon. I'm not sure you'd be able to hire someone on such short notice."

"See? That's so considerate, I'd be a total ass if I said no."

"No to the boxes or no to dating?" She quirked a brow. It felt like a game, and she hoped to God that was the case.

"Both." Kathleen stuck both hands out.

"Okay. You should say yes to the garden and maybe to the dating. Consider the boxes a friendly gesture, and I promise I won't have any expectations." Though trying to avoid them had gotten them into this confused state in the first place.

Kathleen's eyes narrowed. "You'll let me buy the materials."

Logan laughed because making light seemed less likely to send Kathleen skittering in the opposite direction. "You drive a hard bargain, woman. Yes, okay. Deal."

Kathleen glanced at the clock. "Now I'm going to get out of your way so you can go to work."

She didn't wait for a response, heading to the door and putting on her shoes. Logan followed, hoping to sneak a kiss. Kathleen indulged her and wished her a good day. Logan then hurried to get herself together and out the door, goofy smile firmly in place.

She stepped onto the porch just as Jack did. "Good morning, sunshine."

Jack's eyes narrowed. "You got laid."

"How do you know that?" she asked.

"You look smug. Deny it."

"Okay, fine. In the crassest of terms, yes. I got laid." Though it wasn't at all how she would describe being with Kathleen, it technically described the situation.

"Who's the lucky lady?"

"Seriously, dude?" Logan shook her head. "You know I've been chasing Kathleen for the better part of two months."

Jack shrugged. "Yeah, but she turned you down cold."

Also technically true. "Well, she came around."

"Only you, dude. Only you."

"What's that supposed to mean?" He said it like she was some kind of player who made a point of wearing women down, which she absolutely wasn't.

"Actually, I guess not only you. Maddie went and hopped into bed with her client, too. Clearly, I'm the odd man out."

Logan scrubbed a hand over her face. "It wasn't like that."

"Not like the hopping into bed part or the client part?"

She frowned. "We didn't hop."

"Oh, I'm sorry. Fell? Tumbled? Dove headfirst?"

The last thing she wanted to do was encourage him, but she couldn't help but laugh. "Eased in. With intention. And consent."

Jack made a face. "Sounds geriatric."

She could take Jack's needling any day of the week, but something about the word made her defensive on Kathleen's behalf. "Let me assure you there was nothing geriatric about it."

"Hey, I'm not implying your lady is old. I'm implying you're about as smooth as one-twenty grit."

Again, she didn't want to laugh, but she did. "I'd decided to respect her wishes and boundaries. That's all. They just happened to change. And I took advantage."

"God, I hope you're cooler with her than you are with me."

"I'm always cool." Definitely not true.

Jack's face made it clear he agreed with her thoughts more than her words.

"Okay, I'm rarely cool. But Kathleen decided I wasn't so bad, and I knew better than to correct her." Especially after all their false starts and steps backward.

"So, she's a minx, eh?"

"When did you become such a bro? Are you overdosing on the T?"

Jack straightened his shoulders and puffed out his chest. "I'll have you know I'm jaded and sullen, not douchey and misogynistic."

"You're too young to be jaded."

"Antisocial, then." He shrugged. "And I'm not disrespecting Kathleen, I'm simply yanking your chain because it's so easy."

As was his habit. "Be nice or I'm going to tell Maddie you wondered out loud how much of a bridezilla she'd turn into when she and Sy got engaged."

To his credit, Jack looked genuinely mortified. "I never said that."

"I know, but you're jaded and sullen enough that if I told Maddie you did, she'd believe me."

"Low blow."

She shrugged. "You started it."

He stuck out both hands. "Minx is a compliment."

To be fair, it was. Accurate, too. For all that Kathleen had started out shy, she turned the heat up to eleven. Even after a shower and Kathleen's departure, Logan's body practically hummed with it. Still, Kathleen was classy. And she'd be damned if she let her bonehead brother imply otherwise. "Debatable. Either way, I'll say this. It was well worth the wait."

❖

"You're looking particularly glowy this morning," Clover said when she slid into the chair across from Kathleen.

It had become an unspoken ritual, meeting Maddie and Clover for coffee on Monday mornings. Not that they didn't bump into each other at least once or twice otherwise during the week, but this involved sitting for a bit and catching up like old friends.

"Glowy?" Kathleen asked, looking to deflect more than wanting Clover to clarify.

"All aglow? Dewy?" Clover's eyes got big. "Or freshly fucked."

"Who's freshly fucked?" Maddie took the chair next to Kathleen.

Clover did an exaggerated head jerk in Kathleen's direction.

Maddie looked at Kathleen. Kathleen looked at her coffee.

Clover wagged a finger. "Girl, there's no shame in getting a little action, especially in a slim pickings place like Bedlington. Was it Logan? Please tell me it was Logan. If it wasn't Logan, where did you meet them? Who am I kidding. Of course it was Logan. How are you? How was it?"

Kathleen blinked a few times, more overwhelmed by the rapid-fire stream of consciousness than the prospect of her friends knowing what had happened. "Yes. And good."

Clover's eyes narrowed. "You're good, or it was good?"

Heat rose in her cheeks. She'd yet to make eye contact with either of them and couldn't bring herself to now. "Yes."

"Hot damn." Clover smacked her hand to the table, startling the short queue waiting to place their orders. "Sorry," she said to the bakery as a whole.

"Please, can we not make it weird? I don't want things to be awkward."

Maddie laughed. "For Logan, or for you?"

"Yes." The absurdity of the situation made Kathleen laugh, too, even as a panicky sensation vibrated in her ribcage.

"Oh, this is so great," Clover said.

Maddie shook her head. "I'd actually stopped teasing Logan about having the hots for you because I didn't think it was going to happen, and it was starting to feel mean-spirited."

Kathleen winced. "I definitely don't need to know you've been discussing it."

Clover waved a hand. "Just hypotheticals. And mostly teasing Logan about having a crush on you more than specifics of you two having sex."

That was better. In her logical brain—even the prudish part of it—she knew that was better. Still. Her friends, her lovely new friends, were discussing her sex life. Now, with her, but also when she wasn't even around. It was, well, a lot.

"You're not mad, are you?" Clover asked suddenly, as though seeing the realization play across Kathleen's face in all its unflattering glory.

"No." Mad definitely wasn't the right word. And even though mortified came to mind, that was only a small piece of it. Because despite her rather repressed upbringing, she wasn't a prude. Flabbergasted. She was flabbergasted.

"Are you sure?" Maddie looked incredulous.

"I'm adjusting to the fact that I have an interesting enough love life, or sex life, or whatever, that it's worthy of conversation." She nodded slowly. "Big adjustment."

Maddie gave a sympathetic chuckle and Clover howled with laughter. "Congratulations," Clover said eventually, wiping tears from her eyes.

"Thanks?" It felt weird to say, but what other response was there?

"Wait, though." Clover lifted a hand. "You still haven't said if it was a one-time thing or if you're going to hook up again."

Hook up. When had she last used that phrase in reference to herself? Never ago, that's when.

"Or is it more than hooking up?" Clover asked.

"I'm not sure." That time, she was being honest.

"For what it's worth, Logan likes you likes you," Maddie said.

Even before the library ladder and the big reveal, she'd gotten the feeling that Logan wanted more than a roll in the hay. What she couldn't decide was what to do with that. They certainly weren't suited for anything long-term. And while she might be perfectly happy to pass the time and enjoy Logan's company for however long the feelings remained mutual, she imagined Logan wanted a wife and a family and all that, and it felt wrong to keep Logan off the market for any length of time.

"You like her, too, don't you?" Clover asked.

Kathleen cringed. "How obvious is it?"

Clover regarded her with sympathy. "You say that like it's a bad thing."

She made a series of faces—a hem and haw without words.

"What?" Maddie asked, suddenly suspicious. "Is it a bad thing?"

"We're just so, you know."

"We don't know," Clover said gently.

"Different." Which literally said everything and nothing at the same time.

Neither Clover nor Maddie looked remotely satisfied. Maddie's eyes narrowed. "She went to college, you know. She has a degree in design."

Kathleen's mouth fell open. "Oh. No. That's not what I meant at all."

"Oh." Clover's hands flew up in true aha fashion. "It's because Logan is a hopeless romantic and you're not."

That certainly didn't work in their favor. But in her heart of hearts, that wasn't the worry taking up space. "Logan is so young."

"Oh." Maddie and Clover spoke in unison, dragging the word out and making Kathleen feel both foolish and vindicated.

"But you're hot," Clover said like it was the most obvious thing in the world.

She didn't believe middle-aged women were inherently not hot. Quite the opposite, in fact. And it wasn't even that she didn't think she had a certain appeal. In certain circumstances. To certain people. But everything about hooking up with someone like Logan flew in the face of those assumptions. And now, in the light of day, the implausibility felt glaringly obvious. Like, had she really? And, had Logan actually?

Clover waved a hand in front of her face. "Earth to Hottie. Come in, Hottie."

Kathleen snorted—the literal opposite of hot. "I don't know."

"Don't know that you're hot, or don't know that Logan thinks you're hot?" Maddie asked, tapping her finger to her chin like some cartoon detective.

"Both. Neither." Ugh.

"Aw, honey." Clover got up from the table, came around to Kathleen's side, and wrapped her arms around Kathleen's shoulders. "We got you."

Since she couldn't return the hug, she gave Clover's arms a squeeze. "I'm fine. Better than fine."

Clover slipped back into her seat. "We know. You got laid."

She scrubbed her hands over her face. "It's not like it was unexpected, you know? I mean, I sort of decided before we even went antiquing. I was just waiting to make sure Logan was still interested."

"Ha." Maddie practically yelled the fake laugh, then laughed for real. "Sorry. I'm not sure interested does it justice."

It felt good to hear, even after last night. "So, yeah. It was great. I'm just not sure there's much there. Does that make sense?"

Maddie made a face, and Clover shook her head.

"I'm not sure there's more to it than chemistry," she said eventually.

"But you went antiquing," Clover said, as though that explained everything.

"Do you not want a relationship?" Maddie asked. "Or do you not want one with Logan?"

"Even contemplating that question feels a bit premature, no?"

Maddie looked incredulous. Clover, God bless her, offered a sympathetic smile. "If you mean long-term, monogamous relationship, then sure. But otherwise, you're kind of already in one."

She must have looked like a deer in the headlights, because Maddie leaned into Kathleen's line of sight. "My pan and poly friend uses the term very broadly."

She let out a shaky breath and reminded herself this was a perfectly rational adult conversation. "Right."

Clover shoved Maddie until she returned to her side of the table. "For now, you have to decide two things."

Two things. How hard could that be? "Okay."

"One. Do you want to sleep with her again?" Clover didn't continue, ostensibly waiting for Kathleen to answer first.

Kathleen closed her eyes, prepared to be honest but not while making eye contact. "Yes."

"Excellent. Two. Do you want to spend time together doing things other than sex?"

She opened them to find both Clover and Maddie waiting like her answer was the most interesting thing on the planet. Theoretically an easier answer and yet somehow so much more complicated. "Yeah."

"Well, there you go." Clover brushed her hands a few times, as though that solved everything.

Kathleen looked to Maddie, but Maddie merely shrugged. "It's annoying as hell, but she's usually right."

Kathleen slumped, letting the waves of obvious slosh over her like a rising tide. "What am I going to do?"

Clover's head tipped to the side. "Honey, you already answered that."

"I did?"

Clover nodded. "You're going to have sex, probably a lot of it. And you're going to hang out and do fun things that aren't sex, a lot of which would make a great HGTV show."

"Huh." Was it as simple as that?

"And most importantly"—Clover poked her finger to the table to emphasize her point—"you're going to let yourself enjoy it."

Chapter Eighteen

After a bit of back and forth about size and shape and materials, Logan sketched a grid of six rectangular-shaped beds, big enough to sustain a nice mix of flowers, herbs, and vegetables but small enough to tend without having to climb into them. She got Kathleen's approval, ordered the lumber, and arrived at Kathleen's house the following weekend—which happened to be the first of May and a gorgeously sunny Saturday morning—ready to get to work.

Kathleen stood in the driveway wearing a pair of loose overalls, lavender muck boots, and a floppy straw hat. Next to her, a shiny red wheelbarrow and a giant pile of dirt. Logan barely had the truck in park when Kathleen offered an enthusiastic wave.

"Good morning," Logan said.

"Good morning, indeed." Kathleen's smile held a mixture of enthusiasm and determination. "Look at my beautiful soil. It literally got here ten minutes ago."

Logan laughed. "That's a lot of dirt."

Kathleen's smile didn't falter. "I did the math. It's exactly the right amount."

She didn't doubt it. What she did doubt was Kathleen's ability to move it all without hurting herself. Hell, she doubted her own ability on that front. "I hope you'll let me help you move it."

Kathleen waved her off. "I'm saving you for skilled labor. And I'm expecting this to take me the better part of a week."

At least she had realistic expectations. "I won't argue now, but I reserve the right to ask again after you've shoveled fifty wheelbarrows full."

"Deal."

"In the meantime, want to help me stake out exactly where these beautiful new beds are going to go?"

Kathleen cringed. "I may have already done that."

"What do you mean?"

"I woke up super early, and I probably should have done some writing, but I was too excited to focus. I've been here like two hours already."

Logan couldn't decide whether to be amused or incredulous that Kathleen had such a go-getter streak when she put her mind to something.

"Don't be annoyed with me," Kathleen said.

"Oh, I'm not. I'm just thinking about the woman who was so adamant about not wanting to get her hands dirty."

Kathleen stuck out both hands. "Yeah, but I got the outfit."

"It's a very cute outfit at that." Though not as cute as Kathleen's delight in wearing it.

"I'm kidding but not." Kathleen gave a playful shrug. "I've also been hanging out with this woman who's convinced me getting my hands dirty can be fun."

Logan nodded slowly. "I'm not going to lie, I legit love that answer."

"I'm pretty sure I never want to hang drywall, but still."

Logan grinned. "Baby steps."

Kathleen lifted her chin toward the back of Logan's truck. "You want me to, uh, help you move that wood?"

She laughed before she could stop herself. "Ahem. Yes, that would be great."

To her credit, Kathleen held her own as they unloaded two-by-twelves and carried them to the backyard. Logan had taken advantage of Maddie's much fancier miter saw and cut the pieces to length already, which made it easy to assign Kathleen the four-foot pieces while she hauled the eights.

As promised, Kathleen had marked the grass with spray paint, making little L brackets to denote each corner. "Is this okay? I tried to maximize the sunlight they'd get around the house and trees."

The layout was tidy and symmetrical and exactly what she'd expect from a woman like Kathleen. "As long as you're not going to regret giving up so much lawn, I think it's perfect."

"Well, I'm not having kids who'll need to run around, and I'm more likely to become a crazy cat lady than get a dog, unless you figure out how to clone Kiwi. So, yeah."

The emphatic reply caught Logan off guard, though it probably shouldn't have. "Then I think we're good to go."

Kathleen scrunched up her shoulders and let them drop. "Yay."

Kathleen held the boards in place while Logan drove the long screws through each one and into the lengths of four-by-four she'd cut to anchor the corners. After finishing the first two, Logan assured Kathleen she could handle it, and Kathleen went to work shoveling and hauling dirt.

About an hour in, she remembered to put on sunscreen. At hour two, Kathleen brought out glasses of iced tea mixed with homemade lemonade. Logan downed half her glass in a couple of gulps. "Very refreshing. You could give Martha Stewart a run for her money."

A shadow seemed to pass through Kathleen's eyes, but almost as quickly she smiled. "Thank you."

A caveat—or at least a clarification—danced on the tip of Logan's tongue. She bit it back, having gotten herself into trouble enough to finally learn her lesson. "How are you feeling about the progress?"

"Really good." Kathleen nodded with enough enthusiasm that Logan wondered if perhaps she'd imagined the shadow after all.

"What are you going to plant?" Logan asked, figuring that fell into the category of universally safe conversation topics.

"Tomatoes for sure. Some flowers." Kathleen frowned. "I'm going to have to do some research. It's my first garden, and I don't actually know what I'm doing."

As much as Logan loved the idea of swooping in and saving the day, she didn't know much, either. "You know who has a green thumb?"

"Who? And please don't say your mom." Kathleen laughed. "I'm kidding but not."

"Oh, lord, no. I was going to say Leah. I have this great memory of her showing up at our house with a blue ribbon she'd won at the county fair for growing the prettiest squash. You'd have thought it was an Olympic medal."

Kathleen's whole face softened. "That's adorable."

"I'm sure she'd be happy to help," Logan said.

"Will she let me pay her, you think? I'd feel bad otherwise."

"She'll probably say no at first, but you should be able to talk her into it, given the number of diapers she's going to have to buy soon." It was the argument she'd made when finalizing Leah's internship. "If she thinks she's contributing, it'll make all the difference."

"Well, I'm starting from zero, so that won't be hard."

They got back to work—Logan assembling the remaining beds and Kathleen slowly filling them. Logan got the last screw on the last board halfway in when the battery on her impact driver bit the dust. "Damn it."

Kathleen, who'd just dumped a wheelbarrow full of compost into the bed she'd half-filled with topsoil, looked her way. "What? What's wrong?"

"My battery died."

Kathleen came over, stared at the tool, and pursed her lips. "Don't you have a backup?"

She scowled. "That one's dead, too."

Kathleen shook her head. "Isn't the number one rule of power toys to keep a spare battery ready to go?"

Her frustration faded at the Freudian slip. "Don't you mean tools?"

Kathleen gave half a shrug and a full smirk. "Same difference, no?"

Logan hooked the drill on the metal loop of her tool belt and indulged in a rather cocky hip jut. "I guess that depends."

Kathleen lifted her chin. "On the toy?"

"And who's wielding it." They hadn't discussed bringing toys into the bedroom, but no time like the present, right?

"Is that an offer?" Kathleen asked.

She had no idea what switch had been flipped, but she couldn't get enough of this brazen side of Kathleen. "If you're interested, I'm absolutely offering."

"Oh, I'm interested."

"Something in particular?"

Kathleen's gaze flicked to Logan's fly, and she licked her lips. "I defer to you on that one."

The statement could have been bland, disinterested even. But that's not how it landed. No, Kathleen managed to drop the tiniest breadcrumb at Logan's feet and send her imagination into orbit. The thought of Kathleen deferring to her like that felt like a glimpse of Kathleen putting herself in Logan's hands, of letting go. Logan had never been especially invested in power play, but damn. The prospect of even the tiniest bit of submission had her wondering if there was a soft surface in the house she could put to good use.

"Cat got your tongue?" Kathleen batted her eyelashes, all innocence.

"Um." Logan swallowed. "Something like that."

"I have a proposition for you, then. And it involves my bed."

"I'm all ears."

"I'm bordering on desperate to get out of my apartment. How gigantic a pain would it be to get my bedroom set up?"

"Like, today?" She could pull strings, but it would require a whole spool.

Kathleen laughed. "No, no. Like, in the next week or so. I don't need to fully move in, but I'd love to start spending the night here."

Logan's mind raced—the things still to do, the favors she'd have to call in. But for every hoop she'd have to jump through, a single thought pulsed through her. And that thought was giving Kathleen what she wanted. Well, that and all the other stuff Kathleen seemed to be suggesting. "I think I can make that happen."

"Really?" Kathleen's eyes lit up but the rest of her remained wary.

"The biggest hurdle will be the floors, but Maddie and I will be doing them, so I can probably cash in a favor to get the upstairs done quicker." Or ask for one on credit. But Maddie loved having an IOU in her back pocket, so Logan couldn't imagine her saying no.

"I don't want to be a pain."

"It's hard not to make a joke about the pleasure outweighing any pain you might inflict."

For all her teasing a moment before, Kathleen's shoulders dropped with pure exasperation. "I'm serious."

"I am, too. I also get what you're saying, and I promise it won't be that much of a pain." And honestly, if Kathleen was staying in Bedlington, it would probably be easier to coordinate sleepovers. She had a vested interest in that.

"Okay." Kathleen's brows knitted together, but then she nodded. "Okay. My lease is month-to-month, so I only need to give two weeks' notice. You're saying I can do that?"

Logan cringed. "I'm not sure we can accommodate all your furniture quite that quickly."

"Oh, no. That's in storage." Kathleen laughed. "Lord, I didn't mean that. That's basically asking for the whole house to be done."

She lifted a shoulder. "Wilder requests have been made."

"Good to know."

"Trust me when I say all your requests have been more than reasonable."

One of Kathleen's now relaxed brows lifted. "All of them?"

She looked Kathleen up and down, slowly enough that there could be no mistaking her intent. "All of them."

❖

Kathleen sat in one of the rocking chairs on Logan's porch, gently tipping herself forward and back. It was such a soothing sensation, she might have to concede Logan's assertion they were ageless. She closed her eyes and imagined sitting on her own porch with a cup of coffee, some pretty vining flower she hadn't picked yet fragrant and glistening with dew. She'd put up bird feeders and watch the chickadees and titmice flitting about for their morning meal. She'd feel a little silly talking to them but would do it anyway. Logan would tease her, catching her at it as she left for work, before kissing her and wishing her all the good words.

"Are you waiting for Logan?" Jack's voice yanked her back to reality.

Kathleen cleared her throat, as though Jack might be able to sense her thoughts and be judging her for them. "She's running a little behind. She texted me."

"There's a key over the doorframe. I can let you in."

His casual tone reminded her that of course he hadn't been reading her mind. "She texted me that, too. It's such a lovely afternoon, though, I decided to sit here instead."

"It's one thing you have to give us New Englanders credit for, isn't it? We know how to appreciate a nice spring day."

"For sure." She cleared her throat again, unsure if she should make small talk or let him go on his way. "Are you coming from work?"

"Yeah. A rare electric only job. Some lady decided she simply had to have this European bread oven she saw online and didn't realize until it was sitting on her counter that it required special wiring."

Kathleen chuckled. "That's a hell of an impulse buy."

"She promised to make me some baguettes when she got the hang of it, so I kept my mouth shut."

"Wise man."

Jack grinned. "Right? So, your house is coming along?"

He seemed genuinely interested rather than merely polite, so she nodded. "I may have convinced Logan to move up the floor refinishing so I could partially move in."

"I bet she loved that." Jack chuckled. "Or maybe I should say, I bet she loves earning the brownie points that comes with delivering that."

Kathleen opened her mouth, then closed it. Was he teasing her? Or Logan? Or maybe both of them?

Before she could ask, Logan's truck pulled in, and she hopped out. "Sorry to keep you waiting." She jogged over from the driveway and bounded up the porch steps. "Especially if my brother is giving you a hard time."

"Nah, I save that up for you," Jack said.

"Well, at least he has some manners." Logan winked at Kathleen, then leaned in to kiss her cheek. "I hope you haven't been waiting long. Did you not get my text about the key?"

"I did. I was just enjoying the afternoon. And debating whether having both a swing and rocking chairs on my porch would be overkill."

"No." Logan and Jack spoke in unison.

Kathleen laughed. "That was clear. Also, kind of cute."

"And that's my cue." Jack offered a salute. "You two have a nice evening."

Jack disappeared into his half of the duplex, and Kathleen frowned. "Did I offend him? Calling him cute?"

"Nah. If anything, it was us being cute. Anything cutesy and coupley skeeves him out." Logan shook her head. "Total dude."

"Huh."

"He doesn't mean any harm. He's just whatever the opposite of a hopeless romantic is. A cynic?"

Kathleen chewed her lip, wondering whether to admit what she was thinking. "I guess I find it funny is all."

"That he's in his early thirties and already a grumpy old man?" Logan asked.

"No, more that I'm like that, too."

"Like what?" Logan regarded her with confusion.

"Not a romantic." Not really the thing to say to the person she'd just started dating.

"You write romance novels for a living."

Strange how separate the two felt in her mind. "I like the idea of happily ever after. I just think it's rare for it to play out in real life."

Logan's confused look fell into a full-fledged frown. "You don't believe in happily ever after?"

"Not in a bitter, jaded way," she said.

"What other way is there?"

Kathleen canted her head back and forth, grasping for the right words. "I think people fall in love, and I think people can decide to mate for life and make a go of it. It's just the soul mate part, I guess. Most people either break up or stay together out of stubbornness and fear more than a real desire to be with their person forever and always."

"So, you're poly?" Logan asked.

She appreciated that ethical non-monogamy was getting more traction these days. It had the potential to save so much heartbreak and deceit. But the thought of juggling multiple romantic or sexual relationships at a time was enough to give her a migraine. "Oh, no. Not even a little. I'm..."

"You're what?" Logan seemed more worried than irritated, though Kathleen wasn't sure that was much better.

"I'm more of a non-celibate spinster." She'd never put it in those words before, but it fit. Fantasies of sipping coffee on the porch while Logan headed off to work notwithstanding.

Logan cringed. "That sounds bleak."

She bristled, though Logan probably hadn't meant it as an insult. "Not at all. I get to date. I get to be the cool aunt. And I get to live life on my own terms without having to answer to anyone."

"Yeah, okay." Logan continued to frown. "But don't you want someone to grow old with?"

Didn't everyone, at least in theory? She'd simply stopped spending energy chasing it. "I'm not saying it's bad to. I'm saying way too many people make that the end goal rather than being happy, and wind up unhappy in the process."

Logan scratched the back of her neck, clearly unconvinced. "I guess so."

"Anyway, it doesn't matter. We're not talking about growing old together, so we can agree to disagree." Logan didn't look convinced of that, either, but Kathleen knew better than to press it. They'd only end up arguing and alienating each other and blowing whatever they did have to hell rather than enjoying it while it lasted. In other words, time to change the subject. "Is everything okay at my house? Usually things taking longer than you think isn't a good sign."

Logan's face contorted, like shifting gears took physical as much as mental effort. She blew out a breath. "So, I have good news and I have bad news."

"Okay, what's the bad news?" Better to get it out of the way.

"The motor on our floor sander bit the dust."

"Oh, no." That counted as pretty terrible news in her book, unless the good news involved a backup tucked away somewhere.

"The good news is we got the bedrooms done before that happened."

"What does that mean?" Because there was no point getting her hopes up if the end result meant a delay in her plan to move in.

"It means we can finish the rooms themselves on schedule, but the hall, stairs, and landing will have to wait until we get downstairs."

"Oh." Her mind attempted to calculate and deduct meaning but came up short. "What does that do to my plan?"

Logan's shoulders fell. "Nothing if you're prepared to vacate the whole house for the seventy-two hours those areas will take to cure when we get to them."

Logically, it made no sense. She should just commit to her rental for another month and wait until everything was done. "That seems like an awful lot of trouble for you."

"It's no trouble at all. It's you who stands to be homeless for three days." Logan took her hand and gave it a squeeze. "Though I'll do my best to convince you to stay with me."

"How ridiculous is that?"

"I don't know, I thought it might be fun." Logan smiled, but there was something sheepish in her demeanor, like their conversation about spinsterhood had left her less confident.

"I meant the plan in the first place." It screamed high maintenance. Worse, it made her feel like her mother.

"I love that you're eager to be in your house. As your designer slash contractor and as your—" Logan stopped abruptly.

"Person you're dating?" Kathleen went for a cringey smile. She couldn't be certain Logan tripped over saying girlfriend, but the last thing she needed to do was encourage her.

"Yeah, that." Logan's hand returned to the back of her neck. This time she ran it up and over the top of her head before roughing it through her hair.

Little alarm bells sounded, but the fact that Logan had to go and be so damn sweet about it left her insides all warm and gooey. "You're sure it's not too much trouble?"

"I swear it's not."

Logan either meant it, or it was a lot of trouble and she wanted to do it anyway. Either way, who was Kathleen to argue? It wasn't like she was stringing Logan along. Or the other way around? Whatever. It meant she'd get to sleep in her brand-new bed in her very own house. "Will you let me do something nice for you as a thank you?"

"Depends." Logan's expression changed and the melty feeling threatened to spontaneously combust.

"On?"

"On whether getting to spend the night with you counts as something nice." Logan's tone might have been casual, but her eyes were anything but.

See? They could do this. Have fun and not let things get too heavy. "That's nice for both of us, so I'm not sure it counts."

Logan shook her head. "So would you making me dinner."

She had a point. "True."

"It doesn't have to be the first night if you want that to yourself. But I'd like to make love to you in your own space, sooner rather than later."

Kathleen's heart might have tripped slightly over the phrasing—not having sex or fucking or even sleeping together—but she reminded herself it was just that. Phrasing. And whatever Logan called it, it was hot. And she definitely wanted more of it. The rest would sort itself out. "Deal."

CHAPTER NINETEEN

Logan pulled up to Kathleen's just as the last of her crew pulled away. It was barely noon, but she'd only scheduled work for the morning since Kathleen's movers were coming in the afternoon. Della put down her window and she did the same.

"How's the patio?" Logan asked.

"Done." Della flashed a grin. "And she's a real beaut."

"I thought you weren't going to finish until tomorrow?"

Della gave a happy shrug. "A lot less leveling than I thought there would be. Got all the stones in place by ten. Went ahead and swept in the polymeric sand since we've got a nice dry day."

"Did you tell Kathleen?"

"Knew you'd be by, so saved the honor for you." Della winked. "You're welcome."

For a second, Logan panicked that somehow everyone on the crew had sorted out that she and Kathleen had slept together. Were sleeping together? She still wasn't sure.

But no, that wasn't what put the playful gleam in Della's eye. It was that everyone at Barrow Brothers, including all the subcontractors Barrow Brothers worked with, knew this was her first lead on a job. And rather than hazing her, they all seemed to be going out of their way to make things run smoothly. She'd gotten so wrapped up in trying to impress Kathleen, she'd lost sight of how many people had rallied to make sure she looked good. "You didn't have to do that, but thank you."

"Eh." Della waved her off. "I'll take a long lunch over listening to a client gush about how awesome I am any day."

"Give me a couple years of gushing clients, and I'll be right there with you." Though, really, she liked the time with clients. Getting to tell them about or show them a job finished ahead of schedule? That was about as good as it got.

"Have fun being the hero. I hope she finds a way to show her appreciation." Della winked again and drove off, leaving her to wonder whether maybe they knew she and Kathleen were seeing each other after all.

Fortunately, she didn't have long to ponder the possibility. A small moving truck rumbled up and into the driveway. A pair of guys who looked like they might weigh a hundred pounds soaking wet hopped out and went to the front door. Logan held back for a minute, letting Kathleen greet them and give directions, before getting out herself.

"Big day," she called. She walked across the lawn, leaving the paved walk clear for the movers who'd already started to unload. Now that they'd reached the middle of May, it was lush and green and just about ready for a trim.

"So big. I'm as excited as a little kid on Christmas."

Kathleen stepped aside as they hustled by with the first load—a gorgeous wood and wrought iron headboard that sent Logan's imagination darting to satin rope, Kathleen's wrists secured ever so perfectly above her head, and all the things she'd love to take her time doing.

"Was that a dorky thing to admit?" Kathleen asked. "I'm not taking it back, I just want to know."

"Huh? Oh, no. Not at all. Sorry. I got distracted."

"By?" Kathleen regarded her with amusement.

Even if that was a conversation they might have at some point, it sure as hell wasn't one she was prepared to have now. As if to punctuate the point, Skinny and Skinnier emerged from the house and headed back to the truck. "The fact that I get to tell you your patio is finished."

"It is?" Kathleen sounded equal parts surprised and delighted. "I went out to say good morning but got caught up in puttering around the house and didn't make it back out."

"I'm sorry I didn't tell you in time to get any outdoor furniture you might have wanted."

Kathleen shook her head. "Oh, I've never lived anywhere that justified that."

"Does that mean you get to go shopping?" Logan asked. She'd gotten the sense Kathleen wasn't a major shopper in general. But her house? Another matter entirely.

"How did you guess?" Kathleen rubbed her hands with relish. "It's going to be my treat for hitting my word target this month."

Logan was a fan of little treats and rewards for getting things done, even if it got her a heavy dose of teasing from Maddie and Jack. "Sounds like a perfect plan."

"Silly maybe, since it's my work and I have to get it done either way." Kathleen shrugged, like maybe she was embarrassed over admitting it.

"The couch at my house? Reward for learning how to frame and finish a wall to my dad's specifications."

"Seriously?" Kathleen asked.

"Because I went for a design degree, I didn't get the full apprenticeship like Maddie and Jack did. But since we don't do enough volume to warrant a full-time designer, I had to learn how to do some of the dirty work. I didn't mind, but I was terrible at it at first."

"Well, you could have fooled me."

"Thank you. It took months before I was allowed to do anything but demo and hauling materials on and off the truck. Hence, the swanky sofa." One more thing she and Kathleen had in common, one more way they were compatible. Did Kathleen see it that way?

"I'll be sure to choose something that can be delivered." Kathleen smirked, giving none of her inner thoughts away.

"You can, but you have a lesbian with a pickup at your disposal. You shouldn't hesitate to use her."

Kathleen worried her lip in that way she had—a moment of indecision or inner struggle. It shouldn't have been as sexy as it was.

"And I'll happily take all sorts of things as expressions of your gratitude."

Kathleen's eyes went wide. So much for not giving anything away. Logan smiled slow, attempting to drive home exactly the sorts of things she had in mind.

The movers came with another load—mattress this time—grunting with effort. Rather than be annoyed with the interruption, Logan let her gaze flick to it before returning to Kathleen. Kathleen blushed, and Logan loved every second of it.

The truck was empty in under an hour. Kathleen tipped each of the guys and sent them on their way, promising to see them again in a few weeks. Logan followed her upstairs to see what had been left where.

They'd assembled the bed frame and put the box spring and mattress on top, being thoughtful enough to set each post on one of those furniture glide discs. Kathleen nudged it a few feet over and back toward the wall. "That was easy."

"Can I offer you a hand with anything?" Logan asked, wanting to be helpful but mostly happy to spend her afternoon at Kathleen's beck and call.

Kathleen studied the boxes, hands on hips. "I think I can handle it. It's mostly making the bed and putting clothes away."

She wouldn't mind helping with that, either. Not in a creepy way, of course. But definitely an intimate one. "I'm pretty good at folding, for the record."

Kathleen laughed. "I'll keep that in mind. But for now, I'm thrilled to get everything sorted and put away just so."

She could appreciate that. And really, she was mostly just angling to stick around and spend time with Kathleen. "Well, let me know if you change your mind."

Kathleen tapped her index finger to her chin. "I wouldn't say no to some help hanging things on the wall. I'm terrible at the measuring and not all that great with the deciding and arranging."

Logan puffed out her chest. "I'll have you know I aced hanging things on the wall."

"Was that an actual class?"

She laughed. "No, but composition was. Furniture in the room, things on a shelf, stuff on the wall. There's as much science to it as art."

Kathleen nodded slowly. "Okay, maybe I need your help more than I thought."

"I'd love to help with as much staging and decorating as you'd like. Not everyone wants that, but it's part of the package if you do."

Kathleen's eyes narrowed. "With all your clients or just me?"

It was impossible to know which answer Kathleen wanted. "Everyone who has as much of a remodel done as you gets the option. Let's say I have a particular interest in making sure you're satisfied."

One flavor of dubious look gave way to another. "Satisfied, huh?"

She resisted a facepalm even though she no longer feared the insinuation would get her fired. Or send Kathleen running in the opposite direction. Still. "I didn't mean it like that."

"Oh, so you don't want me satisfied?"

Holy crap, Kathleen was teasing her. And not just any kind of teasing. Sexy teasing. "No, no. I'm very invested in that. In any and every way you'll let me be."

Kathleen waited a beat, and it sent anticipation zinging through Logan. "I'd love to have you over. For some arranging." Kathleen waved a hand vaguely, but it seemed to indicate the bed more than the wall. "And some banging."

"I'm at your service."

Kathleen hummed her approval.

"Tonight?" she asked hopefully, willing herself not to toss Kathleen on the unmade mattress right then and there. "Or tomorrow?"

Kathleen gave a small but eager nod. "Tonight."

❖

Kathleen smoothed and tucked the new sheets, laundered fresh in her very own washer and dryer. With the weather finally starting to warm, she went for just the quilt on top. She tugged it into place, thinking about the day she bought it—the same day she put an offer in on the house. It had spent the better part of six months in a box. Having it on the bed felt like its own celebration, a long time in the making.

Any worry over being impractical was long gone. In its place, the deep satisfaction of having a major component of her house done. But also of doing something slightly fanciful for no other reason than she wanted to. Of having that lauded rather than judged.

Maybe it was bad form to have Logan over right away, to not spend at least one night making it her own. But just like moving in early in the first place, it's what she wanted. And since sleeping with Logan in the first place was essentially an exercise in doing what she wanted, why the hell not?

Since enough of the kitchen was complete to use the oven and fridge, Kathleen picked up a chicken to roast, along with a lemon and a head of garlic to stuff inside and carrots and potatoes to cook alongside. It never failed to amaze her how little fanfare it took to make a whole house smell fantastic, and how a single pan could yield a pretty damn impressive dinner.

Logan arrived just after six, knocking on the front door like a guest. "Since when do you do that?" Kathleen asked.

"Since you've moved in. It's your home, now, not a job site." Logan smiled like it was the most obvious answer in the world.

"I mean, technically it's both, but I like the distinction."

Logan continued to smile. "I'd like to get to where we can come and go without the formality, but I'd rather earn that than presume— oh, damn, what are you cooking in here?"

She laughed at the abrupt shift. "Just chicken."

Logan sniffed. "That is definitely not just chicken."

"Okay, gussied up chicken."

Logan quirked a brow, making Kathleen wonder how much she'd dated herself with the word. But then Logan clicked her tongue. "I have this image in my head now of chickens in sequin dresses and full makeup. I hope you're happy."

She laughed again. "I think I am."

They ate at the island on the stools she'd bought the week before. Despite knowing why Logan was there—what they'd agreed to do after dinner—Logan chatted at her like it was just a casual evening. It felt so weird until she realized it was how most people who were dating did it. Hell, even people just sleeping together probably shared a meal now and then before tearing each other's clothes off.

Logan talked about the other project she had going, asked her about her writing. Kathleen cleared the disposable dishes she'd bought to tide her over until the kitchen was finished. Then they stood there, like neither of them wanted to be the one to mention sex first.

"I'm sorry I don't have a nice place to sit yet," Kathleen said.

Logan shook her head. "I don't need to sit."

It felt a little too weird to go right from eating to fucking, so she tipped her head toward the backyard. "Did you see the patio?"

Logan's eyes lit up. "I didn't."

They stepped through the French doors into the cool evening. "Didn't it come together nicely? I'm so glad you talked me into the larger stones."

"You'll be even more glad when it comes time to weed between them." Logan lifted a hand. "Though hopefully that won't be too bad either, between the underlayment and the polymeric sand."

She nodded like she'd known what those words meant before Logan told her. "I'm sure I will."

"Would you rather just hang out tonight?" Logan rocked back on her heels. "Or maybe you'd prefer your first night solo. It's a big deal, and I'd understand if you wanted it to yourself."

"Um." Kathleen frowned.

"Which isn't to say I don't want to stay." Logan quirked a brow. "Or that I don't want to do what all that innuendo from earlier implied we might. I just, you know, don't want you to feel obligated or whatever."

She winced. "How many more times are we going to have to sleep together for you to trust that I'm not going to change my mind?"

Logan's gaze narrowed, and Kathleen imagined her concocting a formula based on the number of times she'd backed off relative to the times she hadn't. But instead of a rational argument, Logan ultimately smirked. "Just one, I think. Maybe two."

The cheeky reply made Kathleen feel silly but helped her relax. "Well, we should get to it, then."

"For the record, you're allowed to want me in general but decide you're not in the mood on a given night."

She appreciated that, though it was hard to imagine not wanting to have sex with Logan now that she'd opened those floodgates. "Good to know."

"But if you are in the mood and just not sure how to move us in that direction, I'm happy to take the lead."

Kathleen swallowed. She'd spent so many weeks telling herself Logan's confidence, her ability to be unabashedly direct, came off as arrogance. But the truth of the matter was she found it sexy as hell. "You should do that."

"Take the lead?" Logan asked, as though needing Kathleen to be extra concrete about it.

"Yes."

Logan's grin spread slowly. "Great. Hey, Kathleen?"

"Yes?"

"I'd love to see your bedroom."

Her breath caught, despite knowing exactly where the conversation was going. So much promise in such an innocent little statement. She held out a hand. "Come on. I'll show you."

CHAPTER TWENTY

L ogan paused in the doorway. "Wow."
   Kathleen turned. "What?"

Logan gestured to indicate the room. "It looks so different."

"Not really. Just bedding and candles. I decided to wait for you to help me hang things."

"It's come together, though. Even without stuff on the walls." Logan gestured to the dresser, where Kathleen had arranged the antique vanity set she'd bought on a whim and a framed adage about being enough. "You're making it yours, and it looks fantastic."

High praise from an interior designer. "Thanks."

Logan's attention shifted back to her. "It's got nothing on you, though."

She chuckled. "That's quite a line, Barrow."

"But is it a line if I mean it?"

"Yes." She lifted a finger. "I'm not complaining. Simply pointing it out."

"Oh, well, then. You're looking exceptionally beautiful tonight. And I'm not just saying that because I'm about to take you to bed."

That was a line, too, but she couldn't bring herself to mind. Because Logan had a way of making her feel beautiful. Of forgetting her soft stomach and stretch marks, the parts of herself that weren't as perky as they once were. Of feeling desired exactly as she was. And unlike their first time together, she'd taken a couple of hours to pamper the skin she was in. The combination made her about as confident as she was going to get, and she had no intention of wasting it. "You should still do it, though. Take me to bed, I mean."

Logan wasted no time, threading her fingers into Kathleen's hair and pulling her in for a kiss. Kathleen's stomach flipped, leaving her to wonder vaguely when that thrill of newness would wear off. But then Logan's tongue traced her lip, coaxing her to open, and wondering gave way to the sort of wild urgency Logan stirred up in her with seemingly no effort at all.

Hands roamed, touching skin and getting rid of any and all clothing that stood in the way. Her dress, Logan's shirt. Her bra, Logan's pants. All the while, kissing. Kissing. Kissing. Seeking, teasing, demanding.

It was the demanding that did her in. Logan kissed her and left no space to wonder if she meant it, wanted it, needed it. Logan kissed her like her life depended on it. Like she was an addict and Kathleen her drug of choice. Like the more she had, the more she needed it.

She could get drunk on Logan's kisses. On Logan's desire. Get drunk and lose herself and not worry one lick about the hangover she might have in the morning.

And why shouldn't she?

She'd already thrown caution to the wind, and it left her feeling more alive than she had in as long as she could remember. Maybe it would all come crashing down in a haze of what the hell had she been thinking. But damn it all if it wouldn't be worth it.

So she threw herself into the kiss. Into Logan's arms. And into the beautiful bed in the beautiful house Logan made feel like the home she'd wanted for longer than she could remember. Okay, she didn't literally throw herself into the bed. She fell back onto it, pulling Logan with her and letting out a little growl of pleasure at how good it felt to have Logan's body covering hers.

Logan broke the kiss long enough to ask, "Did I squish you?"

She shook her head, not willing to waste time on words. She cupped Logan's face in her hands and pulled their mouths together once more. And then it was back to insistent kisses and roaming hands—kneading and grabbing and scratching in all the right ways in all the right places. Logan's hand slipped between them, between Kathleen's legs. Kathleen opened in invitation, her want bordering on desperate.

The first touch sent her careening into orgasm. She clutched at Logan's shoulders, clamped her thighs together, and rode it to a ragged and shaky end. "Fuck."

"You okay?"

She cringed. "Apparently, not being saddled with the will we or won't we question means my body was free for pregaming."

Logan laughed. "That's the best description of an instant orgasm I've ever heard."

"Sorry to be so, you know, eager." She blushed at the admission.

"Don't be sorry. Unless you're feeling one and done? That would be okay, but I'd be a little sad."

"No. No, I'm not."

"Oh, good." Logan's hand shifted slightly, away from her hypersensitive center but not entirely. "Because I'm having a great time and I'd hate for it to be over."

Kathleen nodded, slightly entranced by the slow but firm movement of Logan's fingers up and down her swollen lips.

"Does that feel good?" Logan asked with the confidence of someone who knew full well it did.

Another nod.

Logan continued what Kathleen could only describe as an erotic massage—relaxing as it aroused, soothing as it stimulated. Forget kiss drunk, this was enough to leave her delirious. When Logan slipped a finger into her, she gasped.

Logan stilled. "No?"

"Yes. Yes and more and please." She clutched Logan's shoulders again, trying to express the need that suddenly went beyond the words she could string together to convey it.

Logan added a second finger and curved them, inviting Kathleen's G-spot to the party.

"Oh. God. Yes."

Logan stroked. She kissed Kathleen's neck, her breath heavy and hot. Kathleen rode Logan's hand, forcing the knuckle of Logan's thumb to her suddenly ready for more clit. Logan took the hint, uncurling it to swipe it up and over with each thrust.

She managed a few more yeses, but even they succumbed to whimpers and moans, wordless sounds of encouragement and affirmation and surrender. She craved release and yet held it at bay, riding the edge and tempting the fates of overstimulation and not even caring.

The orgasm crested like a wave—the kind surfers spend their whole lives chasing. It carried her, exhilarating even as it threatened to pull her under. All the words she'd lost came tumbling out. Swear words and Logan's name and all manner of nonsense that hopefully Logan wasn't paying attention to.

Logan held on, held her close. Kept her hand still but her fingers buried deep until Kathleen's body relaxed and she gently nudged it away.

"I think I blacked out there for a second," she said eventually.

Logan kissed her temple. "I'm taking that as a compliment."

"You definitely should." She looked at Logan, but her vision had gone spangly and it took her a moment to focus. "Definitely."

Logan grinned, somehow channeling smug and a little sheepish at the same time. "It's easy to get carried away when I'm with you."

"Carried away? Is that what you call it?" It didn't seem to do justice to what Logan did to her, what Logan made her feel.

Logan shrugged. Kathleen kissed her, an exclamation point to Logan's question mark. Only once she started, she couldn't stop. Logan's mouth, the toned lines of her arms and torso, the salty sheen of sweat on her skin. She'd meant to make a point, but she got lost in the way Logan's body moved next to hers. She wanted—needed—to feel that movement under her.

She swung a leg over Logan's hips, rolling them both until she was on top. She pinned Logan's hands over her head. Not forceful, just insistent. She rocked herself forward and back, letting her full breasts graze Logan's smaller ones. At the brush of nipples, Logan let out a groan.

"I guess I get carried away, too." Kathleen released Logan's wrists and slinked down her body.

Logan's legs spread, and Kathleen wasted no time with teasing kisses or gentle nips. She needed Logan's taste on her tongue, the pulsing of Logan's clit in her mouth. Logan bucked, then stilled, but only for a second. Kathleen didn't slow, and Logan matched her, stroke for stroke. She hadn't meant to be frenetic about it, but she couldn't get enough. The harder Logan arched into her, the more she wanted it, sucking and lapping and wondering vaguely if it was possible to drown in another person.

Logan's fingers slid into her hair, holding her with just enough force to get her own clit twitching again. She worked her hand under her, and held two fingers to Logan's pussy. When Logan all but growled a "yes," she pushed inside, instantly in awe of the way Logan clenched and molded around her.

It wasn't the best angle, but she tried to give Logan a fraction of what Logan had given her. She'd barely gotten her fingers curved when Logan let out a sound so primal, goose bumps exploded over every inch of Kathleen's skin. The tug on her hair almost painful and yet utterly perfect.

Logan went limp, and Kathleen rested her cheek on Logan's thigh. Almost better than her own release, pushing someone to the edge of their self-control. Pushing them past it. She'd never done that before. Never realized she wanted to. And now Logan had given her a taste and she wasn't sure she could live without it.

"You're thinking, I can tell," Logan said feebly.

"Only good things, I promise." Scary as hell, perhaps, but good.

"Come up here so I can spoon you and fall asleep and try not to snore in your ear."

She scooted herself into Logan's arms and tried to ignore the tripping sensation in her chest when Logan kissed her hair.

"I hope I didn't hurt you," Logan said.

"The good kind," Kathleen confessed. "I liked it."

"Your mouth." Logan shook her head. "I don't even have words."

"You addle my brain, too." Because that was a hell of a lot safer than admitting Logan was the best sex she'd ever had.

"I like that. Let's get some sleep so we can get addled again in the morning. Or maybe the middle of the night."

She contemplated getting them each a glass of water, of taking a quick shower, of her nightly skincare regimen. But none of it proved compelling enough to leave the bed. So, she stuck out her arm and reached as far as she could, and it turned out to be just far enough to turn off the light. The room slipped into darkness, and Kathleen let the sex endorphins fade into the sated sleepiness that only seemed to come after sex. She let her mind and her body drift. The rest could wait.

❖

Logan woke to an empty spot rather than Kathleen naked and next to her. She ran her hand over the sheets and frowned when she found them cool. Before she could decide whether to wait or go looking, the door swung open and Kathleen walked in, wearing a tiny excuse for a robe and carrying two steaming cups.

"Is that coffee? Please tell me that's coffee."

Kathleen regarded her with amusement. "I wouldn't inflict tea on you at seven in the morning."

She sat up and accepted the mug Kathleen extended. "For the record, I really do enjoy a nice Earl Grey in the afternoon. Or evening."

"Noted." Kathleen sat next to her. "Good morning."

"Good morning." She took a sip and let out a hum of pleasure. "Damn, that's good."

"Life's too short for crappy coffee."

She chuckled. "Someone should put that on a mug."

"Someone did," Kathleen said. "And gave it to me as a gift."

"Shut up." How hilariously random.

"It was a travel mug, actually. The one I carried when I was schlepping around to different campuses for more semesters than I care to admit." Kathleen got a faraway look in her eyes, like the memory created a domino effect back to that time in her life.

"It's a great sentiment," Logan said, not sure whether wading deeper was a good idea or bad.

Kathleen's gaze focused, warm and easy. "My best friend gave it to me. Part of a pact we made never to settle for a shitty cup of Dunkin' no matter how hurried and harried life got."

She let out a snort. "Isn't it illegal to hate on Dunkin' if you're from Massachusetts?"

"Oh, but I'm not actually from there. It's allowed if you're a coffee snob transplant."

"Wait, wait, wait. I have so many questions." Like where Kathleen was originally from, and how she ended up in Massachusetts before here. And, maybe more importantly, had she secretly judged the cup Logan served her?

"Do you?" Kathleen brought her mug to her lips, all innocence. "And here I was thinking I could ply you with caffeine and get you to fuck me again."

Just as quickly as the questions flooded her mind, they melted away. "I wasn't aware that was on the table."

Kathleen lifted a shoulder. "You've apparently made me insatiable, and I'm hopeful you're going to do something about it."

Insatiable. Such a simple word, but it packed such a punch. Not to mention, she was fairly certain, a state that sat squarely outside of Kathleen's comfort zone. "I would love to do something about it."

Kathleen set her mug on the bedside table and slipped off her robe. "Like what?"

For as bashful as Kathleen had been, she had no hesitation now, standing in front of Logan gloriously naked. "Something. Anything. All the things. Just let me pick my tongue up off the floor and I'll think of something."

Kathleen smirked and fuck it all if it didn't make her even sexier. "I could show you what I had in mind," she said.

"By all means." Logan set her own coffee down. "Never let it be said that I'm not open to suggestion."

Kathleen's hand dipped under the sheet, down Logan's torso, between her legs. Logan didn't like to draw attention to the fact that she usually woke up horny, especially when waking up involved being in bed with a gorgeous woman. But she was hot and hard and wet, and there was no hiding it. Kathleen's eyes widened slightly, and Logan laughed. "Yeah."

"I should bring you coffee in bed more often," Kathleen said.

"Or you could just crawl back into bed naked. Or not get out of bed in the first place." She shrugged. "It all works."

Kathleen laughed then, rich and sexy and sure. "Good to know."

"But if you're going to keep doing that, I'm going to have to tie you up and keep you here all day."

Kathleen angled her head. "I could think of worse things."

Logan had no idea what switch had flipped for Kathleen but damn. She was in heaven. "Do you want to be tied up?"

Kathleen stilled and her face grew serious. "I don't know."

"No pressure," Logan said quickly. "I don't need that sort of thing. But if you want it, I'm game."

Kathleen's hand began to move again, sexy but deliberate. Was that a thing? Deliberate? Well, if it was, Kathleen was certainly the woman who could manage it. "Maybe."

"I don't want you to stop what you're doing, but I'm going to need to flip you onto your back and have my way with you. It only feels right to give you fair warning."

Kathleen quickened her strokes, pulling a groan from Logan. "Are you now?"

"I mean." She willed her brain to focus, but it, along with her vision, had gone fuzzy.

"Seems like you're not about to stop what I'm doing."

Logan thrilled at being under Kathleen's spell and, more, of Kathleen seeming to thrill at it. "It would be rude." She panted out a breath and fell back onto the mattress. "To interrupt."

She didn't last long, coming with a litany of expletives and endearments. Kathleen remained seated, looking smug until Logan delivered on her promise, grabbing Kathleen around the waist and pulling her down to the bed.

Even with Logan's warning, Kathleen's eyes went wide. Maybe it was the speed more than the flipping. Either way, Kathleen didn't argue. Logan contemplated all the ways she might elicit her own string of swear words, earn her own look of smug satisfaction. And then she contemplated what she had time for before work.

Despite her best intentions, she wound up late for work anyway. Fortunately, it was a meeting with her sister to brainstorm an awkward first floor layout for an indecisive client. The fifteen minutes gave Maddie time to clear her email and fodder for giving Logan a hard time. She might not be a math whiz, but it tallied up to a tick in the plus column for everyone as far as she could tell.

CHAPTER TWENTY-ONE

Despite the downstairs work zone, Kathleen coaxed Logan into spending the night again just a few days later. Well, coaxed might be an exaggeration. Logan seemed only too happy to do whatever Kathleen suggested. Though, to be fair, the feeling turned out to be quite mutual. And although Logan had to spend the day meeting with a client and helping Jack rewire a garage, they woke together and managed both a leisurely cup of coffee and a quickie before Logan had to leave.

Kathleen had plans of her own. With Memorial Day upon them, the danger of frost had passed, and it was time to put her new garden beds to use. And Leah, who'd consulted on the types and arrangement of plants, offered to help with the selecting and planting as well. She turned this way and that, assessing herself in the mirror "Are you sure I don't look silly?"

Logan finished buttoning her shirt and came up behind Kathleen, sliding her arms around Kathleen's waist. "You're adorable."

"I'm too old to be adorable." Though the floral-print capri pants made her smile even more than the overalls had.

"No such thing," Logan said without missing a beat.

"Do you need anything before you go? Lunch?" Asking felt strangely domestic, and she didn't entirely mind.

"Nah. I'll grab a sandwich since I'll be at the office."

Logan left, and Kathleen picked up Leah. At the nursery, Leah assured her the shrubs and perennials she got in addition to the veggies and bedding plants counted as an investment. And things like hoses and stakes and tomato cages only needed to be bought every so often. Which meant it was a justified case of going overboard—her favorite.

"You'll have to ask Logan to help you with the rose bushes, though. I'm not in any condition to wield a shovel." Leah shook her head and patted her belly. "It's all I can do to waddle around."

"Are you sure you're up for coming over? I can probably manage. I'll just watch videos online like all you young'uns."

Leah laughed. "No, I'd love to help. With my due date right around the corner, my mom is in full mother hen mode, and I don't want to pick a fight with her right before I'm going to need her for so much."

"That's a very mature observation." More than most of the college students she worked with through the years.

"Practical is more like it. She's warned me how hard it is to function on so little sleep, and I don't want to bite the hand that's offering to hold an occasional bottle and change a diaper during the night."

She'd never had the urge to have children of her own, but she could imagine doing that—lending a helping hand to make the first few months a bit easier. It saddened her that the communal way of raising kids had gotten so lost, at least in American culture. "Well, don't forget she's not your only support. I'm happy to take an afternoon here and there."

Leah nodded, her face suddenly serious. "Thank you. Like, I can't say how much that means to me."

Back at Kathleen's, they each carried a flat of veggies to the backyard. "Okay, where do we start? You just stand there and give me directions. Unless you'd rather sit. I can pull over one of my lovely new patio chairs."

Leah waved her off. "No way. I love getting my hands in the dirt."

A moment later, they knelt side-by-side, trowels in hand. Leah explained the spacing for squash—they needed a lot—and her preference for staking cherry tomatoes and using cages for bigger varieties. "How did you learn all this?" Kathleen asked.

"My mom is an avid gardener. And by avid, I mean she could have been a professional horticulturalist if she'd had the resources to go to school and get a degree." Leah sighed. "I think she's so worried I'm going to give up on school and settle for some entry-level job and never leave Bedlington."

Kathleen tamped the dirt gently around a baby Sungold tomato plant. "Are you worried about that?"

"I'd be foolish not to. I know how easy it is to fall into routine and not have the momentum to change it. Working with Logan helps. It reminds me of the job and the life I could have if I keep working toward it."

"I wish I'd had that insight at your age." And the simple belief that wanting a good job and a good life counted as sufficient ambition.

"Maybe you can remind me of it when all I want to do is take a nap."

Kathleen gave a decisive nod. "I'll do that, and I'll babysit so you can take one and then help you with your papers."

Leah bumped her shoulder to Kathleen's. "Thanks."

"I'm happy to." Which she would have said either way, but it was nice to truly mean it.

"Okay. Let's get this row finished, then we'll get them tied up and watered in," Leah said.

"Whatever you say, boss." She offered a playful salute and got to work on the rest of the plants designated for that bed.

Once they were planted, Leah stayed where she was, and Kathleen pushed in the long bamboo poles that would serve as supports. Leah gave each one a tug and declared them deep enough to get the job done. Kathleen cut short lengths of tomato tape and Leah demonstrated her loop and knot method.

"You have to tie them loosely so they have room to grow." Leah shifted her hips back and forth. "And to wiggle."

"Wiggle. Is that a technical term?"

"Yeah. Super scientific. All the serious gardeners use it. I learned it from—holy crap." Leah's eyes went wide, then squeezed shut.

"Oh, God. What's wrong? Are you okay? Is it the baby?" The rapid-fire questions tumbled out, but Kathleen caught herself and took a deep breath. "Talk to me."

When Leah's eyes opened, they held a mixture of wonder and fear. "I think I just had a contraction."

"Maybe you did. Let's get you off the ground and in a more comfortable place to sit."

Leah nodded and let Kathleen help her up. "I had some pains earlier this morning, but I thought it was indigestion. I definitely ate more jalapeños on my pizza last night than I should have."

"A woman after my own heart. Tell me about the pains. Where were they?"

Leah indicated either side of her belly. "It wasn't even pain really. More like heartburn."

"I think it can all be connected." Kathleen winked. "Or maybe you just have gas."

"That's what my mom said." Leah laughed but stopped abruptly and pressed a hand to the underside of her belly. "Whoa."

"Not gas?"

Leah shook her head. "I don't think so."

"Well, all the internet research I've been doing since we met says you don't need to go to the hospital right away, but I don't think we should take any chances."

"You've been doing research?" Leah grabbed her hand. "That's so sweet."

Sweet sounded nicer than terrified of a moment exactly like this and having no clue what to do. "I'm a big fan of knowing what to expect."

Leah's whole demeanor changed, like she was having an aha moment. "Is that why you write romance novels?"

She chuckled. "One of the reasons."

Leah shook her head. "I love that. It makes so much sense."

"I'd love to talk about it, but how about we call your mom and let her know what's going on and decide whether you're going home first or right to the hospital?"

Leah laughed. "You're such an adult."

Well, in her experience, someone had to be. "That's me."

"But a cool one. I'm glad we're friends."

A rather unlikely friendship, but one that seemed to be good for both of them. "Me, too."

❖

"What exactly happened again?" Logan sat in the hospital waiting room with Kathleen and tried to piece together the details from the series of disjointed texts she'd gotten over the last couple of hours.

Kathleen regarded her with something she'd call amused pity. "Leah was helping me with planting and went into labor. Her mother had come to Bennington for the day to shop and have lunch with a friend, so I offered to bring Leah to the hospital so she could meet us here."

"And she's here now?"

"Yes, which is why I'm out here with you and not in there with Leah." Kathleen tipped her head toward the maternity ward.

For all that Logan loved kids—assumed she'd have her own one day—she didn't have much experience with pregnant people and all the things that happened during labor and birth. "I'm glad you were with her."

"Me, too. She was prepared, but I think she would have been scared by herself."

Logan tried to imagine being in Leah's shoes and failed, on all levels. "Yeah."

"Thank you for coming, and for bringing Leah's things. I know her dad will be here later, but there are a couple of comfort items she really wanted for the duration."

That, she could appreciate. "I'm glad the neighbor had a key and could let me in."

"I can hold onto it until they come out to get it if you need to go."

"Wait, are you staying? Like, until the baby is born?" It seemed unlikely, but she got that impression.

Kathleen shrugged. "I have my laptop, and I do love a change of scenery. I thought I'd work here for the afternoon and see how things progress. She was a good six hours in by the time we got here."

"Huh."

"You certainly don't have to," Kathleen said quickly. "I just thought I would in case she or her mom needed anything."

She knew Leah and Kathleen had bonded, she just hadn't realized how much. "You're really fond of her, aren't you?"

"Do you think that's strange?"

"Not at all. Just, unexpected, maybe." Though, aside from their rocky start, Kathleen seemed to make friends with everyone she met.

Kathleen sighed. "As much as I hated the adjunct hustle, I really did like working with young slash new adults. Most of them, at least. Leah is a remarkable one who I think could use people in her corner."

Logan nodded. "Yeah."

"Like you, I mean. It's so wonderful that you've taken her under your wing. She basically said working for you is helping her keep motivated to stay in school and finish her degree after the baby is born."

"She's a great kid." One Logan would have been happy to take on even if it hadn't been a favor for a family friend.

"But that doesn't mean you need to spend your day hanging around a hospital waiting for her to give birth."

She'd held the day to start staging the job Maddie had wrapping up, but the movers got delayed a day. That left her to work on plans for a basement finishing job or show up at one of Maddie's or Jack's sites and play errand girl. "I have my laptop, too, actually. If you wouldn't mind having company."

Kathleen looked incredulous but not opposed. "Do you want to do that, or do you feel bad leaving me here?"

"I want to be where you are." Logan cringed. "In a non-creepy, non-clingy way."

Kathleen laughed.

"I mean, if we're both going to spend the afternoon on our computers, we might as well do it together, right?"

"Excellent logic," Kathleen said.

Since there weren't any tables in the waiting room, they headed to the cafeteria after Leah's mom came to grab her bag. The coffee was mediocre at best, but the slice of pound cake they shared passed muster. Hours ticked by, and it proved disarmingly easy to sit across from one another, typing and clicking away. Around eight, still no sign of the baby, but dinner options in the cafeteria seemed to be waning, so Logan offered to rustle up something of substance.

The chicken marsala was passable, and a text that Leah was going into delivery had them scurrying back up to the maternity floor. Leah's dad had arrived, along with her best friend from UVM. A thin veil of worry seemed to wrap itself around everyone there but not heavy enough to curb conversation or prevent the swapping of classic Leah stories.

The baby arrived just shy of midnight, and there were hugs and happy tears all around. It made Logan imagine doing this when Maddie and Sy got around to starting a family, which she imagined might happen sooner rather than later. Jack was another matter, of course. He talked about kids sometimes but moved slower than molasses in the relationship department and wasn't even dating anyone at the moment.

Family was such an integral part of her life, she'd spent most of hers assuming she'd have kids. But even as her thirties loomed, the prospect of having her own still seemed like a vague, distant future sort of thing. Even being part of Leah's pregnancy hadn't brought her own desires into any sort of focus. It made her wonder about Kathleen's longings and what they looked like. Made her think about the importance of wanting the same things, or at least a close enough approximation to compromise. They should probably talk about that, eventually.

The vagueness didn't stop her heart from getting all gooey when Kathleen held the baby, cooing and fawning and nuzzling little Nate's nose. She loved that Kathleen had bonded with Leah, become part of Leah's support network. And she loved that Kathleen was becoming such an integrated part of her world. Those feelings lingered, staying with her until they made it back to her place to crash for the few short hours until dawn. "You're such a natural with babies," she said, not sure how to articulate the rest.

Kathleen chuckled. "Maybe in small doses. I love loving on them, and then giving them back."

"Huh."

"I know, not the most maternal thing to say. Any inklings I had toward motherhood evaporated when I turned forty." Kathleen sighed, and Logan couldn't tell if it came from relief or regret.

"I never had the burning desire to birth them, but I always figured I'd have them someday," Logan said. A true sentiment even if it fell a bit flat in the moment.

Kathleen offered a soft smile. "You've got lots of time still."

She wanted to say she was in no rush, but also maybe that she was open. With a side of assuring Kathleen it wasn't too late for her. But none of the words she could come up with felt right. There was also the matter of attempting conversation at two in the morning. Not great for a discussion of any substance. "Well, at the moment, I'm thinking less about babies and more about the time we have to sleep before the alarm goes off at seven."

Kathleen smirked, seeming unbothered by the change of subject. "I thought your alarm went off at six."

"I'm giving myself a little grace. Besides, I worked later than usual this evening on those plans, so I'm ahead of schedule."

"Fair enough. I suppose I can say the same for my word count, though I wouldn't set an alarm either way." She tipped her head towards the stairs. "Shall we?"

"Shower first?" Logan asked hopefully.

"I could be talked into that." Kathleen pointed a finger, but her expression remained playful. "No funny business, though. You're hot, but I'm too old for all-nighters."

"Don't worry, I'm beat, too." Though she'd probably rally if Kathleen hinted at being in the mood.

They peeled off clothes and stepped under the hot spray. What was it about a steamy shower after a long day that felt so very good? She mostly behaved, though she did let her hands slide down Kathleen's soap-slicked torso once. Or maybe twice.

In bed, Kathleen drifted almost immediately, leaving Logan to rehash the day. Reflect, really. Rehash made it seem bad, and the truth was it amounted to a rather fantastic day. Not what she'd expected or planned, but getting to spend it with Kathleen had been a treat. Being there for Leah was great, too, and she'd never held a baby only a few hours old.

And if it left her thinking about her own future—and how Kathleen might fit into it—well, there were certainly worse ways to spend her time.

CHAPTER TWENTY-TWO

The following week passed in a blur of punch list items and final installations at Kathleen's, culminating in the return of the moving truck and the rest of Kathleen's belongings making their way into the house. Logan shooed Kathleen out, making her promise not to be home until at least four. Kathleen huffed, pointing out that she and Logan had done the upstairs together to great success. Logan huffed back, asking Kathleen to do it for her and promising to redo anything Kathleen didn't love. Please and thank you. With a side of get some words and go see the baby.

She didn't do the sort of staging the TV shows did—flawless decor with minimal function, using furniture and props the homeowner didn't even own. It made for a great reveal but rarely tracked to how the owner would ultimately live in the space, which in her mind made it an exercise in futility. Or ego. She had no interest in either.

Her style had mostly to do with arranging what the client already owned or had purchased for the house. She threw in a few of her own finds, little things that underscored the vibe of the design and quirky antiques she'd picked up that reminded her of the client. Soft textiles that made an average sofa cozy and inviting. The perfect lamp. None of that books backward on the shelf nonsense or massive arrangements of flowers that wouldn't last a week.

In the case of Kathleen, she hardly needed to add a thing. Or remove, for that matter. Her upgrade from apartment living had allowed her to pick and choose pieces that spoke to her, and it was all good stuff. Even the chunky metal asterisk—that she would normally dismiss as kitschy—fit Kathleen's writer persona and made Logan smile.

She worked her way through the living room first, creating a gallery wall of the vintage lesbian photographs Kathleen had collected and put into mismatched frames and filling the shelves with plants and pottery and what Kathleen called her suitable for company books. She lingered over the family photos and realized how little Kathleen talked about her parents, her brother. It made her want to know more, like if Kathleen longed for closeness that wasn't there or chose her independence. There were a few of Kathleen with what appeared to be friends, and Logan wanted to know all about them, too.

Had they simply not gotten around to sharing, or had Kathleen held it close on purpose? Did Logan's super obvious and super present family dynamics make Kathleen uncomfortable? Not if Kathleen's friendship with Maddie was anything to go on. Still. They'd been together for over a month—and getting to know each other for two before that—and Logan knew less about the other people in Kathleen's life than she did the characters in one of Kathleen's books. Had Logan dropped the ball of being a caring and curious partner? Or, for all the intimacy they'd built, was Kathleen still holding her at arm's length?

Logan tucked the questions away with a mental note to ask more, listen more, pay closer attention. She made the mistake of taking things at face value—a trait that seemed like a positive but had bitten her in the ass more than once. She didn't want to make that mistake with Kathleen.

Pleased with the living room, she moved on to the kitchen. Kathleen had already put her pots, pans, dishes, and glassware away. Her new buttery yellow Kitchen Aid mixer sat cheerfully on the counter, tucked into the corner nearest the fridge. Logan pulled out the fruit bowl she'd picked up at a local pottery studio. She set it on the counter and filled it with lemons, knowing Kathleen would put them to use beyond providing a cheerful pop of color. A new dish towel on the handle of the oven, a narrow planter on the windowsill over the sink, filled with baby succulents.

When Logan stepped back to assess, she couldn't help but admire. Her touches, yes, but also each and every decision Kathleen made along the way. They weren't always the ones Logan would have made herself, but they worked. The end result was inviting and warm, like the house and been brought up to date but also brought back to life. It was, she realized with a start, the first project she'd ever done that, in the end, felt like home. Not just a home, but a home she'd happily call hers.

❖

Kathleen pulled into the driveway but didn't get out of the car. The front porch, with its freshly painted columns and newly installed swing, welcomed her. The lilac bushes hadn't done much this year, but the weigela hinted at the riot of pink and white they'd put out once they got established. The thick layer of mulch Leah insisted she needed made for a lovely contrast against the plants and the grass and the white of the house.

It looked exactly like it had when she'd left this morning, and she'd spent no small amount of time staring at it as each piece came together, but it felt different now. Silly, really. Knowing the inside was complete shouldn't change the outside. But that argument did little to still the kaleidoscope of butterflies fluttering around in her chest. It was done. Hers. Home.

Logan chose that moment to step onto the porch, and the butterflies had a field day. She looked so good standing there— confident, happy. And like she had eyes for no one and nothing but Kathleen.

More overwhelmed by the prospect of that than her finished house, Kathleen hurried out of the car and up the walk. "Are you finished? May I come in now?"

Logan's smile was sly. "I am. Thank you for indulging me."

Even if she had to rearrange half of what Logan had done, it was an extraordinarily sweet gesture. And who knew? She might be pleasantly surprised, given Logan's ideas for upstairs and the library. "Thank you for spending a whole day to give me a special moment."

"Well, not a whole day." Logan's smile turned into a grin.

"Better part of the day. Time you could have spent on your other projects instead of an already satisfied customer." A fact not lost on her.

"I do this for most of our big projects if given the chance." Logan lifted a shoulder. "But I'd be lying if I said I didn't spend extra since it was for you."

"Do I get to go in, or are you going to keep me out here in suspense?"

Logan stepped aside and gave a big, sweeping bow. "It's all yours."

Since Logan had pulled the door closed behind her, Kathleen opened it—something she'd done probably a hundred times or more since that ill-fated first attempt that had her falling through the floor of the porch. Like all those times before, she stepped inside. Unlike all those times, this time took her breath away.

She'd be hard-pressed to explain it. She'd picked the paint and seen it go up on the walls. The furniture in the living room was hers—a mix of new and old, and even though Logan had weighed in on the sofa, all things she'd chosen. She recognized most of the pictures on the walls and items scattered around the space. Hell, she'd pulled them out of boxes herself, telling Logan what she thought she wanted where.

And yet the whole was so much more than the sum of its parts. Colors and textures, patterns and light. Every element played off or accentuated something else. And the pieces she didn't recognize—a pair of lamps with soft linen shades, a throw blanket the color of the ocean—felt like things she would have bought. Felt like her.

"Logan." She wanted more words, wanted eloquent compliments or gleeful exclamation. And yet that's all she could manage. Logan.

Logan appeared from behind her and took her hand. "You like it?"

"It would be impossible not to." She turned with a smile, but the eager and hopeful look on Logan's face had tears welling. She tried to blink them away, feeling foolish. "I love it."

"It feels like you," Logan said with an earnest nod.

It did. "Thank you."

"You haven't even seen the kitchen yet." Logan's hand cupped her cheek, wiping away a tear that had spilled over.

"Well, let's go, then." Since Logan still held her hand, Kathleen pulled her along. Excitement and anticipation felt a hell of a lot better than whatever that sentimental swell had been anyway.

The kitchen utterly delighted and, thankfully, didn't reduce her to a crying mess. The cabinets she wouldn't have picked in a million years were perfect, offset by the quartz counters and antique brass pulls. Her sink—the one with twin drain boards that had been her sole must have—looked both brand new and like it had been there for a hundred years.

Like the living room, Logan's touch was everywhere. The spice rack on the wall that Logan had promised but not let her see, lined with matching glass bottles and filled with a rainbow of flavors. The succulents on the sill over the sink she'd have considered fussy but looked fantastic. The vase of tulips, happy and bright.

"It's beyond perfect," Kathleen said.

"Thank you for letting me do it for you."

Kathleen turned. Affection and appreciation swirled and swelled and mostly, if not entirely, nudged out the anxiety that came with being the center of attention. Of having someone do something so special for her with no expectation of getting something in return. "Thank you for convincing me it would be worth it."

"I'm sure you'll move a few things around. It's more about having that singular moment of seeing it all come together. There's nothing like it, I think."

"You don't think. You know. And I'm sorry I was stubborn."

Logan angled her head. "I don't mind that you're stubborn."

She laughed. "Did it make it more satisfying when we started sleeping together?"

Logan frowned. "Not like that."

"No?" Kathleen asked. Logan had never treated her like a conquest, but it was fun to tease.

"It's like, you know your mind and you hold your ground. So when you say or do or decide something, I know you mean it."

"You sound like you've been talking to my mother. Only I'm pretty sure she wouldn't mean it nicely."

Logan lifted her chin. "She's wrong then. It's one of the best things about you."

When it came down to it, it was as simple as that. Logan liked her, wanted her, exactly as she was. They might not turn out to be suited for the long haul, but in this moment, it was a hell of a lot more than she'd signed up for when she'd moved to this tiny town. When she'd thrown herself into putting passion on the page instead of her own life. And for now, it was enough. "Will you stay?" she asked.

"Tonight, you mean?" Logan looked surprised but pleased at the prospect.

Kathleen nodded. She'd mentioned wanting a night after everything was done by herself. Sort of a sentimental slash stake her independence mashup. Only, now that the moment was here, she couldn't imagine not sharing it with Logan. "It feels like a celebration. And I want you to be part of it."

"I'd be honored."

She bit her lip. No point being overly sentimental. "Might you be horny, too?"

"For you? Always."

It might be a line, but Kathleen believed it. Logan seemed even more insatiable for her now than their first time together. Which maybe wasn't saying much, since first times were always laced with at least traces of apprehension and wanting to do and be what the other person wanted without yet knowing what that entailed. Still. "Sweet talker."

"Is it working?" Logan regarded her with the confidence of a person who already knew the answer.

"I think you should go home and pack a bag while I make us a light dinner."

"In your finished kitchen?" Logan asked with an unabashed grin.

It proved impossible not to mirror the smile and the sentiment. "In my finished kitchen."

CHAPTER TWENTY-THREE

Logan spent exactly twelve minutes at her house. Just enough time to take a shower, throw some clean work clothes into a bag, and ask Jack if Kiwi could bunk with him for the night. Again.

"Depends," he said. "You getting lucky?"

"You going to say no if my answer is yes?"

Jack shook his head. "No, dude. I'm going to say no if your answer is no."

He wouldn't say no either way, but still. "I appreciate your investment in my sex life."

He shrugged. "I'm glad at least one of us is getting laid."

"You could be, you know. If you didn't shun the prospect of dating, leaving the house, or making conversation with women you don't know."

"That sounds like a deal with the devil, kid. No thanks."

She laughed. "You're hopeless."

"Yep." He offered a playful salute. "You have fun now."

"One of these days, a woman is going to land in your lap and give you a run for your money. And I can't wait to watch it happen."

He grumbled. She returned the salute and let herself out. She was halfway to her truck when she doubled back, took the stairs two at a time, and yanked off the jeans she'd just put on. She opened the bottom drawer of her bedside table and pulled out the silicone cock she kept tucked inside.

Risk? Maybe. Worth it? She'd find out.

She got to Kathleen's a few short minutes later, only to find Kathleen exactly where she'd left her. "Sorry," Katheen said. "I can't seem to stop staring at it."

"There's no need to apologize. I'm so happy that you love it."

Kathleen turned, smile wide. "That feels like such an understatement. Please tell me you weren't gone long, though, or I'll feel silly."

"Mere minutes, I swear." Logan lifted her duffel. "And I packed a bag, just like you told me."

Kathleen smiled. "Is it weird to find that sexy? Like, not because of what it implies so much as because it's practical?"

"It's cute. There's nothing wrong with finding practical sexy."

"Thank you, even if you're lying," Kathleen said.

"Actually, it's not the only thing I packed." She tipped her head and quirked a brow.

It took Kathleen a second but only a second. Her gaze flicked down and, well, no way of missing the prominent bulge straining the denim around her fly. "Oh. My."

She cringed slightly. "A good 'oh, my,' I hope."

Kathleen nodded slowly.

"Good. I mean, it seemed maybe a little presumptuous. But I've been reading your book and, well, between that and the conversation we had in your backyard, I was feeling inspired." Logan lifted both hands. "Not that you have to like or want everything you write."

Kathleen crossed the room and, without hesitation, cupped the bulge in her hand. "I like it. And I like it on you."

Relief spread from her center, and arousal zipped along her spine. "I'm glad to hear it."

"In fact, I'd like very much if you were to do whatever you wanted with it." Kathleen swallowed. "With me."

Logan wasn't entirely sure what she expected to happen, showing up at Kathleen's with a strap-on tucked into her pants. Something good, obviously, or she wouldn't have done it. But Kathleen's eagerness—laced with that tiniest hint of submissiveness—just about sent her over the edge. "Whatever I want, huh?"

Kathleen tipped her head. "I mean, pretty much."

A series of fantasies flashed through her brain rapid-fire. Some sweet and sensual, some creeping into categories of kink she'd only thought about. She tamped them down, not sure whether she was more worried about overwhelming Kathleen, or herself. "I do like the sound of that. But I also want to know what you want, what you like."

Kathleen nodded slowly but didn't say anything.

"Is that not the right thing to say?"

Kathleen lifted her shoulders, let them fall. "I want to be wanted."

Something in the simple declaration socked Logan in the chest with more force than any sexually explicit declaration. She threaded her fingers into Kathleen's hair, cupped the side of her face. "Do you doubt how much I want you?"

"No."

"That wasn't convincing."

Kathleen smiled—a little sheepish and a little resigned. "Yeah."

"You'll have to let me show you."

"That's kind of what I was going for."

The weight of that sank in. Such a gift, but a responsibility, too. "Do you want to eat first?"

Kathleen chuckled as she shook her head. "I figured we'd get to that after."

She loved that was becoming their routine. Not always practical, but always her preference. "So, I can take you upstairs?"

That submissive look returned to Kathleen's face, her smile a perfect blend of invitation and promise. "Yes, please."

She took Kathleen's hand, led her upstairs and into the bedroom. The small lamp on the far nightstand emitted a warm glow against the encroaching dusk. The bed had been meticulously made and the linens turned down. "This is nice."

"Thank you for indulging me, with this early and with everything else."

Logan smiled. "You're easy to indulge."

"And you're okay indulging me now? In bed, I mean?"

Meaning didn't register. "Indulge you?"

"Doing whatever you want. Calling the shots."

Oh. That. Logan's libido roared. "As long as you're okay with me checking in, and you promise to tell me if there's something you don't like."

Kathleen's smile was coy. "I think I can handle that."

"Take off your dress." She smirked. "Unless you need help with a zipper."

Kathleen crossed her arms, catching the fabric in her hands and pulling it over her head. "No zipper."

Logan's breath hitched. She hadn't been the only one to hide a surprise under her clothes. Kathleen wore a sheer lace bra in soft blue. The same lace covered a small swath of skin at each hip but left plenty to the imagination. "You are stunning."

Kathleen shook her head. "You don't have to say that."

"But I want to. I want you to believe it."

"I'll try."

"Maybe you'll let me show you. The question is, shall I do it with care or with intensity?" Not that those things were mutually exclusive, but hopefully Kathleen would understand the distinction she meant.

Kathleen bit her lip, understanding evident. "Intensity."

Logan shut off the part of her brain that tended toward reverence. Perhaps she'd be able to talk Kathleen into letting her show that side of her desire another time. For now, she focused on the throbbing in her clit, the one that had been going since she tightened the straps on her harness. "Unbuckle my belt."

Kathleen did as she was told, bottom lip still caught between her teeth.

"Unbutton my jeans."

Kathleen obliged.

"And the fly. Then take out my cock."

Kathleen did and, when it was free, took the silicone in her hand. She grasped it and rocked her hand slowly, pressing the base against Logan's clit. Logan groaned. Kathleen licked her lips before flicking her gaze up to Logan's.

"Do you like that?" Logan asked.

Kathleen nodded. "I want you to fuck me with it."

The command turned her on more than any show of compliance. "I'm going to. Take off the rest of your clothes, please." She ran a finger along the edge of the lace. "Though you look exceptionally pretty in them."

Kathleen blushed, and it took effort not to toss her on the bed and take her fast and hard.

"There's no need to be shy. You're gorgeous, especially when you're naked."

Kathleen did as Logan instructed, unclasping her bra and sliding it from her shoulders. Her mind whipped to that sex scene she'd written, way more D/s than her usual style. She'd ultimately toned it down for her characters, but traces of it remained in her imagination. For another story, she'd told herself. But maybe that other story was her own. As unlikely as it seemed to have Logan, more than a decade her junior, bossing her around, she liked it. More than liked it. Thrilled at it. "I like you telling me what to do."

"Do you, now?" Logan's gentle tone belied the fire in her eyes.

She nodded, craving the intensity of being tossed around, taken. Driven by sensation until her brain went offline completely. Freed from every thought or wonder or worry that flitted through her mind nonstop. Fucked, quite literally, stupid.

"Take off your panties."

Kathleen slid them down her legs.

"Pull back the covers."

She folded the sheet and quilt with meticulous precision, smiling at the prospect of turning the whole thing into a tangled mess. Before she could turn back, Logan's hand was at her back, pressing gently between her shoulder blades. She instinctively bent at the waist, bracing both hands on the mattress.

"Is that comfortable enough for you to stay for a little while?"

"Yes." Her voice came out breathy, barely above a whisper.

"It's such a lovely view. I'd like to enjoy it for a minute."

She arched her back, letting the stretch slide up her spine and down her legs. Forget yoga, goat or otherwise. It didn't hold a candle to this.

Logan's hands—warm, strong, sure—caressed her skin and rubbed muscles that weren't sore but seemed to melt under her touch. Kathleen rocked slowly, hypnotized and hyper aware at the same time. When Logan shifted her attention to Kathleen's ass, Kathleen braced herself to be taken hard and fast.

Only Logan didn't take her. She continued the massage, kneading at the swell of Kathleen's hips and stroking the backs of her thighs. The cock remained elusive, though, and Logan's hands only brushed between her legs briefly. An afterthought, or a tease.

A small whimper escaped, and it took Kathleen a second to realize it had come from her.

"Are you in a hurry?" Logan asked, clearly in no hurry whatsoever.

"I just—" She sucked in a ragged breath. "I need you."

"And you'll have me. Any and every way you want me." Logan's hands continued to roam, sensual and lazy.

"But I need you now." She'd never—ever—been one to whine, but holy fuck she needed to be fucked.

"What do you need me to do?" Logan asked with an innocence that belied the fact that she had Kathleen bent over the bed like something out of a well-written erotica scene.

"I need you to touch me. To be inside me." The whine was gone, but desperation had taken hold.

"Like this?" Logan's fingers slipped into her folds, circling her clit.

"Fuck." She hissed the word more than she said it. "Yes. No."

"No?" Logan's fingers stilled but didn't disappear.

"I need that. And so much more than that."

Logan chuckled softly, cocky as all get-out. "More? More what?"

It was a game now—her wanting Logan to give it to her without asking and Logan insisting that she did. She let out a ragged breath that hinted at a groan. "Your cock. I want your cock inside me now."

"Now...what?"

Her mind raced, tripping over its own sex-crazed self. And then it hit her, as intensely as if Logan had slapped her ass. "Please."

Logan's hand shifted away. She heard the squirt of a lube bottle and almost told Logan it wouldn't be necessary. But then Logan's fingers were at her opening, the lube mixing with her own wetness and just about sending her out of her skin. A second later, that glorious press of silicone—insistent and firm and promising to fill the throbbing ache that threatened to consume her.

"Please," she said again, as much for herself as for Logan this time.

"You ask so nicely."

Logan eased the cock into her, and Kathleen thrust her hips back, the urgency more than she could bear. Logan groaned. She groaned. And they stayed like that for a second, just soaking it all in.

And then Logan's hands came to Kathleen's hips, and she started to move. Slowly at first. Long, languid strokes that had Kathleen's eyes rolling back and her knees threatening to buckle. Not hard enough or fast enough to make her come, but each thrust demanded her full attention. Each sensation a pinpoint of pleasure.

It was too much, tethering her to exactly who she was and where she was and who she was with. Not things she wanted to forget, exactly, but it forced an awareness that made her feel seen and known and far too exposed. "Harder," she said, desperate for the oblivion that a good fuck promised. "Please," she added, knowing it would make Logan more likely to do it.

And Logan did. Her fingers dug more firmly into Kathleen's hips, pushing their bodies apart and pulling them together with the intensity Kathleen craved. She expressed approval—sounds more than words—thrusting back to meet Logan with as much force as her wobbly legs could manage. The exquisite, individual sensations vanished, swept away by the quiver in her belly and the sprint to release.

She chased it, and Logan was right there with her. Making her wild, making her want. Making her remember and forget and lose everything but this moment and their bodies crashing together like waves pounding the shore.

Kathleen came in a torrent, all heat and surrender and reckless abandon. Logan followed, tensing and tightening and saying Kathleen's name like a swear word and a prayer rolled into one.

She collapsed, no longer up for the herculean task of standing. Logan remained upright long enough to ease the cock away gently, then dropped onto the bed next to her. "Fuck," Logan said.

"Fuck." Agreement trumped redundancy, right?

"Are you okay?" Logan asked.

"Can I be in a coma and okay at the same time?" she wondered aloud.

"It's the best subset of okay, at least after sex." Logan crawled into a more fully horizontal position. "Come here."

She gathered enough energy to do the same and let Logan's arms slide around her. "I'm not sure I'll be able to move tomorrow."

"Are you sorry?"

She smiled. "Nope."

"Oh, good."

They stayed like that for a little while. Her mind, usually so quick to dive into analysis or what next, hummed with a low, satisfied static. She listened to Logan's heartbeat, let her breathing slow to match Logan's. Eventually, even the sex haze couldn't keep her busy brain still.

"What?" Logan asked. "I can tell you're thinking something. And I'm guessing it's not about what we're going to eat for dinner."

"Do you do that often?" she asked, not sure she wanted the answer.

"That?" Logan asked brow raised.

"Be so directive." She flipped her hand back and forth. "Dominant."

"Oh." Logan laughed. "I've never done anything even remotely like that. Ever."

Her imagination came to a screeching halt. "Wait. Seriously?"

"Seriously. I just, I don't know. You looked at me with those big brown eyes and I wanted more than anything to be exactly what you wanted. What you needed. I was winging it and, if I hadn't been so fucking turned on, I probably would have frozen."

Kathleen clamped a hand over her mouth, though there was no need. Logan had left her speechless.

"Was it okay? Enough? Too much?" Logan asked. Gone was the confidence that bordered on arrogance. In its place, a sort of eager earnestness that threatened to turn more than Kathleen's knees to mush.

She dropped her hand, covering Logan's with it. "It was perfect."

Logan frowned, concentration more than consternation. "I don't want to be weird, but like, I can take feedback. Unless that breaks the illusion." She winced. "Not illusion. Vibe? Dynamic? But not like dynamic dynamic. I know that's a whole other thing."

Kathleen laughed, gobsmacked in the best possible way. "I haven't really done that either. It was, I don't know, a moment, I guess. Being able to let go and trust that you knew what you were doing and would take over and take care of everything."

"I do like taking care of things." Logan's smile was sly, bordering on smirk.

"I do, too, but fuck if it isn't a lot of work sometimes. It's exhausting."

"Is it?" Logan considered, like the possibility hadn't occurred to her before.

"You're young still. Just you wait."

She expected Logan to argue, but she merely nodded. "I feel like most of my life has been scrambling for more responsibility, more autonomy."

"In bed?" Kathleen asked, unable to resist.

"Ha ha. I'd never thought of it that way before, but maybe." Logan rolled her eyes. "Like everything else."

Kathleen tucked the sheet a little more tightly across her breasts. "Well, my best friend has been telling me for years to loosen up. So, I guess, we both needed that."

Logan tugged at the sheet, then pressed a kiss to the freshly exposed skin. "It was really hot."

She nodded, reminding herself she didn't have to analyze it to death. At least not right now. "It really was."

CHAPTER TWENTY-FOUR

Kathleen finished slicing tomatoes, adding a pinch of flaky salt to one of the ends and popping it in her mouth. She closed her eyes and let out a hum of pleasure. Fuck, that was good.

"I thought I was the only one who could get you to make those sounds." Logan's arms slipped around her from behind. "Should I be jealous?"

"I'm poly-pleasure-ous."

She turned in Logan's arms. Logan looked incredulous. "Did Clover teach you that word?"

"No, I just made it up."

Logan laughed. "Of course you did."

"Seriously, though. Taste this." They weren't her tomatoes yet, and wouldn't be for a couple of months still, but she'd found some locally grown hothouse varieties at the farmer's market in Bennington, and they smelled and tasted like summer.

Logan took the bite she held out. "Okay, that is good. Not as good as sex, but good."

"It's not a competition," she said.

"Oh. Well. In that case, yum and when do we eat?"

"As soon as I cut up this mozzarella I got from Sy and you pour us each a glass of wine." That had been the inspiration as much as the tomatoes—the first goat milk mozzarella from Grumpy Old Goat.

Logan kissed her cheek, then her jaw, then her neck, getting that spot right below Kathleen's ear that sent a shiver skittering down her spine. "Sorry. I got distracted. On it."

Logan dashed over to the fridge, pulling out the rosé and going to work on the cork. Kathleen stood there for a full minute, half watching and half letting that zing of arousal work its way through her. She'd stopped being surprised Logan had that effect on her, but it still caught her sometimes how easy it all was. Yes, it would hurt like hell when it eventually ended—because surely it must—but it was so much better than she'd allowed herself to imagine. A gift. She'd enjoy it until it was time to move on, and then she'd pick herself up and go back to the worlds she created, where HEAs happened whether or not they defied the general rules of reality.

She finished arranging the plate of cheese and tomatoes, drizzling them with olive oil and balsamic, and finishing with flaky salt, pepper, and basil. She snagged the loaf of ciabatta she'd warmed in the oven and carried it out to the patio, along with the new linen napkins she'd also scored at the farmer's market.

"Feels like summer," Logan said, turning her face into the sun.

"It really does." She did a little basking of her own before tearing into the bread and putting a hunk on each of their plates.

"Have you started writing outside?"

"I tried, but between the birds, the flowers, and my resident chipmunk, I'm finding it hard to concentrate."

Logan laughed. "I think I'd get caught up in that, too. Unless I'm on such a roll that I'm scrambling to get my ideas on paper before they flit away. Then I can focus no matter what."

"I wish I had that setting. I'm the plodder. Slow and steady, needing to wander around after every few hundred words."

"I don't know. That sounds kind of nice."

It got the job done, so she didn't complain. "It is, but I long for those bursts of creativity, you know? Staying up half the night possessed with something that has to get out and won't let you rest until it does."

Logan licked a smear of vinegar from her thumb. "It's overrated."

"Because you pay for it the next day?" She didn't like to admit it, but she could be a total bear when she didn't get enough sleep.

"That and the stuff that seems so amazing at three in the morning often doesn't stand up to the light of day."

Kathleen snickered. "You know, I feel like I've said that exact thing to students. I just figured it wouldn't apply to me."

Logan shrugged. "I say, if your method works, it works. Why mess with it?"

"Yeah." Though, her relationship with Logan was basically the exact opposite of that. "Speaking of work, I'm going to be away for a few days next week."

"You are?" Logan looked alarmed at the prospect.

"Are you going to miss me?"

"I mean, yeah. But not in a weird, creepy way." Logan gave a toothy grin that could just have easily been a grimace.

"Nothing about you is creepy."

"That's not what you said when I asked you out the first time."

She frowned. "That wasn't creepy. It was forward. It triggered all my spinster instincts, and I went into possum mode."

"Possum mode?"

"You know, there's fight or flight or freeze. I'm freeze. Like a possum. Play dead and hope the scary thing goes away."

Logan laughed like it was the funniest thing she'd ever heard. "I'm stealing that for future use."

"Be my guest."

"Sorry. Didn't mean to get sidetracked. Where are you going? Family visit? Exotic vacation for one?" Logan's tone remained lighthearted, but her eyes went wary. Like she maybe suspected the latter but also didn't want to have it confirmed.

"Writing conference."

Logan visibly relaxed. "Oh. That's cool. Where?"

"Boston. And my publisher is setting up a signing at one of the bookstores there since I'll be there on my release date."

"Wait, wait, wait." Logan set down the bite she'd been about to put in her mouth. "You have a book coming out?"

"Yes, my third. I finished it last September, but that's how long the production calendar is." A process she found maddening with her first book but now appreciated.

"But why didn't you tell me?" Logan looked genuinely confused, not to mention hurt.

"About the trip? I guess I haven't been all that focused on it." She made a sweeping gesture, encapsulating both the back garden and the house. "And I guess I'm not used to reporting my comings and goings to anyone."

Logan's features softened. "I meant the book. I feel like I know what you're working on, and you made a passing reference to edits, but I had no idea you have a book coming out."

"Oh." Silly, really. She hadn't forgotten exactly, but she'd yet to get on doing the social media and such for it, so it was more a vague knowing than a front of mind situation.

"Unless I'm supposed to know and I somehow missed it. Because if that's the case, I'm really sorry. I haven't been a writer's girlfriend before, and I might need to be trained." Logan gave a big smile and two thumbs up. "But I'm told I'm a quick learner."

Kathleen shook her head, unsure whether to laugh or cry or dole out an apology of her own. "You weren't supposed to know. I mean, not as in I was keeping it a secret. More like I wasn't really thinking about it at all."

Logan's eyes narrowed. "Are you one of those women who has to be dragged kicking and screaming to celebrate her successes?"

"No." She bit her lip, working out an honest and not simply reflexive answer. "No."

"But?"

She took a deep breath. "But I'm used to celebrating them with myself. Or maybe my best friend."

"You hate being the center of attention." Logan's smile held wisdom beyond her not quite thirty years.

"Something like that." Because when you're a perpetual disappointment to your parents, it's never the good kind of attention.

"Hmm." Logan frowned.

"What?"

"I'm trying to decide whether I should respect that or put up a fuss because you'd actually like it deep down and just aren't used to it."

"I'm not sure what the answer is, but it means a lot that you care what it is instead of plowing ahead with whatever yours would be."

"Thanks." Logan angled her head, a wry smile replacing the frown. "For what it's worth, I prefer a lot less attention than the average youngest child."

Kathleen laughed. "That's good to know. My brother is, well, not that."

Logan nodded slowly, as though the small observation held a wealth of relevant information. Which, she supposed, it did. "Okay, well, you think on it. I'd love to throw you a small party if you're open to it, with as many or few people as you'd like to invite. Oh, and I'm happy to look after the house and water the garden and stuff while you're away."

"Thanks." Such unexpected dinner conversation. And yet, pretty basic couple stuff.

"But no thanks?" Logan smirked.

"I didn't say that." Even if it had been her first instinct.

"You can say yes to the house and garden and no to the party. You won't hurt my feelings."

She would, though Logan wouldn't let on. That was the thing about letting people do nice things for you. It was nice for them, too. She might be better at giving that advice than taking it, but there was no time like the present. "You know what? Yes. I'd love a party. As long as it's small and low-key."

Logan's eyes narrowed. "Define small."

"Fewer than ten people?"

"Twenty," Logan countered.

"I don't know twenty people in town yet."

"Of course you do. And isn't the point of a book release to have people you don't know show up and buy your book?"

Technically, yes. And that's exactly what her signing in Boston would be. Doing that with her friends and neighbors? Ew. "No. And

I have a second caveat. No sales. I'll bring some of my comp copies for anyone who wants one."

Logan didn't say anything, and Kathleen got the impression she was strategizing.

"I'm firm on that. It's a celebration. I'm not asking people to buy something if they come to my celebration."

"Fine, fine." Logan nodded slowly. "I get what you're saying."

She folded her arms, oddly excited about the whole thing. "And you've already learned that arguing with me is fruitless."

Logan lifted her chin. "I wouldn't go that far."

She wouldn't either. She and Logan got off to a bumpy start, but they'd landed on equal footing. It made whatever this was between them feel like maybe not such a terrible idea after all.

❖

With Kathleen gone, Logan seized the opportunity to catch up with her siblings—plus honorary sibling Clover and practically a sibling-in-law Sy—over drinks at Fagan's. She expected some ribbing over spending all her free time with Kathleen and boy did they deliver. She soaked it up though. She might be the baby of the family, but she had more pair up and settle down vibe than the lot of them put together. Well, save Maddie and Sy, perhaps, but even then only recently.

Clover lamented yet another dating debacle, Maddie and Sy floated their plan of moving in together before winter, and Jack joked about adopting Kiwi permanently. Logan offered some good-natured sympathy, help with heavy lifting, and a promise to start taking Kiwi to Kathleen's. "I'm sure she'd be welcome. She just hates the car so much."

"If by hates you mean pukes on trips longer than two minutes," Jack said.

"Yeah, that." Poor girl.

"I'm mostly harassing you." Jack punched her bicep lightly. "I love having her around."

Kiwi had that effect on people, even those who didn't like dogs. Something about being adorable and sleeping most of the time. Still, she missed those low-key couch cuddles she got with Kiwi. If only she could have both.

Conversation drifted, but Logan's thoughts remained fixed on the idea. What if she could have both?

"How do you ask someone to move in with you if you've just finished giving them the house of their dreams?" Logan asked no one in particular at the next lull.

"You don't," Jack said, as though it was the most obvious thing in the world.

"But how do I float the idea of moving in with her without making it seem weird?"

"Again, you don't." Jack shook his head.

Maddie rolled her eyes. "What he means is, you gently broach the subject of moving in together, then the unspoken where becomes obvious once you agree you want to."

"That's not what I meant," Jack said.

Clover gave his bicep a pinch. "You know, one of these days, some woman is going to come along and sweep you off your feet, and you're going to have to stop being such a grumpus."

"I'm not a grumpus," he said grumpily.

"He prefers the term curmudgeon." Logan sighed. "Seriously, though. Is it weird to broach the subject? Like, is it too soon?"

"Soon is relative," Sy said.

Clover, who sat next to Sy, elbowed her. "But also not."

"You hush." Maddie reached across Sy to poke Clover in the arm. "You don't want to live with anyone ever, so you don't get a vote."

"Well, then, he doesn't either." Clover lifted her chin at Jack.

Maddie looked from Clover to Jack before turning her gaze to Logan. "Not to change the subject from your problem, but can we take a moment to enjoy these two being on the same page on something regarding relationships?"

Logan laughed. It was a rarity. Jack was a consummate bachelor and Clover a solo poly romantic. They might be friends by association, but they almost never agreed on anything, relationships or otherwise. "Yes, because I'm not sure I should be asking for advice in the first place."

Clover propped her chin on her fist. "Because you should be having honest and open dialogue with your partner?"

Maddie pressed her lips together and Jack didn't even try to hide the snicker. Clover had a gift for making the hardest parts of relationships seem the simplest and most obvious. The thing was, it was hard to find fault with her logic. "Yeah."

"When's she home again?" Clover asked, then lifted both hands defensively. "Not that I'm assigning you a deadline or anything."

"Monday." Not even a week and somehow it felt like an eternity.

"What's the welcome home?" Sy asked.

"Uh. Was I supposed to plan one?" Was that a relationship rule she'd missed?

Maddie sighed. "No, Sy's just still traumatized from her homecoming when I acted all moody and sullen."

Logan chuckled at the memory. "Don't worry. I'm not dumb enough to ask for a break."

Everyone at the table laughed, including Sy. "I'm glad everyone agrees that was not the right move," Sy said.

"Ha ha." Maddie rolled her eyes. "I'm glad we can all still get a chuckle at my expense."

Clover, who'd gone thoughtful and quiet, tapped the tip of her finger to the table. "You have to decide if you're going to be cool or make it nice."

Maddie and Sy might have worked it out, but when it came to the basic dos and don'ts of relationshipping, Clover was her guru. "Okay, vague-book. Tell me what that means."

Clover laid out one hand, palm up. "Cool is basically, I'm glad you're home. Let's have sex and get back to life as usual tomorrow." She mirrored the gesture with the other. "Nice is fancy dinner waiting, an I-bet-you're-beat massage, extra sensual sex, and breakfast in bed the next morning."

"Damn." Jack shook his head. "She hasn't been gone that long."

Maddie made a sweeping gesture. "And this is why you never get laid."

"Not never," he grumbled.

"Which would you do?" Logan asked, definitely wanting to be more like Clover than Jack.

"Well, since you're looking to take things to the next level rather than maintain the status quo, I think making things nice signals that. You still need to talk, of course, but your gestures say—"

Jack didn't let her finish, inserting instead: "I'm a sucker, prepared to wait on you hand and foot."

"Such a hater, dude." Sy shook her head.

"Grumpus," Maddie and Clover said in unison.

They all ribbed on Jack for a bit, giving Logan time to contemplate Clover's advice. She could make Kathleen's homecoming nice and see how Kathleen took it. That might give her a sense of things? Though, if Kathleen was a little weird because she always seemed to be a little weird when Logan lavished too much attention on her, that could backfire. On the other hand, finishing the library was what got Logan her first kiss, so Kathleen clearly wasn't immune to such things, or incapable of accepting them completely.

Sy, not yet comfortable with the intensity of the family harassment being doled out, caught her eye. "Are you thinking about the welcome home sex or what you're going to make her for dinner?"

Logan nodded slowly. "Yes."

"You're a goner. You know that, right?" Jack asked.

She continued to nod. "Also yes."

Clover's fingers drummed the table. "Does Kathleen know you're a goner? Not that you're a goner who wants to nest, obviously, but the goner part?"

She had no illusions of being as relationship savvy as Clover, but she aspired to it. Or a monogamous version of it, at least. Because in her heart of hearts, she was, as Clover would say, a nester. She might be shy of thirty still, but she already couldn't wait to come home every night to the same woman. And it was getting easier and easier to imagine Kathleen as that woman. "Not yet."

Clover pursed her lips. "You should probably start with that."

"Oh, I will. As we've discussed, I'm not afraid of feelings."

Everyone laughed except Maddie, who groaned. "I'm never going to live that down, am I?" she asked.

A chorus of nopes and not a chance rose from the table.

Maddie shot Logan a defiant look. "For the record, your eagerness to share your feelings got you the cold shoulder at first. Don't pretend it's all smooth sailing and sunsets."

Logan cringed. "Do we have to bring that up?"

"Yeah." Jack, not usually one to rush to her defense—at least in matters of love—gave a devilish grin. "Besides, that was mostly about lust anyway."

It was Logan's turn to groan while everyone else got a laugh. Clover cleared her throat. "We'll take mercy and change the subject." Good old Clover. She could always be counted on to swoop in.

"Yeah, let's talk about the woman who's stopped by Jack's twice now and been shooed away in under five minutes both times," Logan said.

All eyes turned to Jack, who promptly insisted he needed the bathroom and disappeared.

With him gone, the table turned to Logan for the details. She shrugged. "It's a client, but one who happens to know him from high school. The first time, he'd left his phone at her place, and she returned it. This week, she brought over a plate of cookies to thank him for finishing the job. Poor thing obviously has a crush, and Jack just acts like a deer in the headlights."

"Is he aromantic?" Sy asked. "I mean, I'm not in the business of assigning labels, but maybe he's legit not interested."

Maddie gave Sy's hand a squeeze. "Oh, no. Just socially awkward around pretty women."

"And a grumpus," Logan added. "As we've established."

They agreed not to give Jack a hard time when he returned, if for no other reason than he'd been known to bail entirely when too much attention got directed his way. Clover asked if there were any updates on the Rich and Cherry situation, to which everyone mumbled and shrugged. They'd already stayed in Bedlington longer than Rich had initially said they would. Other than a brief mention of Cherry wanting to experience Vermont, he hadn't said much.

It was all beyond strange. Cherry was clearly not the gold-digging floozy Maddie's imagination had conjured. And Rich, God love him, was proving significantly more tolerable with Cherry around. They'd decided to stick around at least until the end of July, and his kids had agreed to drive up for a big family barbecue. Logan had no idea how it was all going to go, but from where she sat, it would likely be the focal point of the party, which meant her plan to bring Kathleen might go off with minimal fanfare. And while she'd no longer classify Kathleen as skittish, there was no point in giving her any reason to bolt. Or backpedal. Or any of those other words that implied the opposite of taking things to the next level.

CHAPTER TWENTY-FIVE

K athleen sat at the small table, a stack of her books in front of her and a poster of the cover propped on an easel to her right. It wasn't her first signing, but it was the first she hadn't had to orchestrate on her own. The first where an employee of the bookstore greeted her with eager enthusiasm and offered to get her something from the café in the back. The first where people queued up as soon as her reading was over and asked for selfies in addition to having their books signed.

It was magical. It was thrilling. It was exhausting.

Between two hours of nonstop chatting with readers, plus the pre-signing lunch she'd had with her agent, she couldn't remember a time she'd been so peopled out. Funny, really. She spent more time talking with students at midterm most semesters. Though, those chats were about them—their work and their goals. As much as she'd tried to show genuine interest in the people who'd come to the signing, this was all about her. It made her realize how much of her life she'd spent deflecting.

She finally made it back to her room a little after ten. She showered off the makeup and the city feeling before crawling into the crisp sheets of the hotel bed. It took less than a minute for her mind to veer to Logan. To the prospect of hotel sex—because, obviously—but also to everything else. How easy it was to spend time together. To the fact that Logan seemed to want her exactly as she was, in bed and out. To the fact that they'd slid from sleeping together into spending more nights together than apart. To what it all meant.

It left her staring into the semi-darkness and worrying the inside of her cheek. How long could they go on like that? Logan didn't seem in any rush, either to break up or take things to the next level. Which was all well and good, but what if it simply delayed the inevitable? People Logan's age believed they had all the time in the world—to build their careers, to see the world, to start families.

She no longer enjoyed that illusion, or the hubris of living with it. But was it her job to disabuse Logan of those notions? To remind her that, at the end of the day, being together kept Logan from pursuing things she really wanted?

Trudy had been adamant it wasn't her responsibility, part of her wholesale critique of Kathleen's penchant for worrying about things that weren't hers to worry about. But much like Kathleen's insistence Trudy didn't have to climb the administrative ladder if she didn't want to, some things were easier said than done.

She shook her head on the overly puffy pillow, tuning her mind back to hotel sex like she would adjust the radio dial to find a new station. Unfortunately, the analogy made her think about the fact that Logan probably had never even seen a radio dial, and she was back at square one. Or negative one. It was hard to keep count while kvetching in the dark. She grabbed one of the extra pillows and pressed it over her face, letting out a groan of frustration.

Are you still awake?

The text from Logan brought the argument with herself to a halt. She smiled at the words glowing on the screen. *Yeah. A little wired I think.*

I could try to help you relax.

She imagined Logan's hands on her neck and shoulders, rubbing away the tension she'd managed to put there all by herself. *Wish you were here.*

Oh, yeah? What would you ask me to do if I was?

Thoughts of a massage vanished. In their place, thoughts of, well, an entirely different sort of massage. *I'd ask you to touch me.*

Where?

She closed her eyes briefly, imagining Logan's strong, sure fingers on her skin. *My neck. My breasts.*

Anywhere else?

A low pulse started between her legs. *My clit.*

I hate to make you get out of bed, but you should open the inside zipper of your purse.

Kathleen frowned at the odd request, but curiosity won out. A minute later, she held a dark blue bullet vibrator in her hand. *I've been carrying a sex toy around all day!*

Logan responded with several laughing emojis. *I almost told you at lunchtime, but I didn't want you distracted for your signing.*

She would have been, too. Not merely by its presence but the memories that came with it. Logan pressing it to her clit while fucking her with her cock. Kathleen returning the favor a short while later. Well, with the vibrator, not the cock. They hadn't discussed switching yet, and she didn't feel any burning need to.

How would you feel about touching yourself with it now?

Her thighs clenched at the prospect, at Logan suggesting it. *I feel very good about it.*

How would you feel about recording yourself for me?

The flare of self-consciousness didn't stand a chance against the swell of arousal. *Really?*

I love the sounds you make. It would be a nice treat to tide me over until you get home.

She'd never had a lover make that sort of request. It managed to feel both a little naughty and deeply intimate.

I'd return the favor…if that was something you wanted.

The idea of listening to Logan touch herself, hearing her come, sealed the deal. *Oh. Yes. Please.*

We could do it live, but I like the idea of being able to listen again and again.

Weirdness over recording herself seemed less weird than knowing Logan was right there on the line. Plus, yeah, the option of instant replay appealed. *Let's do voice memos.*

I'm going to stop texting you now. But I'm already touching myself, thinking about that perfect hot mouth of yours.

Kathleen let out a groan for her own benefit before engaging the mic. When she turned the vibrator on and slipped it under the sheets and between her legs, she gasped at how wet and ready she was. She told Logan as much, closing her eyes and letting her imagination take over.

❖

For all her initial talk of not wanting a party, Kathleen worked the room like a pro. Logan stood to the side and simply watched. Easy conversation, lots of laughter, and the sort of low-level bashfulness that came off as charming rather than awkward. It felt like a mutual warm welcome—like a housewarming if it had been at Kathleen's house rather than the café.

Logan hoped that was Kathleen's experience of it, one that made her feel like part of the community she'd decided to call home. Just like Logan hoped Kathleen felt like Logan's planning of it had been an act of love.

Love.

She'd sort of danced around that word until now, but what was the point? She was utterly, completely, head over heels in love with Kathleen Kenny.

She'd have expected it to feel like an explosion, or at least an arrival. Pulling into the station of big feelings and realizing with a start that she'd made it to her destination. This was quieter, like going through the motions of a new skill or hobby so often and for so long that she missed the moment of finally getting the hang of it, of being good at it. The joy of knowing the practice had paid off and it was engrained now, as much a part of her as the color of her eyes or the birthmark on the inside of her left thigh.

"Dude, you're zoning." Jack, who'd appeared out of nowhere, elbowed her in the ribs.

"You zone all the time," she countered, "especially in social situations."

He tipped his head, as though conceding the point. "Yeah, but this is your party."

Logan shook hers. "No, it's Kathleen's party. I just handled the details."

"She does seem to be holding court." Jack lifted both hands. "In a good way, I mean. She's so good with people."

"Yeah," Logan said, slightly in awe. She'd have expected nothing less, given Kathleen's almost two decades of teaching. What she hadn't expected was that Kathleen would enjoy it enough to genuinely relax. And yet that's exactly what she seemed, chatting and laughing with Maddie and their parent's neighbor, Martha. Martha picked up a copy of *Kiss and Tell* and held it out to Kathleen, who picked up her pen and scribbled something inside before handing it back.

"And kind of famous. Like, probably the most famous person in Bedlington."

She laughed. "I think that honor belongs to Uncle Rich."

"Naw. I don't mean famous in Bedlington. I mean legit famous who happens to live in Bedlington. Think about it."

It wasn't a high bar. Of the few thousand residents who called their little town home, most had lived there their whole lives. And people who did move here—like Sy—might be making their mark, but not like that. Not in the thousands-of-people-knew-her-name way. Not in the people-wanted-her-autograph way. But Kathleen was. Beautiful, bashful, self-conscious about the silliest things Kathleen.

It was no wonder she'd fallen in love. And by some wondrous magic of the universe, Kathleen loved her back. Well, at least something close to it. Logan had only embraced the word herself just now, so Kathleen might not be there yet. But no way would she deny she and Logan had something special.

"You're supposed to say, 'you're right, Jack.'"

Logan nodded vaguely. "You're right, Jack."

He made a clicking sound with his tongue. "It's so much less satisfying when you're not even paying attention."

She looked at him and shrugged. "Sorry."

"How in love with her are you?" he asked, as though reading her thoughts.

She let out a sigh. No point lying. "All the way."

Jack shook his head. "You could do worse. Does she love you back?"

"We haven't used the word yet, if that's what you're asking."

"What word?" Maddie, who'd snuck up behind them, asked, joining the conversation seamlessly.

"Love," Logan said.

"Sure, yeah." Maddie nodded. "What other word is there?"

Jack looked indignant. "Literally thousands. Millions, probably."

Maddie rolled her eyes and Logan went for another shrug, her way of agreeing that, when push came to shove, it was the only one that mattered.

"You're going to tell her, right?" Maddie asked. "Like, soon?"

Since she'd used up her shrug quota, Logan cringed. "Maybe? I mean, the time has to be right."

Maddie wagged a finger. "Uh-uh. You don't get to pull that shit after doing a full-scale intervention on me for not saying it."

They had done an intervention—Clover, Jack, and her—when Maddie had pulled the bonehead move of asking Sy for a break rather than being honest about her feelings. But that had been different. Maddie had been an idiot. She was simply playing it subtle with her demonstrably gun-shy girlfriend. "This is different."

"What's different?" Clover asked. She'd left Kathleen with a pair of obvious fans and made a beeline for them.

Maddie hooked a finger at Logan. "This one is trying to say that refusing to tell Kathleen she's in love with her is different from my refusal to do so with Sy."

"Is it?" Clover's sincere tone made Logan want to hug her.

"Yes. I'm not afraid of my own feelings. I just don't want to scare Kathleen with them before she's ready."

"Oh, so you're assuming how she feels without actually asking her." Maddie's deadpan delivery drove home the point, hard.

"Okay, fine," Logan said. It wasn't like she didn't want to tell Kathleen how she felt.

Jack clapped a hand to her shoulder. "I mean, she did agree to come to a Barrow family barbecue. If that doesn't say all in, I don't know what does."

He had a point. Family gatherings were a big relationship step, and she was pretty sure that was a universal thing. "So, if Uncle Rich doesn't send her running for the hills, I'll take that as my sign she's in it for the long haul."

Jack shrugged. "Seems like a reasonable plan."

Clover shook her head but didn't say anything. Maddie's brow furrowed. "You do know it's more complicated than that, right?"

Logan rolled her eyes. "Yes. I'm actually less of an idiot when it comes to relationships than you are."

"That's not saying much," Jack observed, which promptly earned him a backhand smack to the chest from Maddie.

Logan raised a hand. "To be fair, I was a bigger idiot in the beginning."

"Yeah, you were," Maddie said.

"But I have the advantage now because I'm not afraid of my feelings."

Everyone nodded, including Maddie, which Logan took as a combo concession and vote of confidence. But Clover's expression remained worried.

"What?" Logan asked.

"I love that you embrace your emotions and aren't afraid to talk about them." Clover gave her forearm a squeeze.

"But?" Because nothing said "but" like a reassuring gesture.

"But I can't help but wonder if the same is true of Kathleen."

"Wait." Jack looked from Clover to Logan and back. "Doesn't she write romance novels for a living?"

Clover cringed. "Write them? Yes. Believe in them? Less so."

"She doesn't?"

"Not like a total cynic," Clover said quickly.

"Just a partial one?" Kathleen had alluded to that at one point, but Logan attributed it to the fact that Kathleen was trying to avoid getting involved with her. Not some permanent ban on committed relationships.

"Partial." Clover gave a decisive nod, as though that both explained the situation and made it better.

"Sounds like you've got your work cut out for you, kid." Jack gripped her shoulder once more. "Now, if you'll excuse me, I'm going to go congratulate your partial cynic girlfriend on her book and make my exit."

Jack crossed the room, leaving her with Clover and Maddie. Both gave her the sort of vaguely encouraging but uncomfortable smiles that were perhaps the least heartening thing ever. She brushed off the low-grade anxiety threatening to take up residence in her rib cage. They knew the Kathleen who'd first come to town. She knew the Kathleen she'd woken up with that morning. The one who'd given herself to Logan in so many ways already. A bit reserved, sure, but with so much passion and playfulness beneath that cool exterior. That was the Kathleen she'd fallen in love with—the whole magically messy package.

CHAPTER TWENTY-SIX

Thank you for tonight," Kathleen said as Logan drove them home. Well, to her home. Though Logan spent so much time there—and had played such a role in making it what it was—it practically felt like theirs sometimes. For all her regular admonishments not to get too invested, too attached, she liked it. Slow mornings, shared meals, doing the dishes side by side. It was everything she told herself sounded better than it was, only it turned out to be pretty fucking fantastic.

"Thank you for letting me." Logan glanced at her briefly before returning her focus to the road. She reached over the center console and squeezed Kathleen's hand.

"I confess I didn't expect to have fun, but I did."

Logan nodded. "For the record, you were nothing but graceful."

Kathleen laughed. "That might be the first time anyone has used that word to talk about me."

"What are you talking about? You're beyond graceful."

She shifted in her seat and folded her arms. "Like the first time we met, you mean?"

Logan wagged a finger. "Okay, that wasn't your fault."

Since the café was all of three minutes from her house, she didn't have the chance to argue before Logan pulled into the driveway. Still, as they made their way to the side door, she couldn't help but ask, "So, you'd have fallen through, too? And gotten stuck?"

Logan reconsidered. "I very well could have fallen through. Rotten wood doesn't care who you are. And I'm sure I would have benefited from a helping hand even if I technically could have wiggled my way out."

Kathleen grabbed Logan's arm and pressed their bodies together. "That's the sweetest bullshit I've ever heard."

"It's not—"

She swallowed Logan's protest with a kiss. Long, hot, hard. Because if she let the sweetness take root, she'd be done for. And she was pretty far gone already.

When she finally pulled away, Logan eyed her with a mixture of curiosity and lust. "If you ever want to win an argument with me, just do that."

"What if we aren't arguing?" she asked.

"You should do that anyway."

Kathleen quirked a brow. "Then take me inside so I can."

"I was trying to," Logan said.

"I'm sorry, are you arguing with me right now?" Kathleen asked. Then she held out her keys as though presenting Logan with a gift.

Logan snagged them, unlocked the door, then dropped them back into Kathleen's outstretched palm. "Depends. What are you going to do about it?"

She tugged Logan inside and pushed the door closed. "Come on, I'll show you."

Kathleen didn't let go until they were up the stairs and in her bedroom. Even then, she only let go so she had both hands available to tear at Logan's clothes. Shirt? Gone. Belt? Unbuckled but left in place because who had the time to pull it from all those loops? She unbuttoned Logan's pants and yanked the zipper down just enough to get her hand inside.

She might have been sloshing around in feelings, but Logan's attention was clearly on the physical. She was hot and wet, and her clit pulsed under Kathleen's fingers.

"Fuck," she said when Logan let out a groan. This. This she understood. This she could handle.

Logan thrust against her a few times but then stepped back. "Don't mind if I do."

She quickly rid Kathleen of her dress and slip, bra and panties. Being naked in front of Logan no longer left her feeling self-conscious and exposed. Which was a good thing given how close she'd come to tumbling out the contents of her heart. Talk about exposed.

But this kind of want fueled her. And as much as it terrified her at first, now it made her feel safe. Like she was on steady ground with crisp, clear lines marking exactly where she stood.

She backed toward the bed, willing Logan to toss her down—kiss her and touch her and fuck her until all that remained was sensation and the white-hot race to release that would leave her body sated enough for her mind to rest. Her body revved at the prospect, almost loud enough to drown out the rest. The little voices in her head that screamed that none of this was safe. None of it was sure.

Only Logan didn't take the hint, didn't toss her. Hell, she didn't even nudge. She eased Kathleen onto the bed without letting go. The word that flashed like warning bells in her mind was reverent.

She couldn't handle reverence right now.

"What?" Logan asked. "Why are you shaking your head?"

She stopped. "I'm not."

"You were."

"Just turned on," she lied. "I still can't believe how much you turn me on." At least that part was true.

Logan narrowed her eyes but didn't argue. Instead, she kissed Kathleen. Her eyelids, her jawline. Again, there was a reverence to it, one that threatened to leave Kathleen coming apart at the seams. She took Logan's face in her hands, pulling Logan's mouth to hers. She channeled all the insistence, the urgency, she could muster.

Logan matched the thrust of her tongue, the nip of her teeth. But her hands roamed almost lazily. The swell of Kathleen's hip, the softness of her belly. Kathleen arched and writhed with the subtlety of an animal in heat. To no avail. Logan refused to rush. And to make matters worse, she kept murmuring compliments in Kathleen's ear. Endearments.

Kathleen's pulse tripped and trembled. At least she told herself it was her pulse, skittering with desire and arousal and any other word that implied something other than the freefall her heart seemed to be in.

When Logan's fingers slid over her clit, into her, everything stilled. The voices in her mind went silent, her breath shuddered. And for the first time in perhaps her entire life, she felt whole.

The sensation couldn't have lasted more than a minute. Probably not even that. Logan didn't stop the thrust of her fingers—slow and sure, stroking places Kathleen hadn't even known she had. She clung to Logan for dear life, kissing and biting Logan's shoulder and murmuring a few endearments of her own. Nonsense, mostly, but enough meaning must have come through because Logan gave her exactly what she needed.

And her body did what it did every time Logan fucked her. It followed along with eager enthusiasm, with some innate conviction that Logan knew how to please her, knew what she needed. Only this time, her heart followed along. And she was utterly powerless to stop it.

"That was…" Logan grasped for a word that would do what they'd just done justice and came up woefully short.

Kathleen nodded, seeming to share her loss for words.

"Exquisite," Logan said. "Epic. Earth—"

"Don't say shattering." Kathleen poked her lightly between her breasts. "It's cliché."

"Yes, Professor." Logan kissed the top of Kathleen's head, happy to be schooled on such matters. She would be in general, seeing as Kathleen was brilliant but managed to be cool about it. This was different, though. Whatever had just happened between them maybe hadn't shattered her world, but it had given it a good healthy shake. What started out as a nice slow and thorough fucking had turned into a hell of a lot more, and she felt it in every fiber of her being.

"Don't call me Professor." Kathleen poked her again. "I'm not a professor anymore."

"What worshipful nickname am I allowed?" Logan asked, not really wanting to slip into banter just yet. But she wasn't sure how to talk about the way Kathleen had given herself just now without turning into a blabbering fool about it.

Kathleen let out a happy sigh, and her eyes drifted closed. "No nickname required. Just me."

"What about a pet name? Am I allowed one of those?"

"I suppose."

"Honey feels trite, though you are incredibly sweet."

Kathleen lifted her head and regarded Logan, a blush creeping across her cheeks. "I'm not. Not really."

"Sure you are. I've seen you with Leah, and with Nate. Pure gold."

"If you want." Kathleen shrugged the shoulder not tucked in the crook of Logan's arm.

"I want you to like it." She kissed Kathleen's temple. "But you don't have to decide right now."

"You did make my brain go a little fuzzy there," Kathleen said, her gaze softening in a way that had Logan wanting to do it all again.

"I like you fuzzy." Kathleen wore it well, to be sure, but Logan also liked the idea she could put Kathleen's very active brain in a languid state.

"Well, it makes it rather hard to think." Kathleen frowned but didn't seem all that bothered.

"Yes, I'm sure you want to think on it. And I'm happy to talk it through, try a few on for size." She was sort of kidding but not. She loved the sweet things couples called each other and hoped Kathleen did, too. For its own sake but also for what it signified. Not a big relationship decision like moving in together, but a rite of passage. Plus it was the sort of thing that tended to stick, and it would serve them both to choose well.

"Let's not talk anymore." Kathleen rolled, hooking one leg over Logan and coming to a seated position, straddling Logan's hips.

"No?" If part of her was disappointed at the abrupt shift, the rest couldn't find fault with her current position. Or Kathleen's.

"No." Kathleen didn't elaborate, at least not with words. Her body, on the other hand, had plenty to say. She slinked her way down Logan's body, leaving a faint trail of wetness across Logan's thigh. She made quite a show of it, doing a slow shimmy of shoulders and hips that would have been at home in any striptease.

Logan opened her legs and Kathleen settled between them, licking her lips. Yeah, nothing to protest here. Besides, she hadn't imagined the shift between them. Kathleen might not be eager to talk about it, but she wasn't denying it, either. There'd be plenty of time for talking after. Or maybe in the morning, over a nice cup of coffee.

Thoughts of morning and coffee and talking evaporated at the first press of Kathleen's tongue to her clit. Logan let out a hiss, the pleasure so intense it bordered on pain. Kathleen eased off in terms of pressure but nothing else. She lapped and sucked, working Logan into a frenzy. Only to change the angle and do it all over again.

Logan buried her fingers in Kathleen's hair, mumbling encouragement and swear words along with the sweeter ones she'd used earlier. Because her feelings were the same, but dear God, Kathleen's mouth. Soft and hot and wet and everywhere and driving her absolutely mad. She came with a force that left her body quaking and her breath ragged. So good, and not unlike the dozens of times before but somehow totally different.

As Kathleen reclaimed her spot curled against Logan, Logan couldn't help but wonder if she felt it, too. Wondered if she'd use the same words Logan would to describe it. Not earth-shattering, of course. They'd established that. Profound, maybe. Complete. And of course the elephant in the room: love.

She knew better than to declare her love in a haze of sex endorphins, but she wasn't one to hide from the truth. Especially not her own. For the first time, though, she believed more than hoped that Kathleen was on the same page. It allowed her sex buzz to mellow into a warm and happy feeling that promised more than a good night's sleep.

Later, with the lights off and Kathleen breathing in the soft steady rhythm Logan had come to cherish, she kissed the top of Kathleen's head and held her the tiniest bit tighter. And she whispered the words that had been growing in her chest like one of the weeds Kathleen insisted popped up the moment her head was turned. "I love you."

CHAPTER TWENTY-SEVEN

Kathleen tugged at the neckline of her dress. It was modest to begin with, but she didn't want even a suggestion of cleavage. Even if half of Logan's family knew what they got up to in the bedroom—at least in the most general terms—there was absolutely zero need to be putting herself on display.

Logan strolled in from the bathroom, holding the belt Kathleen struggled to look at without thinking about unbuckling it. "Stop fussing. You look amazing."

She stopped tugging but resumed the smoothing she'd done prior to tugging and now had to redo. "You're sure it's not too revealing?"

"You're not revealing anything. I'll have to get you home and stripped if I want to see any skin."

"Stop. I'm showing plenty of skin." Specifically, her arms from the elbow down, her calves, and a modest scoop below her neck that showed off nothing more than the freckles she'd picked up with all the gardening she'd been doing. In other words, the perfect amount for a party in which she'd be meeting her girlfriend's parents.

Well, not meeting meeting. She'd met Logan's mom at the book party and her dad, if briefly, the day the porch got rebuilt. But this was different. This was a family function. This was a big deal. Capital B, capital D.

Logan came over and nuzzled her neck. "Hardly any. But that doesn't mean I'm not going to enjoy it."

Kathleen giggled. "You're tickling me."

"Am I?" Logan asked, all innocence.

"You know you are."

"Yeah." Logan did it again. "It's your punishment for showing so little skin."

"I'm meeting your parents." What was she thinking agreeing to this?

"So? They've been dying to meet you. Or rather, spend time with you."

She let her shoulders slump even though it gave Logan unfettered access to her neck. "They're going to see I'm closer in age to them than to you."

"One, they wouldn't care."

Kathleen hmphed. Easy for Logan to say.

"Two, that's entirely untrue. They're in their mid-sixties."

She settled for a "hmm" this time.

"I'm serious. I'm the youngest, remember?" Logan nibbled this time, just below Kathleen's ear.

Kathleen let out a yelp. "Okay, fine."

Logan stepped around to face Kathleen and put a hand on each of her shoulders. "Seriously. Is that what you're worried about?"

She gave a flick of her wrist. "One of many."

"Oh. Babe. You're amazing. Everyone is going to love you. Maddie already does. And Clover. And Jack more than tolerates you, and that's saying something."

She laughed in spite of the churn in her gut. "Parents are different."

"Maybe, but mine are an easier audience than Maddie and Jack, so you don't have anything to worry about."

"Okay. You're right. Fine." She didn't believe it, but haggling wouldn't get her out of the afternoon. It might put off the inevitable for a bit, but then they'd be late, and she'd have that to worry about too.

Logan's eyes narrowed. "You're just saying that so I'll stop trying to pump you up, aren't you?"

She nodded. "Not at all."

It was Logan's turn to laugh. "Come on. We want to get there in time to snag good spots for our chairs."

Kathleen nodded again. She could do this. It might be unpleasant, but it certainly wouldn't be the first time she navigated an uncomfortable social situation. And Logan was right—she did get along with both Maddie and Jack. Better than with her actual brother, in fact. Plus Clover. Hopefully, between them and the couple dozen other people Logan said would be there, she could survive on the small talk skills she'd picked up through the years, courtesy of countless faculty socials and adjunct organizing events.

As promised, a half dozen vehicles already sat in the driveway and on the street in front of the house. Logan gathered their camp chairs and the bottles of rosé she'd picked up earlier in the week. Kathleen stacked the plate of brownies on top of the veggie platter she'd assembled that morning, and they made their way around the house to the backyard.

Earth, Wind & Fire blasted from a speaker she couldn't see, and conversation and laughter filled the air. If part of her found the sheer volume of people and sound overwhelming, the rest of her appreciated the anonymity of arriving to a party already in progress. In short, nothing like the polished outdoor dinner parties her parents hosted. For all her fretting, she relaxed and laughed at herself.

"What's so funny?" Logan asked.

"Just a moment of should have known better."

Logan's gaze narrowed. "That sounds ominous."

She laughed. "No, in a good way. I was expecting uptight."

"Oh. Well, then. Yes. You definitely should have known better." Logan winked. "Come on."

They made the rounds. With each relative, each family friend, Logan introduced Kathleen as her girlfriend. They hadn't discussed it, but Logan said it with this mix of confidence and affection that left Kathleen feeling bubbly.

Cherry and Rich took up most of the oxygen and attention, laughing and telling stories about how they met and their disaster of a first date. She was happy to mingle on the periphery, chatting with Maddie and Sy and asking Clover about the newest kids on the farm. Logan remained attentive without hovering, checking in but not clinging to her side. For all her nerves, she felt not only welcome but easy, like she belonged.

They filled paper plates from the abundance of food spread out on several tables, then balanced them on their knees in the camp chairs Logan set up in the shade of a massive sugar maple in the corner of the yard. Logan got pulled into an argument about when the distressed wood look would fall out of fashion, and Kathleen excused herself to wash her hands inside.

She emerged from the house to find Leah and Logan surrounded. Logan held Nate, making goofy faces and soliciting smiles from the adults if not the baby. She made her way over just in time to hear Logan's mom say, "You're a natural."

"You really are." Martha, the woman who lived next door to the Barrows, beamed. "And you'll be even better with your own when the time comes."

Kathleen froze, a good ten feet away from the conversation. She had no desire to join but wasn't sure where else to go.

Logan lifted her free hand. "Let's not rush that, shall we?"

Logan's mom, Cathy, regarded Logan with affection. "No rush at all. You're a young one yet."

Both of Maddie's hands went up. "Which doesn't mean you should be rushing me just because I'm older."

"But you and Sy have started talking, haven't you?" Clover asked.

All eyes went to Maddie. "I mean, we've talked about both wanting kids at least."

"Have you?" Cathy asked.

"Sy's got to get the tasting room up and running and we're probably going to do the whole get married thing before the making babies thing. But yeah." Maddie shrugged, looking slightly uncomfortable but not like she really minded the line of questioning.

"Thank God for older siblings." Logan made the comment directly to Nate, but everyone laughed.

Kathleen's chest constricted, like someone had taken one of Logan's ratchet straps and secured it around her ribs, clicking it tighter and tighter. Since no one had seen her yet, she fled back into the house, locking herself in the powder room off the kitchen.

Hot splotches crept up her neck and covered her cheeks. The rest of her broke out into a sweat and left her unsure whether she was about to throw up or having a hot flash. She yanked the faucet handle, swearing when water sloshed up onto the vanity and splashed the front of her dress. After adjusting the flow, she thrust her wrists under the tap, willing her blood to cool. The tears pricking at her eyes were another matter. A fat pair spilled over and ran down her cheeks.

Do not cry. Do not cry. Do not cry.

By some miracle—or perhaps merely years of practice—Kathleen pulled herself together before her makeup became a lost cause. She did the slow deep breaths thing for a minute or two because it was stupid but worked, then dried her hands and dabbed at her eyes. One look in the mirror told her what she already knew: she was a mess.

But it was only a matter of time before someone knocked politely and asked if anyone was in there, so she blew her nose and returned to the backyard. It wasn't like Logan's plan to have a family came as any real surprise. And it wasn't like she'd never concocted a story about a contact lens going rogue to justify why her eyes had gone all red and puffy. She just needed to get through the rest of this party, then she could fake a headache and have her desperately needed pity party in peace.

❖

Logan sat at the table in Kathleen's backyard, the way she had more mornings than not for the last month, save the week Kathleen had been away. It had become such a nice little routine, basking in the cool air and soft light—and each other—before heading off to work for the day. One she imagined would give way to cozy mornings with a fire when the weather turned. One she could very happily imagine enjoying every morning for the rest of her life.

Only this morning, it didn't feel like basking. And the night before hadn't felt like any variation of the knock her socks off sex they had. In fact, things felt so off, she stopped halfway through to check in. But just like the day of the barbecue, and just like the evening after when Kathleen had claimed a headache and begged off spending the night together at all, Kathleen remained evasive.

It was starting to give her a low-grade headache of her own.

Logan set down her coffee, drummed her fingers on the table. "I can tell something's bugging you. Why won't you talk to me?"

"Nothing's wrong. I'm fine." Kathleen sipped her coffee as though that proved her point.

"Come on. I'm not an idiot. If you're mad at me and I should know why, I'm sorry. If you tell me, I promise I'll try to make it right."

Kathleen pinched the bridge of her nose, pressing the tips of her thumb and index finger to the corners of her eyes. "I'm not mad at you."

"What is it then?"

"I'm stressed is all. Deadline looming and feeling the crunch."

She wanted to believe that, to trust that even calm, cool, and collected Kathleen could paint herself into a corner with a deadline and then have to negotiate her way through the consequences. Only it didn't track. Kathleen was meticulous with her writing schedule and, in the time Logan had known her at least, ran ahead of schedule. "Did something happen to put you behind?"

Kathleen canted her head back and forth. "Changed up a few things with one of the characters' backstories. Makes for a lot of revision."

A perfectly logical answer, one she had no way of verifying. "I'm happy to be a sounding board, you know. I'm not an expert, but I love a good story. And I've read all three of your books now, so I have context."

Kathleen offered a weak smile. "Thanks, but I think I have to slog through this one on my own."

Again, a perfectly logical answer. Assuming they were talking about Kathleen's book. But Logan couldn't help but feel like Kathleen implied a hell of a lot more than she said. "Well, the offer stands."

Kathleen gave a brisk nod and stood. "I'll keep that in mind."

She picked up her cup and the saucer that had held her toast and headed inside, leaving Logan scrambling to down her coffee and follow. Not that she should have bothered. Kathleen made some comment about wanting a shower and disappeared upstairs without so much as a kiss good-bye.

Logan went about her day and tried not to brood—two meetings with clients, a little bit of heavy lifting at one of Maddie's sites when a member of the crew called in sick, and helping Jack pull wire for the hot tub Clover had insisted every farmer of a certain age deserved. Since she and Maddie hadn't had more than two seconds alone, it left her with Jack in the role of confidant. Not her first choice, but if she didn't talk to someone, she might literally crawl out of her skin.

"Maybe she really is stressed about work." Jack shrugged his dismissive, women are nothing but trouble shrug.

Logan shook her head. "It's more than that. I get the feeling it's about me. Or us."

"You and me us?" Jack pointed to himself. "What did I do?"

"Not you and me us, you idiot. Kathleen and me."

"Oh." Jack nodded. "That makes more sense."

"Yeah. Only I can't figure out what I've done wrong."

He finished capping the connections and arranged them in the junction box. "Maybe she's being cagey because she wants you to propose, and you haven't."

"If only." Despite having no clue what had Kathleen so on edge, she'd wager a week's salary that wasn't it.

"All right. Maybe she's worried you're going to propose, and she doesn't know how to let you down easy."

"You're literally the worst. You know that, right?" But even as she said it, his words landed heavy. How many times had Kathleen mentioned not wanting to get married? No, she hadn't used those exact words, but the sentiment had come in loud and clear. Plus being past the wanting kids phase, or maybe never being in it in the first place. Logan didn't have a burning desire for babies, but having a partner to nest with was definitely part of the equation.

That was the problem. When she thought about "the equation," she was talking about her equation. Her life plan.

Kathleen didn't even want to discuss what constituted her equation. What did she do with that? Or, worse, what did you do when you and the person you're in love with wanted different things? She didn't know if that was the case, but what if it was?

It was one of those obnoxious questions with a glaringly obvious answer that hid its potential to gut a body. Sure, sure, one could hope for mature conversation and compromise. But just as possible was realizing that being in love didn't mean there was a foundation to build a life on. And she knew enough about building things to know that no foundation was a no go.

Jack smacked her in the arm. "Dude, did you buy a ring?"

"What? No. Of course not. We've been together like two months." Which isn't to say she hadn't thought about it, but Jack didn't need to know that.

"You want to, though."

For all that Jack grumbled about not liking people, he could be pretty damn insightful. She both loved and hated that about him. "I can imagine a future with her. How's that?"

"Practically a proposal." Any disdain Jack might feel about the prospect got lost in his satisfaction over being right.

"But not yet. And sure as hell not when something is bothering her and she won't even talk to me about it."

It was the not talking that got under her skin more than the idea that Kathleen might be upset about something. She might not be the most intuitive or savvy person on the planet, but she liked to think she had the maturity and willingness to have hard conversations and find common ground. At this point, she didn't even know if Kathleen was upset with her or about something that had absolutely nothing to do with her. She didn't like it. Not one bit.

Chapter Twenty-eight

After yet another day of wringing her hands and finding no magic solutions, Kathleen stood in the kitchen, not wanting to taint the space with a fight but no longer seeing a way to avoid it. She and Logan had been dancing around each other for days and, other than a shadow of worry in Logan's eyes and a seemingly endless desire to please, they'd carried on as though nothing was wrong. Well, sort of. They'd gone through the motions at least.

"This isn't working," she said eventually, hoping maybe Logan would agree, and then they could both be relieved and get on with life and the unpleasant task of getting over each other.

"What's not working?" Logan asked, tone light but eyes wary.

"This. Us. This charade of a relationship." She regretted her choice of words the second they were out of her mouth. This was why she didn't like to fight.

The wariness disappeared and something dangerous flashed, making Kathleen think of the sea in a storm. "Is it a charade to you? Because it sure as hell isn't that to me."

She sighed, suddenly exhausted. "I didn't mean it like that."

"What did you mean?" Logan closed the distance between them, clasping both her hands. "Please explain it to me, because I don't know what's wrong and until I do, I can't fix it."

The earnestness killed her. "There's nothing to fix."

"There's always something to fix. I built my whole career on that being true."

"You want children. I don't. That's not going to change. From where I sit, that falls into the realm of irreconcilable differences." She'd known this from the beginning, but having to say it out loud felt like a fresh blow.

Logan shook her head. "Maybe I don't want them. I've just always assumed I would have them. That's not the same thing."

"No." She let out a sad sigh. "But it's close. And I'm not going to let you talk yourself into something you're going to regret."

"I might not regret it," Logan said.

"It's your life, Logan. Your happiness. It's not a risk I'm willing to take." Because being resented would be far worse than being alone.

"So, your answer is to break up now before we even talk about it?" Logan lifted her chin, a hint of defiance poking through. "That hardly seems fair."

She didn't have the heart to say she knew exactly how that conversation would go. Or that any decisions Logan thought she might make now would be under duress and subject to change. "Not break up. Just accept that we don't have a future."

"How are those not the same?" Logan's eyes narrowed. "Unless you're giving me an expiration date. Like, we can have this amazing life together, but only for another week. Or month. Is that what you're saying?"

"You're trying to make me sound ridiculous." Which instantly put her on the defensive.

"I'm trying to understand what feels like a ridiculous logic."

She took a deep breath and tried to channel the older and theoretically wiser person she was. "What we have feels good now, but it won't when you decide you're ready to have children. And not only will you have wasted time finding someone you might have them with, you'll resent me from holding you back from that."

Logan dropped her hands and took a step back. "That's a big leap."

"Is it?"

"Yeah." Logan's voice had gone edgy. "You're breaking up with me, but you don't even know what I want. And you're giving me zero chance to figure it out."

"I know that your answer will be influenced by me if we're together." She shook her head. "And that's not fair to you."

"So, you'd rather just break my heart either way." Logan's voice had an edge now.

"You still have your entire life ahead of you. Infinite choices, infinite possibilities." And Logan was too damn young—too damn stubborn—to see that sort of thing didn't last forever.

Logan lifted her chin with what felt like defiance. "What if I don't want infinite choices?"

"What is that supposed to mean?"

"What if I only want you?"

"Oh, Logan." She'd told herself she'd be sad when it was all over, when she could fall apart in the peace and comfort of solitude. Why wouldn't Logan give her that?

"I love you, Kathleen. Big L love. Would a future with you look exactly like I vaguely imagined my future to look? Maybe not. But from where I sit, what we have is worth reevaluating all that. Because being with you makes me a thousand times happier than I ever thought I could be."

Had she ever had that level of stubborn optimism? She didn't think so. She'd learned at a painfully young age that some things were for the select few. Well, for those that weren't her at least. And truth be told, she'd given up being bitter about it. She'd built a life that she loved, on her own terms. She'd defined success and happiness and family in ways she could attain. Had attained. She wasn't about to let some far-fetched fantasy upset her entire apple cart. "We've been together for barely three months."

"And?"

"And we're still in the honeymoon phase. We haven't started fighting about money or chores. We haven't had to deal with what will happen when the sexual novelty wears off." She swallowed. "Or when I hit menopause just as your biological clock starts to tick."

"I'm not asking you to marry me. I'm asking you to give us a chance."

"That chance would rob you of too many others. I can't let you do that."

"Kathleen, please." The defiance had drained from Logan's voice. In its place, something that felt like desperation. "Can't we talk? Aren't lesbians supposed to talk about everything all the time?"

"I think you should go." Because surely that would hurt less than this. Less than Logan standing in front of her wanting the impossible.

"You don't mean that."

"I'm not saying I never want to see you again. But emotions are high and we're not going to solve anything trying to convince each other that we're right." In the deep corners of her imagination, they'd have come to a mutual agreement and maybe managed to still have a little fun together. Such a foolish notion.

Something shifted in Logan's eyes then. Resignation, maybe? Defeat? Whatever it was left Kathleen feeling like she had a knife in her chest, but also like she'd managed to jab one into Logan's as well. "Kathleen."

"Please." The word came out barely above a whisper. If Logan kept saying her name like that, she'd crumble. And then where would they be?

Logan didn't answer but didn't move, either. Kathleen stood statue still, sure that any motion would shatter her resolve, if not the rest of her, in the process. She glanced at Logan but had to shift her gaze. Logan's eyes, so intense and so intent on hers, hurt too much.

Eventually, Logan sighed. "I'm going to leave because I respect that's what you're asking me to do. But I believe we can make this work. I believe what we have is worth fighting for, and I'm not giving up."

Kathleen closed her eyes, as though shutting off one of her senses might make the onslaught of emotion more bearable. It didn't, but it did spare her having to see whether Logan looked determined or anguished. She wasn't sure which would be worse, but she knew she wouldn't be able to take either.

She knew the moment Logan left. The soft close of the door announced it, but it was more than that. A change in the air, in the energy of the room. Like a draft that left her chilled, inside and out. Kathleen went to the door and slumped against it. She expected every drop of energy to drain from her, along with the fight. That's how it always went. Defeat and exhaustion. Only that wasn't what happened this time. This time, a burning sensation took hold in her chest, expanding and pressing against her ribs. Her muscles joined in, hot and tight.

She grabbed the first thing that came to hand and threw it clear across the foyer and into the wall. Unfortunately, it was her cell phone. Even more unfortunately, the cute case she'd let herself buy didn't stand a chance. It bounced a couple of times, landing face up with an intricate spiderweb of cracks covering the screen.

"Fuck."

Gone were the days when a cracked phone screen meant a month or two without any of the little luxuries she enjoyed—wine that came in bottles instead of boxes, a nice wedge of brie. Still. She hated futility and waste, and this was both. The energy did drain then. But rather than feeling empty, as she usually did when life handed her something awful, her entire body seemed to fill with tears. And out they came, in the sort of torrent that left her eyes red and head aching.

It was bad enough to realize there was no way she and Logan could make a go of things. Not in the long term. Not in a way that would make Logan happy. But it was so much worse to be the only one who understood that, to be the bad guy on top of it all. And to be the one left, standing alone in this beautiful space that was only beautiful because Logan made it that way.

The need to get away, to get out, swelled until it felt like a creature unto itself, clawing at her insides in search of escape. She grabbed her purse, shoved aside a fleeting thought about packing a bag, and left.

❖

Logan went home and sulked. Okay, she didn't sulk. She paced and prowled like a caged animal, channeling her energy into keeping full-fledged panic at bay instead of the design she should be working on.

How had she blown things so epically?

Despite replaying the conversation a thousand times in her mind, she couldn't pinpoint the moment when things had gone sideways. She suspected it had something to do with people dropping hints that she'd be a great parent. But seriously, that hadn't even come from her. Why was Kathleen acting like it had?

Given how useless Jack had been when she'd tried to suss out Kathleen's feelings in the first place, she opted to call in the big guns. Unfortunately, Clover and Sy were off on a cheese delivery to Northampton, which left her at Fagan's, sandwiched at the bar between Maddie and Jack. At least the new pale ale they had on tap was a winner. At the rate she was going, she was going to need several.

"It's impressive you scheduled your own intervention," Maddie said, bumping her shoulder to Logan's.

"It's not an intervention." She sounded petulant even to herself but didn't care.

"No?" Maddie blinked a few times, all innocence.

"No. An intervention means the person is in denial about having a problem in the first place. I know I have a problem." Because problem made it seem fixable. As opposed to a broken heart she'd spend the next however long trying to mend.

"Okay, so what's your problem? I assume it starts with a K."

Jack chortled. "And ends with -athleen."

Logan groaned but left her irritation at that because she had bigger fish to fry. "She's convinced that if we stay together, I'm going to regret not having children, resent her for it, and then we'll both be miserable."

Jack made a face. "That's intense, dude. Not to mention like ten thousand steps ahead of where you are."

"Right? She won't even give us the chance to see how things go. Says I'll waste all my other chances in the meantime."

Maddie winced. "I mean, she's not totally wrong."

"Seriously? You're going to take her side right now?" She'd expected Jack to be no help. But Maddie? Surely, her bossy but protective big sister should have more to offer than that.

"Hey, I'm team Logan. Every time." Maddie's tone was adamant but hinted at something more.

"But?" She hated knowing there was a but.

"But Kathleen is certain she doesn't want kids. And she's of an age."

Logan rolled her eyes. "I'd never expect her to literally carry children. If we decided we wanted them, I'd do it."

Maddie shook her head. "I don't think it's about that."

"What do you mean?"

"I mean, I think when you hit forty, your feelings on the matter tend to be pretty set. I don't think Kathleen wants kids. Period."

Kathleen had implied as much, but they'd never actually talked about it. The fact that Kathleen had felt like she could confide in Maddie—and not her—hit her like a sucker punch. "Yeah."

Maddie put a hand on Logan's arm. "I know it's hard, but try to set your feelings for Kathleen aside for a second."

She let out a snort. If she'd been capable of that, she wouldn't be in this predicament.

"I know, but humor me. If Kathleen wasn't in the picture and I asked if you wanted kids, what would your answer be?"

Logan groaned. "I. Don't. Know."

Jack let out a low whistle and concentrated on his beer.

Maddie regarded her with sympathy, but it was the kind that came with dropping hard truths more than figuring things out. "Can you see how that puts Kathleen in a terrible position?"

"I know." Another groan. "But why won't she let me spend some time sorting that out before ripping my heart out and kicking it to the curb? Why can't we talk about it? Talk about what a future together might look like?"

She glanced at Jack, who shrugged the beats me shrug he defaulted to. Well, at least she wasn't the only one without a clue.

"She's scared," Maddie said eventually.

"Scared of what, though? That I'll change my mind and break up with her? She already broke up with me, so I'm not sure how that spares either of us any grief."

Maddie sighed a knowing sigh. "Scared she'll fall all the way in love with you and build a life with you and then have it come crashing down."

"Like you did with Sy." It still sucked, but at least she could understand the logic.

"Exactly," Maddie said with the certainty of someone who'd fucked up but come out the other side.

"But she's the one who ended things. How does knowing that help me?"

"Well, it doesn't." Maddie frowned. "At least not logistically in the short term."

"So, I sit around and be devastated and hope she comes to her senses?" She did not like her odds with that plan.

"You could reach out, but you should probably give her some space first."

"How much space?" she demanded, petulant once again.

Maddie shrugged. Jack shook his head. "Don't look at me. This is exactly why I don't get involved," he said.

She rolled her eyes. Maddie did, too. They'd had plenty of sidebar conversations about Jack's affirmed bachelorhood and how long it would last. But that was something to ponder another time. Hopefully when her own love life wasn't in shambles.

CHAPTER TWENTY-NINE

Kathleen made it to the Massachusetts border before a reality check had her pulling into the parking lot of a gas station. She parked at one of the pumps since she happened to be teetering dangerously close to empty, but instead of getting out, pressed her forehead to the steering wheel. What was she doing?

It was the same loaded question she often posed to her students. Sure, she was talking about poor attendance and half-assed essays when she posed it to them. But it usually served as a prompt for bigger quandaries—what they wanted out of her class, the degree they were working toward, their lives. Sometimes, they clutched her feedback on thesis statements and citations and booked it out of her office like their hair was on fire. Sometimes, they'd cry. Often, they'd linger for the better part of an hour and unload a mountain of dreams, doubts, and everything in between.

She'd always chuckled over the runners. The ones afraid of the great big wide world in front of them. The ones who couldn't decide if they wanted too much or not enough and were terrified that all the lines they'd been fed about potential and promise would dry up and leave them stranded in a sea of disappointment. And yet here she was, doing the exact same thing. Literally.

The best part was she didn't even know where she was running to. Trudy's? That was the vague direction she'd headed, but she would never show up on her best friend's doorstep unannounced. And certainly not the week before the chaos of a new semester started. Not that she doubted Trudy would welcome her with open arms. More that Kathleen would rather eat her shoe than be the sad sack who needed that.

The knock on her window had her head jerking up and a yelp of surprise making her feel doubly foolish. She put down her window and tried for an apologetic smile. "Sorry."

The attendant, an old school butch-looking woman in coveralls, offered Kathleen a smile that would make her swoony under other circumstances. "We're not full serve, but I'm happy to pump for you if you'd prefer."

"No, no. I don't mind. I just, I got—" She waved a hand. "I'm fine."

The woman dipped her chin. "If you say so, ma'am."

She had half a mind to bare her soul right then and there. *I've fallen for a woman more than fifteen years my junior and, as expected, it's ended terribly. You look like you've broken a few hearts in your time. Any words of wisdom for being less devastated?* Fortunately, the other half had the good sense to do nothing of the kind. "Just had my head stuck in the clouds for a moment. I'm good."

Another nod. "I'll leave you to it, then."

She disappeared, and Kathleen blew out a shaky breath. Then she got out of the car, pumped her gas, went into the convenience store, and bought herself a Diet Coke. Because she was a fucking adult, and having meltdowns at gas stations in the middle of nowhere was not how she rolled.

Before pulling back onto the road in the opposite direction, she pulled out her phone, only to slice her finger on the cracked screen—a glaring reminder that maybe she wasn't such a fucking adult after all. She berated herself for a minute, then called Trudy, knowing Trudy wouldn't pick up. Only she did.

"I've never been so happy to see your name pop up," Trudy said.

"Aren't you supposed to be at convocation? Or something else that requires regalia and a fake smile? I was ready to leave you a message."

"I'm hiding in my office before the wine and cheese social for new faculty."

Of course she was. "God, I don't miss that."

"Girl, I'm tenured and I don't wanna."

Kathleen laughed.

"So, were you calling to brag about your non-academic lifestyle, or have you invented something new to stress about?"

She hated being so predictable. "Same stress, new development."

"Let me guess. Logan did something really thoughtful and you're tripping."

Kathleen pinched the bridge of her nose. "How is it you have a million-dollar vocabulary but can bring me to my knees with dated slang?"

"I'm a woman of many talents. Also, you're evading. Spill before I have to go rub elbows and drink budget cabernet."

"We broke up." She thought maybe saying it out loud would help, but it only hurt worse.

"Uh-uh. That implies a mutual decision and I'd bet my sabbatical that isn't the case. Did she break up with you or did you break up with her?"

"The latter. But only because it was inevitable. You should have seen it, Trudy, at her family's party. Holding the baby like a natural and everyone falling all over themselves to tell her how great she looked and how her time was coming and what a great parent she'll be." Relaying it brought all the images flooding back and made her heart ache.

"And then you two had a heart to heart about it and she admitted that she wouldn't feel fulfilled as a human unless she had babies of her own. That's rough." Trudy's delivery was deadpan, making it impossible to tell if she was sincere or baiting.

Kathleen waited a beat. "It didn't go exactly like that."

"No? You mean you just made it up in your head?"

Goddammit. "Logical inference isn't the same as making things up."

"Did you talk about it at all?" Trudy asked.

"Not until we had a huge fight, and I broke up with her." Which she hadn't exactly meant to happen the way it had, but it was too late to be more delicate about it now.

"Ah." Trudy tutted. "And that's where she said she needed to have babies to be happy."

"She said she didn't know." Which was clearly kicking the can down the road. Logan might not recognize that at her age, but Kathleen sure as hell did.

"And?"

"You're really not going to cut me a break here, are you?" A fact she loved more than loathed about her best friend, at least under normal circumstances.

"I will the moment you start making sense."

She let out a growl of frustration. "I seem to be the only one who is."

"I have to go in a minute, but I'm going to tell you a story for you to mull over while you're feeling sorry for yourself, and when I get home, we're going to have a nice long therapy session over several glasses of wine. Deal?"

Like she had any choice. "Deal."

"I wanted kids at Logan's age."

"Stop." Childless by choice was one of the things she and Trudy had first bonded over.

"I did. Partially because I knew I liked young people if not babies. Partially because I'd been raised to think being a mom and a successful professional was the ultimate fuck you to the patriarchy." Trudy let out a dismissive laugh.

Kathleen did, too.

"I'm not saying I know the depths of Logan's heart and mind. Though I do feel pretty confident she's over the moon in love with you. I'm saying that people change, especially as their circumstances and life choices evolve."

Kathleen swallowed the sob that rose in her throat. "Don't you see that's what I'm terrified of? That she'll be fine for a while and five years from now decide she really does want a family."

"And five years from now, you could decide you want to move to a tiny village in the English countryside and Logan declares she can't relocate. You never know what the future will hold, good or bad."

"Ugh." She knew that, preached it to her students day in and day out. She still hated it.

"There's a whole middle ground between doom and gloom and the sailing into the sunset bliss you give your characters. But you're only going to get the good stuff if you take some risks."

Trudy was right. She knew this without a shadow of a doubt. But it didn't make the prospect of gambling with her heart any easier. "I just wanted to be a happy little hermit, writing my stories and living in worlds I can control. Is that really too much to ask?"

"Eh. You can live that life, but I think it's going to come up short in the happiness department. You have a lot of passion, and I don't just mean the sexy kind. Ever since you started sharing it with Logan, you've blossomed."

She wanted to poke fun at the flowery language, but she was too busy crying to form words.

"Maybe Logan is your soul mate, maybe she isn't. Maybe soul mates are a bogus concept to begin with. But running away based on the chance of future heartbreak? You're better than that."

Was she? She honestly didn't know.

"Okay, I really do have to go. Sorry to drop hard truths and run, but I'm going to call you later."

"Go." Kathleen sniffed. "And thanks. I love you."

"Love you, too."

Kathleen tapped at her phone, toggling away from the ended call and back to her GPS. She'd literally just driven it but didn't entirely trust herself, so she pulled up the directions for home. The answers wouldn't be waiting for her there and neither would Logan. But it was home, and there was something to be said for that.

❖

"Maybe you need to let it go," Maddie said, cringing like Logan might smack her for such a suggestion.

"I don't want to let it go." Her voice sounded whiny rather than desperate, which felt like an upgrade.

"Why not?" Mom asked, head tipped and a look of genuine curiosity on her face.

She'd had this conversation already with her siblings, hadn't intended on sloshing her heartbreak around the Barrow Brothers office. But here she was, pathetic and heartbroken enough to make it blindingly obvious to anyone and everyone around her that's what she was. "Because I love her."

Maddie sighed. Jack made a show of staring at his computer screen. Mom regarded her with that special brand of sympathy only moms could muster. "That'll do it," she said.

"It's your fault, you know," Maddie said, looking pointedly at their mother.

"I'm sorry?" Mom poked her fingers into her chest, clearly surprised and also a little offended.

"You were fawning all over Logan and Nate and talking about what a great parent she'd be. That's what made Kathleen freak." Maddie shrugged. "Though it was probably only a matter of time."

Mom looked to her for confirmation. Though there might have been a kernel of truth in Maddie's initial assessment, there was equal validity in the second bit as well, and the last thing she wanted was her mother feeling responsible for her mess. "She's struggled with the age difference. That just pushed her over the edge."

"Logan, I'm so sorry. I didn't mean to upset her. Or you." Mom frowned. "I mean, I figured you wanted kids eventually, but maybe you don't. I never meant to make you feel pressured."

"I didn't." Logan blew out a breath. "Feel pressured, I mean. To be honest, I hadn't given it a lot of thought. Obviously Kathleen did. And when my feelings didn't immediately and completely line up with hers, that was the end of it."

"I can see why she'd take that to heart." Mom nodded slowly. "It's one of the biggest decisions a person makes. I'm sure she didn't want you making one you might regret."

She threw both hands in the air, patience finally snapping. "You know what I regret? Losing the woman who feels like the one. Having a hypothetical future conflict ruin the best relationship I ever had. And having my family basically say they see her point."

No one said anything. They just stared at her with varying degrees of pity and regret.

Logan dropped her arms, and her whole body slumped. "I want a family. But I feel like I don't really care exactly what it looks like or how it comes together. Does that make sense?"

Everyone—her mother, Maddie, Jack—shook their heads.

"Like Leah. I love being part of her support system and helping with Nate. Not like some random babysitting here and there. Like family." She lifted her chin at Jack. "Like that trans kid who stayed with you for a few weeks when his parents kicked him out. I feel like people say chosen family only when their actual family sucks, but I want chosen family and my family family. And I don't need to raise a baby from birth to get that. And I really fucking wish Kathleen would understand."

"Have you tried explaining it?" Mom asked gently.

"Yes," Logan said instinctively, then, "well, sort of."

Her mother's shoulders straightened, like no one she'd raised would speak such wishy-washy drivel. "What kind of answer is that?"

She winced. "Not a very good one."

That got her a nod of approval. "What are you going to do about it?"

The whine returned, full force. "I want to talk to her, but she won't see me."

"Won't?" Jack asked, his fascination with disaster outweighing his desire to avoid all talk of feelings.

"I texted her. She says she doesn't want to hurt me any more than she already has and doesn't think it's a good idea."

Jack let out a low whistle. Maddie made a face. Mom continued to nod. "That does make things difficult."

The thing about her mother was that she could take the wind out of a person's sails in two seconds flat. Mostly in a good way, deflating a tense situation before it exploded. Now, though, it made Logan want to scream. "What am I supposed to do? Show up on her doorstep?"

Maddie raised her hand. "That does not sound consensual."

Mom tutted. "Agreed."

"Well?" She looked at the two of them with exasperation, not even bothering with Jack.

Maddie looked to their mother as the universally acknowledged source of wisdom in the family. Eventually, she said, "You remind her in the most unobtrusive way possible that you want to talk, to work things out. And you give her space."

It was pretty much the least satisfying proposition she could imagine, short of Maddie's suggestion of walking away entirely. But what choice did she have? None, really. At least she had the language that might actually convince Kathleen of what she wanted. Assuming, of course, Kathleen came around enough to give her the chance.

CHAPTER THIRTY

When the sounds of Nate stirring came through the speaker of the baby monitor, Kathleen resisted the urge to hop up from her computer. He fussed for a few seconds, then went quiet, and the little picture on the screen confirmed he'd fallen back asleep. She smiled at his chubby little cheeks and returned her attention to the screen in front of her, where her characters remained convinced things wouldn't work out and were utterly miserable about it.

Just like her.

No, that wasn't fair. She was only kind of miserable. With the exception of Logan, everything in her world was exactly as she wanted it. Okay, maybe not exactly but close. By the rules of how she lived her life, breaking up with Logan should be nothing more than an unpleasant blip.

So why was she walking around with this hollow feeling in her chest? As though Logan had yanked her heart out and taken it with her, only to toss it away like some paint chip she'd picked up but decided wasn't the right shade after all. She'd ended things exactly so that wouldn't happen.

She scrubbed her hand over her face. Miserable and resorting to crappy metaphors. Great.

Nate stirred again, but this time he didn't settle. Kathleen pounced on the diversion and went to the guest room where she'd set up the portable crib. "Hello, young man. Are you ready for your afternoon snack?"

He continued to fuss but extended his arms and waved them about. He probably didn't have the wherewithal to mean it as a signal to be picked up yet, but Kathleen smiled and scooped him up. "It's okay, sweetheart. I just need a minute to warm it up."

She set the pouch of breast milk in a cup of hot water the way Leah instructed. Nate entered full meltdown mode, but she remained unfazed, talking and humming to him as though he might pause his wailing long enough to listen. The second she had him situated in the crook of her arm with the bottle in place, he was a changed man. He stared at her with his doe eyes and tear-stained cheeks, and she fell even more in love with him than before.

It struck her how much she loved this baby. This role. Not quite aunt, more than friend. Still safely shy of grandma territory. Being part of a child's life but not solely responsible for it. And being there for someone like Leah. Sure, Leah had supportive parents, but what about the young moms who didn't?

With it came the question of whether Logan might ever find that satisfying. Or satisfying enough. Slippery word that was. So often, what people wanted to be enough fell profoundly short.

Nate finished his bottle, and Kathleen shifted him to her shoulder for burping. He promptly did, along with just enough spit up to make her regret not snagging a towel first. She returned him to the crook of her arm. "It's okay. You can't help it."

He cooed and waved his little arms.

"Life's a complicated mess sometimes. You don't have to worry about that yet, but I feel like you should be warned in advance."

His face scrunched up with intense concentration. Or maybe it was poop. A minute later the smell invaded her nostrils. Yep. Definitely poop.

They repeated the nap, bottle, diaper, cuddle cycle once more before Leah arrived. "I can't thank you enough," Leah said before telling Nate how much she loved him, how badly she'd missed him, and what a good boy he was.

"How was the first day of classes?" Kathleen asked when they'd all settled on the sofa.

"Other than missing this little guy way more than I thought I would, it was great." Leah's shoulders scrunched up almost to her ears with excitement. "My classes are great. I mean, as great as gen ed requirements can be. And I already met another mom who's only a couple years older than me."

Kathleen felt her own excitement bloom. Excitement that Leah was embracing community college as a means of not getting too far behind, excitement that community college seemed to be embracing her. And even though she had a little pang for some of the deeply meaningful connections she'd made with students throughout the years, excitement that it was Leah starting a new semester and not her. "I'm so glad."

"I told my creative writing professor I had this writer friend who'd nudged me to give it a try, and then she asked me if it was someone published. She asked me who, and I told her, and she'd heard of you."

Kathleen laughed at the way Leah described it, like she'd been able to brag about knowing a celebrity. "Officially my biggest brush with fame."

"Oh, stop," Leah said.

Kathleen shrugged. "Okay, second biggest. Getting a good review in *Publishers Weekly* is still at the top of my list."

Leah clearly didn't know what that was or what it meant, but she smiled anyway. "How was your day?"

Kathleen gave her more detail than necessary, but Nate had done so many things to delight her, and she knew enough about babies to know the minutia of feeding and pooping mattered at this age. Leah soaked it in, like stepping into sunlight after a long day indoors. "I know your mom is your go-to, but I'm really happy to watch him anytime, and not just when you have class. You need to make time for studying and some for yourself, too."

Leah reached over with her free hand and gave Kathleen's arm a squeeze. "I can't tell you how much it means to me."

A lump formed in her throat, and she had to work to speak around it. "It means a lot to me, too."

"Speaking of." Leah looked at Kathleen, then Nate, but she didn't continue.

"What is it? What's wrong?"

"Nothing's wrong with me." Leah blushed. "I was going to ask about you."

Kathleen tried to connect the dots and failed. "What about me?"

"You and Logan? It might be none of my business, but I saw her yesterday and she was totally miserable. And you don't seem miserable, exactly, but I have the feeling you're better at hiding it than she is."

Her first thought was to tease Leah about getting overzealous with her intro psych class, but she bit it back. Mostly because it would be an insult to Leah's maturity and perceptiveness. Also because Leah may have taken intro psych at some point, but she wasn't taking it this semester. So Kathleen glommed onto her second instinct—denial. "I'm not miserable."

"But I don't think you're as happy as you were." Leah hesitated. "As you could be."

"We want different things," she said before she could filter herself. "That's the sort of thing you can pretend isn't a big deal, but it only sets you up for bigger disappointment down the road."

Leah frowned.

"I know that's a hard thing to come to terms with, but surely you've already had your own experiences with it."

"Not really." Leah shrugged. "Nate's dad didn't want to be a dad, and as nice as it would have been for him to be in Nate's life, he's definitely not the kind of guy I want to marry."

"See? That's what I mean. You knew that trying to make it work between the two of you would only make things worse in the long run."

"Yeah, but he was a douche. Logan's not that."

Kathleen chuckled. "No, she's not."

"I'm just saying," Leah said, as though that validated her argument.

She managed a smirk because she was good at hiding. "I am, too."

Leah huffed but didn't argue. They chatted a bit longer before Leah had to get herself and Nate home for dinner with her parents. "Thank you again," Leah said after tucking Nate into his car seat.

"Anytime. Literally."

"You know, I hope it's not overstepping to say I think of you as family."

"Not at all." Kathleen's heart swelled yet again. "I'm all about chosen family and I consider you that, too."

"Then I hope it's not overstepping to say that I don't think you and Logan do want different things. It's just that maybe how you've been thinking about family isn't exactly the same." Kathleen opened her mouth to argue, but Leah shook her head. "Just think about it."

❖

Logan looked up from where Nate cooed in her arms. "She didn't budge an inch?" she asked Leah.

Leah's shoulders lifted and fell. "I'm sorry."

Logan shook her head. "Don't apologize. I didn't expect you to plead my case."

"I didn't." Leah frowned. "Or at least I hope it didn't come off like that."

She wanted to ask Leah for a blow-by-blow, for every word Kathleen uttered. She'd already analyzed every conversation they'd had to death and could use some new material to obsess over. But she didn't want Leah to feel obligated or stuck in the middle or anything else gross. And she certainly didn't want to give Kathleen the impression she needed others interceding on her behalf, especially if the one doing the interceding was even younger than she was. "I'm sure it didn't. Kathleen would have called you out if it had."

Leah laughed. "Truth."

"So, how are you? How's school?" Because that had to be more compelling conversation than her sorry state.

"It's good. I mean, I miss my friends and UVM and the carefree college student life we all thought was plenty stressful. But I like my classes and being around other students with kids and jobs and stuff is nice. I don't feel like a freak."

She'd thought about the logistical challenges of Leah's situation and, to a certain extent, the emotional ones. But it was social, too. Not just the time she had for a social life but how she navigated being a parent when surrounded by those who weren't. Her admiration for Leah ticked up a few notches. "Nothing about you is freaky."

Leah snorted. "Thanks."

"I mean it," Logan said.

"I do, too. I also mean it when I say thank you for being so willing to babysit. My mom jokes about it taking a village, and I thought I understood what that meant, but man, I didn't have a clue."

The tightness that had taken hold of Logan's ribs the last week or so intensified. Partly because Leah was such an incredible person and getting to be part of her life—and Nate's—felt like a privilege. And partly because that was exactly the point she so desperately wanted Kathleen to understand. Family was so much more than two parents and a picket fence. More than a uterus and a birth and being called mom. It was this. It was what she hoped to have as an aunty someday. It was the life she wanted to build with Kathleen even if it didn't involve raising a kid together. "I'm glad I get to be part of your village."

Leah's eyes went glassy and she sniffed. "Me, too."

"Do you want to do some schoolwork while Nate is still enamored with me?" She'd taken the morning off and didn't need to be on site until two.

"Yeah?" Leah looked hopeful.

"Totally. I'm not quite ready to give him back, but I'm sure you have better uses of your time than listening to me whine about my love life."

Leah offered a good-natured grimace. "I do have stats homework. And a paper coming up."

Logan laughed. What did it say that statistics was less painful than listening to her? "Better you than me. I'll take the infant while you sort out regressions."

"Is it bad that I actually don't mind either of those things?"

"No." She thought about her own life choices. The fact that she'd take the hard with the good if she could just convince Kathleen of the same. "I think that means you're doing something right."

Leah's expression softened, and it hit Logan just how hard she was working to make a life for her son, but for herself as well. "Yeah."

Logan continued to cuddle and coo at Nate. She really did love him. Babies in general, really. But she also loved that moment of giving them back and going about her life exactly the way she wanted. The conversation she'd had with her family—the one she so desperately wanted to have with Kathleen—echoed in her mind.

When Nate fell asleep, she settled him into the crook of one arm and pulled out her phone. Leah typed away on her laptop, working on some math problem or essay. Maybe it was time to try an essay of her own.

Chapter Thirty-one

*C*an *we talk? Please?*

Kathleen frowned at her phone. Logan had texted her some variation of that each day for the last week. Never more than once a day and never aggressive, but she hadn't missed a day yet. They usually came in the morning, like they'd become part of Logan's getting ready for work routine. She appreciated that, oddly. Like it assured her Logan meant to send them. Unlike a few of the texts she'd just barely thought better of after a glass of wine and good cry. She'd ignored a couple of them but had mostly responded with her own variations of not thinking it was a good idea and not wanting to hurt Logan any more than she already had.

Only this time, Logan hadn't led with that. Well, she had, in her morning text. But then at eight forty-eight in the evening, she went and poured out her heart in the most thoughtful, mature, loving missive of a text Kathleen had ever seen. Wanting a family, but not necessarily a traditional one. Wanting to build a life with Kathleen more than anything, or at least wanting to try. Understanding why Kathleen felt so much pressure to think about what future Logan might want but begging her to trust Logan to know her own heart and to be honest about it.

She'd ended with the simple plea. *Can we talk? Please?*

Kathleen read it again and again, willing answers and certainty that refused to come. Over the course of the last twelve hours, she'd laughed, cried, and sent screenshots of the whole thing to Trudy. What she hadn't managed to do was sleep. Or make any decisions. Or text a reply.

Oh, she'd wanted to. She'd wanted to text yes in all caps, over and over. She wanted to say sorry a million times—sorry for pushing Logan away, sorry for deciding what was best for both of them, sorry for being stubborn and jaded and all the other terrible things she'd been. But she hadn't. Not yet, at least.

It felt too easy. Like a cheat. Or a trick. Like she'd get her hopes up only to have them dashed again.

Unfortunately, her characters continued to slog through their own dark nights of the soul and offered little reprieve from the angst clutching her vital organs and making it difficult to breathe. The fact that she could control their fates should have offered some consolation, but it only served to remind her that happy endings happened way more in fiction than real life. At least Logan hadn't shown up on her doorstep, hoisting a boom box over her head and declaring her undying love. Not that Logan was even old enough to get that reference.

Ugh.

Grand gestures were great in movies and on the page. In real life, they came with a heavy dose of cringe. At least she imagined they would. Having technically neither delivered nor received one.

The page. That's where her attention needed to be. Writing wasn't something she simply did to feed her soul anymore. It was her job. Literally, the way she fed her actual self. She needed to get it together.

She stared at the sentence she'd rewritten three times already before picking up her phone. No morning text from Logan. Not that she expected one. She did have one from Trudy, though. And one from Leah.

For all the ways Leah and Trudy were nothing alike—close to three decades apart in age, several degrees, life experiences—their takes on the current situation were disarmingly similar. Basically amounting to the argument that Kathleen was being a stubborn cow and needed to let Logan decide what she actually wanted rather than presuming the worst and acting on said presumption as though it was fact. If it wasn't so damn annoying, she'd find it rather endearing.

Leah managed to be more subtle. Probably because she saw Kathleen as an adult if not an actual mother figure. Plus, they'd only known each other a few months. Trudy, on the other hand, let loose. Poking. Prodding. More than a few references to allowing her family baggage to ruin a perfectly good shot at happiness.

Unfortunately, the haranguing only served to dig her hole of sadness and self-pity deeper. The people she cared about most in life didn't understand her feelings or her choices. Insisted she was being nothing but stubborn and cowardly. It was harsh and insensitive, and it added insult to injury.

Didn't it?

Suddenly, every argument with herself fell flat. Every half-assed pep talk that she was doing the right thing deflated. Like a single flick to a house of cards, it all collapsed around her.

She expected to feel devastated, as she often did when discovering she'd been colossally wrong about something. This felt like relief. Like she'd been working double-time to maintain a facade and didn't have to anymore. It was gone. And now that it was, the harsh truth looked her right in the eye. She'd built a wall to protect herself, and it had done a shit job.

What did she have to lose? Logan? Well, she'd already done that by pushing her away. Her heart? It had pretty much hopped a ride when she'd shown Logan the door. What, then, was she so fucking afraid of?

It might have been a rhetorical question to the universe, but Kathleen's mother appeared in her mind as though summoned by name. All her sighs, all her subtle digs at Kathleen's success, or rather lack thereof. Patricia Kenney had resigned herself to having a queer, East Coast liberal, spinster of a daughter, and Kathleen had made peace with that. Or at least she'd convinced herself she had.

But had she? Had she really? The last year had felt like vindication—finding success as a writer and buying the house of her dreams. Sure, they weren't what her mother would have wanted for her, but they were things she understood and, in a small way at least, respected. Logan fell squarely outside all of that. Blue collar, or at least her mother's definition of it. So very much younger. Kathleen could almost hear the disdain in her mother's voice as she asked whether Kathleen had decided to become a cougar.

Idiot. She was such a complete and utter fool. And oblivious on top of that.

It was strange how revelations worked. Everything that seemed so murky and impossible became clear in a flash. The myriad of unanswered questions resolved themselves with a single answer. And for her, in this instance, that answer was Logan. That answer was love.

❖

Jack elbowed Logan in the ribs. "Dude, you have a visitor."

Logan looked up from the wire she'd been stripping, pretty sure it was no one she wanted to see. What she saw had both the stripping tool and the section of wire falling from her hand. Kathleen walked toward her with purpose. But also apprehension. Was that a thing? She didn't care if it was. Because Kathleen moving in her direction rather than running the opposite had to be a good sign.

She'd managed to keep herself in the patiently optimistic headspace. Because it had been less than twenty-four hours since she'd sent her soul-baring missive. And while she'd have liked an immediate reply, Kathleen was the kind of woman who'd think things through before answering. And she had enough faith in what she and Kathleen had to trust that somehow things would work out. Unless Kathleen had decided to sell her house and move away and never look back and had decided the least she could do was tell Logan to her face.

Okay, so mostly optimistic.

"Dude." Jack elbowed her again. "Go meet her halfway."

He meant it literally, but her mind raced to metaphorical meaning, to the possibility of compromise on all the fronts Kathleen insisted they were hopelessly incompatible. "I'm going."

Since her hands were empty, she strode down the driveway, stopping a few feet short even though every instinct told her to pull Kathleen into her arms and never let go. Kathleen did the same.

"Maddie told me where I could find you," Kathleen said.

Logan nodded. Kathleen could have just as easily gotten that information by texting or calling her directly. Why hadn't she?

Kathleen laced her fingers together, then took a deep breath and blew it out. "I'm sorry to barge in on you at work."

As desperately as she wanted to read Kathleen's presence as the start of kissing and making up, a knot of anxiety twisted in her gut. "I don't mind."

"The thing is." Kathleen looked at her feet.

"Yes?" This was bad. It had to be bad. Though, honestly, she wasn't sure how things could be worse than they already were. Well, aside from the selling her house and moving away bit. The prospect of never seeing Kathleen again hurt even worse than the prospect of not being together. Even if seeing her would feel like torture.

Kathleen looked up, worry and wariness clouding her eyes. "I'm an idiot and an ass, and it seemed better to own that immediately after having the revelation."

"You're neither of those things," Logan said instinctively, even before the meaning sank in.

"Oh, I've been both. Not to mention arrogant."

Not the words she'd use, but considering what Kathleen had put her through in the last week, she couldn't bring herself to refute it. "Stubborn, maybe."

Kathleen chuckled softly, and the smile that lingered seemed wry. "I'll take that."

The desire to touch, to connect, won out, and she reached for Kathleen's hand. Even though she had no idea what else Kathleen had to say, or what it meant. "I'm glad you're here."

"I'll take that, too."

"Do you want to go somewhere? So we can talk?" She didn't know where, exactly, but that felt like an insignificant detail.

Kathleen chewed her lip. "I don't want to interfere with your work."

She stole a glance at Jack, who'd been staring but quickly looked the other way. "I think they can manage for a few minutes without me."

"Okay." Kathleen nodded as though that was the best news she'd heard all day.

"How about over there?" The cluster of maple trees at the edge of the yard offered shade and a bit of privacy if nothing else.

More nodding and, when Logan gestured for her to go first, Kathleen headed in that direction. They got there and stood, facing one another but not saying anything. Logan figured Kathleen would want to go first but maybe not. She fought the instinct to apologize since she didn't technically have anything to apologize for. Because as much as she wanted to wipe the worry from Kathleen's eyes, Kathleen had shut her down and shut her out, seemingly without a second thought.

"So, like I said, I was an idiot." Kathleen blew out a breath, as though saying it offered her some relief.

"I was, too." Naive, at least, to assume such big things didn't matter as long as they loved each other.

"You weren't." Kathleen angled her head. "Well, maybe you were in thinking our age difference didn't matter."

She opened her mouth to double down on that argument, but Kathleen lifted a hand.

"But I was more of an idiot because I jumped from it matters to it's insurmountable. Without giving either of us the benefit of an honest and heartfelt conversation about the specifics."

That's all she'd asked for, really. "Okay."

"And maybe you'll decide you do want children and it will be the reason we break up, but you deserve to make that decision yourself and not have me make it for you. And yes, it will hurt like hell if you arrive at that in five years, but we could also break up for a thousand other reasons between now and then."

Logan's optimism wavered as Kathleen specced out the myriad of ways they might not end up together. But talking about why things might end implied they hadn't already. That had to count for something, right? "Or not?"

Kathleen smiled. "Or not."

"Is this your way of un-breaking up with me?"

"It's my way of asking if you'll have me back after breaking up with you out of fear. And asking you to forgive me for acting out of fear and not trusting you or us to navigate that together." Kathleen took a deep breath and blew it out in a huff. "And asking you to trust me enough to have the hard conversations that arise instead of resenting me in silence even though I haven't given you a lot of reason to do that up to this point."

"Wait. You lost me on that last one." Though it probably had as much to do with her heart beating in her ears as the convoluted language.

"I want to be with you, and I'm desperately hoping you'll have me. But, I—wait. And. And I hope we can be honest with each other if or when we want different things. Talk about them."

Logan smiled. "And maybe compromise?"

"And maybe compromise." Kathleen nodded. "I've been afraid you're the kind of person who will set aside what she wants for the sake of others to the point of being unhappy."

She didn't know all the hurts and heartbreaks that had given Kathleen such an outlook, but it looked like she might get the chance to. And, just maybe, she'd get to help heal some of them, too. "I can't promise an ending like in one of your books, but I can promise to try."

Kathleen shook her head. "Those aren't really the endings anyway. They're just the moments when the couple decides that loving each other is better than going it alone, even when it's scary."

She'd never thought of it that way, was pretty sure a lot of people didn't. But she loved it, loved what it implied. "I'd rather love you and have you love me than go it alone, even when it's scary or hard or anything else."

The tears started then. Big and beautiful and vulnerable, they spilled over and ran down Kathleen's cheeks even as she smiled. Only then did Logan realize it was the first time Kathleen had been genuinely vulnerable with her, which in turn made Logan feel like she could conquer the world. "That," Kathleen said with a sniff. "Exactly that."

It might not have been like the end of one of Kathleen's books, but Logan kissed her like it was. Long and slow and deep and filled with every ounce of promise she'd been holding from that first night Kathleen stayed over at her house and didn't have sex with her.

When the whistles and cheers started, Kathleen pulled away, though she seemed reluctant about it. Logan slipped her arm around Kathleen's waist and pulled her close. "Don't worry. They're happy for us. Like all the furniture turned back to life at the end of the movie."

Kathleen laughed and buried her neck in the crook of Logan's shoulder. "I'm pretty sure that makes me the beast."

"Hmm. That would make me Belle, so I'm going to go with no. Generic happy villagers?" She quirked a brow. "Or has this whole analogy gone sideways?"

"Definitely sideways."

"Just lift a hand and wave. You can pretend you're my beautiful princess or not. Your call."

Kathleen laughed again but did as she was told. The cheers intensified, then Jack—considerate and also painfully unromantic—corralled everyone's focus back to work.

Logan took Kathleen's hand. "Thank you for coming."

Kathleen angled her head, a sly smile on her lips. "I'm sorry it's not more of a grand gesture."

"What do you mean?" she asked.

"You deserve something big and showy, something public that makes it blindingly obvious that I'm in love with you. Like in the movies."

"What makes you think I'd want that?"

Kathleen frowned. "Maybe you wouldn't."

"You showed up on my job site." A big deal in her book, especially for someone like Kathleen who tended toward the quiet and the private.

"It's not all that grand."

"Yeah, but Jack and the crew are going to tease me about it for ages. That's got to count for something."

Kathleen winced. "Are they? I'm sorry. I didn't mean to put you in a weird position."

"Oh, no. It'll be the best kind of teasing. The kind where I get to gloat. Though, if you wanted to make it up to me by inviting me to your place tonight, I wouldn't say no."

"Please come over. I'll make you dinner and we can talk and…"

When Kathleen blushed and didn't continue, Logan took a chance. "Make up for lost time?"

Kathleen nodded, and the flush in her cheeks intensified, tempting Logan to take the rest of the day off and follow her home now. But just like it had been worth the wait for Kathleen to come around in the first place, she could bide her time for a few hours. Because what had started to feel like a lost cause had suddenly become infinite promise, and she had all the time in the world.

CHAPTER THIRTY-TWO

The oven timer beeped. Kathleen ignored it, not about to delay typing the words she'd been writing toward for the past several months. THE END. She took exactly two seconds to relish the way they looked on the screen while the beep sounded a third time, then hustled to the kitchen. The aroma of butter, sugar, and fresh peaches wrapped around her like an end of summer hug. Sure, apple season was knocking firmly on her door, but she hadn't been able to resist the lone box sitting at the farm stand when she stopped to get ingredients for dinner. Like a happy little omen.

She'd intended to make Logan a peach pie before things had all gone to hell. Or, perhaps more accurately, before she'd shoved them off a cliff. Better late than never, though. For pie and for coming to her senses.

She opened the oven, flinching at the wave of heat when she leaned in too quickly for a deeper sniff. She grabbed the baking dish with a pair of mitts and moved it to a cooling rack near the window. It looked as good as it smelled, and she hoped Logan liked it.

Her phone buzzed with a text from Trudy, who'd been stuck in meetings all day but required an update on what she'd dubbed operation Modest but Meaningful Gesture. Kathleen paused meal prep long enough to fill her in and was rewarded with a string of heart and happy emojis. She got a second in response to her finished manuscript announcement.

I'm still your favorite beta reader, right?

Kathleen laughed. *You're my only beta reader.*

I'll take that, too. I'm penciling you in to keep me company on the flight to the assessment summit in Tampa.

She shuddered. *I'm so sorry you're even using the words assessment, summit, and Tampa in a sentence together.*

Trudy used the shrug emoji. *That's why they pay me the big bucks.*

Better you than me. On so many levels.

Gotta go. Have fun with your make-up sex.

Since she knew better than to protest that's how she hoped to be spending her night, she wished Trudy a good afternoon of meetings and got back to the task at hand: making Logan a special dinner that wouldn't make the last few days go away but would hopefully make Logan feel appreciated. Feel loved.

God, she'd been so scared of that word for so long. Or, rather, what the word signified when it came to romantic relationships. She'd genuinely convinced herself that she wasn't made for that kind of love. Didn't want it. When really, she'd been terrified that no one would want to love her that way. Would want her and love her just as she was. And she'd been utterly convinced that someone Logan's age couldn't possibly know, couldn't possibly understand. And yet Logan was the one who'd taught her—taught her to love with her whole heart and trust that the universe had good things in store. Taught her that it might take work, but she deserved that kind of love just as much as the next person.

Her mind threatened to slip into a spiral of just how close she'd come to losing it all. She yanked herself back from the edge. If for no other reason than she had a lot to get done—including clean sheets on the bed and a nice cool shower—before Logan arrived.

She'd just finished slipping into her favorite dress when Logan's tires crunched in the driveway. She hurried downstairs, feeling as nervous as the first day of school. The mix of anticipation and trepidation that held so much promise but could also cut her at the knees.

She opened the front door and found Logan standing in the driveway with a look of confused indecision. "You okay?" she called.

Logan shook her head but smiled. "I was having a minor crisis over which door to use."

A twinge pinched in her chest. She'd made this amazing woman, who'd done nothing but love her, doubt if and how and where she belonged. "Whichever one will get me in your arms faster."

Logan didn't hesitate then. She bounded up the walk and took the porch steps two at a time. She slid both arms around Kathleen's waist and pulled her close. "Hi."

Her breath caught, desire and delight chasing away the unpleasant sensation. "Hi."

"I've missed you."

She nodded, emotion swelling in her throat. "I've missed you, too."

It was so easy to imagine this moment playing out every night. Logan coming home at the end of her workday, Kathleen greeting her at the door. Knowing she was about a thousand steps ahead of herself didn't stop her from seeing it. Wanting it.

They went inside and Logan shed her boots. "What smells like heaven?"

"Pie." Kathleen angled her head. "I thought the least I could do was make you a nice dinner."

"It's not like that. You don't need to do nice things for me."

"I want to." She worried her lip. "I was such a jerk."

"You weren't. I mean, you were stubborn and closed off, but I understand why. And I was, too."

"You definitely weren't either of those things."

"Okay, fine. I was stubbornly naive. We have some big life stuff to navigate if we're going to be together, and I just wanted to pretend it would magically work itself out."

Since there was a kernel of truth in the admission, she didn't argue. "It didn't help that I was so fatalistic about it all. And that I refused to communicate."

Logan grinned. "My sweet, jaded romantic."

She'd always thought those words couldn't go together, but they suited her to a T. Leave it to Logan to see that in her. To love her for it, not in spite of it. "I'm trying to focus less on the jaded part."

"A noble endeavor. I'll work on being less dewy-eyed and we can meet in the middle."

Again, she could argue that Logan wasn't that, but she liked what it implied. That they both wanted this and were willing to put in the work to make it last. "I like meeting in the middle."

Logan's gaze flitted over her, like she might be trying to solve a puzzle. Or maybe just soak Kathleen in. They'd only been apart a couple of weeks, but she felt like she couldn't get enough of Logan, either. Like she needed to recommit every detail to memory. Eventually, Logan's gaze landed on hers. "You know, I didn't get to kiss you the way I wanted earlier."

Kathleen's stomach flipped, making her wonder if and when that thrill of being wanted would ever subside. "No?"

"No."

"You probably should, then."

Logan nodded. Then her hand cupped Kathleen's cheek in that way she had—gentle without being too tender about it, fingers sliding into Kathleen's hair and to the nape of her neck. And then Logan kissed her, and it was like all the kisses they'd ever shared rolled into one. Timid and sure, lazy and urgent, sexy and sweet—a slow assault on her senses that left her knees weak and her heart quivering.

And the feeling that pulsed through, filling her up like a fuel tank on empty, was that Logan wanted her. Wanted. Her. No caveats or conditions, nothing held back. Love and desire and hope and joy.

When Logan pulled away, her eyes held that wanting along with a glimmer of mischief. "I'm going to stop now because if I don't, I'm going to drag you to bed. And as nice as that would be, you went to all this trouble to make a nice dinner and I want to show my appreciation."

She had, though honestly she couldn't care less about it now. But they had all night. And the night after that. And as many nights as she could imagine. Because Logan wanted her and she wanted Logan, enough to hash through whatever hard stuff they encountered. She might have gone out of her way to mess that up, but here they were.

She poured wine and had Logan sit at the table she'd already set. It only took a couple of minutes to sear the scallops and plate everything.

"This is fancy," Logan said when Kathleen placed the plate in front of her.

"I bought them when I was in Boston and put them in the freezer to have when I finished my book."

"Aw. You didn't have to use your celebration scallops on me."

"I didn't." She grinned. "Well, not entirely. I finished my book, too."

"You did?" Logan asked, something resembling awe in her voice.

"To be fair, I was pretty close." And had been for the better part of two weeks. "I may have been stuck on the ending."

"That's amazing. I'm so proud of you." Logan lifted a hand. "Assuming that's okay to say, of course."

"It totally is." And maybe one of those things she fantasized about when she was awake and alone in the middle of the night and let her imagination meander unchecked.

"Are you happy with it? The ending, I mean?"

"I am." She thought about her characters, so stubborn they'd painted themselves into opposite corners. She hadn't been able to conjure a resolution where one didn't give up an essential part of herself. Turns out the answer had been there all along—expanding their realities to have room for hopes and dreams that seemed incompatible. Just like with Logan.

She sat and Logan reached across the table, taking her hand. "Where did you go just now? You had this dreamy look on your face."

Was it silly to admit? Probably. But Logan didn't seem to mind her silly side. Or her overly serious one. Logan liked all her sides. How marvelous was that? "I was thinking about how you restored my faith in happy endings."

"Even when they take communication and hard work?"

She been such a fool. "Especially then, because I'm pretty sure those are the only ones worth having."

Logan nodded slowly, that gorgeous smile going all the way to her eyes. Just like it had that first day when she'd rescued Kathleen from her crumbling porch. "Indeed they are."

About the Author

Aurora Rey is a college dean by day and award-winning queer romance author the rest of the time, except when she's cooking, baking, riding the tractor, or pining for goats. She grew up in a small town in south Louisiana, daydreaming about New England. She keeps a special place in her heart for the South, especially the food and the ways women are raised to be strong, even if they're taught not to show it. After a brief dalliance with biochemistry, she completed both a BA and an MA in English.

She is the author of the Cape End Romance series and several standalone contemporary lesbian romance novels and novellas. She has been a finalist for the Lambda Literary, RITA®, and Golden Crown Literary Society awards but loves reader feedback the most. She lives in Ithaca, New York, with her dog and whatever wildlife has taken up residence in the pond.

Books Available from Bold Strokes Books

A Case for Discretion by Ashley Moore. Will Gwen, a prominent Atlanta attorney, choose Etta, the law student she's clandestinely dating, or is her political future too important to sacrifice? (978-1-63679-617-8)

Aubrey McFadden Is Never Getting Married by Georgia Beers. Aubrey McFadden is never getting married, but she does have five weddings to attend, and she'll be avoiding Monica Wallace, the woman who ruined her happily ever after, at every single one. (978-1-63679-613-0)

Flowers for Dead Girls by Abigail Collins. Isla might be just the right kind of girl to bring Astra out of her shell—and maybe more. The only problem? She's dead. (978-1-63679-584-3)

Good Bones by Aurora Rey. Designer and contractor Logan Barrow can give Kathleen Kenney the house of her dreams, but can she convince the cynical romance writer to take a chance on love? (978-1-63679-589-8)

Leather, Lace, and Locs by Anne Shade. Three friends, each on their own path in life, with one obstacle...finding room in their busy lives for a love that will give them their happily ever afters. (978-1-63679-529-4)

Rainbow Overalls by Maggie Fortuna. Arriving in Vermont for her first year of college, an introverted bookworm forms a friendship with an outgoing artist and finds what comes after the classic coming out story: a being out story. (978-1-63679-606-2)

Revisiting Summer Nights by Ashley Bartlett. PJ Addison and Wylie Parsons have been called back to film the most recent Dangerous Summer Nights installment. Only this time they're not in love and it's going to stay that way. (978-1-63679-551-5)

The Broken Lines of Us by Shia Woods. Charlie Dawson returns to the city she left behind and she meets an unexpected stranger on her first night back, discovering that coming home might not be as hard as she thought. (978-1-63679-585-0)

Triad Magic by 'Nathan Burgoine. Face-to-face against forces set in motion hundreds of years ago, Luc, Anders, and Curtis—vampire, demon, and wizard—must draw on the power of blood, soul, and magic to stop a killer. (978-1-63679-505-8)

All This Time by Sage Donnell. Erin and Jodi share a complicated past, but a very different present. Will they ever be able to make a future together work? (978-1-63679-622-2)

Crossing Bridges by Chelsey Lynford. When a one-night stand between a snowboard instructor and a business executive becomes more, one has to overcome her past, while the other must let go of her planned future. (978-1-63679-646-8)

Dancing Toward Stardust by Julia Underwood. Age has nothing to do with becoming the person you were meant to be, taking a chance, and finding love. (978-1-63679-588-1)

Evacuation to Love by CA Popovich. As a hurricane rips through Florida, so too are Joanne and Shanna's lives upended. It'll take a force of nature to show them the love it takes to rebuild. (978-1-63679-493-8)

Lean in to Love by Catherine Lane. Will badly behaving celebrities, erotic sex tapes, and steamy scandals prevent Rory and Ellis from leaning in to love? (978-1-63679-582-9)

Searching for Someday by Renee Roman. For loner Rayne Thomas, her only goal for working out is to build her confidence, but Maggie Flanders has another idea, and neither are prepared for the outcome. (978-1-63679-568-3)

The Romance Lovers Book Club by MA Binfield and Toni Logan. After their book club reads a romance about an American tourist falling in love with an English princess, Harper and her best friend, Alice, book an impulsive trip to London hoping they'll each fall for the women of their dreams. (978-1-63679-501-0)

Truly Home by J.J. Hale. Ruth and Olivia discover home is more than a four-letter word. (978-1-63679-579-9)

View from the Top by Morgan Adams. When it comes to love, sometimes the higher you climb, the harder you fall. (978-1-63679-604-8)

Blood Rage by Ileandra Young. A stolen artifact, a family in the dark, an entire city on edge. Can SPEAR agent Danika Karson juggle all three over a weekend with the "in-laws," while an unknown, malevolent entity lies in wait upon her very skin? (978-1-63679-539-3)

Ghost Town by R.E. Ward. Blair Wyndon and Leif Henderson are set to prove ghosts exist when the mystery suddenly turns deadly. Someone or something else is in Masonville, and if they don't find a way to escape, they might never leave. (978-1-63679-523-2)

Good Christian Girls by Elizabeth Bradshaw. In this heartfelt coming of age lesbian romance, Lacey and Jo help each other untangle who they are from who everyone says they're supposed to be. (978-1-63679-555-3)

Guide Us Home by CF Frizzell and Jesse J. Thoma. When acquisition of an abandoned lighthouse pits ambitious competitors Nancy and Sam against each other, it takes a WWII tale of two brave women to make them see the light. (978-1-63679-533-1)

Lost Harbor by Kimberly Cooper Griffin. For Alice and Bridget's love to survive, they must find a way to reconcile the most important passions in their lives—devotion to the church and each other. (978-1-63679-463-1)

Never a Bridesmaid by Spencer Greene. As her sister's wedding gets closer, Jessica finds that her hatred for the maid of honor is a bit more complicated than she thought. Could it be something more than hatred? (978-1-63679-559-1)

The Rewind by Nicole Stiling. For police detective Cami Lyons and crime reporter Alicia Flynn, some choices break hearts. Others leave a body count. (978-1-63679-572-0)

Turning Point by Cathy Dunnell. When Asha and her former high school bully Jody struggle to deny their growing attraction, can they move forward without going back? (978-1-63679-549-2)

When Tomorrow Comes by D. Jackson Leigh. Teague Maxwell, convinced she will die before she turns 41, hires animal rescue owner Baye Cobb to rehome her extensive menagerie. (978-1-63679-557-7)

You Had Me at Merlot by Melissa Brayden. Leighton and Jamie have all the ingredients to turn their attraction into love, but it's a recipe for disaster. (978-1-63679-543-0)

All Things Beautiful by Alaina Erdell. Casey Norford only planned to learn to paint like her mentor, Leighton Vaughn, not sleep with her. (978-1-63679-479-2)

Appalachian Awakening by Nance Sparks. The more Amber's and Leslie's paths cross, the more this hike of a lifetime begins to look like a love of a lifetime. (978-1-63679-527-0)

Dreamer by Kris Bryant. When life seems to be too good to be true and love is within reach, Sawyer and Macey discover the truth about the town of Ladybug Junction, and the cold light of reality tests the hearts of these dreamers. (978-1-63679-378-8)

Eyes on Her by Eden Darry. When increasingly violent acts of sabotage threaten to derail the opening of her glamping business, Callie Pope is sure her ex, Jules, has something to do with it. But Jules is dead…isn't she? (978-1-63679-214-9)

Head Over Heelflip by Sander Santiago. To secure the biggest prizes at the Colorado Amateur Street Sports Tour, Thomas Jefferson will do almost anything, even marrying his best friend and crush—Arturo "Uno" Ortiz. (978-1-63679-489-1)

Letters from Sarah by Joy Argento. A simple mistake brought them together, but Sarah must release past love to create a future with Lindsey she never dreamed possible. (978-1-63679-509-6)

Lost in the Wild by Kadyan. When their plane crash-lands, Allison and Mike face hunger, cold, a terrifying encounter with a bear, and feelings for each other neither expects. (978-1-63679-545-4)

Not Just Friends by Jordan Meadows. A tragedy leaves Jen struggling to figure out who she is and what is important to her. (978-1-63679-517-1)

Of Auras and Shadows by Jennifer Karter. Eryn and Rina's unexpected love may be exactly what the Community needs to heal the rot that comes not from the fetid Dark Lands that surround the Community but from within. (978-1-63679-541-6)

The Secret Duchess by Jane Walsh. A determined widow defies a duke and falls in love with a fashionable spinster in a fight for her rightful home. (978-1-63679-519-5)

Winter's Spell by Ursula Klein. When former college roommates reunite at a wedding in Provincetown, sparks fly, but can they find true love when evil sirens and trickster mermaids get in the way? (978-1-63679-503-4)